# HOUSE
# OF ASHES

ALSO AVAILABLE BY LORETTA MARION

*The Fool's Truth*

# HOUSE OF ASHES

## A Haunted Bluffs Mystery

## Loretta Marion

CROOKED
LANE

NEW YORK

Copyright © 2018 by Loretta Marion

Published in the United States by Crooked Lane Books, an imprint of The Quick Brown Fox & Company LLC.

Crooked Lane Books and its logo are trademarks of The Quick Brown Fox & Company LLC.

Library of Congress Catalog-in-Publication data available upon request.

ISBN (hardcover): 978-1-68331-843-9
ISBN (ePub): 978-1-68331-844-6
ISBN (ePDF): 978-1-68331-845-3

Cover design by Erin Seaward-Hiatt
Book design by Jennifer Canzone

Printed in the United States.

www.crookedlanebooks.com

Crooked Lane Books
34 West 27th St., 10th Floor
New York, NY 10001

First Edition: November 2018

10 9 8 7 6 5 4 3 2 1

*For Geoffrey, the curmudgeonly but loveable bibliophile who shares my world*

Light is the lighterman's toil,
As his delicate vessel he rows
And where Battersea's blue billows boil
To his port at fair Wapping he goes;
Yet deem not the lighterman's heart is as light
As the shallop he steers o'er the severn so bright.

For love he has kindled his torch,
And lighted the lighterman's heart,
And he owns to the rapturous scorch
And he owns to the exquisite smart;
And the Thames Tunnel echoes the lighterman's sigh,
And he glides mid the islands of soft Eelpie.

*Curiosity is lying in wait for every secret.*
—Ralph Waldo Emerson

Eighty years ago ~ Whale Rock, Massachusetts ~ Cape Cod Bay
Friday, December 13th

Percival Mitchell balled up the telegram and threw it into the blazing tavern fire. It had arrived that morning, but he'd yet to share the devastating news with his wife. He needed some Dutch courage before he found the words to tell Celeste that now the last of their three boys had been killed.

"A shot of Old Crow, Lloyd," he said to the barkeep, then downed it, glad for the punishing burn in his throat. He'd loved all his sons, but the youngest, Ambrose, had been most like him, with a love of the sea and a desire to see the world. They'd struck a deal: Ambrose would enlist in the Navy, but after three years' time he would return to Whale Rock and assume his rightful place at the helm of the family business. Yet only weeks later, while Ambrose was stationed in China on the USS *Panay*, there'd been a surprise attack by the Japanese on his ship. The attack was allegedly a mistake, and the USS *Panay* just an unfortunate target—but what consolation would that be to Celeste, who had already lost her other two sons?

Lloyd poured Percy a second shot, but before the glass was touched, a commotion broke out in the main street of Whale Rock. The fire bell was ringing, and someone yelled in through the tavern door, "There's a fire up on the north end! Battersea Bluffs. We need all the hands we can get!"

"No, it can't be," Percy whispered. The Bluffs was his home. He leapt from the barstool and ran for the street, bumping into a stranger as he passed through the tavern door. The man's eyes were ominously familiar to him, but with more pressing concerns, there was no time to bring to memory why. He had to get home to Celeste.

It sickened him to see the flames as his Ford pickup rounded the top of Lavender Hill. How hard he and Celeste had worked to build this house, a grand Victorian with a widow's walk and a proud front porch facing out to sea. Fire trucks were already there, and men he'd known these many years were working hard to contain the blaze to the southwest corner—Celeste's beloved kitchen and keeping room. Others had the presence of mind to remove some treasured possessions, which he saw scattered on the lawn.

As he ran toward the house, it came to him who the stranger in the tavern had been, and later one of the firefighters would recount that Percy had screamed: "Damn that lighterman's curse. Damn you to hell, Robert Toomey!"

Nobody was quick enough to keep Percy Mitchell from entering the inferno. Moments later he emerged, his clothing and hair afire, carrying a charred human form. Any man would have been delirious from the pain, but as the firefighters looked on in shocked disbelief, Percy walked with a purposeful bearing and a swift gait toward the bluffs. A few men chased after their friend, but before anyone could stop him, Percy reached the ledge and cried out, "I am not finished!"

And then, with his already dead wife in his arms, he hurled them both into Cape Cod Bay.

# 1

Present day ~ Whale Rock, Massachusetts ~ Cape Cod
September ~ three days since the disappearance

**"I** warned you months ago about taking those strangers into your home, Cassie." It wasn't the first time Whale Rock's police chief had made his feelings on the subject known, nor was Brooks Kincaid the only one to scorn my decision to take in the young couple who had fortuitously appeared at The Bluffs nearly four months ago, on a day I'd found myself in a rather desperate place. But nobody understood what a godsend they'd been. Vince and Ashley Jacobson had been my lifeline in saving The Bluffs. More than that, they'd rescued me from a very bleak place. But my descent into darkness was a well-guarded secret. Only Vince and Ashley knew.

And now they were missing.

Three days earlier, my young tenants had packed a picnic lunch and set off on their bikes for a day trip to Provincetown—and never returned. This morning I'd been summoned to a long-forsaken barn down at Kinsey Cove to identify two abandoned bicycles. The sight of the familiar picnic basket sent quivering fingers of dread up my spine, and I knew in that instant something bad had happened to them.

"There are no answers here." Brooks was trying to persuade me to go home. "It's very possible they'll still just show up at your place. You should be there in case they do."

3

"I can't just wait around. You need to let me help look for them," I pleaded with my old friend.

"You've already done all you can."

I shook my head. It hadn't been enough. When Ashley and Vince didn't come home, I'd set out to find them myself, driving all the way to Provincetown in case they were stranded on the roadside. When there was no sign of them in P-town, I'd checked Wizards, their favorite local hangout, but nobody there had seen them either. I'd sorted through their personal items for some type of clue or contact information. But all my sleuthing had dead-ended.

Brooks placed a calming hand on my shoulder and nodded toward the team of police who had assembled and were busy securing the scene and collecting evidence. "Leave this to the experts."

"Yeah? Tell me, where were the experts when I first reported my friends missing?" The police had refused to get involved until my tenants had been missing for twenty-four hours.

"Your *friends* hadn't been gone long enough to be considered officially missing at that point." He swept the dark blond hair from his forehead in a lifelong habit. "Give us a break. We've been doing all we can, with essentially no clues to follow."

"Something's very wrong." I held a fist to my knotted-up stomach. "I can feel it."

"There are countless explanations for where they could be."

"Without calling me? Or checking on their dog? How do you explain the bicycles? Ashley and Vince were always careful with their bikes. They never would've left them unlocked." Their bikes had instead been left simply tied together by a knotted rope that had also been used to secure the picnic basket to the back fender of one of the bikes. I flipped it open to peer inside. *Empty.*

"This was my grandmother's picnic basket. They knew it was special to me, and there's no way they would've left it behind. Something is amiss, Chuckles."

I watched the police chief's ears and cheeks flush pink as his first patrolman stifled a snicker. I mumbled an apology for using his detested childhood nickname in front of his subordinates. He'd earned the

4

name in grammar school because of an uncontrollable deep chuckle that erupted whenever he was nervous or excited. Everyone had openly called him Chuckles Kincaid until his sophomore year of high school, when he'd returned after summer break with a hulking form from a summer job with a moving company. He became a star defensive tackle for the Whale Rock High football team, and since then all he need do was glare at anyone who dared to resurrect the old nickname, and they were silenced. A select group of close friends could still get away with it in private—I was grandfathered in, since Brooks was my sister Zoe's first boyfriend—but I'd crossed the line today.

"Maybe they'd taken all they needed from the Mitchell gravy train and moved on," he snarled as he untied the knotted rope and thrust the basket into my grasp. "We've already gotten what we need from this."

"Touché." I looked down at the basket, feelings of hurt and anger at battle.

He pulled me aside. "Did you ever ask for references, like I advised?"

"No. Feel better now?" I snapped.

"Actually, I was hoping to be wrong because then we'd at least have a starting point for tracking them down." He glanced around the scene, his lips a tight line, before he asked, keeping his voice intentionally low, "Is anything missing from your house?"

"They didn't steal anything." I self-consciously tucked my bare right hand into the pocket of my jeans. I had absolutely no reason to believe Ashley or Vince had anything to do with my grandmother's missing ring. So I deflected by posing a different argument. "In fact, they left behind everything they owned, including their dog. Don't you think that's a bit suspicious?"

"You're correct, Ms. Mitchell. It is suspicious."

I turned in the direction of the unfamiliar voice and found a man sporting a navy windbreaker. It took a minute for the FBI emblem to register.

"Agent Daniel Benjamin, ma'am." His smile was measured, official, meant not to detract from the seriousness of the situation.

I took the FBI agent's proffered hand and managed, "Glad to meet you."

"You're in charge here?" Agent Benjamin asked Brooks.

"Yes. Chief Kincaid." The two men shook hands, but Brooks looked peeved. "Who contacted your office?"

Agent Benjamin turned his eyes toward me and ever so slightly cocked his brows. It was a subtle gesture, passing the ball to my court.

"That might have been me," I answered meekly. Then, feeling somewhat emboldened by the presence of a federal agent, I added, "I didn't feel you were taking me seriously."

"I can assure you, the Whale Rock PD takes every case seriously." Brooks addressed the agent, then glared at me.

While Daniel Benjamin consulted his notebook, I held my hands up innocently and mouthed, *What?*, which Brooks dismissed with a disgusted shake of his head before directing his attention to the FBI agent. "I didn't realize this was a federal matter."

"It's a nice day. I like the Cape. When the call came in, I decided to take a ride out and see if I might be able to help." His response was ambiguous, his demeanor cavalier. "Bring me up to speed?"

"Sure." Brooks gave a reluctant nod.

Agent Benjamin then said to me, "Could I stop by your house after I speak with the team here? It might help if I take a look at the Jacobsons' belongings." He turned to Brooks and added, "That is, if you don't mind."

"We haven't been out to the house yet." Brooks's tensed jaw told of his displeasure. Then to me, but maybe for the agent's benefit, "We'll be out shortly, so please leave everything as it is."

"Of course." I'd 'fess up later about already muddling up practically everything in their room in my search for clues.

The agent checked his notes and lifted a brow. "Battersea Bluffs at Lavender Hill?"

"My ancestors were British," I answered, as if that alone explained the name. "Now most everyone calls it just The Bluffs. I'm heading back there now. Chief Kincaid can give you directions."

When I left, Brooks was filling the FBI agent in on plans for

6

gathering special teams and bloodhounds to explore woodland areas and rocky shorelines. My stomach lurched as I heard one of the officers call out, "Hey, Chief! Found a couple of phones ditched in the barn."

\*   \*   \*

Back at home, I took a good look at my beloved Battersea Bluffs, with its towering widow's walk and double chimneys, several large bay windows, and impressive wrap-around porch. It had become part of Whale Rock's lore that the majestic Victorian sitting high above the cliffs on the craggy northern end of town was possessed by the spirits of my great-grandparents, Percy and Celeste Mitchell, its original owners. The legend evolved from a rumor initiated by my father when he was trying to take back his rightful home. It had been a successful strategy, but he could never have guessed how prophetic his fable would become—or maybe he'd already sensed the mysterious aspects of the old house. To be fair, Papa and I had never discussed the lurking scents and sounds presented by the spirits sharing our home.

I unlatched the gate, to a warm greeting of soft whimpers and an exuberant tail.

"You're missing them too, aren't ya, buddy?" I reached down to stroke the German shepherd's glossy black fur, those usually erect ears momentarily relaxed. I widened the gate. "Let's go, Whistler."

I followed the dog to the ledge of Percy's Bluffs, so named after my great-grandfather's dramatic leap from the cliffs overlooking Cape Cod Bay. I stared down to where the waves were crashing against the rocks below. Through the years, this spot had become my refuge, where I'd come to contemplate decisions or brood over troubles. Exhausted and numb, I sank to the ground and idly fingered an abandoned champagne cork, probably left here the night Vince and Ashley moved in with me. We'd brought a bottle down to the cliffs to toast our new alliance and the home they were going to help me save. I closed my eyes to bring to memory the feel of the fizzy liquid against my tongue, the first I'd tasted in years. There'd not been much to celebrate in recent times. But that night, a sense of hope had returned to me.

It had all happened so suddenly. Looking back now, it was amazing how immediate our connection had been, and how quickly the loose ties of a mutually beneficial arrangement became tightly woven into bonds of friendship.

I sat a moment longer, gazing at my bare hands. My wedding band was tucked away in a box somewhere, but I could come up with no logical explanation for what had happened to my grandmother Fiona's emerald ring. I didn't suspect my tenants and hadn't wanted to mention it to Brooks, for surely Ashley and Vince would stand accused by those who didn't trust them.

I considered how little I knew about their lives. Had I been so consumed with my own problems? Upon honest reflection, regrettably, the answer was yes.

On my walk back to the house, I took the picnic basket from my car and fingered the tangled line that had been used to secure it to the bike. It might have been the same rope I'd used to teach Vince about sailing knots. "That's strange," I mumbled, pondering the incongruous series of knots.

After removing the rope, I returned the picnic basket to its proper hook. A moment later, Whistler stood and growled an alert, which was followed by a knock at the door. The dog sprang forward, offering the fierce greeting reserved for strangers.

Agent Daniel Benjamin jumped back when I opened the door. "Does he bite?"

"Only federal agents." I cringed the moment the clichéd joke escaped my lips. "Kidding. Just give him a moment to get familiar with your scent, and he'll be fine."

"If you say so, Ms. Mitchell." He gingerly opened the screen door and offered his hand to the dog. After a few whiffs, Whistler was wagging his approval.

"Please, it's Cassandra, or Cassie."

"If you'll call me Daniel."

"Thank you, Daniel, for taking this seriously, for coming out so quickly."

He dipped his head. "You sounded desperate. I couldn't refuse."

He stood close, encroaching on my personal space, perhaps to intentionally unnerve me. He had piercing gray eyes, and was what my grandmother would have described as a ruggedly handsome sort of fellow. I was unnerved by the sudden warming of my cheeks. *This was not good.*

I swiveled away and picked up the kettle to fill it. "Care for a cup of tea?"

"Do you mind if I have a look at where your tenants were staying, first?" He glanced around the house.

"Sure. This way." With Whistler at our heels, I led him up the narrow back stairway, contemplating whether I should admit to my sins. However, one glance into the room, and it was fairly obvious their belongings had already been disturbed. "Here's their room. And there's an en suite through that door."

"Thanks. I can handle it from here." A not-so-subtle dismissal.

"Of course." I tried to cover my dismay. "Yell if you need anything."

"Will he be okay?" he asked, pointing to the dog.

"Come on, boy." I patted my leg, but Whistler seemed disinclined to follow me. "He's good."

Agent Benjamin did not look convinced. But having been abruptly dismissed, I didn't really care if Whistler bit him. No matter how attractive I found him.

"Find anything?" I asked when the agent returned to the kitchen fifteen minutes later.

"Just this." He held up a clear evidence bag containing a small slip of paper. "A receipt."

"For what?" I tried to get a look, but all I could make out before he pocketed it was a glimpse of the store name. *Sincere House, maybe?* I'd never heard of it.

"Don't know yet. I'll get my team working on it."

"Where was it?" I asked, trying to determine how I'd missed it during my search of the room.

"You must not have looked under the bureau." His eyes crinkled into a half wink.

I frowned, recalling Brooks's displeasure when it had become clear Agent Benjamin intended to involve himself in the case. "What about Chief Kincaid?"

"I'll make sure the local guys are informed."

"Were the phones found in the barn—?"

"—your friends'? It's the most probable scenario." Daniel sniffed the air. "Oatmeal raisin?"

"I beg your pardon?"

"You've been baking something." He shrugged. "Cookies was my guess."

"Baking is my way of dealing with stress," I said, covering my surprise with a small fib, while breathing in the sweet familiar scent wafting through my home. I'd never told anyone—not my sister, Zoe, not even my Granny Fi—about the smell of burning sugar, which always accompanied the hovering spirits of my ancestors and original owners of The Bluffs. I'd only recently come to understand the nuances of those scents. Could it be that Agent Benjamin was especially intuitive? More likely, he had a particularly good nose and was picking up on the same hints of sugar and vanilla from the old converted pantry. "And right now my stress level is pretty high."

"As it should be." He rubbed his hands together in what appeared to be a habit.

"So what do you think happened to my friends?" I brought the discussion back to Ashley and Vince. "Are they in trouble?"

"Too soon and too few clues to answer." He pulled out his notebook and was poised to write. "But you can help by telling me everything you know. What brought them to Whale Rock?"

"They'd just finished graduate school. They'd never been to the Cape before and thought it would be a fun place to explore before settling into real jobs."

"So where were they from?"

"I'm, uh, not sure. Maybe the Midwest? I think Ashley was a Southern girl originally."

He consulted his notes. "Chief Kincaid mentioned that people around here didn't feel quite so positive about your tenants."

"Nobody *knows* them like I do." My annoyance flared. "Vince and Ashley are more than tenants. They're my friends."

"And just how long have you been associated with these *friends*?" The sarcasm was underscored by his dubious expression.

I forced myself to swallow a smart response. "Four months."

"Not all that long, and yet . . ." He left the thought dangling, but I understood the implication: I should have known a few personal details—at the very least, where they were from.

My face warmed from a mixture of shame and anger. "They've been busy doing reno work for me, so we didn't spend a lot of time talking about their lives."

The agent's brows popped up in a doubtful way. I had to agree, it was flimsy.

"They're pretty . . ." I hesitated, searching for the right word.

"Secretive?"

"No, not secretive." My defensiveness provoked another eye raise, so I softened my tone. "They're just intensely private people." The kettle whistle offered a momentary save. I filled two cups to steep before adding, "The Jacobsons rallied round me at the lowest point of my life. And they would never leave without an explanation. Something isn't right."

Agent Benjamin flipped the notebook closed and blew out a deep breath.

"You're right," he agreed, staring hard. "Something is very wrong here, Cassie. But the biggest problem is that there's no record of your Vince or Ashley Jacobson. According to the US government, they don't exist."

# 2

Present day ~ Whale Rock ~ Cape Cod
Four months earlier

"Losing The Bluffs? How did your life get so out of control, Cassandra?"

I was used to my sister's disapproving tones, but today her patronizing attitude was especially disheartening, considering the reason for my call.

Not wanting to alienate the only lifeline for saving my home, I tamped down a smart-ass reply.

"We haven't lost it yet, Zoe."

"So it's *we* now?" No doubt my sister was referring to all the unsolicited advice I'd rejected through the years.

"You have every right to be disappointed in me." I tried to sound remorseful.

"I heard that," she chastised.

"What?"

"The 'nobody understands me' sigh. Don't forget, I was as much a mother to you as Mama."

This time I did sigh, but not audibly. With a decade between us when I was born, Zoe had treated me as her own private living doll from the start and had never abandoned her protective yet bossy role. If she'd had her own children, the maternal grip might have loosened. That hadn't been in her proverbial deck of cards, however.

She never understood that it wasn't a second mother I needed, but a real sister I desperately wanted, a best friend to whom I could confide my secrets, my dreams, my fears. And it would have been helpful to have someone with whom to share the burdens of family obligations.

I was only seventeen when Mama died, but by then the Cape was firmly in Zoe's rearview mirror. She'd rushed into marriage five years earlier with a spring break fling, the overly charming and handsome Oliver Young, who'd been on a fast track to a promising future in a prestigious San Francisco firm. At first glance, it appeared my sister had stepped into a fortunate situation, but the enviable role of a young executive's wife had its hidden costs, and soon she was barely treading water in a sea of demands: keeping up with the other executives' wives, joining the Junior League, hosting cocktail parties to impress the boss, shopping for outfits to impress the boss's wife.

She'd barely made it back to Whale Rock in time to witness the last breath of life drift from our mother's ethereal being. Zoe returned again three years after Mama passed, for Papa's funeral, but that was her last trip home. She couldn't even be bothered to make it back when Granny Fi died. I swallowed the bitter taste that always accompanied a reflection back to the difficult time in our past. Resurrecting the grudge would not serve me well today.

"It's time to put The Bluffs on the market. Free yourself from the lurking shadows of Percy and Celeste," Zoe said.

I was momentarily taken aback. Zoe had always eschewed my notion that the spirits of our great-grandparents were a presence in the house.

"So you're finally admitting they exist?"

"Of course not," she clucked with disdain. "But there is something sinister lurking within those walls, and your attachment to that house is unhealthy. Its kept you firmly tethered to a provincial Cape Cod existence, strangling possibilities. You're only thirty-seven. There's a big world out there, waiting to be explored."

"Yeah, I know. 'The world is my oyster.' I've heard the speech before."

"Well you might try listening to me occasionally," she pouted, strapping me with feelings of guilt on top of all my other shortcomings. "Regardless, I see no other way out but to sell." When I said nothing, she added, "You're always welcome to come live with us for a while."

I nearly gasped. Move in with her and Oliver? Not happening! I'd live on Papa's sailboat first.

"Selling would be disrespectful to Papa's legacy."

"Legacy? Pfft. For whom are you proposing we preserve that antiquated monstrosity?"

I winced at the sharpness of her words, knowing Zoe's strong reaction reflected bitterness over her inability to conceive a child. And she was right that there were no future heirs to the stately Victorian our great-grandfather had lovingly built for his family. My mother had tried her best to fill it with children, suffering seven lost and debilitating pregnancies, with only Zoe and me surviving. I myself was perched precariously on the end of the last dying limb of the Mitchell family tree. That our bloodline was on the threshold of extinction was the fulfillment of a prophecy, a century-old curse cast upon Percival Mitchell by a lifelong nemesis and rival for his wife's affection. *The lighterman's curse.*

"This is a beloved historic home, and it would be a dishonor to let it slip away." I sucked in a deep calming breath before pressing on with my appeal. "I have a proposal."

"Why do I have a bad feeling?"

"Please hear me out?"

"Fine," she sighed.

"I realize you don't share my love for The Bluffs, or Whale Rock for that matter, but this is the only home I've ever known, and I'd like to make a try at saving it." I let that sink in before adding, in the most matter-of-fact voice I could muster, "I just need a small loan."

"What on earth happened to your trust fund?" The dressing down continued. "I can't believe that trustee, what's-his-name, didn't request an accounting for where the money was going. Or at the very least some tangible evidence of an investment."

Evidently she'd forgotten that control of the trust fund set up by our maternal grandparents had been turned over to me on my thirtieth birthday. My sister was careful with her money and incapable of grasping the notion that anyone could let a million dollars slip through her fingers. I did the math. And yes, it *was* inconceivable to think all my money was gone in just seven years. It wasn't lost on me that my marriage had only lasted as long as my trust fund.

"Zo-Zo, at the moment I need a solution." I managed to choke back, *Not an "I told you so."* Our differences aside, my sister was the only one left I could turn to; even when my soon-to-be ex-husband was still around. Ethan had been the ultimate dream weaver, one failed venture following close behind the last. Then—*poof!*—he was gone. And so was all my money. The most significant remnant of my marriage was a staggering mortgage.

Ethan saw himself as a real estate speculator, and his enthusiasm for his visions had been contagious. As it turned out, he was an ideas man—big ideas with big budgets—but unfortunately he was *not* a follow-through guy. He seemed to lack even a basic understanding of what was required to be successful in the real estate game. It was his final investment in a waterfront condominium project prior to zoning approval—which was never granted—that had sunk us completely. To make it worse, he had lied about his plans for using the money. It was a hard lesson, one that had come too late for me and with devastating consequences.

My sister clicked her tongue. It was possible she was seriously considering my plea, but just as likely that she was suppressing a scolding retort while searching for the suitably nurturing words of refusal.

To fend off an inclination to refuse me, I forged ahead.

"I'm thinking of renovating the carriage house. Turning it into a rental to cover upkeep expenses."

"Not Mama's studio," she protested.

It was an infuriating objection. I was the one who'd inherited our mother's artistic gift, and after she died, Papa had turned her studio over to me. Mama had been prolific in her painting, and even now it seemed I couldn't turn a corner in Whale Rock without running into one of her works, including those donated to the Whale Rock Art Museum or on permanent display at the LK Gallery, owned by local art dealer Lu Ketchner, another of Zoe's many high school bosom buddies.

It would be a great personal sacrifice to surrender my sanctuary, but I'd do anything to hold onto this house.

It took some restraint to leave such thoughts unspoken, but I was desperate.

More tongue clicking, and then, "I don't know, Cass. Maybe it's worth considering." Was she softening a bit? "Morning, sweetheart. There's a fresh pot brewing."

Evidently my brother-in-law had blessed my sister with his Oliver-ness. I looked at the captain's wheel clock, which had been a fixture in our kitchen since I was a little girl. Seven AM on the West Coast.

"I need to get ready for a meeting, Cassandra." It was back to Cassandra. Not the best of signs. "Let me mull it over a bit."

This would translate to Zoe lamenting to Oliver about the mess I've made of my life, and should she give in and lend me the money or offer up a dose of tough love, forcing me out of my sheltered existence in Whale Rock?

After ending the call, I sat dejected, staring into the murky dregs of my long-cold coffee, as if it held answers, until my phone buzzed on the table, waking me from the pall.

"Go away, Billy," I groaned after checking the screen and pressing the ignore button. *Why had I agreed to see him again last night?* I had an unshakeable habit of avoiding problems, and Billy had long been my go-to diversion. When he'd called yesterday, it was right after I'd received the papers from the bank. The reality of losing my home was weighing heavy, and it had been easier to surrender to Billy's charms than to think about my problems.

Until yesterday, I'd been on a strict Billy Hughes avoidance diet for the past three months—ever since the day Ethan found out about us. I shuddered at the shameful memory. And yet, my affair had been but the final splinter in an already fractured marriage.

I wished I could talk to Brit Winters, my best friend since kindergarten. But Brit had abandoned me in my greatest hour of need. Shortly before Ethan and I split, during the roughest of marital oceans, Brit had enrolled in a professor exchange program from Providence College and was having the time of her life in Milan, Italy. As happy as I was for her, the timing sucked. She alone knew every detail of my decades-long saga with Billy, except for this most recent dalliance.

"Damn." I rested my head onto folded arms. I'd screwed up big-time. Looking objectively at my choices, it cast an unenviable impression. Viewing it through my sister's critical orbs, it was abysmal. Thirty-seven years old. Soon to be divorced. Childless. Alone. Broke. Strike that—not just broke, but on the precipice of homelessness. Aside from the occasional portrait job that came my way, I possessed few other marketable skills, unless unrigging and washing down whale-watching boats counted. I'd avoided admitting to Zoe about the scut work I'd been doing to earn grocery money.

*What would become of me if she said no to the loan?*

\* \* \*

I sought refuge in the sanctuary of the studio, but immediately regretted it. If I did turn the carriage house into a rentable space, I would have to face the prospect of packing up all my art supplies. Painting had become a refuge from my pain, and I credited it for getting me through these current tough times.

I took a quick inventory of the canvases, so many unfinished. *What would I do with them all?* I inspected my current work in progress, set up on the easel. It was a portrait of the Bartlett family, a Whale Rock institution, and I'd been lucky to get the work. Commissioned portraiture wasn't exactly a booming business on the Cape. I'd best finish it up quickly so I could get paid. Every dollar counted these days.

Until my recent financial woes forced me to abandon my land- and seascapes, the only portraits I'd painted were of my own family. There were several of my parents, and two of Fiona, one each for Zoe and me. And, of course, several portraits of Ethan. Perhaps I'd ship them off to his snooty mother one day. If Brit were here, she'd probably suggest a symbolic gesture like taking them out on the sloop for a proper sea burial.

Granny Fi always told me my painting would never pay the bills. *'Find a practical job,'* she'd said many a time. But then, she was a practical woman. How I'd hate for her to see the mess I'd gotten myself into now.

The sound of barking interrupted my dispirited reverie. I went out to investigate, and saw two twenty-something strangers and a dog sitting on the ledge of the sea cliffs overlooking Cape Cod Bay. The couple were spellbound by the stunning view and didn't hear me approach. It was the striking black German shepherd who noticed me first and immediately assumed a defensive posture. The low growl was enough of a warning for me to halt.

"Whistler, down," the young man commanded, and the dog promptly obeyed.

The woman offered a sheepish shrug. "He's a bit overprotective."

"Once he trusts you, he'll be your forever friend." The man patted the head of his devoted canine companion. "Right, boy?"

The dog maintained a wary stance, so I suggested, "Until then, maybe keep him on his leash?"

"I hope we're not trespassing." The woman leapt to her feet and dusted off the seat of her pants. "We seem to have gotten lost while hiking."

"You wouldn't be the first hikers to miss the trail turn." I pointed toward where I assumed they'd made their mistake. "When you get back to the tree line, you'll see a crumbling stone wall. A few yards beyond that is the trail marker."

In no hurry to leave, the young woman looked toward the house and said, "I have to ask. Is this Battersea Bluffs?"

When I nodded, she turned to her companion. "I told you we were close."

"Are these the famous Percy's Bluffs?" He pointed toward the cliffs.

"That's right." I fought from rolling my eyes. *More curious tourists.* "Are you staying in town?"

A glance passed between them before they both nodded.

"The Hilliard House?"

They seemed a bit spooked by my guess. "How did you know?"

"Aside from the fact she has the only dog-friendly cottage rental in town, Evelyn Hilliard enjoys sharing all the juicy Whale Rock history with her guests. Did she send you out here?"

"Not exactly." The young woman pulled a folded piece of paper from her pocket and handed it to me. "I wanted to see the haunted house."

I glanced at the paper, recognizing a printout of a familiar article from over a decade ago.

~

October 31, 2005, *Cape Cod Times*, "Happenings at Battersea Bluffs"
Written by Edgar Faust, author of *The Enduring Mysteries of Cape Cod*

I was recently a lucky guest at Battersea Bluffs, the proud estate of the Mitchell family, which sits high on Lavender Hill at the north end of Whale Rock. When I walked through those stately doors into the grand entrance hall, I couldn't deny feeling like a trespasser on a private history. Local legend claims the house is haunted by the spirits of the original owners, Percy and Celeste Mitchell. Does an evil curse continue to breathe its affliction through the genetic fiber of the Mitchell family? Celeste Mitchell alluded to said curse in a letter to her son, and when Percy arrived home to find the manse in flames, he damned the man who'd cast the wicked veil upon his family.

My own grandfather spoke with some of the witnesses who were at The Bluffs to help douse the fire. One man claimed to have been physically forced back by a wall of heat that surrounded Percy Mitchell when he burst out of the house carrying his dead wife. Others believed Percy was in a state of delirium from the pain and could not have been in his right mind when he leapt from the cliffs.

But I must pose this question: How did a man who was literally on fire have the physical or mental capacity to leave his own personal footnote? "I am not finished!" was his declaration to the world. Perhaps he's still not finished. Perhaps he is unable to rest until he can be sure the curse against his family has been lifted.

If his spirit lurks within the bones of that grand old Victorian, I say let him be. Let him leave on his own terms this time.

I'm not a clairvoyant or a spiritualist, nor do I go in search of otherworldly beings. But I must give my readers the account of one strange incident that occurred when touring the Mitchell home. As I ambled through those noble hallways, I swore I detected a faint whiff of crème bruleé, which, as it happens, is a favorite dessert of yours truly. If you don't believe me, ask Chef

Henri at Café Muse. (Wink!) Could it have been subliminal? A seed planted in my brain from long-ago newspaper accounts of the tragic fire I uncovered while doing my research for this story—that men who worked to put out the fire reported smelling the strong sweetness of burning sugar? Celeste's talents as a baker were well known, and later it was surmised the smell came from the large stock of baking ingredients she'd just had delivered to her pantry. But the sweet caramel scent that followed me like a shadow from room to room, though mild, was persistent. I've given serious thought to the experience, having read about the phenomena of specters presenting themselves as aromas significant to their lives. And I had to wonder: Was the lingering scent a presence, perhaps even a means of communication? Was the ghost of Celeste Mitchell trying to send me a message? Then again, perhaps I was just hungry.

I'm sure once this article goes to press, I will be asked if I believe the house to be haunted. Some readers may think I've already answered the question. Others who know me well will not be so certain. I'm a romantic, and I love the idea of Celeste Mitchell's essence reaching out to me with her ephemeral tentacles of sweetness. But truly, does it really matter? Unless, of course, you're living there.

~

"That story follows me closer than my own shadow," I said. "I'm Cassandra Mitchell. Cassie to my friends."

"Vince Jacobson." He offered his hand, then nodded toward the woman, who smiled broadly. "My wife, Ashley."

"Is it really haunted? The house?"

The young woman was obviously intrigued by the possibility. *Why not indulge her?*

"You should read Edgar's book." I pointed to the byline as I handed back the article. "This was printed about the time the book came out, probably as a tease to get readers to buy it. Our story rates right up there with other local legends like Lady of the Dunes and The Black Flash of Provincetown."

"For sure I'll have to check it out."

I gazed up at the sky, contemplating the wisdom of inviting them to the house. They seemed a pleasant young couple. What harm could come from it? Besides, I could use a healthier diversion from my miseries than responding to Billy Hughes.

"How long have you been out today?" I looked pointedly at the German shepherd, who was panting from the arduous hike.

"We started early. Probably around seven thirty."

"Time for a break then. Let's get you something cold to drink." I gestured toward the dog. "And a fresh bowl of water for the devoted Whistler."

By the time my guests were settled on the large open-air porch, I was already annoyed with myself. Never before had I invited wayward hikers to stop in for some Mitchell hospitality. Had I become so pathetically lonely that I was now seeking companionship from total strangers? I tried to assuage my misgivings while filling glasses with tea, the crackling ice cubes echoing the cacophony of conflict in my head. Seriously, what shame was there in offering a bit of rest to some hikers and their weary pooch?

During this internal argument, I became enveloped by the aroma of burnt sugar, always a reminder I wasn't alone in the house. The spirits of my great-grandparents apparently felt the need to rouse themselves from a recent state of dormancy. I walked to the kitchen window and took a long, hard look at the strangers who'd found their way to my doorstep. But what message were Percy and Celeste trying to send?

Conversation was easy while we sipped our tea in the fresh bay breezes. My guests were enchanted by the Mitchell family history, and not at all timid with their questions.

"I love the widow's walk." The young woman shielded her eyes and gazed upward. "It gives a romantic touch."

"I'm told it was the one detail my great-grandmother had insisted on. She fancied the notion of being able to look out to sea where her husband and sons were out in their sailing vessels, to wave them home at the end of the day. However, it was also said that after her two eldest sons died in a tragic boating accident, she never returned to her beloved widow's walk."

"So you're a descendent of the original owners?" Vince asked.

"Yes, Percy and Celeste Mitchell were my great-grandparents."

"It's both horrible and romantic, isn't it? Percy leaping off the cliffs like that, holding Celeste in his arms, both of them in flames." Ashley closed her eyes as if trying to envision the scene.

"The legend of Percy and Celeste is woven into Whale Rock's history. People still come out here every December to toss wreaths of flowers down into the surf."

"Do you mind?"

I shook my head. "They'll never be forgotten. Nor should they be."

"So your family has lived here in this house for almost a hundred years?" Vince relaxed into the cushions of the porch chair, prepared for a story.

"Actually, no. A wealthy architect was first to take ownership after the fire. Thankfully, he was painstaking in his goal to restore the Victorian to its original grandeur."

"It seems he accomplished that goal." Ashley stepped off the porch to admire the house. "She's an eccentric old lady, isn't she?"

"The architect apparently spent a good deal of time interviewing people who'd visited the house about specific details. Later, he sold it to a family who only used it during summers, and then it was sold twice more to other out-of-towners."

Vince now leaned forward with a searching look. "So how did you end up back here?"

"It's a bit convoluted and way too long a story for today." I didn't even want to think about how close I was to having to give up my home.

They were both visibly disappointed, but Ashley cheerfully suggested, "Another time?"

"Sure." I returned her smile, finding the hopeful feeling sprouting within me both comforting and worrisome.

They helped me gather the glasses and cart the dog's water bowl into the kitchen.

"At any rate," Ashley quickly added, "we need to make the most of our last days of leisure."

"Heading back home?" I asked.

They shared an uncertain look then, and as Vince began rinsing out the glasses, he told me their plight. "We'd actually love to hang out here for the rest of summer, but we'd need to find jobs and a cheap place to live."

I didn't want to discourage them, but most seasonal jobs in Whale Rock and surrounds were secured months in advance by college students looking for a Cape experience during their summer breaks. As for inexpensive dog-friendly rentals? Forget it.

"If you know anyone who needs a carpenter, Vince is quite handy," Ashley mentioned casually, picking up a dish towel to wipe off the splashes from the countertop. "He once helped his grandfather build a cottage."

"It was a *small* cottage." Vince shrugged off the compliment. "But I learned a bunch about construction."

Before I knew it, we were touring the carriage house as I explained my visions for converting it from art studio to income-producing rental.

"Wow, Cassie, you're really talented." Vince held up a painting of Whale Rock Harbor and pointed to a Mitchell Whale Watcher tour boat. "I think we went cruising on that boat."

"It was once my family's business." I held up my hands to fend off questions. "Another story for another time."

"I love your portrait work." Ashley was checking out the Bartlett painting. She added in a joking tone, "Maybe you could paint us?"

I considered the suggestion. Vince and Ashley would make excellent subjects: Ashley, with her wholesome farmer's daughter face, and Vince, who was just short of handsome with a shade of inscrutability. Now that she'd mentioned it, I itched to paint them.

Vince brought the conversation round to the renovation. He was generous with design ideas, and his enthusiasm for the project convinced me that my plan had substance. When he suggested that he and Ashley do the work in exchange for room and board, the combination of their eagerness and the persistent sweet scent of Percy and Celeste was so compelling, I found myself readily agreeing.

Now all I had to do was convince Zoe to come through on that loan.

# 3

Present day ~ Whale Rock

The next day, my new lodgers showed up with loaded backpacks and a duffel bag crammed with Whistler's necessities. We started right in on the carriage house, with Vince hauling down dusty boxes from the attic to sort through.

My breath caught after prying the top from a crate of paintings only to find Ethan's once-irresistible bedroom eyes gazing back at me.

Ashley sidled up and observed in an admiring tone, "Nice-looking guy."

I glided my hand across the surface, clearing away dust and recalling the day when I'd hastily tossed all his portraits into this crate and nailed it shut.

"Sad memory?" Ashley asked, intuiting this from my silence.

I nodded, not trusting myself to speak.

"Here, let me." In a fluid movement, she replaced the top and began tapping the nails back into place.

Vince had descended carrying another stack of boxes and, with a quick read of the scene, heaved the crate aside. "To the barn for this one?"

I don't know what affected me more: the sudden and unexpected longing for Ethan or the swift and compassionate intervention of these relative strangers who so easily grasped my despair.

They hovered like protective mama birds over a wounded fledgling,

Ashley gently draping an arm across my shoulders and murmuring, "Just toss those troubles off the bridge, and watch them float far down the river."

She sounded so much like my grandmother, for an instant I thought it was a memory of Fiona's voice echoing in my head.

"At least you're smiling." Vince handed me a tissue.

"My Granny Fi used to say things like that." I wiped away the wetness. "And she was always right."

"Funny how that goes." Vince winked, then hefted the crate and left to stow it out of sight in the barn.

Ashley gave me a squeeze, then let go and walked over to a box marked "Fiona Patrick." She dragged it over to me and opened it. "These were her things?"

"Mm-hm." I lifted out a feathery-soft afghan and held it to my cheek while Ashley flipped through an old photo album, stopping at a faded color image of a man posing in front of a sailboat. "That's the only photograph I have of my grandfather, Ambrose Mitchell."

"Anyone could see where you got those stunning green eyes." She looked up from the album. "But where did that gorgeous hair come from?"

My thick mane with its rich russet tones was my one vanity, and yet still I was flustered by the compliment. Vince entered with the save, appearing with a block of cheese and a loaf of bread. "Time for a break. I raided your kitchen."

Vince poured us each a glass of wine, glancing first at his wife and then at me. "Maybe you'll tell us now how your family returned to The Bluffs?"

"Yes, please." Ashley leaned in eagerly

A smile played on my lips as I recalled Granny Fi frequently recounting the tale during my curious youth. If not for her, I'd never have learned anything about my family's history.

I smoothed my hand over the afghan as if to connect with her spirit. "My Granny was the only daughter of the local grocers, an overly protective father and a pious mother. To hear her tell it, a mere glance in the direction of a boy brought out her mother's rosary beads and her father's threatening scowl. My grandfather, Ambrose Mitch-ell, had been the only boy in town brave enough to risk the wrath of both God and Mr. Patrick to pursue Fiona's attentions."

"Here's to Ambrose." Vince lifted his glass in salute, provoking a playful rebuke from Ashley.

"Shh. Don't interrupt."

"Anyhow, my father was conceived just days before my grand-father left for the Navy. As Granny Fi liked to tell it, when Ambrose shipped out, she'd sent him off with a taste of her womanhood, and he left behind his planted seed." I made a face.

Ashley giggled. "What a character she must have been."

"Oh yeah." I had to chuckle. "But people respected her, which was unusual for an unwed teen mother in those days."

"What happened to Ambrose?" asked Vince.

"He was killed while serving on a US patrol boat in China that was mistakenly bombed just days before the tragic deaths of his parents."

"A freak accident?"

*No accident. The lighterman's curse.*

~

Eighty-five years ago ~ Cape Cod Bay

"Untie her, Ambrose, me boy," Percy instructed his youngest son, and then glanced with concern at Celeste. Wearing a mask of sorrow, she clutched tightly to her breast the urns holding the ashes of her two older boys.

"Can I take her today?" Ambrose asked eagerly. Taking the catboat out had been the only way to cheer him in the days and weeks following the tragedy. But he knew this sail had a somber purpose.

"Let's get her out a ways first and see what the wind has in mind for our lady of the sea."

There was a nice easy breeze, so Percy relinquished the rudder. "Steady now." He ruffled the boy's hair and settled in beside Celeste.

"He's a natural," she said, pushing aside strands of auburn locks that had blown loose from her braid.

"That he is." He took her hand, and she finally met his eyes.

"We don't have to do this," Celeste pleaded.

"Where else but the sea should we set free our boys' spirits? It's where they loved being most while they were living, and it's where they'd want to be now they're gone."

"But it was the sea that took my boys from me."

He'd held his tongue and refrained from saying, *'No, it was Robert Toomey's curse that took them.'* His wife had shouldered enough guilt for that curse; he didn't need to be reminding her of it now. Instead, he soothed her. "We'll be with them every time we take the *Femme Celeste* out for a sail. We'll remember them every time we watch the sun setting over the bay."

"Coming about," Ambrose shouted, and they ducked their heads. The boy radiated sheer joy. There could be no doubt a kinship with the sea coursed through his Mitchell veins.

"How will we keep him safe?" Celeste wondered aloud.

*How indeed?* Percy thought.

When the wind died down, he instructed his son to bring down the sail. The boy did as he was told, the earlier joy now clearly doused by the understanding of what was to come next. Ambrose had adored his older brothers and was stricken by their deaths. Edwin and Jerome had been taken by a sudden storm when their fishing boat wrecked into the rock formation from which the town had taken its name.

Percy, Celeste, and Ambrose shared the ritual of releasing Edwin and Jerome Mitchell into Cape Cod Bay, each whispering his or her own private meditations before Percy solemnly repeated The Lord's Prayer. For a time afterward, Percy let the boat drift, until a stiff wind kicked up and he was forced to raise the sail.

On the way to their private dock at Bluffs Cove, Percy steered the *Femme Celeste* into Whale Rock Harbor.

"Your mother needs a few things from Patrick's." He tied a bowline knot to the cleat.

"I'll get them for you, Mum," Ambrose volunteered with enthusiasm.

She eyed him suspiciously. "All right, then. I need a dozen eggs and two pounds each of flour and sugar. Oh, and a bottle of vanilla extract."

The boy scurried up the dock.

"And come back directly," she called after her son before he rounded the corner of Main Street.

"What do you suppose that was all about?" Celeste asked.

"I'd say it might have something to do with pretty little Fiona Patrick. She's always at the store, and I've caught her making eyes at young Ambrose." Percy smiled.

"Oh, Percy. Don't encourage him. He's just a boy."

He was just a boy now, but he would grow to be a man. And Percy prayed to God each night that his Ambrose would be the one to break the curse of Robert Toomey.

~

Present day

"He never knew about the baby?" Ashley asked in a hushed voice.

I shook my head. "But I think we can believe he'd have been happy." I handed Ashley a yellowed envelope from amongst Granny Fi's mementos, addressed *To Fi, My Love*. Ashley slipped out a letter written by the bold and steady hand of my grandfather, its pages diaphanous from age and frequent readings.

After reading aloud Ambrose's declaration of undying love and vow to return to his one true Fiona, she sighed and took Vince's hand.

The natural intimacy sent a stab of envy to my gut. Rubbing my bare left ring finger, where my wedding ring had been, I studied the emerald ring on my right hand, a symbol of my grandfather's promise to return to Granny Fi.

"When my father found out about Ambrose and his family, he made it his quest to claim the Mitchell legacy. Even if paternity testing had existed back then, there was no DNA available for proof, since Percy, Celeste, and all three of their sons ended up buried at sea."

"Granny Fi told me the people of Whale Rock had willingly accepted Papa as a true descendent. Very little escaped the eyes of small town folk, especially when it involved a forbidden courtship. And while my father's given name was James Mitchell Patrick, it had been shrewd of Fiona to name Ambrose as the father on the birth record."

I glanced out the large bay window of the carriage house, to where my home was cast in the rosy glow from the lowering sun.

"It has an eerie beauty, doesn't it?" Ashley followed my gaze.

"The kind that easily possesses you," agreed Vince.

I couldn't help but wonder if they too would come to sense a mystical presence within the bones of Battersea Bluffs.

"How did your father reclaim the house?"

"He had the devious idea of planting a rumor about the house being haunted."

"So that's how it all started?" Vince nodded approvingly.

"*From a small seed a mighty trunk will grow.*" Another of Fiona's legendary sayings. "People believe what they want to believe. When the last outsiders tried to sell, the rumors of a haunting had taken root and there weren't any takers. The value eroded to where my father was finally able to afford it."

It occurred to me that maybe mere rumors of a haunting weren't totally to blame for the revolving door of ownership. Maybe, instead, the true unsettling nature within its walls was what sent people packing. I rather liked thinking that Percy and Celeste might've had a hand in restoring Battersea Bluffs to its rightful heir.

"Brilliant!" Ashley clasped her hands together delightedly, then asked in mock dread, "Should we be frightened?"

"I've lived to tell the story, haven't I?" I joked, but the question gave me pause. I hoped the otherworldly presence in my home would pay little attention to the new residents.

Vince raised his glass. "Cheers to your father's happy ending."

Not wanting to spoil the moment, I kept quiet about whether it could be considered a happy ending, given Papa's despondency when Mama took ill, how he never recovered from her death and followed her to the grave just three years later. And then, so soon afterward, losing my Granny Fi too.

I busied myself replacing the items we'd taken from Fiona's box. Ashley returned Ambrose's letter and said, "You miss her, don't you?"

"More than anyone." Tears burned to be released.

"I get it." Vince's face clouded. "I miss my grandfather. He was my beacon, and it's been hard navigating without him."

Ashley's sad eyes traveled between us, her mouth working in search of the proper consoling words. She settled on a notion as insightful as it was comforting.

"They are both still with you in the special imprints of themselves within each of you."

Ashley's suggestion that Fiona's essence had somehow transferred to me had me considering the serendipitous way the Jacobsons had happened upon The Bluffs, their eager helpfulness and intuitive concern, how quickly I was drawn in by their compelling aura. My nostrils filled with the comforting scent of caramel. I'd felt Granny Fi's firm steering hand at my back countless times as I lost my way after her death. And I'd always managed to get back on track . . . at least until Ethan had derailed me. But with Percy and Celeste vigilantly watching over me, Fiona's spirit alive within me, and the support from these burgeoning friendships, dare I hope my course would once again be righted?

# 4

A week later

I was in the barn, sorting through my canvases. Vince had suggested moving my studio out here, and actually, it was a pretty fair space. I'd have to do something about temperature and humidity control down the road, but the light was excellent.

A car horn sounded in several short toots, bringing me outside to investigate. My heart sank when I saw a familiar powder-blue Mini Cooper convertible.

"Yoo-hoo! Anyone home?" Evelyn Hilliard was on the porch, peeking in through the kitchen door, when I approached from behind.

"Right here."

She swirled around, holding her hand to her heart. "Why, Cassie, you scared me half to death."

"Sorry, Ev."

"Never mind." She good-naturedly waved the worry away and moved in for one of her famous hugs.

Evelyn and her husband, George, had been high school sweethearts and classmates of Zoe's. When George's parents grew tired of inn keeping, he and Ev willingly took over running the Hilliard House, ideally located in the center of the village.

"We missed you at our Memorial Day cookout." It was their big annual to-do, kicking off the summer season. It was not to be missed. Except, that is, by me.

"I was kind of busy."

"No worries, Baby Cass." She patted my cheek as I cringed inwardly at the enduring nickname my sister's friends had dubbed me when I was just a kid.

"Lord, we had so much food left over." She reached down to pick up a large basket overflowing with goodies. "So I brought the cookout to you."

"You are too kind." I took the basket from her grasp and motioned for her to follow me inside. I began to store the food, glad I now had two tenants with whom to share the bounty. "Can I fix you something? I've got some coffee left in the pot."

"No thanks. I have to hurry back to the inn." She stood at the window, looking curiously out at the carriage house. "We heard you were going to convert your studio to an apartment."

*My, word traveled fast.* "So, you've been talking to Zoe?"

"Mm-hmm. Hey, I know that dog." Evelyn was still peering out the window.

"Who, Whistler?"

"What's he doing here?" She looked at me askance.

"He belongs to the couple I hired to help with the renovation work." I sidled up to her, deciding to feign ignorance about Ashley and Vince having stayed at Hilliard House before moving in with me. "Ashley and Vince Jacobson are their names."

"Yes, I know. They stayed in our cottage for a while." She was facing me now, arms folded.

"Oh? How were they as guests?"

"Fine. Fine." She chewed on her lip.

"And they took good care of the cottage?" I returned my attentions to the generously filled basket of food.

"Why, yes. Yes, they did."

"Good to know. Oh! Your brownies." I removed one and took a bite. "Yum."

"Look, Cass, I would never dream of overstepping—"

"Thank you, Evvie." The perfect opportunity to cut her off. "You don't know how much I appreciate that. And what a relief to hear they were such good guests at the inn."

This had the desired effect of leaving her momentarily speechless.

"All this food you've brought will be a tremendous help in feeding my new hired hands." I returned the empty basket. "I can't thank you enough."

"Well, good. I'm glad it won't go to waste," she said as I walked her to the Mini.

"That it won't." I looked about, but Whistler was nowhere to be seen. Neither were Ashley and Vince for that matter.

"You know, Baby," she glanced once more in the direction of the carriage house, "if you ever need anything, *anything at all*, George and I are only a hop, skip, and a jump away."

"Duly noted. Means a lot, Ev."

I waved her off and headed back to the barn. Moments later, Vince rolled in with two more crates atop the dolly. I couldn't help wondering if he and Ashley had intentionally made themselves scarce while Evelyn was here.

"Where do you want these?" he asked.

"I'm not sure what they are," I said, picking up a hammer to pry off the tops. "Where did you find these?"

"The crawl space." He wiped the sweat from his face with a bandanna, then tucked it into his back pocket and helped me open the crate. "Wow."

*Wow, indeed.*

"These are"—he stared in fascination—"dark, right?"

I fingered the signature in the lower right corner of the eerily exquisite works: *Jacqueline M.*

"My mother's," I whispered.

"Have you seen these before?"

I shook my head. These were so unlike any of Mama's other paintings, which had mainly been of quaint seaside villages in the primitive Americana or folk art style. The works before me now were more like Edvard Munch's famous painting *The Scream*. There was indeed an ominous nature to the paintings, and the unknown subjects were obviously tormented. Was that why they'd been hidden away? Dark and disturbing as they were, however, these were by far Mama's best work.

"Can I help you put these somewhere?"

"Your time is more valuable back at the carriage house."

I gestured toward the disarray of boxes and supplies. "Only I can put sense to this mess anyway."

But more than that, I craved a bit of solitary time with those paintings.

*  *  *

Sometime later, I was startled from a daze by my cell phone's ship bell ringtone.

"You comin' in today or what?" Johnny Hotchkiss sounded irked. "The boats are in."

I'd been a cruise tour guide, starting as a teenager, back when my father still owned Mitchell Whale Watcher Boat Tours, and even when my father abandoned the business, I'd continued on with Johnny until Ethan arrived on the scene and I'd quit to help with his real estate ventures. When I'd recently gone back to beg Johnny for a job, I'm sure he'd felt obligated to offer me something, considering he'd gotten such a good price for the business way back when. There just wasn't much available. So he let me help with the unrigging and cleaning of the boats at the end of the day, and occasionally I filled in when they were shorthanded for crew. It was hard work and the pay stank, but I needed every penny I could scrounge together.

"Already?" A quick check of the time had me stunned by how late it was. *Had I really been sitting there for three hours?* That seemed inconceivable. "I'll be there in ten minutes."

I hoisted myself from a cross-legged position in front of my mother's mesmerizing canvases and forced myself to head out the door before they had the chance to take ahold of me again.

However, when I returned from working at the harbor, exhausted and in desperate need of a shower, instead of heading for the house, I made a direct beeline back to the barn.

*  *  *

"Come on, Cassie!"

I dreamed that someone was leading me away from a fire. But who? I tried to focus through the smoke.

"Always a fire," I murmured. The invariable theme, of being caught in a fire and desperately searching for an escape, no doubt had everything to do with the fate of my great-grandparents. I'd learned the story about Percy and Celeste when I was quite young, and the nightmares had persisted ever since.

I still couldn't see who was tugging me by the arm through the haze, but I blindly followed.

"Wake up," a soothing male voice coaxed. Then the man said, "Get a blanket. She's shivering."

Moments later, my head was gently lifted.

"Just a dream, Cassie." A woman talking now.

"Zoe?" I finally forced my eyes open to find not my sister, but Ashley tending to me. I must have fallen asleep out in the barn and had one of my recurring nightmares about being trapped in a fire. When fully roused, I covered my face with my hands. "I'm so embarrassed."

"Don't be. We were worried when you didn't come home," Ashley scolded kindly, "so we came out here to look for you."

"That must have been some nightmare." Vince looked relieved. "You kept moaning about the burning and the smoke. What were you doing out here at this hour?" He helped me to my feet.

"I'd hoped to get some work done." I glanced about, disappointed to find nothing had changed since Vince brought everything over from the studio. I must have become distracted by my mother's paintings again.

"Who are these people?" Ashley now had her eyes fixed on my mother's art.

"They aren't familiar to me." But how could I tell with those agonized expressions distorting their features?

"These were some tortured souls." Ashley couldn't seem to look away.

Or maybe it was the artist who was tormented? I wondered about the timing of these paintings that had been secreted away. Were they created during the last years of my mother's life, as the cancer was progressively invading her body? Was it her way of exorcizing the terror of death's approach?

Vince began to cover my mother's canvases with a drop cloth. It seemed I wasn't the only one who found the images intriguingly disturbing.

# 5

Early June ~ three months before the disappearance

"So what's this about complete strangers moving in with you?"
Zoe's reproachful words when I called to thank her for coming through with the loan proved the old adage of no good deed going unpunished.

"You've been talking to Evelyn?"

"What? No."

*Right.*

"Who among your Whale Rock cronies are you going to send out next to spy on me? Lu?" As a bicoastal art dealer, Lu Ketchner's frequent trips to the West Coast had kept the connection between her and Zoe strong through the years.

"You're being ridiculous, Cassandra." My sister proceeded with the interrogation. "What are you thinking? What do you even know about these people?"

"They're a couple of nice kids having a summer of adventure before they're forced to settle into the real world of nine-to-five jobs, long commutes, and all the crap I'd probably hate." I'd become spoiled by my Cape Cod lifestyle.

"I wouldn't be so concerned if they were local kids." She made a tsk-tsk sound. "Whose idea was it they move in with you?"

"It was a mutual decision." The lie was necessary since Zoe had already reached a Code Red level of suspicion. Besides, two weeks in and it was working out more beautifully than I could have dreamed, so what difference did it make?

"Evelyn thinks—"

"So I'm right. Evelyn *is* your snitch."

"If you must know"—she lowered her voice—"it was Brooks who first told me."

"Interesting." In imitation I lowered my own voice. *Of course, Evelyn would have made sure everyone in Whale Rock knew by now.* Brooks had shown up on my doorstep not two hours after Evelyn's surprise visit.

"Don't read anything into a simple phone call," she hissed.

Oh, I was reading something into it, all right.

"So what else did Chuckles have to say?"

"Don't call him that. He's a grown man, for Pete's sake."

"And you should see what a fine specimen of a man he's grown into. Without a doubt Chuck—uh, Brooks is the most sought-after bachelor in the Rock."

"He should find the right woman and marry her."

"He did. Find her, that is. But I don't suppose anyone can live up to Zoe Mitchell in his mind." How I wished to see my sister's flustered face. But why torture her further? "So what did he want?"

"He's worried about you. As am I. Your overly trusting nature always lands you in trouble."

"Ethan didn't set out to take advantage of me, you know? He loved me. He was just a . . ."

"A leech?"

"Ouch. I was going to say 'mirage chaser,' but 'leech' is a much more elegant term."

It took great restraint for me not to bring up Zoe's own questionable choice in marital partners. Oliver had strayed earlier in their marriage, but who was I to judge? I lived in a glass house on that account.

We were both quiet for a moment before I asked, "Has Brooks called you before about me?"

After a pause in which my sister was either ignoring the question or stalling, I pressed: *"Zo-ee?"*

"He was concerned when Ethan left and suggested I might want to come back and check on you."

"So why didn't you?" I whispered, stung by the obvious rejection. Ethan had been gone for over three months now. Plenty of time to squeeze in a sisterly visit.

"Cass? Are you there? This darn phone," she grumbled before disconnecting.

I chose not to pick up when she called back. Aside from wishing to avoid the resumption of a lecture, I was overcome by a petulant need to punish my sister for abandoning me again. To escape the persistent ringing, I slipped out to check on the renovation progress.

The Jacobsons were huddled over a project and hadn't seen or heard me come in. They were both wearing tank tops that revealed matching shoulder tattoos of a bird with brightly colored plumage.

"Do you think he's gone yet?" Ashley's tone was thick with angst. "It's been over two weeks now."

"We don't even know why he was here. Maybe it's a coincidence?"

"Doubtful."

"What's a coincidence?" I asked.

Ashley stood quickly, her natural smile dismissing any suggestion of concern.

"Oh, just some people we met at Nauset Beach from upstate New York."

Vince winced, then shook his hand when he noticed me looking at him.

Though it seemed contrived, I still felt obliged to ask. "Hurt yourself?"

"Just caught my thumb."

"Nauset Beach is lovely, but don't forget the beautiful beaches practically out our front door."

"We like biking to Orleans. It's a good workout."

"I wish I had as much energy as you two." I turned my attention to Vince, who was devising some sort of pulley system with ropes.

"What kind of a knot is that? I know a ton of sailing knots, but I've never seen that one. What do you call it?"

"The Dead Man's Hand. It's used in climbing, specifically for rescue work. Some people call it a backup knot."

"You're a mountain climber?"

"He used to be." Ashley had taken the Shop-Vac up to the loft and called down, "It was a condition of marriage that he quit."

"Too many close calls?" I lowered my voice so Ashley couldn't hear.

Vince offered a sheepish grin. "Have you seen the movie *127 Hours*, about the rock climber who had to cut off his own arm to survive?"

I shuddered. "I remember it."

"Well, it might have done me in."

"And for good reason," I admonished him gently. "There are less dangerous ways to get your thrills. Have you ever sailed?"

He shook his head. "Not many opportunities for sailing where I grew up. My grandfather used to take me lake fishing on a rowboat when I was a kid, but that pretty much sums up my experience on the water."

"Maybe later this week we can take the Cat out."

"Cat?"

"My sailboat. It's a catboat, technically a sloop." It was a cherished heirloom, and one thing I'd never let Ethan talk me into selling. My great-grandfather had christened her the *Femme Celeste*, and the sailboat had remained with the house each time it changed owners. Papa had renamed the sixteen-foot sloop *Queen Jacqueline* after my mother, though she rarely joined him on the water, whereas I was barely walking when I'd started going out with him on the bay. But it had been ages since I'd sailed, and I was excited for an opportunity to introduce my new friends to its exhilaration.

I'd lost confidence in solo sailing. Ethan had had an irrational fear of the ocean and not only refused to go with me but also insisted I take a friend along on my outings. Unfortunately, I'd chosen the wrong "friend" . . . being out on the boat with Billy had proven more

temptation than I'd been able to resist. He'd always had a way of causing me to go against my better judgment. And I was seriously regretting the last rendezvous with my old flame—*was it already three
weeks ago?*—especially now that my period was worryingly late.

"We'll take it out soon. But for now, let me show you an Oyster-
man's knot. It might work better." I changed the configuration of the
rope and handed it back to him. "And so you won't forget, it's also
called an Ashley knot."

"Perfect."

*  *  *

Whistler began barking an alert, and moments later, Whale Rock's
finest pulled up. I turned around to say something to Vince, but he'd
already disappeared up into the loft with Ashley.

"Well, if it isn't Deep Throat," I called out as a greeting.

"Who?" Brooks leaned down to offer the German shepherd a
head pat.

"Never mind. What brings you out this way?" *As if I didn't already
know.* It was, after all, his third stop out to The Bluffs since Ashley
and Vince had moved in. Brooks had been an extended member of
the Mitchell family since the day he fell head over heels for my sister
in junior high school. Even though Zoe eventually broke his heart,
over the ensuing years he and I had formed a companionable friendship. Then after my parents died, Brooks stepped naturally into the
role of protective big brother. Though there were times I'd rather he
be less attentive to my affairs, it was a great sense of security to have
someone watching out for me.

"Just checking in." He craned his neck to look beyond me to the
carriage house. "Where are your new best friends? They always seem
to make themselves scarce when I'm around."

"You're imagining things." I hooked my arm around his elbow
and steered him toward the house. "Besides, I get the feeling you are
intentionally trying to intimidate them."

"Not true. I just don't know them well enough to trust them." He
gave me a pointed look. "Do you?"

"I'm sure you've already done some type of background check on them." I poured us each a glass of lemonade and lowered my voice dramatically, "So what evil deeds turned up?"

"Their names didn't show up on any wanted persons lists. No outstanding warrants that I could find." He paused then added. "But many unscrupulous people don't have criminal records. Taking advantage of someone's generosity isn't usually a prosecutable crime, or else—"

"I know," I said before he could drag Ethan into this. "I get that you don't think I'm a good judge of character. But I do think the world of you, and there's nobody I'd trust more with my life, so I must have a touch of good sense."

Brooks turned his hangdog face away and took a chair at the kitchen table. He then said contritely, "I'd hate for you to lose this house. The Rock would be a lonely place without you."

That might have been true years ago, before I'd unwoven my personal threads from the fabric of Whale Rock. Nonetheless, I was touched and reached over to squeeze his arm.

"Where would I go?" It wasn't the first time in recent months I'd asked the question.

"Anywhere but down at the docks." Brooks brought the conversation around to my job working for Johnny Hotchkiss. "That's no work for you, Cass. The least Johnny could do is give you your old job back."

I'd asked Johnny to keep the scut work I was doing for him on the down low, but obviously I wasn't fooling anyone, at least not Brooks.

"I'd prefer if nobody knew," I now told him. "Especially Zoe."

"Good luck with that." He tapped his fingers nervously on his glass before returning to the subject of Ashley and Vince. "There's something you should know about your new roomies."

"Oh? And what's that?"

"They'd already moved out of Hilliard House when they *so conveniently* became lost on your property. It seems they left rather abruptly at that." He waited for a reaction but got none, so he continued. "Apparently they became visibly rattled at breakfast one morning.

41

About what, George couldn't tell. But within an hour those two were checked out and gone, even though they still had a week left on their reservation."

"So?"

"I'm just sayin'." He lifted a shoulder.

"Well, you're not *sayin'* it very clearly."

"Look, something doesn't add up. George told me when they settled the bill, the girl said they'd miscalculated their expenses."

"I'm still not following."

He sighed deeply. "They may be taking advantage of you. It's not all that hard to figure out where The Bluffs is and how to reach it through the trails."

I narrowed my eyes. "And they simply jumped to the conclusion the owner was in need of a couple with some carpentry skills?"

He looked down at his shoes. "It's a small town, Cass."

It finally sunk in.

"So I'm now a juicy topic for the Whale Rock gossipmongers? To the extent that complete strangers are hearing about my troubles?"

"I don't need to tell you how Hilliard House is the hub of town chatter."

Not only was it a popular B&B, but Evelyn had created an open-door policy for locals to congregate in her gathering room for "coffee and a catch-up," as she called it. In other words, it was the clearinghouse for unofficial town business.

My face burned.

Brooks understood he'd stepped into a briar patch and began a quick retreat.

"If people are talking about you, it's only because they're concerned."

"And they show their concern by attacking a couple of newcomers who've offered to help me out during a tough time?" Might as well lump Zoe's friends in with the rest of the natives. Whale Rockers drew a very distinct line between visitors and locals, unreceptive to outsiders until tourists opened their wallets. It was the reason they'd been so opposed to Ethan from the beginning. *A Chicagoan living in our midst? Gasp!* That they'd pretty much been on target about him was irrelevant.

"Nobody's attacking them. But they do have reservations about you being out here alone with two strangers." He scratched his head. "Don't you get that people in this town really are on your side?"

I refused to let unfounded suspicions taint my regard for Ashley and Vince, but I didn't trust myself to speak again, and Brooks read my silence well.

"Okay, subject dropped." He looked toward the carriage house as he stepped out onto the porch. "Just keep your eyes as open as your heart, Cass."

I watched as Chuckles drove away, inhaling the powerful aroma of my great-grandparents.

But so focused was I in pushing aside the warnings of Zoe and her friends, I didn't pick up on the subtle change in scent, and the possibility that it was alerting me to a danger.

It was the next day that I came upon the abandoned campsite in the woods.

# 6

Late June ~ nine weeks before the disappearance

When one of Johnny Hotchkiss's crew up and quit, he offered me the extra hours until he could find a replacement. Considering my desperate financial situation, I willingly accepted.

My days began at sunrise, and I didn't get home until past dinnertime—and even later when scheduled for the sunset cruises. Working long days and staying up to all hours in my studio was starting to take its toll. I'd worked nearly every day the past few weeks, and now full into tourist season, I could see no break in sight. If it hadn't been for Ashley and Vince, I might have starved.

One night at dinner, Ashley said, "Don't hate me for saying this, but you look exhausted, Cassie."

"You're working too hard," Vince agreed. "And I've seen the light burning in the barn well past midnight."

"Guilty." I offered a sheepish shrug and then added excitedly, "But I'm in such a good place with my art right now, following a very long drought I might add." I'd accomplished little during the end of my marriage. And what time I had spent in my studio had not been productive, leaving me with a slew of unfinished paintings. But these past weeks I'd been prolific. I wasn't sure what to credit it to: the move to the barn, the easing of some financial burdens? Or perhaps I was just more creatively fertile at night.

Chewing on a bite of grilled chicken, I also chewed on the most

44

significant change during this creative burst and pointed my fork at Ashley and Vince. "Hey, maybe you two are my muses."

"Well, if that's the case," Ashley said, pushing her plate aside, "when are you going to let us have a peek at your work?"

"You *have* been rather mysterious lately," Vince added, refilling his own plate with a huge second serving of broccoli.

"You'll have to wait until they're finished." I had become protective of my work, even taking to covering the canvases and locking the barn lately, attributing it to concern over whoever might be prowling the nearby woods.

A few weeks ago, I'd stumbled upon a couple of abandoned campsites, one near where the trail abutted my property and another in a shallow alcove further into the woods. Camping was strictly prohibited in the preserved land trust, but I chose not to report it.

The Jacobsons took Whistler out on the trails every morning, and they'd reported nothing suspicious except finding a pocket field sharpener, which arguably could belong to anyone who walked the trails. Brooks was already paranoid, and I didn't need him or his troop of not-so-merry lawmen breathing down my neck.

Still, though I'd never been frightened of being alone, the thought of a stranger creeping about near my property made me uneasy. I couldn't deny how reassuring it was to have a strapping young man in residence.

"Have you seen any signs of our elusive visitor?"

"Nothing." Vince shrugged between bites. "Let's hope whoever it was has moved on."

"Good riddance." Ashley shivered, looking more relieved than she sounded. "I mean, it's just so secluded out here."

The Bluffs *was* remotely positioned. Sitting on the very outskirts of Whale Rock, the drive up from the main road was nearly a mile. The house faced westward over the cliffs, and the property was bordered along its southern boundary by hundreds of acres of land trust woodlands. The northern edge gradually swept down into a large marsh. *Lots of places to hide, but nowhere to run.*

"No more talk of strangers prowling the woods," Vince commanded. "You two will have nightmares for sure."

I didn't mention my own relentless nightmares and how the late stays in the barn had as much to do with avoiding my bed. I was also trying to ignore the change in scent I'd noticed; the once-comforting sweet smell of burning sugar had become acrid, almost chokingly pungent. But fatigue was interfering with my ability to interpret the messages Percy and Celeste were trying to convey.

\* \* \*

Johnny unexpectedly gave me a weekend off, and I took the opportunity to hole up in my studio and finish the Bartlett family portrait. I hated to slow the momentum on the new series of paintings I'd been working on, but I had no choice but to tear myself away to finish commission work.

*If only I didn't have to pick up that package today.* I was not looking forward to a foray into Whale Rock, but I needed those oils I'd ordered if I was to finish the portrait and get paid. The electric bill awaited. As did the gas bill and the phone bill. The goal was to slip in and out of town without being noticed.

But in line with how my luck had been running lately, I exited the post office just as Lu Ketchner rounded the corner of High Street at breakneck speed.

I tried to duck into the Shipyard Sweet Shoppe before she saw me.

"Well, look who found her way to town," Lu called out.

*Crap. Too late. How did she walk so fast in those skyscraper heels?*

"Oh. Hi, Lu. I didn't see you."

"Uh-huh." She raised skeptical brows. "So what brings you out of hiding?"

"I'm not hiding," I answered a little too defensively. "I've just been busy finishing up a painting."

"Anything I can exhibit?" Lu was always on the lookout for her next commission.

I shrugged.

"You have got to stop with the silly portraits and get back to your true talent," she scolded.

"It pays the bills." *Just barely.*

"Your mother would hate that you're wasting the gift she passed on to you." Lu clicked her tongue. "What I wouldn't give to have some more of her work."

If only Lu knew what I'd uncovered in those long-hidden crates. But I wasn't ready to share Mama's mysterious paintings yet, and hoped I never reached such a desperate point to be forced to sell them.

I slipped away after promising Lu a peek at some of my new paintings once they were finished. Who knew? Maybe the new series I was working on would show potential.

At least I'd avoided an encounter with Billy. I wasn't sure how much longer I could blame long work hours and lack of sleep for my late period. How often these past few weeks I'd wished I hadn't slept with him that last time—or ever. *'If wishes were horses, then beggars would ride.'* Granny Fi's oft-spouted rebuke rang through my head.

* * *

Late Saturday afternoon, there came a light knocking on the barn door.

"We have a surprise for you." Ashley poked her head in, subtly looking past me to where my paintings were set up.

"What kind of surprise?" I quickly turned the easel and walked toward the door, blocking ingress into my private retreat.

"Something we found hidden in the carriage house," she said in her honeyed voice, and made a playful spinning gesture with her finger. "Now go clean your brushes and then come down to Percy's Bluffs."

"Time for a shower?" I held up my paint-smudged arms. "I'm an untidy artist."

"Genius is often messy." She gave an impish wink. "Whenever you're ready."

I arrived on the bluffs awhile later to find a small makeshift fire pit blazing, to fend off the evening chill. They'd carted over an old folding table, swathed it in white linen, and set upon it fine china, crystal, and silver.

I caressed an antique dish, then held a crystal wine glass so that the lowering sun glinted off its rim.

Ashley was beaming. "They're Percy and Celeste's, right?"

"How could I have forgotten about these?" I fingered the initials "PMC" engraved on one of the knives.

Men working the fire had removed some of Celeste's finer belongings from the house, but with the whole family presumed dead—or so everyone thought until Fiona's secret was revealed—many of those treasures had disappeared. Over the years, Granny Fi had collected the odd piece here and there until a good portion of the missing sets had been recovered. Before she died, she told me, "Check with Archie from time to time. More might show up." Archibald Stanfield owned the local antiques store and had been the source of many of her acquisitions. Knowing how hard Fiona had worked to reclaim these family legacies, I'd hidden them years ago when Ethan began to blow through my money.

Tears threatened, and I was glad for my sunglasses.

"May I present the first course?" With dramatic flair, Vince removed the cover from a silver serving dish to reveal a display of colossal shrimp.

"My favorite." I dipped one into a small crystal bowl of cocktail sauce.

"We couldn't have picked a better night." Ashley delighted in the stunning view of Whale Rock Harbor. Typical of this time of year, there seemed as many sailboats coming in after a long day's sail as those heading out for a sunset cruise.

The offerings were delicious, and when we'd finished, the sun had set, but the sky was still blazing a deep rose to match the blush wine I sipped.

"You must have scrambled to pull this off. I mean, we didn't even know I was going to have a free weekend until last night."

"We had help," Vince admitted. "You've heard of La Table over in Wellfleet?"

A sudden heat rushed to my cheeks. There was no way they could have known my history with the caterer who prepared the luscious meal we'd just enjoyed, or that he'd been involved in the breakup of my marriage.

"Yes, the owner, Billy Hughes, is an old friend." I tried to sound casual. "You didn't by chance mention where you were staying?"

Ashley shook her head. "Should we have?"

"No!" It came out a panicked croak. Further talk of Billy would put a damper on the evening, so I redirected the conversation. "It's all lovely."

"It's a way to thank you for giving us a place to"—Vince shrugged—"hide out this summer."

"And for taking a chance on us," Ashley added. "We'd been nomads searching for a purpose, and you made that happen for us."

"You never said where this roving journey of yours began."

"Where haven't we been?" They shared an elusive smile. It wasn't my first attempt to get them to open up, but Vince and Ashley persisted in their usual pattern of skirting personal questions.

"How did you end up on the Cape?"

"My college roommate's family spent time out here every summer," Ashley said. "She'd go on and on about how wonderful it was."

"Where did her family summer?" I asked.

"I never thought to ask," she admitted.

"We're going to sound like the hayseeds we are," added Vince, "but we honestly didn't realize the Cape was so large."

Ashley made an "Aren't we silly?" face and nodded her agreement.

"Why don't you call her and find out? People *never* give up their Cape rentals. They could be out here now," I suggested, excited for them at the possibility of reconnecting with a friend. "And maybe not too far away."

"We've lost touch." Ashley was dismissive, a shadow darkening her face, making me feel I'd overstepped in my eagerness.

"I get that. Life gets busy, and we lose track of people." I wished to return to the happier mood of the evening. "Thank you again for tonight and for all your hard work on the carriage house." Except for me selecting the finishes and driving to Hyannis to pick up supplies from the Home Depot, they were handling the entire rehab project. When I wasn't working at the harbor, I'd cocooned myself in the studio.

I raised my glass, then swallowed the last sip of wine.

"To Battersea Bluffs." Ashley added her own toast.

"We're making good progress," Vince said. "At this rate, you should be able to rent it by early fall."

"I could draft an ad for you," offered Ashley.

"Start with this line: 'Seeking two wandering souls looking to end their nomadic existence to take up permanent residence in prime Cape Cod locale.'"

The sky was darkening now, with only the stubs of two candles casting light, and I questioned whether the look that passed between the couple was sad or disturbed, real or imagined.

"Seriously, why don't you put an end to your roving ways and rent it yourselves? You already know the landlady's a pushover."

"We love it here."

I sensed the hovering rejection to my proposal, and after an awkward hesitation Vince provided it.

"Ashley has an internship that begins in October."

"That's great news." When there was no response, I added, "Right?"

"Yeah, sure, it's all good," he said.

It sounded not at all like an endorsement to my ears, but then again, I didn't want them to go. I'd grown quite fond of and accustomed to having them around.

"I presume this position isn't within commuting distance?" Probing, but not too aggressively.

"Not by a long shot." Ashley pouted.

Vince stood and began to gather dishes. "You two relax, and I'll handle the cleanup," he said.

"Don't be silly." I stood and began to help. I'd put a damper on the magic of the evening and wished for a chance to take back my prying questions. "As Granny Fi used to say, *Many hands make for a lighter load.*"

We worked in silence until Vince began pulling the overfilled cart across bumpy terrain, the china and crystal tinkling harmoniously. While passing the wooded boundary to my property, I felt the eerie sensation of eyes upon us. I pulled my pashmina shawl tighter and began to sing a melody that had calmed me since childhood. *"Light is the lighterman's toil, as his delicate vessel he rows."*

"That's a pretty tune."

"Fiona taught it to me. She said my grandfather used to sing it to her when they were courting." I continued singing, *"Yet deem not the lighterman's heart is as light, as the shallop he steers o'er the severn so bright."*

"What *is* a lighterman?" Vince asked.

"They captained cargo boats called 'lighters' on the Thames River. It was a job for lower-class boys, but it required great skill and an intimate knowledge of tides and currents. Before a lighterman could acquire his own license, he had to apprentice with a master for many years. It's what Percy did before he left London. There's an image of a lighter engraved on his grave."

"How interesting. I'd love to see it sometime," Ashley said.

"Sure—why don't I give you a little tour of the Mitchell burial grounds tomorrow?"

"Hey, Ash, more material for your—" Vince began, then broke off.

"For what?" I asked but then remembered Ashley's journalism degree. "Are you writing something about my family?"

"Just a short story. Loosely based on the tragedy at Percy's Bluffs." She was flustered. "I'm not sure if it will develop into anything. I was going to tell you about it." An awkward moment passed before she added, "But if you'd rather I didn't . . . ?"

"Let me think about it." I wasn't certain how I felt. *Deceived? Gratified? Violated? Honored?*

We walked on as I finished the song. *"For love he has kindled his torch, and lighted the lighterman's heart, and he owns to the rapturous scorch."*

I'd have to sleep on it.

But sleep was elusive, mostly from anxiety over somebody hanging out in the woods. I should probably mention those campsites to Brooks.

In my wakefulness, a recent conversation with Zoe about Ashley and Vince popped into my head, one I couldn't seem to banish.

"You want to prove me wrong so badly that you'd put yourself in jeopardy," she'd accused, and then went on to say, "Have you ever asked them what they're really doing there, Cassie? You are far too trusting."

The truth was, I *had* asked but was never able to pin them down. I hated that my sister's disapproving attitude was unconsciously influencing my feelings, and I'd answered by directing the blame on her. "You just have a distrustful nature."

It was the same old argument, only I'd hit closer to the mark than she had. If it weren't for Zoe and all her friends, particularly Brooks, constantly planting the seeds of doubt, I wouldn't have given a second thought to Ashley wanting to write a story about my ancestors. She wasn't the first person to recount the Mitchell family tragedy, nor likely the last.

Unable to shove aside all my misgivings, I tossed off the covers to seek pharmaceutical assistance. The next morning, after a more peaceful sleep than I'd had in months, I made my decision.

I was frying bacon and mixing batter for pancakes when my sleepyhead tenants came down for breakfast. Vince poured two cups of coffee and set one down before his young bride.

"It was the mouthwatering smell of bacon that woke me from my dreams."

"Speaking of dreams," I said, offering the platter of crisp bacon, "you have my blessing for the story."

"That's awesome!" Ashley sprang from her chair, nearly knocking over her coffee cup, and threw her arms about me, making me feel small for having doubted her motives. "I promise to let you read it before I do anything with it."

"I'm sure I'll love it." I flipped a stack of pancakes onto Vince's plate, and he attacked them with his usual relish. "After breakfast, let's walk over to the graveyard. I can offer a more personal version of our family history than what you'd dig up at the library."

"No pun intended?" Ashley laughed.

I was happy for the return of goodwill, even if it was to be short-lived.

\* \* \*

I walked Vince and Ashley over to the graveyard, directing them first to Percy and Celeste's gravesites. Ashley had brought along some sheets of white paper and a black crayon. "I thought a grave rubbing would give me inspiration."

"Clever idea for a book jacket," I suggested.

She rolled her eyes in a self- effacing way. "Let's see how the short story develops first."

While Ashley did her rubbing, I began roughing out a line drawing of her in my sketchbook. When I finished, she was no longer working at my great-grandfather's grave. I glanced about and spied her standing with Vince at the southern corner of the cemetery. When I reached them, they were kneeling and brushing away dirt from one of the stones.

Ashley read the epitaph: "'Thief of life, with burning strife, actions caused for mourning rife.'"

Vince pointed to the stone. "Who was R.T.?"

"Robert Toomey." My nostrils filled with an acrid burning smell, sharper and more intense than ever before. Neither of my friends seemed to notice, so I assumed it was a signal form Percy and Celeste, though I'd never known them to venture so far. Was it a sign of their contempt for the man?

"Was he a relative?" Vince asked.

"No. Actually, he was Percy Mitchell's worst nightmare."

"I know who it is." Ashley stood and dusted the dirt from her hands. "The Englishman who started the fire at The Bluffs."

"Allegedly. Nobody saw him do it. But he had arrived in Whale Rock that very day, and Robert Toomey is the name Percy damned before rushing into the flames to try to rescue Celeste."

"How did he end up buried here, in your family plot?"

"He died soon after the fire and before the property had been purchased by the architect who restored the house. A local pastor arranged to have the body buried on the grounds, assuming there'd never again be a Mitchell living there. Fiona wasn't about to protest, since she hadn't yet told her parents she was pregnant. At the time, the only markers in the private graveyard were Edwin and Jerome's. It was my father who later put up the stones for Percy, Celeste, and Ambrose."

"But why would Toomey do something so horrible?"

"Unrequited love." I knelt down to inspect the stone. "Celeste's family had promised her hand in marriage to Robert Toomey, who worked for Celeste's father, the owner of a fleet of lighters. But she'd spurned Robert's affections."

"Because she'd fallen in love with your great-grandfather?"

I nodded. "As the story was told to me by Granny Fi—who I imagine heard it from Ambrose—Percy became enchanted with the young beauty who was always hanging about the London docks. And Celeste was equally charmed by the handsome Percival Mitchell. She also had a strong will, and a heart and mind of her own, with every intention of marrying for love."

"So this Robert Toomey sought revenge?"

"His pride had been wounded, and he struck out at Celeste by attacking her virtue. Her parents threatened to send her off to a convent to preserve the family honor."

"Until true love prevailed and Percy came to the rescue?" Vince wore a sardonic grin.

"My husband, the *skeptic*, doesn't believe in 'happily ever after,'" Ashley said. I wondered if Vince's cynicism was the product of a broken home. Divorce can certainly devastate idealistic notions.

"You were the first woman who at least made me optimistic about the prospect of 'together forever.'"

"Good to know." Ashley gave him a good-natured backhanded smack. "Go on, Cassie."

"Well, he did come to the rescue. And it was said they were happy, but as you know, the ending was tragic. That should satisfy both the skeptic and the romantic."

"Did they come to America to escape the wretched Robert Toomey?"

"Yes. But they almost didn't make it."

~

Over a century ago—London, England

"Celeste, m' love, wake up. Now is the time."

Her eyes fluttered open, and she gasped when she saw Percy standing over her.

He held a quieting finger to her lips. "We don't want to wake your mum and da."

She rubbed her eyes before asking in a hushed tone, "What time is it?"

"Early enough. Do you have your bag packed?"

She pointed under the bed.

Percy tugged the overstuffed satchel from beneath the bed boards. "Are you taking your mother's silver now?"

She hit him playfully with her pillow, then hissed, "You said one bag. That's my one bag. And I'm not going without it."

"If ye say so," he murmured. "Hurry up now. If I'm to save you from life in the convent, we must be at the shipyard within the hour."

Percy had managed to secure passage on a merchant steamer sailing from Southampton to Boston. A friend had arranged for a relative who lived in a town called Whale Rock in Massachusetts to sponsor them. To begin the journey, Percy had called in a favor from the owner of a small clipper setting out before daybreak with a cargo shipment.

"What a queer name. How do ya suppose they came up with it?" Percy had asked his pal.

"When the tide is low, there's this fantastic rock about a half mile from shore, 'tis the spitting image of a blue whale," Smithy replied. "Me cuz tells me it's been the cause of a few shipwrecks."

When Percy told Celeste about the name of their new home, she'd been intrigued. "Are there real whales there?"

"Imagine so."

"And what will you do there? How will we get by?"

"We'll be living near the ocean, and I'm a damn good sailor. I'm sure to find work."

During the short walk to the boatyard, Celeste uttered one small lament. "I guess I'll never have a house on Lavender Hill, as I'd always dreamed."

"We'll have our own Lavender Hill. I'll build you a fine home, and that's what we'll call it."

"But I've already decided on a name for our place."

"You have? And what might that be, m' love?"

"We'll call it Battersea Gardens so we never forget where we came from, and I'll fill the gardens with lavender instead."

Percy was finally breathing easier when the docks came into view, where three of his good mates were waiting for them.

"Smithy, Peter, what are you two handsome lads doing strolling about at this hour?" Celeste teased.

They both stammered a response, and had it been daylight, they surely would have been glowing like summer roses. Celeste had that effect on men.

"And Michael O'Connell, you must have skipped the pub last evening to be here before the crack of dawn. Does Mattie know what you're up to?"

"I'm as tight-lipped as a man without a tongue. We wanted no trouble getting you to your launch."

Someone's lips had been loose, however, for somehow, Robert Toomey had learned of their plans. From an alleyway now he pounced, taking the group off guard.

"Trying to pull a fast one on me, are ye?" He rammed Percy in the stomach, and they both sprawled down to the ground with a thud.

"Stop this foolishness," pleaded Celeste as the two men wrestled in the dirt.

Peter and Smithy were quick to pull Robert away and pin him down while Michael did his best to usher Percy and Celeste away from the scene and to the boat awaiting them.

They were still within earshot when Robert Toomey spit out his curse.

*"May your sons all die young, and your grandsons, and any generations to come whilst mine will thrive, knowing the seed of Percival Mitchell shall never endure."*

~

Present day

Percy died believing the curse had come true, as all three of his sons were young men with promising futures when they were killed. Ambrose died in the Navy, and his two older brothers had died at sea during a storm, crashing into—of all places—the rock formation for which the town was named.

"The curse mentioned in Edgar Faust's book?" Ashley looked at me.

I merely shrugged. I didn't want to talk about the lighterman's curse today with Ashley and Vince. It was all so complicated. Was our long family history of tragedy somehow tied to a century-old curse? It seemed implausible that a superstitious spell was responsible for wiping out an entire family's bloodline. And frankly, this talk was venturing too close to the question I was avoiding regarding my reckless night with an irresistible old boyfriend.

"Such a long way to travel to seek revenge."

"I've often wondered what Robert Toomey's intentions were in coming here. But that is destined to remain one of life's unsolved mysteries."

"No charges were pressed for setting the fire?"

"He was questioned, but there were no witnesses, no proof."

"No Percy or Celeste to refute his story." Ashley sighed lightly.

"Only circumstantial evidence. Not enough to prosecute." More legalese from Vince.

"But enough for the town to turn against him. Nobody would hire him, and he didn't have enough money to leave. What little money he had left, he apparently drank away in the town tavern. Granny Fi herself witnessed the man's rapid descent into madness, then death."

Vince read the inscription again. "Harsh sentiments."

"At first there was a simple flat marker engraved with his name and date of death, but it was replaced with this stone in the early 1990s. One day when Granny Fi was visiting Ambrose's grave, she noticed it had been changed, but nobody ever knew how or why."

"My goodness. Look at all these tiny grave markers." Ashley bent down to inspect them more closely. They each said the same thing—"Mitchell Boy"—followed by a date. "Seven?"

"My brothers." Four died between Zoe's birth and mine, and three died after I was born. "Most were late-term miscarriages. One stillbirth. Another lived only a couple hours."

I pointed out the nearby marker of Ambrose and those of his two brothers, Edwin and Jerome, who died in a freak boating accident. "There are many sad stories here."

Ashley ambled over to the only other grave not belonging to a Mitchell. Her shoulders slumped as she read the inscription and rested her hand upon her heart.

Vince noticed and moved to her side. "What is it?"

She nodded to the marker and grasped her husband's arm, leaning into him.

I knew how it read: "Bless this unknown boy who washed upon our shores."

They hadn't asked, but the silence was unsettling, so I began telling them the story behind the sad little grave.

"My father was the one who first spotted the boy's body. He'd been moving a sailboat that day. The coast was too rocky to approach, so he sailed to the nearest inlet where he could dock and run for help. He guided the sheriff and a rescue crew back to the location on foot."

"How old was the child?" Vince asked.

"Fiona said he was probably five or six. The old timers still refer to him as 'Barnacle Boy.'"

Ashley grimaced. "Nobody ever claimed him?"

"There was a widespread effort to find out who he was, where he came from, how a child could've drowned and never been reported missing. But nothing ever came of it."

"Why was this little boy buried in your family's private cemetery?"

"It was the same year my parents bought back our house, and since my father had been the one to find him, they arranged to have the child buried here. Granny Fi took charge of the funeral. Nearly everyone in Whale Rock turned out for it."

We stood in silent reverence until Ashley said, "It's an idyllic resting place for an unclaimed soul."

My young friends had apparently had enough of the cemetery tour and begged off for an afternoon at the beach. I stayed behind to pay tribute to those who had lived and died before me. The gravestones of my great-grandparents, their sons, my grandmother, and my parents were all shaded by the cedars and faced out to sea. Percy's large stone with the lighter boat etching, was engraved with his last words: "I am not finished." Celeste's was slightly smaller. "Femme Celeste, his lady true." My father's: "A Mitchell born, a Mitchell died." And my mother's: "Our Beloved Queenie. Rest her fragile soul."

Two leaping dolphins flanked either side of Fiona's headstone. It bore the fitting inscription: "Her heart was as large as her life." The woman who'd done so much to help others had no special requests for herself. As her death drew near, she'd told me, "What does it matter? I'll be gone from here. Do what you think best." So I threw a party on Percy's Bluffs in honor of the unofficial town matriarch.

I turned toward a twig-snapping sound. My scalp crawled with the feeling of being watched again. I marched in the direction of the trees bordering the graveyard, but whatever—or whoever—had been lurking there hastened away.

I was still unsettled when I arrived back at the house. Vince and Ashley had not yet left for the beach, and my sense of foreboding intensified when I overheard their conversation as I passed underneath the kitchen window.

A bottle cap popped. "Sip?"

"Honey, it's not even noon," I heard Ashley say.

"I know. But I'm a little freaked out." Gulping sounds followed by a beer belch.

"You don't seriously think he's still around?"

"It's unlikely, right?" The sound of another gulp. "We still don't know why he was here."

"I guess." She sounded unconvinced.

"And we can't be sure he said anything."

"True."

"Hey, are *you* okay?"

"That little boy's grave, it just . . ." Ashley said cryptically, "made me a little shaky, but maybe we came upon it for a reason. It could be a good place."

*A good place for what?* I pressed my body flat against the house, not wishing to be caught in the embarrassing act of eavesdropping.

"I dunno. We need to be certain it's not a risk."

"Let's at least consider it for a while." She sounded serious, gloomy almost, a striking contrast to her usual cheerfulness.

"Not too long, babe. We don't have the luxury." The beer bottle, now presumably empty, clanged onto the table. "Let's get out of here."

I laid a hand over my racing heart and slid down to the ground as all kinds of scenarios began whirling around in my head. Did they suspect more about whoever had been hiding out in the woods than they were telling me? If so, chances were it wasn't just a harmless camper.

The bitter odor had pursued me from the graveyard and was now so pervasive I'd begun to cough. I pulled my shirt up to cover my nose and fled to the barn in hopes of shaking free of the nasty smell. But it was not to be. The haunting odor had now invaded my sanctuary. Was there nowhere I could go to escape it?

# 7

Mid-July ~ six weeks before the disappearance

Ever since the cemetery visit, there'd been a melancholic cloud hovering over Ashley and Vince. Although I remained anxious about what I'd overheard that day, I decided to bide my time and hope whatever was troubling them would resolve without my interference.

There were no more indications of anyone hanging about in the woods, so I'd been able to talk myself down from the panic, convincing myself that whatever had been hiding in those trees was most likely a deer or coyote. It's amazing how the distance of time can sway perceptions.

Good progress continued on the carriage house, and it was a bittersweet realization that the project was nearing completion. Even though my two lodgers had become withdrawn of late, I dreaded the looming goodbyes.

When not working, Ashley and Vince took off on their bikes and often didn't return until evening. For the first time since they'd arrived, I felt lonely. Making it worse was the absence of Percy and Celeste's reassuring aroma, now replaced by the stench that had haunted me since the day at the cemetery.

"The new closet doors are in," Vince announced one morning as he scraped the last bit of eggs from the frying pan. "Can you pick them up this morning?"

It was selfish of me, but I'd been looking forward to spending time in my studio. "Why don't you take the truck and go? Maybe pick up some paint chips while you're there?" I suggested, to save me yet another trip to Home Depot. Facing summer Cape traffic in sweltering heat was not an appealing prospect.

"I'll come with." Ashley stood and began clearing the breakfast dishes.

"No. You stay here." He cut her off but softened his tone when he noticed her wounded expression. "We need to start prepping the walls, babe. You can work on that while I'm gone."

Shortly after Vince departed on his errand, a familiar Whale Rock PD cruiser pulled up the drive. With two coffee mugs in hand, I met Brooks at the door and motioned for him to take one of the porch rockers.

"I was worried you'd forgotten about me." I handed him one of the mugs. "Or have you finally come to the realization that Vince and Ashley aren't trying to rob me blind?"

My old friend frowned. "There's a lot going on in the Rock."

"Anything interesting?"

"If you could bother to drag yourself away from the docks for a real visit now and again, you might learn something." I was getting the gist of his visit: a scolding for keeping my distance.

My absence from Whale Rock social circles had little to do with the hours I'd been keeping. I was still smarting over being the butt of local gossip, but mostly I wished to steer clear of Billy as I continued to shove away anxiety over an unplanned pregnancy.

"You know as well as I do that the summer crowds are so thick, nobody would even notice if I were there or not."

"I noticed," he said before taking his first swig of coffee.

"So what's up, my dear Chuckles?"

His initial scowl morphed into a reluctant smile when he realized I was using the nickname affectionately.

"A lot of vandalism in the National Sea Shore, even in the preserve here." He pointed to the land trust bordering The Bluffs. "Brush fires from kids starting campfires and leaving them unattended."

"Any major damage?"

He shook his head. "Fortunately, they were quickly contained." He took another gulp of coffee. "And we've got ourselves a party house this year. A group of young punks crammed into a beach house and causing lots of late-night disturbances."

"Close to town?"

"Yep. And someone stole one of Johnny Hotchkiss's Mercury boats." In addition to whale watching and sightseeing boat tours, my boss also owned several small sailboats used as rentals.

"When?" Johnny had finally hired someone to crew full-time, which left me out of the loop. Rubbing at calluses from being relegated back to limited hours of stinky grunt work, I pondered this new information.

"Yesterday."

"Are those boats docked now?" That would make them fairly accessible.

"No, they're still moored out in the harbor. Whoever stole it would've either had to swim out or be dropped by another boat."

Never, to my recollection, had there been a boat theft from Whale Rock Harbor.

"It's kind of hard to hide a sailboat, even a Mercury. Any leads?"

"I'm hoping to connect the theft to our party-house occupants so we can evict them."

I picked up his empty mug. "Time for a refill?"

He nodded and followed me into the kitchen. "You okay? You look pale."

"I'm fine." I waved away his concern.

His phone rang, and as he listened, his hand shot out over the top of his mug. "Sorry—gotta run."

I waved him off, having failed to tell him about the unidentified camper who may have been hiding out in the nearby woods. It might have helped him make a connection to the vandals who'd been wreaking havoc on his summer.

I decided to take a walk out to those campsites to see for myself if there'd been any recent activity. At the site closer to my property, there were a couple cigarette butts I didn't recall from before, but any inconsiderate hikers could have left those. There were no signs anyone had been hanging out at the alcove further into the woods. As much as I wanted to believe it was a group of rebellious teens who'd been loitering near my property, there'd been none of the normal partying paraphernalia, like food wrappers or beer bottles, left behind.

*  *  *

Around noontime, I sought out Ashley in the carriage house. It was time to break through the strange force field that had been erected.

She was bent over her notebook, so intent in her focus that she didn't notice me until Whistler stood and whimpered a greeting.

"Sorry, I didn't hear you." She jolted alert and quickly shut the notebook to hide what she'd been writing.

I waved away her apology. "I often lose myself to my painting. I suppose you do the same when you write."

She fixed me with a confused look, then followed my gaze to her notepad and shook her head. "Yes. Of course. Happens all the time."

"I made some sandwiches." I held up a small cooler. "Want to take them down to Percy's Bluffs?"

"Sure." She looked at her watch, brow furrowing. "Wonder what's taking Vince so long?"

"He's probably stuck in traffic." A perpetual problem on the Cape in the summer. "Yesterday there was a three-mile backup at the Route 6 light."

"I'll just call him quickly to check."

I squatted down to pet Whistler while she made the call.

"Straight to voicemail." She bit her lower lip, as was her tendency when puzzling over something.

"If he's still in Home Depot, he won't get service."

"That's true. Maybe they misplaced the doors like they did with your vanity."

"Or he's become hypnotized by the Glidden color wheel." I smiled, then made a beckoning gesture.

"I'd better leave him a note," she said, still chewing that lip.

"I expect he'll figure out where we are."

"You're right." She hesitated before ripping a sheet from her notebook. "But still, I wouldn't want him to worry."

She jotted *With Cassie*, then tacked the paper to the door.

"It's the perfect day, isn't it?" I said as we walked toward the water. "I'm really going to miss it here."

"And I'm going to miss you when you have to leave." We smiled at each other regretfully, amiably bumping shoulders. "You never did say where your internship is."

"Actually, I'm not certain of the exact location yet."

This struck me as odd, especially since she had earlier implied it wouldn't be near the Cape. "I misunderstood. I thought you already knew."

"I'll know fairly soon. They haven't made the assignments yet."

"They?"

"It's a, um, start-up online media company."

Two questions immediately came to mind. Since it was an online company, why couldn't she work remotely? And start-up or not, wouldn't they have established a business location?

My confusion must have shown, for she quickly expounded. "They're going to set up satellite sites, and I had to agree to be flexible."

"I admire you for that. Not knowing would drive me crazy. How does Vince feel about waiting?"

"Waiting?"

"To look for a job."

"Oh, he'll find something. As you know, he's pretty handy, and there's always a need for carpenters and odd-jobbers."

"Isn't he eager to start teaching?"

Her perplexed look had me questioning my memory. I was positive he'd mentioned education as his area of study, having just finished his master's.

"High school psychology? Or was it history?"

Ashley nodded. "That's right. History. But, um, he hasn't finished his thesis yet."

The dog ran ahead of us. "So did the two of you get Whistler together?"

"He came as part of a package deal." She peered at her phone.

"Is it two years you've been married now?"

"Almost. Gosh, we're practically an old married couple."

"Hardly."

"My parents wanted us to wait until after we finished graduate school, but Vince thought it would make it easier to concentrate on our studies if we were settled."

"So it was *the skeptic* who pushed for the marriage?" We'd arrived at the cliffs, and sat down on a large rock to take in the view.

"Good memory. He has a grim view of commitment. His parents fought a lot when he was growing up. There were many separations and reconciliations. He spent a lot of time with his grandfather. But as much as he protests, he really does crave stability. And besides, I wouldn't just move in with him. My father's a Baptist minister." She raised her brows in a meaningful way. "Daddy can be quite the intimidating figure."

Another check of the phone.

"You guys met in college, right?" I had assumed they weren't high school sweethearts, with Vince's slight Midwestern twang and Ashley's accent with hints of sweet Southern tones.

"Yep." A wistful smile crept across her face. We both heard the noise of a car door slamming, and looked up to see Vince approaching in his long, easy stride. Ashley's smile multiplied exponentially, and I had the feeling she was not only happy to see her husband but also relieved.

When she jumped from her perch to give him a smooch, it further occurred to me that these two were rarely out of each other's sight.

"Cassie made us lunch," she told her husband.

"I've been hearing all about your courtship." I began unpacking the food.

He shrugged nonchalantly. "Not much to tell."

"It was fate." Ashley beamed. "I was wait-listed and had almost given up hope of being accepted. Of course, Vince was a triple legacy and—"

I looked up because she stopped abruptly. Ashley was flushing deeply, and I didn't think it was from the heat of the midday sun. I wasn't sure what I'd missed, but there'd been a definite shift.

"Did Ash tell you about our wedding?" Vince asked. "Her father is a minister, and he wanted not only to escort his daughter down the aisle—and rightfully so—but he also wanted to perform the ceremony, select the music, and sing a solo."

"Where was this?" I asked after he finished sharing the humorous aspects of their wedding day.

"It was a destination wedding," they said in perfect unison, as if rehearsed.

"Bermuda," they said again, then laughed at their parroting. "We do this all the time."

I envied them this sense of unity.

"I hear it's beautiful."

"September is the best time to go."

"So you're coming up on your anniversary? We'll have to celebrate before you leave."

A look passed between the two, and I realized my gaffe.

"That's silly, isn't it? You'd want to be alone." I was embarrassed for intruding.

"You'd be more than welcome to join us." Vince smiled warmly. "But we were married on the twenty-seventh and might be at our next port of call by then."

"I knew I'd make a sailor out of you eventually."

He blushed uncharacteristically. "Trust me. I've a long way to go before I'm ready to call myself a true sailor."

"You're being modest." We'd only managed a few outings, but Vince had taken to sailing as if he'd been born with a mainsheet in his hand. "Regardless, I hope you won't be too far away to come back for visits."

Another of those enigmatic gazes passed between them, making me feel the outsider.

"I hope so too," Vince said, then rubbed his hands together. "I don't know about you guys, but I'm starving."

"What's new?" I teased.

The outing had served its purpose, and the awkwardness had evaporated. But I still had the distinct impression neither of them was ready to start their next chapter. Perhaps it was jitters about a new job in an as yet unknown location. Or maybe they'd become subconsciously enchanted by the essence of Percy and Celeste. I could think of stranger possibilities.

# 8

Late July ~ five weeks before the disappearance

The mordant odor seemed to strengthen. I had to find ways to escape the haunting stench before it drove me mad. When I opened the can of paint thinner to clean my brushes, I inhaled deeply—which was a mistake, for it made me dizzy and caused me to stumble. Next thing I knew, I was being carried from the barn. It felt similar to my fire dreams, which were always incredibly realistic, but when I saw Ashley and Vince run back inside to snuff out a small fire along the side wall, it became all too real.

It took some effort to pull myself up, but I managed to stagger back to the door. The fire was already out, and I watched Vince gesture toward my newly finished paintings.

"Look at what she's been working on."

Ashley walked over to take a closer look. "Are you sure these are Cassie's?"

"You mean because they look so much like her mother's?" He shook his head and directed his chin to the rear of the barn. "I moved those to the back stall the night she collapsed."

"Weird. I could swear these were the same agonized-looking people." Ashley's voice seemed filled with wonderment as she slowly turned toward Vince. "Maybe Cassie's copying her mom's paintings for some reason?"

"If so, she has a great memory—or she could be working from photos? Still . . ."

The blare of fire sirens fast approached, and Vince began to cover the canvases with some opaque plastic sheeting. As they made to leave, they found me propped against the door.

"My God, Cassie, you're bleeding!" Ashley rushed to my side. "We need to get you to a doctor." She was panicked.

"We called nine-one-one. There'll be an ambulance," Vince reminded her as he rushed past me to greet the arriving vehicles. Or so I thought.

I looked down to see the red wetness staining the front of my pants and was filled with relief.

I grabbed Ashley's arm before she could follow. "It's just my period." *Finally.*

She looked again at the bleeding. "Really? It's awfully heavy."

"Trust me, I'm fine." The sirens were closer now. "Please stop Vince from saying anything to the EMTs."

I quickly threw on a smock to cover the blood just as the volunteer firefighters charged in with their equipment. After a few moments of dazedly observing the flurry of activity, I looked about for Ashley and Vince, but they were nowhere to be seen. From the fire squad chief, I learned a call had come in from a frantic female, who they'd presumed was me. I didn't correct that notion because a WRPD cruiser skidded to a halt, and out leaped Brooks.

"You okay?" His genuine concern nudged me to the edge, and I crumpled into his outstretched arms and began to sob.

Brooks murmured calming words as he escorted me to the house and then returned to the barn to tie up matters with the fire department. After I stripped off my bloody clothes and showered, I found Brooks waiting for me on the porch.

"Do they know how it started?" I asked, pulling my sweater tight from a chill within.

"They have some suspicions."

"Arson?" This was too much to take in.

He shrugged. "It's possible."

"Who would want to set fire to the barn?"

He answered by looking beyond me into the house first and then fixing me with a meaningful stare.

I shook my head vehemently. "Absolutely not. They called nine-one-one and got me out of the barn."

"What were you doing in there?" he asked.

I explained how I'd been painting and became faint from inhaling the turpentine.

"So what happened to them?" Again he pointedly gazed into the house.

*Good question.* But I deflected by asking what evidence there was.

"It appears the fire started where you've stored some nearly empty bottles of solvent. However, solvents don't automatically combust."

"Did they find any matches?" I motioned for him to follow me inside.

"No." He leaned against the kitchen counter. "Could've been a lighter."

"What about the vandals you told me about a few weeks ago? Didn't you say they'd been setting fires?"

He frowned skeptically. "We'll start by questioning *your friends.*"

We heard voices approaching from outside, and seconds later Vince and Ashley came in through the porch, with Whistler in tow on his leash.

"So sorry for deserting you, Cassie." Ashley gave me a hug. "Are you okay?"

I nodded.

"Whistler bolted," Vince explained as the dog dropped to the kitchen floor, panting roughly, briars clinging to his thick black coat. "And it was hell trying to find him in the dark."

Ashley was now sitting on the floor and had taken Whistler's head in her lap. "It's okay, baby."

I lifted my eyebrows to Brooks, who'd been quietly watching from the sidelines. I didn't think the kids even noticed him until he cleared his throat.

"Oh, sorry, Officer." Vince held out his hand, inspected it, and withdrew it when he noticed how dirty it was.

"I can come back tomorrow if you'd prefer," Brooks offered.

Ashley looked up, quizzically.

"Chief Kincaid needs to question us all about the fire," I told them. "But if you'd rather wait?"

"Now's good," Vince said. "No reason for you to make an extra trip."

Brooks indicated the table, where we all took a seat except for Ashley, who was still ministering to Whistler and gently removing thorny twigs from his fur.

"Cassie says you called nine-one-one about the fire?"

"That's right."

"Where were you and how did you come to notice the fire?"

"We'd ridden to Eastham for some burgers, and as we came back up the lane, we smelled smoke. It was dark, so we didn't see anything at first until we rounded the bend and noticed the lights in the barn."

Ashley picked up the story. "Cassie's been working late out in the barn, so we checked on her there first, and that's when we found her passed out by the work bench and some flames over on the side of the building."

"Ash called nine-one-one, and I carried Cassie outside. Once we were sure her pulse and breathing were normal, we ran back into the barn to smother the fire until the pros arrived. Thankfully, it was a small fire. I don't think there's any damage." Then Vince looked at me with concern and asked, "Did the EMTs check you out?"

"I'm good." I answered and quickly diverted the conversation. "Where did you find Whistler?"

"In some brush on the side of the marsh."

"Is there anyone who can corroborate your whereabouts this evening?" Brooks asked, resuming control of his interrogation.

"Teddy at Wizards in Eastham." Ashley responded a bit defensively.

Brooks arched his brows at this but said nothing as he jotted the name in his notebook.

"I think that'll do it for now." And then, possibly to make amends for the interrogation: "Cassie was lucky you arrived when you did."

Vince swept his hair to the side and shared a sincerely relieved expression with Ashley while I shuddered, considering the horror of being stranded in an all-consuming fire as had once happened to my great-grandmother.

"If you're finished, we'd like to take Whistler upstairs. It's been a pretty traumatic night for him."

"For all of us," I agreed. "Thanks for rescuing me." *Again.*

"I hope you're satisfied now that they mean me no harm," I said to Brooks after they went upstairs.

But he quickly dashed those hopes, raising his notebook and saying in a dubious tone, "Let's wait and see if their story checks out."

* * *

It was past eleven when the frantic call from Zoe came in. I'd made Brooks promise not to tell her, but in small town Whale Rock, where nosy parkers abound, there was no containing the chatter. All the more so when it involved a fire at the legendary Battersea Bluffs.

"You have got to get out of that house," my sister pleaded with me. "I'll wire you plane fare. Just pack a bag right now and leave."

How could I explain to her? As much as Zoe hated to come home, I never wanted to leave.

"I'm staying here, Zo-Zo." She started to protest, but I cut her off. "I don't know what you have against Whale Rock, or maybe just The Bluffs, but I don't share your aversion."

"You'd never understand."

"Why don't you enlighten me?"

"When I'm in that house . . ." She hesitated. "Oh, Cassie, it's too hard to explain."

"Try," I urged.

"It's a feeling of—I don't know—like I'm always gasping for air." She sounded miserable. "It's that pervasive smell."

"What smell?" I asked, though I was convinced I knew what she was going to say. What else could it be but the telltale calling card of Percy and Celeste? At long last I would be able to put my sister's mind at rest. She'd no longer need to be afraid. Zoe could come home at last.

"Of burning . . ." But she was unable to complete her thought.

So I finished it for her. "Burning sugar."

"What?"

"The scent. It's a sweet burning smell, like boiling caramel, right?"

"No. That's not it at all." She paused so long I didn't think she would tell me. "What haunts me in that house is the smell of burning flesh."

I sat on the bed in a haze of disbelief. Burning flesh? How could Zoe and I have completely different perceptions of the presence in this house? And then I considered the unpleasant odor that had been shadowing me lately. *Was that what I was now smelling? Had our great-grandparents* wanted *Zoe gone from The Bluffs? Do they now want me gone too?* As I was mulling the possibilities, a most disturbing thought sprang to mind: *What if the manifestation in this house wasn't the spirits of Percy and Celeste at all?*

~

Eighty-three years ago ~ Whale Rock
Three years before the tragic fire at Battersea Bluffs

Percy had arrived home earlier than usual.

"'Twas the weather that kept everyone away today. There'd be no shortage of whales to be seen. Especially with the size of the herd we saw yesterday."

Celeste had not looked up from the letter that lay in her lap as Percy poured himself a cup of tea from the pot and took the chair across the old oak table from his wife.

"What is it?"

"There's news from home. Not good, I'm afraid." She finally looked at him through tear-swollen eyes.

"Is your mum or da ailing?" He reached across to lightly stroke her hand.

She still thrilled to be touched by those hands, but today it was the comfort they offered she needed most. "Both, I'm afraid."

"I'm sorry." And she knew he was, even though neither of Celeste's parents had ever forgiven him for kidnapping their daughter, despite her countless declarations that she'd gone willingly.

"There's been a fire. The entire fleet of Da's lighters was destroyed."

"No! What happened?"

She drank in her husband's handsome, sun-weathered face, predicting his reaction before answering. "It's thought Robert Toomey might have done it."

"What? Why would he do such a thing? Your da treated him like a son."

"Apparently someone else has been nicked for it."

"So why do they think it was Robert then?"

"Your old mate, Smithy, overheard him bragging about it in a pub after a few tankards. Smithy's mum told mine."

Percy slammed his fist hard onto the oak surface. "Damn that Robert Toomey! The man is mad, I tell you. Mad as a hatter."

Celeste nodded in agreement. What else would push a man to do something so monstrous, if not madness?

"They'll come live with us. We'll send them money for passage."

"You are a good man. And thank you for offering, but they'll not come. To do so would be to admit they were wrong about you."

"Even now, when their beloved Robert Toomey has come under suspicion for their ruination? Still, they cannot find it in their hearts to forgive *me*?"

"They are proud people."

"Pride won't help them in the poor house now, will it?"

In the end, nothing would help. Celeste's parents died in an influenza epidemic the following winter. Had they been able to afford the coal to keep their flat properly heated, they might not have succumbed. The money Percy insisted on sending them had been returned.

Celeste was struck with overwhelming guilt for leaving her parents, for not being there to prevent their deaths. But she was most repentant for her part in bringing down upon her family the evil curse of Robert Toomey.

~

Present day

I was unable to escape the awful burning smell, yet I couldn't keep away from my studio. Still, I had a difficult time concentrating on my work because of the severe menstrual cramps.

It was Ashley who found me doubled over in pain.

"Cassie, I'm worried. You're so pale."

"It's just an exceptionally heavy period," I insisted, but then we both noticed blood had seeped through my jeans again.

She took me by the arm and tugged me toward the door. "You need to see a doctor."

I didn't argue, but not wanting to be recognized at the nearest clinic in Orleans, I directed her to the urgent care facility several towns away in Dennis.

Three hours later, a doctor was explaining to us what an ectopic pregnancy was.

"And the baby?" I asked, still not believing I wasn't completely barren after all. It was unfathomable to think that, after years of trying to conceive with Ethan, it was Billy's sperm that ended up working the magic.

She shook her head. "It's not a viable pregnancy, Ms. Mitchell."

I sat in stunned silence. But if the embryo hadn't gotten stuck on the way to my womb, what then? I'd marry Billy and we'd live happily ever after? Talk about implausible scenarios.

The doctor interrupted my brooding.

"I don't think surgery will be required. Your fallopian tubes are still intact, which is good news for your future reproductive health." She handed me some informational pamphlets and went on to discuss the treatment. "We're going to treat this pharmaceutically. It's good you didn't delay further in coming in. Blood loss is a serious complication, and you got here just in time."

\* \* \*

During the drive back to Whale Rock, Ashley seemed to understand that I didn't want to talk. But as we approached The Bluffs, I turned to her and said, "I'd prefer nobody else know about this."

"I won't even tell Vince." She reached across and took my hand, tears brimming. "I'm so sorry, Cassie."

I squeezed back and then shared the briefest history of my affair and the end of my marriage.

"Since we were teenagers, Billy's had this hold on me," I confessed and then went on to explain how this predicament had occurred. "When things went south with Ethan, I was just too weak to resist. I admit it's not a very good defense, but I'm good at avoidance."

"Sometimes we don't think with our minds, do we?" She said this in a remorseful tone, prompting me to wonder if she'd had a similar personal experience.

"Have you ever been involved with someone like that?" I asked. "Someone who can possess you?"

"There's only ever been Vince." Which wasn't really an answer.

# 9

Early August ~ a month before the disappearance

I scowled at my ghostly reflection staring back from the shiny metal teapot. At least the bleeding had finally stopped. Now, if only I could get a full night's sleep. But I couldn't seem to escape that enduring odor of decay, and Zoe's words haunted me, especially at night. *It's the smell of burning flesh. But where was it coming from? Another spirit in the house? Robert Toomey?* How I longed for the return of the uniquely pleasing burnt sugar scent.

Johnny was none too pleased when I took a leave during the height of summer season. I was simply too weak from the combined results of the blood loss and the side effects of the injection to terminate the unviable embryo lodged in my Fallopian tube.

I was waiting for my tea bag to steep when Ashley and Vince burst through the door.

"Cassie!" Ashley yelled before seeing me in the kitchen. "You'll never guess what I found."

"You've got to see this," Vince added, as keyed up as his wife.

He motioned for me to follow, and I obeyed, but I lagged way behind. My slow progress offered only a peek of a gray Jeep kicking up a trail of dust as it took the bend of the lane.

When I reached the barn, I stopped to catch my breath. "Who was that?"

"Just a friend who delivered these for us." Ashley could hardly contain her excitement.

I stared blankly at two old-fashioned portraits of a man and woman I'd never seen before . . . yet curiously, there was a hint of familiarity about the couple.

"I was doing research at the library for my story," Ashley explained, "when I noticed these portraits being carted from the basement storage area."

"They're having a tag sale tomorrow," Vince added. "And they were cleaning out everything that had been stored there for decades."

"Remember how you said people tried to save valuables from the house during the fire? Like the crystal and silver and stuff, but then it all got kinda scattered?"

I nodded.

"Well, I read that among the things removed were some paintings of the Mitchells from the front hall, but nobody knew what happened to them."

"You're saying these are Percy and Celeste?" I turned back to the portraits, astonished at the thought I could be looking at my great-grandparents. "What makes you think so?"

"The article indicated a local artist named C. Arnold Slade painted their portraits." Ashley pointed to the signature. "Here's the real proof. This was taped to the back of Percy's portrait." She handed me a weathered envelope.

I removed a slip of yellowed notepaper and read a letter penned by Caleb Slade to my great-grandfather, presenting the portraits in exchange for Percy having ferried the artist and his wife around the Cape. So he bartered for them. *What a clever man you were, Percy.*

"Apparently these portraits slipped away unnoticed after the fire. Speculation was they'd been removed with the intention of making a profit, since Slade was an artist of some note and they might've had monetary value."

"But all along, they were safely tucked away in the library basement?" I wondered when they were stashed there and by whom. I remember Fiona's tireless fundraising work on the capital campaign for the library expansion when I was just a child. It had to have been after she died, or surely she would have reclaimed them for the family.

The longer I gazed at the images sitting before me, the more I could see my father's likeness in the portrait of the man. And Zoe's features closely resembled those of the woman.

"I guess we now know where your auburn hair came from," Ashley pointed out.

But it was Vince who revealed the most significant reason they looked familiar by propping up one of my mother's paintings next to the portraits. The figures depicted in her art were distorted perspectives of the portrait subjects.

Then Ashley brought over one of my newer canvases and set it beside my mother's.

The similarities were undeniable. A sudden wooziness came upon me. I stumbled back onto the bench and continued to study the works before me. But how could I have painted people I'd never seen before? Or how could my mother, who'd also never met Percy or Celeste? Though Fiona might have recognized the faces when my mother painted these. Was it she who'd had them crated up and hidden in the carriage house attic?

So many questions were swirling inside my head, but the two I tried to push away were the most devastating: Had something other-worldly possessed my mother and manifested itself through her painting? Was the same thing happening to me?

*   *   *

For the next few days, I avoided the barn. Though it was hard to resist the strong pull of those paintings, I needed to recuperate. The vile odor seemed less intrusive. Or maybe I was just getting used to it. A longed-for respite from my recurring nightmares, likely the result of pharmaceutical assistance, was allowing me to sleep through the night.

I'd awakened early but wasn't ready to traipse down for breakfast, so I picked up the folder of articles Ashley had given me from her research into my family. I puzzled over something written in the margins and, hearing morning noises in the kitchen, went down to ask Ashley about it. But when I heard her mention my name, I stopped halfway down the back stairway.

"Cassie seems so lost."

"Lost? More like a walking zombie," Vince observed.

"Do you think it has something to do with those paintings?" she asked.

"Dunno. They sure creep me out."

Feeling wobbly, I lowered myself onto a step.

"There's got to be something we can do to help snap her out of this trance that's taken hold."

"Well, whatever it is, we need to act fast because there's no way we can postpone."

"You're right, the timing stinks." They were both quiet for a while before Ashley added, "I wish we didn't have to leave at all."

His response was stern. "You know we do."

Was Vince pressuring Ashley to leave? And if so, why?

The sounds of chairs scooting across the floor were followed by "Better get back to work."

I remained on that step for the longest time, contemplating the miasma that had enveloped me. The only way I could think to shake free was the very thing that was making me crazy. I needed to find a way back to my painting. And I needed Percy and Celeste to find their way back to me.

# 10

Mid-August ~ two weeks before the disappearance

Whistler's barking drew me to the window, where I saw him leaping playfully beside Vince and Ashley as they pushed my garden cart in the direction of the family cemetery.

*What were they up to?* I could think of no reason to follow without it being painfully evident I was spying on them. So I poured myself a fresh cup of coffee, took the morning paper out to the porch, and waited rather impatiently for them to return. An hour later, I was still pretending to read the front page when at last their heads popped above the horizon. The duo waved, and Ashley jogged over to join me while Vince rolled the wagon to the barn.

"Good morning." She settled herself in the porch rocker opposite mine.

"Coffee?" I offered.

"I'm off the poison this week." She leaned forward rubbing her face with her hands. "I haven't been sleeping well lately—thought I'd try drastic measures."

"Mornin', Cassie." Vince approached with the shepherd at his heels.

"Skipping breakfast today?" There'd been no evidence of their presence in the kitchen.

Ashley rolled her eyes. "As if."

Vince laughed good-naturedly before explaining. "We needed some grouting compound, so we thought, why not treat ourselves to breakfast at The Hatchery?"

"I hope you don't mind our borrowing the truck without asking," Ashley said.

"You know you can take it whenever you like." Their ancient Subaru had died shortly after they arrived on the Cape.

They didn't seem inclined to mention what they'd been doing with the garden cart, so I asked, "What's on the agenda today?"

"We can't do anything more until the flooring comes in. Are there any other chores you might have for us today?"

"Can't think of anything. Unless you consider taking the Cat out a chore?" The sea air might just be what I needed to escape the persistent shadow of gloom.

Vince's eyes popped. "Are you kidding?"

My new friend had caught the sailing bug, and with each sail he'd become more daring, heeling the Cat and reveling in the thrill of it. Today the winds were favorable, and it would be the perfect occasion to let Vince take the helm.

"Do you feel okay to sail?" Ashley asked me.

"Much better." Physically, I was nearly back to normal. I sent her a furtive thumbs-up to indicate my follow-up doctor visit had gone well. I stood and gathered my cup and paper. "I've got a quick errand to run. While I'm out, I'll pick up some lunch. Why don't we meet down at the *Queen* at noon?"

"That will give us time for a ride."

We departed together, they on their bikes and I in my old but faithful Mazda Miata. After several circuits of the main streets, I finally found a space to park, and just as I reached for the door handle, a familiar swagger approached on the sidewalk.

*Damn.* I pretended to sort through my purse, hoping the tinted windows would be adequate camouflage. But alas, he recognized the car; not surprising, since I'd been driving the Miata since high school.

Billy Hughes drummed his knuckles against the window.

I turned on the ignition to open the window, not trusting my legs to get out of the car.

"Hey, babe." He leaned in close enough for me to take in the alluring scent of Old Spice.

"Taking the day off?"

"I can't work every day. You know what they say about all work and no play."

"A dull boy you will never be, Billy."

He fixed me with a suggestive smile. "You free today?"

"Nope."

He glanced up at the sky. "Perfect day for a sail. Are you sure you can't shake free?"

"Positive." I kept my focus trained on the parking meter.

"I hear you've found some new playmates."

It wasn't a question, so I didn't respond.

"You should probably know," he said, glancing around the street, "folks in the Rock aren't exactly enamored with your new buddies."

I did look at him now. "Well, you know how it is. Unless you have Whale Rock blood cursing through your veins, you're a nobody and can't be trusted."

"Mee-oow".

I was back to staring at the parking meter.

"Too bad you're not in the mood to play." His tone implied it would be my loss.

"See ya." I pushed the window button, leaving him standing there awkwardly until he gave the hood of the car a fond farewell tap and sauntered away.

As I watched Billy disappear into the throngs of tourists, I contemplated the recent pregnancy scare. All the possible ramifications, had it been viable and the baby carried to term, started playing out in my head. What type of father would Billy have been? How involved, if at all? Who would the child have resembled? Would it have been a boy or a girl? Had I lost the baby because of the curse Robert Toomey had cast upon my great-grandfather? Was that why Percy and Celeste had abandoned me? And how might it all tie in to the eerie happenings at Battersea Bluffs? I despaired to think it was the most recent consequence of the lighterman's curse. I was tiptoeing toward a slippery slope of dangerous speculation.

*You can't go back.* I was channeling Fiona now. There was no way to undo my shameful betrayal, so I might as well move on. Besides, Ethan and I had been teetering on a precarious edge for some time, and I had no doubts he'd have left by now anyhow, since my bank account had been completely tapped.

Too miserable to conduct my errand, I shifted into reverse, pleasing the driver of a Ford Explorer swarming with sightseers and circling like a vulture. Such was the seasonal downside of living in a beautiful harbor town on Cape Cod. I made a quick stop at Town Line Deli for sandwiches, arriving back at the house well before noon. With time to kill, I decided to pay a visit to the cemetery to see what Vince and Ashley had been up to with the garden cart.

At first glance, everything looked much the same, although my mother's perennial garden needed weeding; I'd tended it the many years since her death but had been derelict this summer.

"Sorry, Mama." I began to tidy it a bit until something caught my attention by the stone wall border, and I discovered what my friends had accomplished: on either side of the unknown boy's marker were freshly planted daisies and baby's breath, fitting floral symbols of innocence for the poor abandoned child who'd washed up on our shores decades ago.

More surprising was the bronze statue of Winnie the Pooh placed in front of the grave. Winnie was part of the fabric of Main Street Whale Rock, where the statue had delighted scores of children for years from its prominent display in the window of Coastal Vintage Wares. I'd never considered that it might actually be for sale, and couldn't begin to think how my friends would've convinced Archibald Stanfield to part with his prized Pooh. Not to mention what it must have cost them.

I stood before this memorial to an unclaimed child with hand on heavy heart, conflicting emotions at war within me. I was immensely proud of Ashley and Vince for this generous act, while I also chastised myself for never thinking to make such a heartfelt gesture of remembrance. I'd placed cut flowers at the grave on Memorial Day and laid a wreath of greenery at Christmas, but never anything of a more permanent nature. I took a closer look around the hallowed grounds and also noticed a newly planted shrub between the stones of my great-grandparents. *A burning bush.* I leaned down to sniff the flower of the shrub, which emitted a light, clean lemon scent, whereas the air surrounding me was heavy and with just a hint of familiar burnt sweetness. I was afraid to hope Percy and Celeste had returned. If they had, what were they communicating through this more complex essence? Approval? Appreciation? Were they mourning all the losses they'd experienced during their own lives and witnessed from beyond the grave? Or was it the scent of regret?

~

Eighty years ago
September ~ three months before the tragic fire

Percy paced, then halted; turned, then paced again. This went on for several minutes before he finally asked his son, "What if I forbid it?"

"Then I'll not go." Ambrose looked at his shoes.

Percy had raised obedient and respectful sons. In return, he had always been generous, even indulgent. But how could he give in to this request, especially with that damn curse hanging over their heads like a French guillotine?

He loved his son and wanted to keep him near to protect him. And Celeste had never fully recovered from the deaths of Edwin and Jerome. Would she ever forgive him if he agreed to let Ambrose ship off as a blue jacket to far-off lands?

Percy knew it was prideful to want his good name to live on after he was pushing up the daisies. But he wanted nothing more than for his own son to outlive him and for his grandsons to outlive Ambrose.

"What about the Patrick girl?" Percy had never seen his son blush until that moment. Perhaps she was the key to convincing his son to abandon his dream. "You've been spending time with her?"

"When she can escape the watchful eye of her folks."

Percy gave his son a stern look.

"She's a good girl." Ambrose said.

"Have you made any promises to her yet?"

"No." Ambrose fingered something in his pocket. "But I care deeply about her."

"Yet you're willing to leave her behind with a broken heart?"

"I won't be gone forever. She may wait the three years for me."

"A pretty girl like Fiona turns a lot of heads."

Ambrose was quiet for a moment, which bolstered Percy's confidence, until his son's next deflating words.

"Haven't you always told me a man must be true to himself? What good would I be to Fiona if filled with regret? Not going would eat away at me until it killed me. Wasn't that how it was when you left England for America?"

"But it was *with* your mother I came to America. I didn't leave her behind."

The two men stared hard, waiting for the other to end the stalemate. It was the older, more mature Mitchell who finally laid down his sword.

"Would you promise to give it up at the end of the three years? Will you come back and take over the business, settle here in Whale Rock?"

"I promise." Ambrose, the victor, smiled broadly. "Thank you, Father."

"And"—Percy pointed a warning finger—"you will write to your mother every week."

"Yes, sir."

Percy prayed his son's promise would be enough to assuage Celeste's heartache when he summoned the courage to tell her. But he knew it would take more than prayer to ensure the safe return of his son. He wondered whether a deal with the devil would serve him better. Percy lowered his weary head and sobbed as the stunning truth descended upon him. He had brought this plight on his family by defying that vile curse. For wasn't Robert Toomey Beelzebub himself?

~

Present day

On my walk back to the house to gather items for the sail, I had to stop myself from automatically turning toward the barn. I'd been avoiding the studio ever since Vince and Ashley gently suggested a break from painting after finding me rolled into a ball and sobbing in front of my new series. They were right to be concerned about my unhealthy obsession. For now it was best to steer clear altogether.

At least the harsh, acrid odor that had been shadowing me for months had finally diminished. Which brought my thoughts to the burning bush. Such a symbolic acknowledgment of Percy and Celeste's deaths . . . yet it seemed strange that Vince and Ashley would presume to do something of such a personal nature without first seeking my permission. It was different for the unknown boy—my family had merely provided a peaceful place for his remains to rest, and anyone had a right to pay tribute to his short life.

I was struck with a disquieting thought: *Was it possible Ashley and Vince had lost a child?* It could explain why they'd assemble such a meaningful memorial. And Ashley's distress at the clinic might have been from her own painful memories. I decided against mentioning the plants or statue. If my theory was correct, I had no wish to rekindle the grief of these two people I'd grown so close to so quickly.

\* \* \*

I arrived at the dock first and was surprised to find the rigging loose and the mainsail cover on the *Queen Jacqueline* partly undone. I thought immediately of the vandals Brooks had complained about, then Johnny Hotchkiss's stolen Mercury, and finally, whoever might be creeping around in the woods. I would definitely report this to Brooks first thing after we got back from our cruise.

I felt subdued during the sail and was glad to have Vince captaining with Ashley as first mate. I lazed on deck and looked more closely at their matching tattoos.

"What type of bird is that?" I pointed to the artwork that graced Ashley's shoulder when she took a rest from her crew labors.

"The phoenix. You know, from Greek mythology?"

"The one that sets itself on fire at the end of its life and is reborn from the ashes?"

"That's right."

"What's the significance?"

"The short version of the story is we lost something important in a fire, and we handled it like the immature college kids we were: by finding the nearest bar and getting drunk." She shook her head with dismay. "The next morning we woke up with these. I suppose after several shots of tequila, it all made perfect sense."

"You regret it?"

She cast an admiring gaze toward Vince. "Not at all."

"Coming about," Vince called out, and his first mate leaped up to assist as I ducked from the boom with Whistler.

I envied their way with each other, how easily they seemed to communicate. Had I ever felt so in tune, so relaxed with anyone, like these two were? I mentally filed through my short list of romantic failures. The answer was an unqualified no. I'd been in a brooding mood before we set sail and was even more dispirited when we glided back into our small cove.

Vince made swift work of the cleat hitch as he tied the *Queen Jacqueline* to the dock, then used a thief knot to secure a small bundle to his backpack.

"I see you've become a master of sailing knots."

"I've been studying the book you loaned me." He'd borrowed my father's copy of *The Art of the Sailor.*

"My man's a quick study." Ashley hopped off the boat and leaned down to plant a spontaneous kiss. "I, however, can't seem to remember how to tie a bow knot."

"The bow knot *is* the most useful one in sailing. Here, let me show you." I took the end of a line attached to a fender and demonstrated my technique. "Now, you try."

Ashley took the rope and managed a fair attempt. "I'd better keep practicing, since my husband has discovered a love of the sea."

He smiled up at her. "One day we are going to have our own sailboat."

"I'm game. We'll just have to be sure to plant ourselves near a suitable body of water."

"Maybe you'll be lucky and end up on the coast, or at least near a large lake. Have you found out your assignment yet?"

"Still waiting to hear."

With October less than two months away, I thought it unfair of Ashley's employers not to give her more details about her new job.

"Why don't you come with us to Wizards?" Vince suggested, expertly securing the mainsail.

"Where?" I looked up from my task of wiping down the hull.

"It's a tavern we found in Eastham," Ashley explained. "Mostly locals."

"It's not a place that draws in tourists," added Vince.

"I've never heard of it, but sounds like my kind of spot."

"The beer is frosty, and the burgers are to die for." Vince indeed looked as if he'd gone to heaven just thinking about scarfing down a juicy burger—or three.

"Please come with us," Ashley pleaded.

"Why not? I could go for a cold brew." I was sun-drenched, wind-burned, and thirsty. More importantly, I didn't want to be home alone. Nor did I trust myself to refrain from phoning a certain bad influence, one who just happened to have the day off.

* * *

"Dudes." The sandy-haired bartender's lazy smile reminded me of someone, but I couldn't place it.

"Hey, Teddy." Ashley walked behind the bar for a hug.

"Hands off my wife, Theodore." Vince reached in for a fist bump.

"Not easy, man." The bartender raised his hands in surrender.

Ashley kept her arms snuggly around the young man's waist. "Don't be jealous."

Teddy, or Theodore, was obviously enjoying the repartee. "Dudes. Dudes. I'm a peace-loving man."

"Okay. You can keep her for a while. This is Cassie," Vince said as an introduction before guiding me to a corner booth. He called over his shoulder, "A pitcher of Genesee? Three glasses."

"I can see why it was okay to skip the shower." I took in the clientele. "A very, um, casual crowd indeed."

"These guys are mostly fishermen. They stop in after selling their catch at the local fish markets and before handing over their take to the missus."

"Here we go." Ashley set down before us a tray with the beer and a large basket of popcorn. "First round is on the house."

"Teddy's never going to get out of this place if he keeps throwing his money away."

"We'll make it up with the tip. Cheers." We clinked frosty mugs and quickly downed the first round.

"What's his story?" I was still trying to place whom he resembled. "Is he from around here?"

"He pretends to be a proud native Cape Codder, but he's actually a transplant from Boston."

"He certainly carries off the surfer dude persona."

"Teddy is really quite bright, just not very motivated," Ashley said, coming to his defense.

"You know him well, then?" I asked, stealthily sneaking another peek.

"He's a friend of sorts." Vince lifted a shoulder. "We've known him since we discovered this place, back when we first arrived at the Cape."

"What's his last name?"

Ashley sent Vince a searching look. "Do you know?"

"No, do you?"

She shook her head, and they both laughed. "I guess it never came up."

For the next couple of hours, we drank from the oft-refilled pitcher and munched on burgers, with fries smothered in malt vinegar, while my two friends told stories about the various regulars at Wizards.

Our boisterous laughter provoked Teddy to throw a lime at Vince. "If the story's so funny, why don't you share it with the rest of the gang?"

"Yeah. What's the joke?" A shaggy man ambled toward our table, glass in hand. "Come on, kids—spill."

That was when I noticed Brooks sitting at the far end of the bar. I stood and gestured grandly for the man to take my place. "My pals here will tell you all about it. I have to say hello to an old friend."

As the man squeezed into the booth next to Ashley, she mouthed a sarcastic *Thanks*.

I shrugged innocently and tottered to the other end of the tavern, then hopped up on the unoccupied barstool beside Brooks.

"Buy a girl a drink?"

He fixed me with a cool look. "It appears you've had enough."

I made a pouty face. "Come on, Chuckles."

He reddened, and I laid my arm atop his shoulders, bringing my lips close to his ear. "Sorry, old buddy. You know, old habits die hard, and all that."

"Funny you should mention old habits." He took a swig from his bottle. "Wasn't that Billy Hughes I saw sniffing around you earlier?"

My back went rigid. "You're mean. And besides, that's very old news."

He pursed his lips and cocked his head. "Depends on what you consider old."

The thought of Brooks knowing about my brief but life-altering affair with Billy sobered me quickly. "What are you implying?"

"I'm not *implying* anything." He gave me a knowing look.

But how could Brooks possibly know? I looked down at my hands, twisting my ring as I considered. It was doubtful Ethan had told anyone, and besides, he'd packed up his things and driven back to Chicago right after we filed the divorce papers. As for Billy, it didn't reflect well on him to have been involved with a married woman, even one with whom he had a long history. The people of Whale Rock could be unforgiving. Just ask Robert Toomey. Billy was smart enough to understand that a rep as a home-wrecker wouldn't be good for business; despite his narcissism, Billy would never put La Table in jeopardy.

The only person I'd told other than Ashley was Brit. I became queasy as a memory smacked me in the face: my best friend had confessed to a careless fling with one of Whale Rock's finest right before embarking on her great Italian adventure. She hadn't said who it was, and under no circumstance could I have imagined it had been with . . . I looked searchingly at Brooks.

"Yep. It was Brit. And I might add, neither of you handle alcohol well." Brooks waved Teddy over. "I'll have another Sam Adams, and could you brew a pot of coffee for my friend here?"

"Forget the coffee. I'll have a shot of tequila."

Brooks gave a subtle shake of his head, but the bartender answered with a look of defiance. He poured the golden liquor and placed the shot in front of me along with a salt shaker and wedge of lime. "On the house."

I downed it and slammed the glass on the bar.

"Thanks, Teddy." I smiled, taking in those deep blue eyes and the lopsided grin. In the brief clarity that comes only in an alcoholic haze I knew with certainty whom the young man resembled. Then—*snap!*—just as quickly as the revelation had come to me, it was gone again.

# 11

Later that night

"**W**here are you taking me?" It was dark, I was drunk, and I didn't have a clue in what direction Vince was driving. "Grand Funk Ink," he answered.

"You mean Grand Funk Railroad?" I managed, then collapsed into hilarious laugher.

"I think you turn right here." Ashley was sitting in the middle of the backseat and pointed, hitting my nose and sending us both into another fit of giggles.

Vince steered the truck down a side street and parked in front of a brightly lit shop, remarkably still open at—what time was it? Midnight?

Ashley placed a reassuring hand on my arm. "You do not have to go through with this."

*Go through with what?* I was hazy about the past hour or so.

Vince hopped out of the driver's side and trotted around the front to open my door. "Just come in and take a look around. If you don't feel comfortable, we'll leave."

It wasn't until we stepped through the door that I finally remembered our mission.

I'd shared a friendly drink with Brooks at Wizards, although the "friendly" aspect had quickly dissipated after he admitted sleeping with my best friend. The shock was compounded when I learned Brit had betrayed my confidence about the affair with Billy Hughes. This inspired anger of the red-seeing variety and thus provoked the hasty and defiant downing of not just one but also a second shot of tequila before I rejoined Vince and Ashley at the booth. Somehow the conversation drifted to the subject of their tattoos, which I'd admitted a fascination with, and from there the plan was hatched to drive to Provincetown and get myself inked too.

The artist working late that night appeared relatively hygienic and was in possession of a full set of teeth, one of which was capped in silver. His thick black mane bore a shocking white streak and was pulled back into a sleek ponytail. The man himself was surprisingly ink-free, save for one mesmerizing serpent creature coiling around his lower left arm.

"I can't do all three of you tonight," he informed us gruffly.

"Our friend here is the only one who'll be getting one." Ashley told him.

I gave a little wave. "I'm Cassie."

He nodded once. "Skunk."

I managed to stave off another eruption of giggles, not wishing to offend the person who would be applying a sharp needle to my body.

"Have a seat," he instructed and then returned his attentions to the only other customer in the shop. A twenty-something Pink wannabe was having a guardian angel tattooed on her shoulder.

"Any pictures she can look at for ideas?" Vince asked.

"Over there." He jutted his chin in the direction of the counter.

As I perused the images in the notebook, the giggles returned, partly a reaction to the more seamy choices, but mostly from nerves.

"She been drinking?" Skunk asked Vince.

"Last time I checked I was still here." *Where had the sudden bravado come from?* "And clearly of an age to make my own decisions."

"Just don't want you waking up tomorrow with two hangovers." He sent me a pointed look. "One that'll be permanently etched across your ass."

Now there was a sobering thought.

"Where should I get this done?" I whispered to Ashley.

"I guess it depends on which tattoo you pick." We flipped through the pages, but none of them really spoke to me.

"Will it hurt?"

"Can't remember," she admitted.

Vince added, "We were pretty far gone the night we got ours."

"Believe me, you'll feel it," the tattoo artist interrupted.

I was beginning to think Skunk was hoping to scare me off so he could close up shop. If that was his intent, he'd misjudged me, because now I was all the more determined. But what image could I live with into perpetuity?

Ashley turned a page and pointed to an image of a phoenix. "Why not join our elite club?"

It was the flames that drew me in as much as the phoenix itself. Hadn't fire been an integral part of my heritage? It would be like a Mitchell family branding iron seared into my skin forever.

"I nearly got a tattoo when I was in high school," I admitted.

"What happened?"

"Granny Fi overheard me plotting with my best friend, Brit, and foiled our plans." She'd been quite firm, saying, "Nobody should get a tattoo until they are at least twenty-one." But she did promise to give her blessing, and even pay for it, if I still wanted one on my twenty-first birthday.

"What would you have chosen back then?"

"I was into Metallica at the time, so I planned to get their emblem tattooed on my ankle."

"Seriously?" Ashley was amused. "I'm having a hard time imagining you a heavy metal fan."

"I had an unsavory boyfriend at the time."

"In that case, it's probably wise you listened to Fiona."

I twisted my ring. "I completely forgot until just now about my grandfather's tattoos. He got them before he left to join the Navy, and Fiona once described them to me."

"What were they? Your grandfather's tattoos?"

"He had one of Vulcan, and the other was Neptune. The Roman gods of fire and water."

"That's so cool. Back home there's a statue of Vulcan on top of Red Mountain."

"Where's that?" I asked. "You've never said."

Before she could answer, Skunk called out, "Next."

~

Eighty years ago
Three months before the fire at Battersea Bluffs

"Fi, you must come out and meet me tonight," Ambrose Mitchell whispered in the ear of sixteen-year-old Fiona Patrick.

She looked around cautiously, making sure neither of her parents were anywhere to be seen. "Where?"

"I'll be at the pier by the *Femme Celeste* at nine o'clock."

"So late?"

"Can you manage? It's important."

"Fiona!" Mr. Patrick's voice boomed as he rounded the corner of the market. "The produce has been delivered, and your mother needs you."

"Yes, Pop." Fiona scurried away, turning back once to mouth the words *I'll try.*

"Are you not working today, Ambrose?" Mr. Patrick fixed him with a stern look.

"I've just returned from Boston, sir. I've joined the Navy and will be shipping out the day after tomorrow."

"Not soon enough for me," Fiona's father grumbled under his breath. "And leaving your father to run the business himself, aye?"

"Only a three-year tour. My folks and I struck a deal. I'll go off and see the world and then come back to take over, settle down here in Whale Rock, get married, and have my own family."

"Suppose you'll find the right girl while you're away, then?"

"No sir. I reckon I've already found her."

Mr. Patrick narrowed his eyes. "You best not be talking of my Fiona. She's too young for you. Too young for anyone."

"But she won't be when I get back now, will she?" Ambrose had been emboldened by his new status of enlisted naval man. "She'll be nineteen and of a consenting age."

"That may well be, if she'd settle for the likes of you. But for now, you keep your distance, Ambrose Mitchell."

\* \* \*

Ambrose had been waiting for more than an hour and was fast losing hope of seeing his lovely Fiona. He stubbed out his last cigarette and rose to his feet. He'd be leaving in two days and finding another opportunity to say goodbye would not come easily. He felt the sway of the pier and knew at once Lady Luck was with him.

"Fi?" he called out softly.

"Yes, Brosie, it's me." She fell into his arms and began to cry.

"Hey, my darlin' Fi." He took her chin and turned it toward the moon. "What's all this about?"

"Pop said you're leaving. Is it true?" She tilted her tear-stained face upward.

Why was it that the romantic notions of women prevented them from seeing the practical side of a man's vision?

"If I don't go now, I'll always be wondering what's out there. It would burn a hole in my soul. Besides, your pop will never let me see you until you're of age."

"But I can't bear three years without you." She buried her face in his shoulder.

"We will write to each other. Make our future plans through our letters. Time will pass quickly. And when I return, we'll be married." He fished from his pocket a small box and handed it to her.

"What's this?" Fiona's innocent but tear-filled eyes widened as she gently lifted the top to display a ring set with a green gem.

"It's a promise ring. I mean to make you my wife when I come back to Whale Rock. That is, if you'll wait for me."

He removed the ring from the box. "I chose an emerald to match my eyes. When you look at this ring, I'll know you're thinking of me."

"It's beautiful. But even if it were just a chip of sea glass, I'd still find it beautiful because it's from you."

"So do you promise to wait for me the three years I'll be gone?"

"I'd wait for you forever."

He leaned in for a kiss, but the sound of the harbormaster's approaching steps interrupted his intentions.

"We gotta hide," Fiona whispered.

"The *Celeste*." Ambrose hopped into his father's catboat, lifting Fiona in after him. They pulled the tarp over their heads until the coast was clear. When they freed themselves from the covering, the moon cast its light on Ambrose's arm.

"Whatever is this?" Fi gently caressed the image.

"I had it done in Boston. I thought it would make me look like a real sailor."

"But what is it?"

"This fella here, rising from the flames? He's called Vulcan."

"A funny name."

He pointed to his other arm. "They're both mythical figures."

"You got two?" Fiona exclaimed. "Did it hurt?"

"Nah. But this one's my favorite: Neptune, the water god. He's half man, half ocean wave. They're symbolic."

"How so?"

"They're the two vast powers that could ruin a man. We should always respect and even fear them." He'd learned that from his father. Both forces of nature had left their mark on the family. His grandfather's fleet of cargo boats had been wiped out by an arsonist back in England, a tragic act of revenge. The man who lit the match gave new meaning to the phrase "carrying a torch," as Robert Toomey had once done for Ambrose's mother. And a few years ago, his two older brothers had been enjoying a carefree day of sea fishing when a sudden turn of weather ended in tragedy. The storm had been violent, sweeping the splintered remains of their small boat ashore along with the broken bodies of Edwin and Jerome. His parents were heartbroken, and the accident left Ambrose an only child. It had taken all his courage to ask his father for permission to join the Navy, knowing how hard it would be for Percy to run the business on his own. And the toll the news took on his mother had been almost unbearable.

Fiona continued to caress Ambrose's arms.

"You'd best be getting back, Fi." He nuzzled her neck.

\*     \*     \*

It was nearly dawn when Fiona finally untangled herself from Ambrose's arms and climbed out of the *Femme Celeste*. She'd wanted to make a lasting impression to ensure her love would keep his promise and return to her.

Two days later, she joined the many other well-wishing town folk who'd gathered at the center of Whale Rock to see Ambrose Mitchell off to serve his country. From the sidelines, she blew a surreptitious kiss to her beloved, who made a secret gesture of catching it and bringing it to his heart. In her pocket, she fingered the letter he'd slipped to her earlier, certain his intentions were sincere. But then Fiona caught sight of Celeste Mitchell's tormented expression as she released Ambrose from a tender embrace, and she'd shivered as if the cold finger of death had tapped her on the shoulder.

~

Present day

While Skunk prepped the workspace for his final artistic creation of the night, I considered how the powerful forces of water and fire had perpetuated the ruination of so many in the Mitchell family. The tragic loss of all three of Percy and Celeste's sons to the sea and then, of course, their own ultimate demise by fire. And metaphorically, the cancer that coursed like a wildfire through my mother's body, the fluid buildup from pneumonia that virtually drowned my father, Ethan setting my trust fund to flames, and my affair with Billy that was born at sea. And most recently, the fire at The Bluffs that might have taken my life had I not been rescued by Ashley and Vince. *It was time to break the spell.*

Skunk was rubbing his hands together. "So what are you going with?"

He nodded approvingly when I handed him the image.

"It's symbolic," I told him, though he didn't ask what it symbolized, and probably didn't care.

What he did ask was, "Where?"

I gulped and pointed.

"Brave girl," was all he said as he led me to the table.

Was I brave? Or was it simply a matter of what I needed to do? Either way, I was ready to rise from the flames, be reborn, start anew. And who knew? Perhaps this bold act would defy the curse of Robert Toomey.

\* \* \*

The next morning I did awake with one massive hangover, and Skunk's forewarning of a second reverberating in my already throbbing head. I sought Advil and strong coffee before even considering a peek at the consequences of last night's escapade. When I finally stepped before the full-length mirror, I slowly loosened the belt of my robe and braced myself as the satiny fabric slid off my shoulders to puddle onto the floor.

I cast an appraising eye at the artistic creation, now a permanent addition to my body.

"Hmm. I don't hate it." I gingerly touched the skin between my pelvic bones, surprised there was no pain. "In fact, I don't mind it at all."

Hearing footfalls on the back stairway, I slipped on sweat pants and a T-shirt, grabbed my now empty coffee mug, and joined my accomplices in the kitchen.

"Another close encounter with a Great White at Nauset Beach." Vince waved the front page of the *Cape Cod Times*. "And to think, we were just at Liam's the other night."

"And you didn't bring me back an order of quahogs?" I feigned a pout. Liam's was the best clam shack on the Cape, but I rarely braved the crowds.

"We didn't know you were such a clam fan."

"I was practically reared on them. But I hate to think of you two out there swimming with the sharks."

"Are you kidding? Ash won't wade out further than ankle-deep water."

"I don't even like it when *you're* out there body surfing." Ashley's face darkened.

"But you don't seem to mind sailing." I refilled my coffee mug.

"That's different." She changed the subject to ask, "You don't have tattoo remorse, do you?"

"What I have is a horrific headache. But this?" I patted my lower tummy. "I must admit, at first I was afraid to look. But believe it or not, I'm pleased with it."

"Whew!" Vince made the dramatic act of wiping his brow. "We've had friends who've awoken the morning after being inked and totally freaked out."

Ashley nodded. "We're just glad you don't hate us."

"Well, I now have more incentive not to gain weight. Wouldn't want Mr. Phoenix to get all distorted and bloated looking."

This brought a chuckle from the young couple.

"Well, you might decide to have a baby one day," Vince said. "That would redefine the image for sure."

Ashley and I shared a meaningful look. I opened the cupboard to pull out the frying pan, knowing full well he was teetering on starvation. "Who's hungry?"

Vince put the paper aside and grinned.

"That's what I thought. How does scrambled eggs, bacon, toast, and grits sound?"

"Like breakfast heaven." He rubbed his hands together in anticipation, reminding me of Skunk before he started my tattoo.

"It's late enough to call this brunch." I checked the captain's clock. Nearly eleven o'clock.

"I know somebody else who's probably starving," Ashley reminded Vince.

"Sorry, buddy." He gave Whistler a rub before filling his bowl with a generous serving of kibble.

"By the way, what was it you said last night about Whistler and how you arrived at his name?"

"Did we say?" Ashley didn't look up from her task of cracking eggs into a bowl. "I don't remember talking about it."

"We did." The subject had come up while I was being tended to by the tattoo artist. "But I'm fuzzy on the answer."

Vince frowned first, then laughed and said, "Oh yeah, that was one of the many subjects we discussed to distract you from your pain."

"It didn't hurt as bad as I thought it would. Likely the anesthetizing effect of tequila."

"Don't. Say. That. Word." Vince placed his hands on his head. "No Wizards for a while."

"So, are you going to remind me?" I asked, adding grits into a pan of boiling water.

He gave me a questioning look.

"The story about Whistler's name?" I prompted.

"Oh, that." He gave a casual wave. "It's not much of a story, really."

Ashley handed me the bowl of whipped eggs, which I poured into a sizzling skillet while Vince drank down a large glass of orange juice and then wiped his mouth with the back of his hand.

"The place I got him from was called Whistler Farms. He was the last remaining puppy from the litter, and the breeders had already started calling him Whistler. I kind of liked the name, so I kept it."

I couldn't summon to memory the story he told last night, but this version did not sound authentic. Mostly, it seemed unlike Vince to leave the naming of his pet to someone else.

I must have looked unconvinced because he lifted his hands in apology. "I told you it wasn't much of a story."

There was something else Ashley and I had been talking about, but it too would remain adrift in the after-haze of intoxication.

"Do you remember agreeing to let us crate up all those paintings?" she said, interrupting my ruminations.

"My mother's?" They'd been pestering me to return the spellbinding works to the carriage house attic now that the upper floor had been completed.

"Those"—then, tentatively—"and also your new ones?"

I didn't look at her but nodded my assent as the smell of smoke wafted to my nostrils.

"Who's manning the toaster?"

Ashley said, "I will."

I turned to see that she hadn't started toasting the bread yet. I looked about to see what else might be burning, but everything was cooking as it should be.

*What was the message this time? And more importantly, who was sending it?*

*　*　*

It was a humid, windless day, so another sail wasn't in the cards, even if our stomachs could have survived an outing on the Cat. Unable to face the crating of my paintings, I sent Vince and Ashley to the barn to do the deed on their own. While they did that, I set about hanging the newly discovered portraits of my great-grandparents. They came in to help me finish, and as we stood back to admire the images, a wonderfully sweet scent surrounded me. The relief was nearly dizzying.

"Do you smell that?" I whispered. "That sweetness?"

"Yeah," Ashley said, tugging me toward what used to be the pantry in the days before my mother converted it to a closet. "Vince noticed it when we were searching for some old rags."

I breathed in the faint combined aromas of sugar and vanilla, but it wasn't the distinct scorched scent that had shadowed me through The Bluffs since childhood. I had no desire to delve into the complicated subject of the spirits in the house, but it was time to admit the truth behind why I selected the phoenix tattoo.

"Let's take a walk down to the cliffs," I suggested. And there I shared more about the fire dreams that had haunted me since childhood and how I believed they were somehow connected to the curse.

"Maybe Robert Toomey's spirit is haunting you." Vince said this half-joking and half-seriously as he echoed my own fears these past weeks since Zoe mentioned the burning flesh smell that sent her fleeing across the continent.

"Have you ever thought of having the house spiritually cleansed?"

I knew what Ashley meant. There were rituals of burning sage or sprinkling holy water throughout the house. But I would never do anything that might chase Percy and Celeste from their beloved home.

"I don't believe it's necessary."

"What about that book and the claims about the curse?" Vince asked.

"So much of what Edgar wrote is based on inference and speculation." It was Ashley who answered, having read it more recently than I.

"If enough people believe in something, it becomes their truth," I said.

"Did Fiona believe in the curse?" Ashley asked.

I nodded. "She blamed it for losing the love of her life, and she was a hawk when it came to watching over my father." I took in a deep breath. "And there were all my mother's many miscarriages."

"Seven lost babies." This was barely a whisper from Ashley.

"My grandmother never spoke of the curse until the end of her life. In a way, I think she felt that talking about it gave it more power. But she also wanted me to know that she believed the curse could be defied. Granny Fi's dying words were *'You may be a Mitchell, Cassandra, but don't you forget about the Patrick blood also coursing through your veins. And it's Patrick blood that kept your father with us for many years.'*"

"I agree with Fiona," Vince declared.

"Well, something feels different today. I have this weird sense of rebirth."

"Maybe returning the happier portraits of Percy and Celeste to their rightful place has something to do with it," suggested Vince.

"Or . . . maybe your tattoo has exorcised the spirit of Robert Toomey?" Ashley leaned in, excited by the possibility.

"Could be. It's why I chose the phoenix." I rubbed my tummy again. That's exactly what it felt like. An exorcism, whether real or simply imagined. I felt lighter, freer, and—best of all—like Percy and Celeste had returned to me. And for that, I had Vince and Ashley to thank.

I wasn't sure where they spent the rest of the day, but I cocooned myself in my favorite spot in the house: the sleeping porch off the master bedroom, which overlooked the cliffs to the bay. It offered a stunning view but was also the best place to try to catch a breeze. I fought to stay awake to finish the mystery I was reading, but kept nodding off. I roused myself around six o'clock, with still no sign of my two roomies or Whistler. After heating up a can of soup, I took myself to bed early, too tired to wait around and see if they'd show up.

It was as I was brushing my teeth that I noticed Fiona's emerald ring was gone from my finger.

# 12

Late August ~ one week before the disappearance

I'd been searching endlessly for Granny Fi's emerald ring, my most beloved possession aside from Battersea Bluffs. And now that Percy and Celeste were back, they weren't letting me be. A constant cloud of burning sugar followed me from room to room, and there was a persistent clattering in the bathroom pipes, another of their warning signals that had remained dormant for some time.

"What are you looking for?" Ashley had found me tearing frantically through kitchen drawers the first morning after I realized the ring was missing.

"I've lost Fiona's ring." I held out my naked hand as proof.

"I'll bet you just misplaced it." She offered to help look, and we thoroughly sifted through the contents of the occupied areas of the house but came up empty.

"I'm sure it will turn up." She tried to encourage me.

"I hope you're right. I just can't imagine what happened to it."

"You have lost weight. Maybe it slipped off?"

Later, Vince said, "I haven't even noticed you wearing it lately."

I was certain he was mistaken, for rarely if ever did I take it off.

"Have you checked the car?" he asked.

"The car, the truck, the studio. I've looked everywhere twice and maybe three times."

"Maybe you lost it on the sail," he'd suggested after giving the Mazda and the truck another once-over for me.

"I think I had it on at Wizards." Though how could I be certain after two shots of tequila and who knew how many beers?

"I'll bet it shows up where you least expect it."

Their indifference to my lost treasure bothered me, but considering their minimalistic attitude about possessions, perhaps I was expecting too much. Neither of them wore any jewelry, not even wedding bands. It was possible they didn't understand my emotional attachment to Fiona's ring.

I didn't broach the subject again with Ashley or Vince, and I dared not mention anything to Zoe or Brooks, knowing full well who they'd blame. Which left me forced to swat away on my own the annoyingly unwelcomed question darting into my mind about how these two wandering paupers had afforded that bronze Winnie the Pooh statue.

*   *   *

A week or so after the tattoo outing, the three of us were homebound on a stormy night. We'd just finished dining on several frozen Totino's pizzas left over from an impromptu gathering last New Year's Eve. I'd kept the unsavory detail of their expired shelf life to myself. Not that Vince seemed to notice, having put away three of the pies single-handedly.

"Do you two have any interest in watching this?" I held up a DVD of *Drive*. "I'm a huge Ryan Gosling fan, but haven't seen this one."

Ashley reached for the DVD cover. "He's *so* hot."

"Down girls." Vince gulped the last of his Dogfish Head IPA and said, "I can't believe you can buy this out here on the Cape."

He'd been thrilled when I brought home a six-pack, having selected the brew based on its amusing name.

"Awesome!" he'd exclaimed, popping the cap off the first bottle and savoring the amber liquid. "I haven't had one of these since Johnny Brenda's."

"What's that, a microbrewery?" I picked up a bottle and attempted to read the small print.

"Not sure. I only know that I like it."

"Want another?" I asked.

"If you're offering."

"How about some dessert with the movie?" Ashley suggested. "Butterscotch sundaes?"

"I'd rather have popcorn with my beer," Vince tossed an Orville Redenbacher into the microwave while I loaded the movie into the DVD player.

But five minutes into the movie, as sirens wailed on screen, Whistler began to whimper and prance frantically, putting an end to our viewing.

"I guess we'll have to wait to see if Ryan Gosling outruns the police."

"Or takes his shirt off in the film." Ashley wiggled her brows suggestively.

"Right?" I smiled and reached down to pet Whistler, now resting calmly at my feet. I was struck with a flash of comprehension. "So, that's why he bolted the night of the barn fire?"

Ashley nodded and got down onto the floor to murmur sweetness into the dog's ear.

"Poor guy. Has he always been frightened of sirens?"

"Just since graduate school." Vince set an ice cream dish in front of Whistler, who happily lapped up the remains. "We lived on the same block as a fire station."

"It was a fabulous loft," Ashley added, wistfully. "It's just too bad it wasn't soundproofed. Huh, boy?"

"The first time that fire alarm went off in the middle of the night? Whistler went nuts."

"And each and every time after that." Ashley frowned.

"Whenever we'd get home from class and couldn't find him, we knew there'd been a fire. He'd be curled up in the corner of the closet or hunkered down in the bathtub."

"That's one good thing about being out here." Vince automatically took his wife's hand. "The quiet."

"It is peaceful," she agreed. "I'd stay here forever if I could."

I knew better than to extend the invitation again. They both became uncomfortable whenever I brought up the subject of Ashley's internship.

"So, did you have to give up the loft?"

"Apartments weren't plentiful in the Fish Town area, so we had to tough it out for a while. We'd leave the stereo on during the day, and that seemed to help."

"Fish what? Where was this? I keep forgetting to ask where you guys went to grad school." Just then, my phone rang. I checked caller ID and saw that it was an international call. *Brit.*

"It's my best friend calling from Italy," I explained before squealing joyfully into the phone. "Brit! Finally."

We'd been trying to connect by phone for weeks, but time zones and Brit's newfound social life had made it difficult. Hearing her voice made me miss her all the more. I'd even forgiven her betrayal and decided not to mention Brooks. I didn't want to waste our precious time on such subjects.

"No, you go first. I want to hear every detail . . . Yes, even if it does make me green with envy . . . You did not!"

Several minutes passed in an excited exchange with my faraway friend before I found myself alone. It was a long call, but not so late when it ended for Vince and Ashley to have called it a night. But the house was still and the upstairs dark. I was on such a high from vicariously experiencing Italy through Brit's eyes, it didn't occur to me until much later that they hadn't answered my question.

# 13

Early September ~ the day of the disappearance

"Here's Granny Fi's old picnic basket." I handed it to Vince. "It will fit perfectly on the fender rack of Ashley's bike."

"It's beautiful, Cassie." Ashley admired the antique basket.

Fiona had loved to shuttle us off to Whale Rock Beach every Sunday afternoon. Zoe and I would practically explode in anticipation of the inspired repasts awaiting us in Fiona's treasured picnic hamper. There was never anything so mundane as a ham sandwich or potato salad. Once she even served us caviar and champagne.

"We can't possibly take this," she protested. "It's an heirloom."

"Besides, we have this cooler bag that serves us just fine." Vince picked up the beat-up insulated pouch and set it on the kitchen island.

"Nonsense. You're going on a picnic; therefore, you must pack a picnic basket."

"It's too special. Have you seen how Ashley rides?"

Ashley took umbrage and pulled a face at Vince.

"I'm a safe rider, and you know it." To me she said, "Seriously, I'd hate it if something happened to it."

"As Fiona would say, *it* is just a thing. Besides, it hasn't been used since"—the memory of my last sailing outing with Billy floated up, but I quickly tamped it down with a fib—"See? I can't even remember the last time I went on a picnic. No further discussion."

Ashley lifted her hands as if to say, *What can we do?* She walked to the door saying, "I need to grab something from the carriage house."

"I'll start the sandwiches." Vince began setting up an assembly line of meats, cheeses, condiments, and rolls.

"I'll leave you to your culinary creations." I winked at him, then hefted the laundry basket onto my hip and took the back stairway up to my bedroom. While folding and sorting, I caught sight of Ashley from the window, but instead of the carriage house, she was in a full sprint, crossing the field toward the graveyard.

Before I could process where she was going or why, the phone rang. It was my attorney calling to report that my divorce decree had been granted. I sank down onto the bed, feeling I might pass out. I knew this was coming. Why then was I trembling and nauseated? I took in several deep breaths and tried to bring to mind Ethan's face. I mouthed the word *ex-husband*.

The last time I'd seen him was six months ago, at the Family Court hearing. He'd stared straight ahead, never once glancing across the aisle to where I was seated with my lawyer. He was alone, having no funds to hire an attorney of his own. When we were dismissed, Ethan had bolted for the door.

I don't know how long I remained in a fugue state before a voice calling my name finally awakened me.

"We're about to head out, Cassie," Vince yelled from the kitchen.

I managed to rouse myself from the bed but took the old, creaky stairs one by one. Vince was filling the cooler bag with sandwiches—at least a dozen.

"That's quite a haul." I tried to make my voice light and cheerful.

"I'm a man with a healthy appetite."

"Even you can't eat that many sandwiches in one sitting. Are you two planning to skip town on me?"

"Of course not." He seemed surprised by the question. "I mean, where would we go?"

"Just kidding."

His easy smile returned. "Well, I had to make at least one sandwich for Ash, didn't I?"

I opened the bread drawer and removed a bag of cookies I'd baked the day before. "Have room for these?"

"Sweet." He took the bag. "Hey, I thought I finished these off."

"Lucky for you, I stashed some away."

We walked outside to where Ashley was waiting on the porch rocker. She was bending over Whistler, who was lying at her feet and wagging his tail in response to her murmurs and pets.

"All set?" Vince asked, gently touching her shoulder. She nodded but did not immediately stop her attentions to Whistler.

When she finally stood, she gave me a searching look. "Is something wrong? You look sad."

If I told them about the divorce decree, they would feel compelled to stay with me, and I didn't want to ruin their plans. But my motive wasn't totally unselfish. I needed the day to pull within my cocoon of misery. So I lied.

"These?" I pointed to what surely were red, puffy eyes. "Ragweed is blowing all over the place right now." It was true; I wiped my fingers across the porch tabletop to display the pale yellow film.

"That must be what's been bothering me too." Ashley rubbed her eyes.

"Let me run inside and get you some Claritin."

When I returned with the antihistamine, Vince and Ashley were standing by their bikes and inserting the cooler bag into Fiona's picnic basket.

"It'll all work out," I heard Vince tell Ashley, and then he lifted her chin and added, "It's now or never."

I cleared my throat to alert them of my approach. Vince clapped his hands together and repeated, "It's now or never if we want to make it to Provincetown by lunchtime."

"Here you go." I held out the medication.

"Thanks, Cassie." Ashley smiled and clasped my hand for a second as she took the pills I was offering.

Vince picked up the basket and looked around, a bit agitated. "Where's the rope?"

"I've got it right here." Ashley untied a line from around her waist, where it had been concealed by her shirt.

With care, they secured the basket to the bike rack. Then each of them squatted down beside Whistler and kissed him goodbye.

"You be good for Cassie, baby." Ashley nuzzled the shepherd's head.

"Don't forget, this weekend is summer's swan song. Traffic will be insane," I cautioned.

"We're going to do some exploring. We should be back by dark unless my romantic husband decides to camp out under the stars with me tonight."

"Or more likely," Vince added, "we'll crash somewhere in P-town if we're too tired for the trek back."

"Either way, if there's a change of plans, we'll call or text you." Ashley smiled sweetly.

Vince gave Whistler one more hug before they quickly mounted their bikes and pushed off.

I held it together until they turned the corner of the drive, before letting the tears flow. It seemed to take all my strength to climb the stairs, where I collapsed onto the bed and pulled myself into the fetal position. I cried myself to sleep and didn't awaken until Whistler began whimpering to tell me he needed something . . . to go out? To eat? Both?

It was completely dark, and I was surprised by the lateness of the hour when I turned on the bedside lamp. Ten o'clock.

"I'm so sorry, boy." I jumped up, a little too quickly, causing spots to appear. I grabbed onto the side table to steady myself. With nothing in my stomach besides my morning coffee, no wonder I felt dizzy.

But Whistler was now prancing and nearly singing, his bladder probably pushed to capacity. I opened the door, and he made a mad dash for the nearest shrub. Meanwhile, I went to prepare his kibble and check for messages. None. Now I was worried. They were excellent cyclists, but still I couldn't imagine them risking a ride on Route 6 in the dark. And Ashley had promised to let me know if they were staying in P-town.

I let the dog back in, and before I could even set his bowl on the floor, he began attacking his food. My friends had both been a little distracted as they prepared for their outing. Could they have forgotten to feed Whistler this morning?

I tried their cell phones but was put through immediately to voicemail. I left messages, then paced the kitchen for another half hour before deciding to take the truck toward Provincetown in case they were stranded on the road.

It was nearly midnight when I returned home, having exhausted all avenues to find them. I'd even stopped by Wizards, but no one there had seen them either. I made a call to the Whale Rock Police Station and spoke to Officer Bland, who told me in a fittingly flat, monotone voice that twenty-four hours had to pass before a missing persons report could be filed. It was too late to pester Brooks at home, so I began to search Vince and Ashley's room in hopes of finding phone numbers of family or friends, local contacts—anyone who might have seen or heard from them. I came up blank and spent the rest of the night through the early morning hours searching on the computer. Still, I uncovered nothing that might help me trace my friends.

After downing my third cup of coffee, I picked up the phone at eight o'clock sharp and called Brooks to get the search rolling. Not surprising, the early bird chief was already at the station.

"I see you called in last night and spoke with Bland."

"Yes, and he told me he couldn't do anything until Vince and Ashley have been missing for twenty-four hours."

"That's correct. What time did you expect them back yesterday?"

"Before sunset. But they actually left early in the morning so it's already been twenty-four hours."

"It doesn't work that way, Cassie."

"But there must be something you can do," I pleaded. "Put out a bulletin with a description. Call the Provincetown police."

"Officially, I cannot put out a bulletin until they've been missing for—"

"Twenty-four hours. Yes, you and the *bland one* have made that abundantly clear."

He ignored the jab at his underling. "I'm feeling generous this morning. I'll call down to P-town and see if there's been any trouble involving your two little buddies."

"Call me as soon as you hear anything, okay?"

"Yes, Cassandra." He sounded exasperated, so I didn't push further.

I thought I'd go crazy waiting to hear something from the Whale Rock PD. With worry over my friends growing as the hours ticked by, I boldly pursued another avenue and placed a call to the Boston office of the FBI.

It was three days after Ashley and Vince disappeared when Brooks finally called me back, but not with news I was hoping to hear.

"Two bikes have been found down at Kinsey Cove. Do you want to come take a look?"

"I'll be right there." But first I ran to the bathroom to empty my stomach. He said two bikes were found. He didn't say bodies. Still, I didn't have a good feeling. I splashed water on my face and grabbed the Miata keys. Five minutes later, I pulled down the lane to the cove and saw Fiona's old picnic basket tied to the fender of the silver bicycle. I ran to the woods and threw up again.

# 14

Three days after the disappearance

"**Y**ou're right, Cassie. Something is very wrong here." Agent Daniel Benjamin told me later that day. He stared hard, and I was regretting my call to the FBI, despite an unexpected attraction to the rather aloof agent that showed up. "But the biggest problem is there's no record of your Vince or Ashley Jacobson. According to the US government, they don't exist."

My life had become as surreal as a Chagall painting. First, my tenants vanish without a trace. And now an FBI agent was standing in my kitchen, making a stunning declaration, one I was about to protest, when he uttered another surprising assertion.

"Until we have more information about the disappearance of your tenants, you might want to exercise some caution, remain alert of your surroundings."

"Are you suggesting *I* could be in some kind of danger?" I'd been too preoccupied with Ashley and Vince's disappearance to consider such a notion.

Either he didn't hear me as he busied himself with the inspection of the door and window locks, or he was evading the question. Regardless, all Agent Benjamin said in the way of an answer was, "These old Vics have a lot of easy entries. I'll check the rest before I leave."

Suddenly, I felt especially glad for Whistler and bent down to give him an affectionate rub.

"He'll be good to have around." Agent Benjamin nodded toward the dog. "Nobody will want to come in here with a big German shepherd standing guard."

"What aren't you telling me?"

"Just some commonsense practices." He passed it off as a minor precaution, but an abrupt change in his manner and the way he averted his eyes made me dubious. "It's always a good idea to keep a house securely locked, especially when you live out here, off the beaten trail, so to speak."

A queasiness came swiftly upon me as my suspicions returned about a possible unidentified person or persons lurking in the woods near The Bluffs earlier in the summer.

He pulled out a chair and motioned for me to sit. "I didn't mean to alarm you."

"I'll be fine." I waved away his concern, though I would definitely heed his advice and keep all the doors and windows locked from now on.

He gave me an uncomfortably long, appraising look before asking, "Something I should know?"

I shook my head, deciding to save the details of the unknown camper for Brooks. I was feeling guilty for contacting the FBI behind his back, and hoped a peace offering might smooth things over. No doubt he'd be livid over my not reporting it sooner, but there'd been no recent signs to indicate anyone was still skulking about.

"I promise we will do our very best to solve this, Cassie." The FBI agent clasped my hand, stirring up pleasantly warm, but unwanted, sensations within me. *Why now, for crying out loud? Wasn't my life messy enough as it was?*

Brooks arrived not ten minutes after Agent Benjamin departed.

"How could they not exist?" I was still digesting the unsettling news.

"It's not that *they* don't exist. But the government doesn't have a record of a Vince or Ashley Jacobson who match the age and description of the two people who were living here with you."

"You knew this already?"

"Not until the FBI agent told me. Dammit," he cursed under his breath. "I should have insisted on a more thorough background check beyond just running their names through the outstanding warrant databases."

"Who's that?" I asked, looking out the kitchen window at the sound of another car.

"The forensics techs. We'll see if we can get some prints, maybe some other evidence."

I escorted them all to the disheveled guest room.

"What happened in here?" Brooks was clearly dismayed by the condition. "I'd have thought the FBI would be more meticulous."

I said nothing and crept slyly down the stairs. Let the FBI take the heat on this one.

"Did Agent Benjamin remove anything?" Brooks asked after the forensics team left with their samples.

"A receipt." I hesitated before adding, "At least that's all he told me he took."

"Do you know what it was for?"

"No, but I did get a quick look at the store name. Does Sincere House mean anything to you?"

"Not off the top of my head. I'll check it out."

"He said he'd let you know the details."

"Did he now?" Brooks leaned against the kitchen counter, arms folded, a sour look on his face. "What else did he tell you?"

"I'm sorry. I didn't mean to go over your head. It's just . . ." I broke down, hiding my crumpled face in my hands.

"Hey, hey, hey. What's all this about?" He put his arms around me in a brotherly way. "We'll find them."

"Everything is such a mess." I took a moment to compose myself before telling him, "My divorce was just finalized."

"Does Zoe know?" He held me back so he could look me in the eyes.

"No, and there's no need to tell her."

He gave me a "Why would I tell Zoe?" look.

I didn't feel like getting into the whys of him being in touch with my sister, so instead I made my confession. "There's something I probably should have told you before."

His expression morphed from sweet concern to seriously stern as I told him about the possible visitor in the woods, making me wish I hadn't brought it up.

"What were you thinking?" he roared, predictably furious with me. "You should have come to me immediately."

"I know." I raised my hands in automatic surrender. "Sorry."

"We know nothing about those people staying here." The lecture continued in earnest. "For all we know, someone may have been following them. You could have been in danger."

I rubbed my forehead, letting what he said sink in.

"Look, what's done is done," Brooks declared in a calmer voice. And then, "Why don't you take me for a look at those campsites?"

* * *

The first location was very near to where the land trust abutted my property. You could barely see any charred wood remains from the campfire. Brooks dug around with the toe of his boot but uncovered nothing of consequence.

"Did you show Agent Benjamin?" he asked.

"No. I thought it best to leave it to you to decide if it's a worthy clue." I was hoping to earn some brownie points. "The second site is further into the woods."

We hiked the trail another fifteen minutes until we came upon the alcove where the fire pit remnants were better preserved. Brooks donned gloves and withdrew a piece of foil, then continued his inspection of the niche, pulling free some black strands tangled on a nearby branch.

"Some type of synthetic fiber like nylon or polyester." He placed his discoveries in two separate plastic evidence bags.

As we walked back to the house, I told Brooks about the

conversation I'd overheard between Ashley and Vince. "You may be right about them being followed. They'd been talking about some man and worried that he was still around."

"Did they mention a name?"

I shook my head. I was now regretting having let it pass.

Before he left, Brooks cautioned, "Just because that little alcove doesn't appear to be occupied now, you can't just assume whoever was hiding there won't return. Make sure you keep everything locked up tight."

The second such warning issued in the space of an afternoon.

Later, as I double-checked the locks, I replayed in my head Ashley and Vince's conversation. *We don't even know why he's here.* Vince said this when they'd been freaking out over the mystery person. Was it the same thing they'd said about the person from upstate New York they claimed to have met at Nauset Beach? Their explanation had sounded flimsy then and in retrospect seemed even less believable. If they were being followed, was it by whoever had been hiding in that alcove in the woods? And if so, where was he now?

# 15

A week following the disappearance

Seven long days had passed since Ashley and Vince disappeared, and there'd yet to be any productive leads.

Search teams had combed the National Seashore. Missing Persons alerts had been issued nationwide. Airport passenger rosters had been checked, and all travelers had been identified and accounted for, none matching the descriptions or the identifications of my friends who had vanished. Brooks had been really good about keeping me informed. As for Agent Benjamin, I hadn't heard from him since the day he stopped out at The Bluffs. But he had been in contact with the Whale Rock police chief.

"I had a call from your friend at the FBI." Brooks phoned me to announce the surprising development. "I'm no longer leading the investigation."

"What? That makes no sense."

"None of this makes any sense, Cassie. I have no clue why the FBI got involved with this case in the first place."

I thought back to the day Daniel Benjamin showed up in Whale Rock. I'd been the one to call the FBI, but he could have blown it off. Instead, he'd made a cavalier remark about liking the Cape and taking a drive out. Was that how the FBI usually worked?

"Did you ask?"

"The FBI isn't beholden to me, and so far they're disinclined to provide an explanation."

We were both quiet a moment, and then Brooks said, "Did I tell you Johnny Hotchkiss's boat has been located?"

"No. Where was it found?"

"It was anchored in an uninhabited cove near Plymouth."

"Any clues?"

"None. No footprints along the beach, but the tide could have washed away any tracks. It was in good shape, everything tied down securely, nothing missing. And wiped down, no fingerprints."

"Well, at least I bet Johnny's happy."

"He will be, whenever he gets it back." His tone was laced with notes of cynicism. "It was confiscated by the FBI."

I'd been sorting through bills and only half-listening to the developments about the missing boat. But now he had my full attention. *Why would the FBI have an interest in the theft of a small sailboat? Unless it had something to do with an active missing person's case in the same small town.*

"Do they think it's connected to Ashley and Vince?"

"I don't know what they're thinking, 'cause they're not talking to me."

I felt bad for Brooks, but I was equally discouraged about the well of information drying up on me.

After the call with Brooks ended, I needed a distraction to keep the worst possible scenarios from monopolizing my thoughts. I took myself down to the dock to spend some quiet time on the *Queen Jacqueline*, and brought along the knotted rope left behind by Vince and Ashley with the picnic basket. Something about the knots had been bothering me. It was possible that Vince or Ashley had been using it to practice sailing knots, but that didn't explain why there were some I didn't recognize. I couldn't shrug off the feeling that this rope had been left behind for a reason. My contemplation was interrupted by a voice calling out from above. Quickly hiding the knotted rope, I shielded my eyes and waved as Agent Benjamin descended the steep hillside steps.

"Have you just tied up, or are you getting ready to take her out?" He crouched down on the dock, level with me, his startling gray eyes piercing me.

"Neither, actually." I forced my gaze away. "Sometimes I just like to come down here and sit on the boat to clear my head."

"Do you have some heavy thinking to do?" he asked. "Should I leave you alone?"

"Yes to the first question, and you can easily guess the subject of those thoughts."

He nodded solemnly but offered nothing on the status of the case.

"But a definite no to the second." I was honestly glad for the company.

"There won't be many more days like this." He was standing now, gazing out to the horizon. "It seems a shame to waste it."

"Don't tell me you're a sailor, Agent Benjamin."

"I thought we agreed on 'Daniel.'" Before I knew it, he'd hopped aboard. "It's been awhile, but I've taken part in a few regattas in my day."

"I'm impressed. And here I had you figured for a city boy."

"Oh, I am that. The worst part of the city as a kid. Ever heard of the Fresh Air Project?"

I nodded.

"Well, I was a Fresh Air kid and an extremely fortunate one. My summer family lived in Marblehead. Need I say more?"

"Sailing capital of the country? I fear my little boat might not prove worthy."

"She's a Cat, right?" He nodded with confidence and began to inspect the vessel more closely. "I got my sea legs on one of these. Not as old a girl as this one." Daniel ran his hands along the gunwale. "She's still in pretty good shape. Someone loved her."

"Lots of people did. You might even say she was a heartbreaker. She originally belonged to my great-grandfather more than eighty years ago. She was the *Femme Celeste* back then."

His head shot up. "Isn't it bad luck to change the name of a boat?"

"It didn't end happily." Of course, her rechristened name hadn't exactly brought good fortune either.

Daniel looked to the sky where a few clouds were skimming by at a good clip. "So, are you game?"

I leaned forward. "You mean, take her out? Now?"

"You have something better to do?" He cocked his head and offered a disarming smile.

"No, but I imagined you might."

"I could use a day off." He began unwinding the line from the cleat near the bow.

"Let's do it." My desire to take the *Queen Jacqueline* for a sail around the Cape won out over a momentary hesitation as I considered how Brooks might feel about my consorting with his rival on the case.

I clapped for Whistler, who'd been exploring along the rocky coast. The dog leapt gracefully onto the bow, taking Daniel by surprise.

"He's sailed before?"

"This guy's an old sea dog." The first time I'd taken Vince and Ashley sailing, there'd been lots of prodding and bribing to get Whistler into the boat, but in the end he feared being left behind more than the unsteady craft. After his maiden voyage, he'd needed no coaxing to come aboard again.

Within minutes, the sail was billowing in a warm autumn breeze. It turned out, Daniel and I were pretty good sailing partners. When we brought the Cat back in and were tying up after our sail, he suggested grabbing dinner.

"I'll come back around six to pick you up."

"You'll never make it back in time." The commute to Boston was a good two hours at this time of day.

"A buddy of mine has a cottage in East Falmouth. He's letting me use it as a base while we're investigating this case. I'll just pop over there and shower."

By a quarter to six, nearly every outfit I owned had been tried and discarded in a heap on my bed. When was the last time I'd actually been on a real date? Ethan and I hadn't exactly had a traditional courtship. We met. He moved in. We married. As for Billy? Our encounters certainly wouldn't fall under Emily Post's concept of proper dates, especially when one of the people involved was already married to somebody else. I swatted the air to chase away the annoying memory.

I returned my focus to the dilemma at hand: finding an acceptable outfit that didn't scream "desperate."

"What will we talk about?" I asked Whistler, who cocked his head and then made a whining sound. "You're right. I shouldn't delude myself. This is business to him."

The last option was my fallback ensemble. Camel slacks and black turtleneck. I'd throw my mother's cashmere wrap around my shoulders. She would have approved of the casual elegance. Papa would have teased by calling it my classic Hepburn look, sort of an amalgamation of the two famous icons—with my wild auburn hair pulled into a casual up-do, there was a slight resemblance to a young Kate, but I'd been blessed with prominent cheeks and a slightly turned-up nose, which were much more Audrey. Neither Zoe nor I had inherited our mother's fair hair and blue eyes. And now that the portraits of our great-grandparents had been discovered, anyone could see that my sister was practically an identical image of Celeste. If only she could be bothered to return to Whale Rock and see for herself. Brooding over Zoe right now would only put me in a mood, so I dabbed on a hint of blush, smacked my lips with gloss, and scrutinized my appearance in the large oval mirror above the art deco vanity.

"It'll have to do." Whistler barked to announce Daniel's prompt arrival, which brought on an unexpected rush of wildly fluttering butterflies. I held a calming palm to my tummy and inhaled deeply, seeking that reassuring scent of warm caramel.

\* \* \*

Maybe it was the wine, but I found myself opening up with Daniel in a way I hadn't expected. I stopped short of telling him about Percy and Celeste—nothing says crazy like talk of ghosts inhabiting your home, even if they are relatives—so when he asked how I'd ended up living alone in the big old Victorian, I skipped over recent events with Ethan, gave a brief account of the long-ago fire, and picked up where my parents' story began.

"My mother's family felt she'd married beneath her station in life. They were wealthy tourists summering on the Cape, and my father was just a lowly sailor running a charter fishing and sightseeing service. Plus Mama was quite a bit younger than Papa." Their unlikely romance had endured by virtue of the couple's strong united front against class differences and attempts to tear them apart.

"It's a familiar story." For a wisp of a moment Daniel's face clouded, making me want to know more about his history. Earlier while sailing, he'd uttered an offhand comment about his ex-wife, but nothing more. "Please go on."

"My mother admitted to me once that she'd intentionally gotten pregnant with my older sister so that her parents wouldn't try to stop the marriage. Of course, Mama *was* delirious on morphine at the time. Otherwise, I'm certain she'd never have confessed such a scandalous deed to her impressionable teenage daughter."

"Did your mother's folks ever accept your father?"

"It took awhile. Their first home was a tiny harbor apartment that Mama's parents refused to set foot in it. It wasn't until Papa bought back Battersea Bluffs, a home they felt was worthy of her background, that peace was finally made."

Bridging the gap between my mother and her parents was yet another motivation my father had had for reclaiming the Mitchell homestead.

"I'm sure they would have come around eventually anyway, though, since my sister and I were their only grandchildren." This was fortunate for us, since they turned out to be exceptionally generous and were in fact the benefactors of our healthy trust funds, even if mine was currently uttering a death rattle.

"So your parents achieved their 'happily ever after'?"

"For a while." I hesitated, but when Daniel inclined his head and offered an encouraging smile, I told him about the sad end of their lives together. "They were very much in love, but my mother had a lot of health problems even before the cancer that she eventually died from, and it wrecked my father. It was hard for the rest of us too, having to watch them in such a hopeless state, knowing their precious time together was approaching the end. It was toughest on my grandmother. She'd always been very protective of her family, my father especially."

~

Eighty years ago
November ~ a month before the fire at Battersea Bluffs

As Fiona rested in her lover's arms under the moonlit sky, that night before he left, they'd laughed off Robert Toomey's curse. She'd been intoxicated in the aftermath of her first night of passion, deluded into the misguided confidence that nothing could interfere with their happiness.

But once she realized that she had a tiny baby growing within her, conceived during that single night's tryst on the aft deck of the *Femme Celeste*, she was determined never to relent to a vengeful curse. Fiona laid a protective hand upon her not-yet-swelling belly and made her own vow. She would do all in her power to ensure the Mitchell family bloodline would remain strong and endure. She and her baby would see to it. Fiona was certain she'd bear Ambrose a son. A Mitchell boy. Percy and Celeste would be welcoming their first grandson in about seven months.

~

Present day

"How old were you when your parents passed away?"

"Seventeen when Mama died, and Papa passed just before my twentieth birthday. Then not long afterward, I lost my Granny Fi."

"So you lived alone in the house for quite a while before you got married?"

This hit a nerve, and yet I was curious. "How'd you even know I was married, let alone when?"

He looked down at his plate and began rubbing his forehead self-consciously.

A blaze of indignation fleetingly blurred my vision. "Isn't it unethical, even for an FBI agent, to intrude on an individual's privacy?"

He met my eyes and took in a deep breath. "Not when they're suspects."

I must have looked as disgusted as I felt, for he rushed to add, "I misspoke. Not a suspect, but a person of interest. In a case like this, we take a close look at everyone associated with the individuals who've gone missing," He reached across and took my hand, which had begun to tremble. "Please understand. It's my job."

At that moment, Brooks walked into the restaurant and likely misread the scene at our table. He made as if to leave, then shrugged and turned back, probably considering it wouldn't take much to set the tongues of our small town wagging all sorts of theories if he made such a hasty retreat. I withdrew my hand from Daniel's grasp as Brooks approached our table.

"Hello, Cassie." He nodded to Daniel. "Agent Benjamin. Any developments in the Jacobson case?"

Daniel frowned. "Nothing worth mentioning. I promise to let you know if we uncover anything significant."

"You do that now." The FBI seizing control of the search for Vince and Ashley had been a bitter pill the Whale Rock police chief was not swallowing gracefully.

Whether intended or not, Daniel's next remark was unnecessarily condescending. "There might be something you and your boys can help us with down the road."

Brooks's tensed jaw suggested how he interpreted the comment. He gave me a thoughtful look and then, with a hint of disapproval I hoped only I could detect, "Have a *lovely* evening."

My friend took a table in the far corner of the opposite side of the restaurant, his back to us. The evening that had begun with such promise had taken an awkward turn, so I decided I might as well give in to it.

"Is there any part of the case you can discuss with me?"

"I can tell you we're pursuing what few leads we have." Daniel then picked up the dessert menu. "Care to share something?"

I became lost in thought for a moment, referee to an internal struggle. Did I risk embarrassing myself by sharing the theory that had been percolating in my head about the sequence of those knots? Or would withholding the idea somehow thwart attempts to locate Vince and Ashley?

In the end my pride gave way to a more pragmatic desire to help find my friends. "There's a rope. It might be nothing. It's probably just a coincidence."

"A coincidence?" He made a rather absurd attempt at a pompous English accent. "The odds are enormously against it being a coincidence."

I tried to suppress a giggle, but it came out a snort.

"You don't care for my Sherlock Holmes impression?"

"Oh, so that's who it was?"

"Now you know why I pursued a career in fighting crime."

"I'll tell you what a crime is. That impression."

"Ba dum bum." He drummed a comedy rim shot. "Tough crowd tonight, folks."

Daniel's attempt to lighten the mood was working. He reached for my hand again.

"Seriously, I believe coincidences only occur in the rarest occasions, if ever. In the FBI, we're taught to investigate even the most improbable variable and to never assume anything is accidental. So what is it about this rope that might help the investigation?"

I took a deep breath. "It was tied to the picnic basket that was left behind. It's just a series of knots. I'd been teaching Vince some sailing knots, and he might have been using the rope to practice, but—"

Daniel didn't prompt me. He simply waited patiently for me to find the right words.

"There are some knots I don't recognize." I hesitated again. "Look, I know this is going to sound as if I've been reading too many mystery novels, but I just have this feeling he left behind a message." There, I'd finally said it, and he wasn't laughing at me.

"Like some type of code?"

I leaned forward. "Exactly."

"You think they left it for you?"

"Maybe. Or perhaps it was a generic SOS,—you know, left for whoever found it."

"I'd have to look at it." He shrugged noncommittally.

My theory wasn't well formed, but I didn't want it to be dismissed. "If we figure out the message, if that's what it is, then we should be able to determine the person it was intended for. Right?"

"Could I take the rope to our forensics team? Let them check it out?"

"Of course. Anything to help."

"Have you told anyone else about this?" I followed Daniel's gaze to where Brooks was now sharing a laugh with the waitress.

"You mean Brooks?" I shook my head. "Should I?"

"For now I think it's best to keep it between us. The agency doesn't share everything with local law enforcement. As much as possible, we try to protect the victims."

"Victims?" It sounded ominous. "And here I thought Ashley and Vince didn't exist."

"They may not have been who they told you they were. But they did exist, Cassie."

"*Do* exist," I insisted.

"We can hope."

\* \* \*

Daniel didn't ask for the rope straightaway when he brought me home, which suggested it wasn't the only reason he came inside.

"Can I offer you some wine or coffee?" I walked to Papa's antique bar and picked up a bottle. "I even have some of the finest tawny port."

"Coffee's fine. It wouldn't be cool to have an elevated blood alcohol level if Chief Kincaid pulled me over. I'm fairly certain he doesn't like me."

"Does that bother you?"

"Nope." He sniffed the air. "Been baking again?"

"Guilty." I lied as Percy and Celeste made their sweet presence known.

I walked through the large archway to the kitchen, where Daniel stopped me and took hold of my hands.

"In my line of work, we're trained to expect the unexpected. It's a mantra of sorts. Always be prepared, because each day holds its own unique surprises. More times than not, I run smack into life's grim realities. On a good day I get to witness a happy ending. But so rarely, in fact, I can't even remember the last time." He shook his head. "The point is, today I failed."

I braced myself for the letdown certain to be coming.

"This morning, I was in no way prepared for the exceptional day ahead of me." He squeezed my hands. "It's been a long time since anyone has taken me by surprise."

Maybe it was the pervasive scent of caramel that sparked such an intense response, but I was unable to hold back. I found my fingers raking through Daniel's thick, dark hair, kissing him with unrepressed fervor. If I'd been watching myself, I might've felt the same vicarious embarrassment one feels when reading a love scene in a bad romance novel, but there was no question I was lip-locked with a partner more than my equal in willingness and enthusiasm, and he didn't seem at all embarrassed. I'm not certain how much time passed before we paused for air, or even how we made it from the kitchen to the library sofa.

"Can I assume I've been forgiven?" Daniel breathed hard.

"Oh yeah." I nestled closer and kissed him again. "All is forgiven."

Just then, Whistler began to bark fiercely from the front of the house.

"Probably a raccoon or a deer." I dismissed the interruption even though I knew the dog wasn't usually bothered by the plethora of wildlife prowling my property.

Whistler ran into the room, whimpered, then left and resumed his post, barking an ever more furious warning.

Daniel smiled apologetically as he quickly disentangled himself from our embrace. "I'll have a look at what's causing such a fuss."

"I'll come with," I said, not letting go of his hand.

We opened the front door just in time to see taillights disappearing at the curve about a quarter mile down the drive.

"Expecting company?"

I looked at my watch, amazed by the lateness of the hour. "At midnight? I think not."

"Maybe someone who got lost?"

"It wouldn't be the first time." But it was a rare occurrence, and my gut was telling me whoever had been here had come with a purpose in mind.

Daniel grabbed a flashlight I kept near the door and walked outside for a check. A sudden chill came over me. I considered telling him about the elusive camper but assumed the Whale Rock PD had shared those details. And then it occurred to me: it must have been Brooks who'd driven out to check up on me. I was relieved, though he probably wouldn't have been pleased to see Daniel's car here so late.

Rubbing the goose skin of my naked arms, it registered that I was partially disrobed. Zoe's unwelcome words of warning echoed in my head. *You're like a Raggedy Ann doll. No spine. You've got to learn to say no.*

Maybe Zoe was right. There was no arguing that the circumstances weren't ideal for romance. But didn't I deserve a bit of happiness? Especially with life serving up a heap of shabby lately.

I shivered again when Daniel came back inside.

"Do you feel safe out here?" He pulled me close, rubbing my arms and nuzzling my neck. "I could stay."

As tempting as it was, the spell had been broken.

"I appreciate the offer, but I'm used to being alone out here." Not that I was ever truly alone under the constant watch of Percy and Celeste. "Besides, as you just witnessed, Whistler's a super guard dog."

Daniel nodded grudgingly to the German shepherd. "Looks like you win, buddy."

"Perhaps another time?" I rested my palm against his cheek.

"I'll hold you to it." He kissed me again and then, with a sigh of defeat, reluctantly released me and draped me in the cashmere wrap I'd dropped by the door.

"Let me make you that coffee." I retrieved my sweater from between the sofa cushions, pulled my disheveled hair up into a bushy ponytail, and walked toward the kitchen. "It won't take but a minute."

"Not necessary." Daniel picked up the tangled line of rope I'd left on the large, oak table. As a sailor, he should be familiar with some of the knots; his furrowed brow indicated he was already trying to decipher a meaning. "I can take this?"

"Yep. Let me know if you can make any sense of it."

He saluted. "Will do."

There was one more lingering kiss before he left. "Lock up tight after me."

I saluted back. "Will do."

I watched the vehicle drive away and brooded over what had created the wall of distrust. I'd let Daniel think he was in possession of the original rope left tied to the abandoned bicycles. Instead, I'd given him an odd piece of line I'd used to replicate the knots myself while trying to decode their message. It was a fair enough copy and would serve its purpose.

I shook my head to dispel the vision repeatedly coming to mind: a hastily knotted rope at the last desperate moment when the two people I'd grown so fond of realized they were in danger.

# 16

Nine days following the disappearance

"Do I have to learn everything about your life from Brooks?" Zoe whined.

I closed my eyes and bit back a cutting response. "Sorry I haven't called. There's been a lot going on."

"I'd say. Let's see, there are your missing tenants, an as yet unfinished and *unrented* carriage house apartment, and—oh yeah, a new man in your life."

"Then we have something in common on that count. It's interesting how often you and Brooks have been in touch lately. Oliver misbehaving again?" The words spilled out before I could catch them.

To the best of my knowledge Oliver had been unfaithful only the one time. However, Zoe had been quite emphatic that if her husband couldn't keep it zipped, she'd help him pack his bags.

Her silence made me consider whether I'd landed the barb too close to the truth.

"Sorry. That wasn't very nice." I softened my voice. "Everything okay?"

"Sure." Was that a sniffle?

"Do you want to talk about it?"

"Nothing to talk about." My sister rarely let anyone see her in a wounded state and handily changed the subject. "But I do want to know, who is this Daniel Benjamin?"

"He's an FBI agent working the disappearance." I might as well tell

129

her about last night since she clearly already knew. "We had dinner. Once."

"And went sailing too, I hear."

*Jeez. Was nothing in my life private?*

"He's a pretty fair sailor at that." I wouldn't let on that the gossip bothered me.

"So what do you think happened to that couple?" Zoe had never called Vince and Ashley by name. They were either "that couple" or "your tenants."

"I wish I knew. It's crazy, Zoe. They vanished without a trace. It's as if they never existed."

"Maybe they had a good reason to leave."

Whistler nuzzled my hand for a pet. "And abandon their dog? No way."

"Well, for their sake and yours, I hope it comes to a good end."

"Me too. They're awfully good kids, Zoe. You would have liked them."

"Brooks didn't trust them," she challenged.

"Brooks doesn't trust anyone."

"I'll give you that." Then it was back to business. "When do you think you'll be able to rent out the carriage house?"

"There's not all that much left to do." Though having not finished the work gave more credence to my thinking Ashley and Vince wouldn't have left of their own accord. "I've hired Steve Morrison to finish the work. Now that summer's over, he's freed up a bit." Steve's father had been Papa's best friend, and his son had taken over his small construction company when the elder Morrison retired.

"I remember Steve. He used to come by the house with his dad all the time. Well if Steve is as good as Mr. Morrison, I'm sure you're in capable hands. Weren't you two friends?"

"Uh-huh." They were capable hands alright. A wicked smile danced on my lips. Steve and I were never an item, just friends who'd experimented in our teenage years. Mama was ill, so Papa hardly noticed where I went and with whom. It was Granny Fi who'd discovered our little trysts, and though she didn't chastise me, she did march me directly to a clinic in Orleans for birth control pills. Shortly after, we fizzled out, and Steve started going steady with Sarah Kimball while I hooked up with Billy Hughes. The birth control pills had not gone to waste.

"Anything else I should know?"

"No, that covers it." I wasn't up for the lecture so I didn't tell her about the notice I'd received from the bank yesterday, reminding me my mortgage payment was late. I'd underestimated the renovation costs and had already blown through Zoe's loan.

"Be wary of rebound relationships, Cass." It was not said reproachfully, but in the weary, knowing way of someone who'd been through it.

"I'll keep it in mind." Had there been more to the end of Zoe's relationship with Brooks and the beginning of her love affair with Oliver all those years ago? Was she hinting at a flaw in her choice? A mistake, rushing into marriage with Oliver? Had she opened her heart too easily to another because Brooks had broken it?

When I hung up, I knocked over the catchall basket on the desk, spilling its contents to the floor. "Damn it."

While collecting and sorting through the hodge-podge, I found an envelope of photographs. I shuffled through them and came upon one of Ethan and me taken on our wedding day. We looked happy. *Oh my God.* I'd completely forgotten. Tomorrow would have been our seven-year anniversary. I rested my forehead in the palm of my hand as an empty feeling threatened to pull me under. All of a sudden, there came a loud clanging on the antique water pipes.

"Okay. I hear you." There'd been no sweet sugary aroma from Percy and Celeste when Ethan entered my life. No scent at all. Instead, this same persistent clattering of the pipes, the source of which no plumber was able to determine. But love had thrown down a gauntlet against their signals, and they'd eventually quieted down.

Another photo was stuck to the bottom of the basket, but this one wasn't of me and Ethan—it was actually a close-up snapshot of Ashley and Vince that had slipped out of her backpack one day. I'd swept it up and had truly meant to return it to her. Only they'd disappeared before I had a chance to remember to give it back.

I examined it more closely. In the corner background of the

picture was a sign, but it was illegible. I sorted through the desk drawer for the magnifying glass but still couldn't make it out.

I picked up the phone to call Brooks, but then put it back down. Daniel had said the FBI preferred to keep some details discreet as a way of protecting the victims. This might well be one of those isolated kernels of information. Daniel's business card was stuck in the corner of the desk blotter, but I hadn't heard from him for two days, since he'd left with the rope. I fingered the card for a minute. *Screw your pride, Cassie.*

I called.

He was quiet when I finished telling him about the photograph.

"I was thinking your team could enhance the image to read the wording on the sign. I mean, wouldn't it be helpful to know where the photo was taken?"

"I'd have to see it." He added nothing more.

I was starting to feel uncomfortable. "Is this a bad time?"

"Just a crazy Monday with a stack of new cases. I've been meaning to call to see if we could get together one night this week." I heard pages flipping, probably his daytimer. "I couldn't make it out there until, uh, Friday night?"

I didn't respond immediately, making the pretense of checking my own calendar. "Hmm. Friday? I don't know. Let. Me. See."

It was subtle, but he must have gotten the point, for he shook free of the caddish attitude.

"I'd really like to see you again." His tone was evocative of the pleasant evening we'd spent together, bringing to life the butterflies. I'd let him off the hook this time.

"Friday it is." I was holding onto the picture and thought to ask before we hung up, "Should I text this photo to you?"

"If you knew my caseload right now?" He blew out a frustrated breath. "I think it can wait until Friday."

What could be more important than finding two young people who'd vanished without a trace? I was tempted to take the photo to Brooks for a look.

Then Daniel said, as if following my thought process, "Let's keep this between you and me, okay?"

When I didn't respond, he added, "Definitely text it, but the image quality might be better on the original. I'll pick it up on Friday."

That should have placated my concerns. Why hadn't it? I had a sick, nudging feeling he was losing interest in finding Vince and Ashley.

# 17

Two weeks following the disappearance

We were lying on my bed, entangled in Egyptian cotton, damp from the swelter of passion. It was Friday night. No, scratch that, it was Saturday morning and our second date was going exceedingly well. It had started at the Café Muse in P-town, and hours later we'd barely walked through the door before tumbling into the sheets.

"I don't know what got into me," I confessed.

"You don't? Then I'm a failure." Daniel bit my bare shoulder playfully.

"You know what I mean. I'll blame it on the Bloody French Martini."

"*Martinis*. Plural."

"But they were so yum, I couldn't resist."

"That's not all you couldn't resist."

"I have no willpower. What's your excuse? The oysters mignonette?"

"That's possible. But it could also be"—he made a roguish face—"the shaky beef?"

"Definitely the shaky beef." I laughed and rolled on top of him, making it clear I was still willing.

He pushed the hair away from my face and kissed me gently. "Give a guy a moment. Don't forget, I've got a few years on you."

"I don't believe the subject of your age has come up." I slowly rolled back to the side. "So, how old are you?"

"Is that a polite question?"

"It is when asking an FBI agent who already knows all the personal details of my life." I pulled at a hair on his chest.

"Ouch!" He grabbed my hand in self-defense. "Let's put it in practical terms. When you were graduating high school I was a first-year field agent."

"Excuse me, but I've had two Bloody French Martinis."

He held up three fingers.

I should have felt ashamed, but the alcohol had numbed that part of my brain. "Even more reason for you to do the math for me."

"I'm forty-four." Seven years older than I was.

"Okay, ancient one. Let's take a break." I rested my head on his shoulder.

"It doesn't seem possible I'll be retiring next year."

"At forty-five? That seems young for retirement."

"I'll have my twenty years in. It's mandatory."

"What will you do?" I didn't know Daniel well enough to be sleeping with him, let alone to understand his ambitions and aspirations.

"I'll probably take a year off before deciding about the next phase of my career."

"You could write a book."

He chuckled. "I have to write a lot of reports, and it's a part of my job I detest. So I'll be taking a vacation from writing."

I assumed the subject was closed, which didn't surprise me since Daniel was much more comfortable asking questions than answering them. But after a thoughtful pause he responded. "I've often thought about buying a sailboat, exploring the Caribbean for a while. Have you ever been?"

"My sister and I went on a cruise of the islands." I didn't admit it was the only time I'd traveled outside the country, lest he think me provincial, which of course I was.

"Is that where you got this?" My skin tingled at his touch as he gently traced the tattooed image of the phoenix's outstretched wings, fiery red and purple plumage, surrounded by dancing flames.

I shook my head.

"It's beautiful. What is it?"

"Out of the ashes the phoenix will rise," I whispered, unsure if he even heard.

"It must have some significance."

He took my silence as the signal it was and directed the conversation elsewhere. "Have you had any more late-night visitors?"

Having convinced myself it had been Brooks, I'd put the incident out of my mind. "Not that I'm aware of. And Whistler would let me know if there had been. Why?"

Daniel gave a half shrug since I had his other arm pinned to the bed.

I raised myself up on my elbow. "Do you have an idea who it was?"

"I always have ideas. That's part of what I do. Contemplate the possibilities and narrow down to the probabilities."

"Well, since you bring it up, I was wondering about a certain possibility and where it stood."

"The rope?"

"Uh-huh."

His chest rose from taking in a deep breath. "So far our decoding guys haven't come up with anything. It very well could be nothing more than a rope your friends grabbed when they needed something to secure the basket to the bicycle."

I slumped down in defeat and rolled onto my back. I'd been researching knots all week and hadn't come up with anything concrete either.

"Hey, I know it's not the answer you wanted to hear. But we've got another expert looking at it this week. Fresh eyes so to speak."

"What about the receipt you found in their room that first day?"

He frowned. "Oh, that. We haven't turned up anything tangible yet."

"And the photo?"

"Still examining it. There might be a solid lead there."

I felt he was humoring me, so I sought his eyes. "Be honest. Is that a *possibility* or a *probability*?"

"I'd like to say the case is solvable, but right now?" His tone was flat. "This is one of the tough ones, Cassie. I wish I could be more optimistic."

We didn't say anything for quite a long time, though he caressed my arm while I played with his chest hair, gently now.

"You're sad." He kissed the top of my head.

I nodded as a tear escaped down into my hair.

He wiped it away with his thumb, then kissed the corner of my eye. "Salty tears wash away your fears."

Daniel did not strike me as the sentimental type, and I was taken aback by the sweet gesture. "What's that from?"

"Nothing." But I could see the shadow of a smile.

"What?" I prodded, threatening to torture his chest hairs again.

He laid my hand flat against his chest where I could feel the thumping of his heart. "My grandmother used to say it to me when I was little."

"You were close?"

"She raised me. My mother worked two jobs to keep us sheltered and fed. A hard worker but not around much. It was my grandmother who kept me on the straight and narrow, and more importantly, out of the system."

"What about your dad?"

"Left before I could walk."

There was much to learn about this Daniel Benjamin, but tonight was not a time for delving too deeply. We had the luxury of time. I jerked upright at the thread of a memory.

"What is it?"

"Something Vince said." But I couldn't put my finger on it. The thought had ricocheted in and out of my brain too quickly to grasp hold. "It's gone. Is this what happens when you get old?"

"Seriously? Abusing me already." He shook his head.

"I'll be good."

He pulled me back down. "That's not exactly what I had in mind."

\* \* \*

The fire was roaring and the sirens screaming. But where was the fire engine? I should be able to see it by now. *Please, please hurry!*

Somebody had ahold of me, but I couldn't see through the flames. "Cassie, wake up."

My eyes shot open. "What's happening?" I gasped.

"Just a bad dream."

"Daniel?"

"Yeah, it's me." He began rocking me gently.

"Oh, thank God." I collapsed against him, breathing hard and my heart pounding so fast my eardrums were vibrating. "It was a fire. There's always a fire. The sirens were sounding."

"That was your phone ringing."

"What?"

"Your ringtone sounds like a fire alarm."

"Damn it, Percy," I whispered.

"Who?" Daniel cocked his head.

"Nobody. Somebody keeps messing with me by changing my phone options."

Percy—or maybe Celeste—had apparently taken an interest in modern technology, driving me crazy with their recent techno-shenanigans. This was the third time I'd had to change my ringtone back. Yesterday it was my laptop that kept powering on.

"Sounds like a case for the FBI," he said affably.

The siren sounded again. I silenced the phone but was unable to suppress a reflexive groan when I saw who was calling.

"Problem?"

"No. Just my sister on the West Coast."

Daniel picked up his watch from the bedside table and frowned. "Ten o'clock already?"

I checked the incoming call history. "Third time she's called."

"Could it be urgent?"

"To Zoe, any opportunity to get under my skin is urgent." I

chewed on my thumb, considering whether I should call her back or let her stew a bit. I glanced about the room. "Hey, where's Whistler?"

"Dunno. Haven't seen him."

I jumped from the bed in a panic. "I did bring him in last night, didn't I?"

"Yeah, yeah." Daniel disentangled himself from the bedding and quickly pulled on his jeans. "I'm pretty sure you did."

But his look of concern had me doubting his memory and wondering how many drinks *he'd* had last night.

"Damn those Bloody French Martinis," I said rushing toward the bedroom door, Daniel at my heels. As we made our way down the hallway toward the stairs, a soft whimpering came from the guest room.

"Oh, poor baby." We found him in the corner of the closet. I kneeled down to stroke his head, and Daniel crouched beside me to inspect.

"Hey there, buddy." He gently checked the dog's legs and joints. "He doesn't appear to be hurt."

Whistler responded to our attentions with an appreciative wag, and after feeling relatively assured he wasn't injured, I stood and clapped my hands. "Outside?"

The dog leaped up and wiggled happily, filling me with relief. It was only then I remembered his fear of sirens and realized my phone was probably the culprit for sending him cowering to the closet.

I brewed a pot of coffee while Daniel supervised Whistler in the yard. When he came back inside, I poured us each a mug and gestured for him to follow me back upstairs to the sleeping porch off my bedroom.

"Nice view." Daniel settled himself on the ancient but comfy overstuffed loveseat and escaped into a caffeine moment. But peace was short-lived.

"Persistent, isn't she?" he asked when my cell phone began sounding the alarm again. "Maybe you should answer that, and I'll grab a quick shower."

"Make yourself at home," I deadpanned.

"I believe I did that last night." He dodged the pillow I threw at him.

"Hey, can you bring me a couple Advil from the medicine cabinet?"

"Bloody French Martini hangover?" He tossed me the bottle.

"Among other things," I murmured, but the shower water was already drowning me out. I sucked in a breath before tapping in Zoe's number.

"Finally," my sister snapped.

"A good early morning to you too, Zo-Zo."

"It's not so early on the Cape."

I tried to stifle a yawn but failed.

"Late night?"

"What? No."

"That's not what I heard."

Who could she have been talking to now? The only familiar faces I'd seen last night at Café Muse were Edgar Faust and Jimmy Collins, and it seemed highly unlikely they would've tattled. Although Zoe probably knew *of* Edgar, I doubted she'd ever met him. He'd written the *Cape Cod Times* article Ashley had shown me that first day, and he'd dedicated an entire chapter of his book, *The Enduring Mysteries of Cape Cod*, to the story of the legendary haunting of my family home. He and his husband, Jimmy, had made a quick stop at our table to say hello on their way out, but I deftly steered the conversation away from any discussions about Battersea Bluffs. I was still leery of Daniel hearing whisperings about the spirits with whom I shared my home.

Could I have missed any other informants? The restaurant hadn't been crowded, and after several visual sweeps of the room, I'd felt confident nobody else from Whale Rock was there. Unless it had been one of Brooks's minions whom I hadn't recognized.

"It wasn't Brooks."

Damn, I hated it when she did that. "Okay, so—what? Did you peer into your crystal ball?"

"Lu was hosting a small exhibit for one of her clients in Provincetown last night at Café Muse. They were enjoying drinks on the terrace when she spied you."

"Interesting choice of words, don't you think? *Spy?*"

Zoe ignored the jab. "She said you appeared to be enamored with a tall, dark handsome stranger."

"I was having dinner with Agent Benjamin."

"Another *business* dinner?" Her chuckle carried the telltale undertones of a cynic. "Any developments in the case?"

"No." My response was clipped.

"Sorry."

"Me too."

"Look, I didn't call to pry into your personal life."

*Yeah, right.*

"I received a copy of your letter from the bank yesterday."

*Crap.* I began a mental inventory of all the Seamen's Bank employees, trying to determine who was my saboteur.

"Hello?"

"Yeah, so?"

"*So*, do you have a plan?"

"Steve should be done soon and I've put fliers around. There's an ad going into the *Penny Saver* next week. Brooks said his niece might be interested in renting it for the winter." Actually, I was pretty pleased with my plan.

"And what about this payment? Do you have the funds?"

The construction costs had surpassed my original estimate. It was painful to admit I'd depleted Zoe's loan, so I said nothing.

"I didn't think so."

I prepared for a lecture, but surprisingly one didn't come.

"Lu and I have come up with an idea."

Daniel came from the bathroom, a towel wrapped round his waist, his dark hair slicked back, and looking irresistible.

"Could it wait?" I asked hopefully.

"This is important, Cassandra. You act as if you don't understand that your future in Whale Rock is at stake."

"I'm only asking for an hour."

There was a pause before she asked, "That Agent Benjamin's still there, isn't he?'

"Um. That would be correct."

I'm surprised Daniel didn't hear Zoe groan from ten feet away.

"One hour. I'll expect your call." At least she had the courtesy not to mention my resemblance to the spineless Raggedy Ann.

\* \* \*

Slightly more than an hour later, after Daniel and I had a lingering goodbye, I found myself racing through the house. When I called Zoe back, she'd informed me that Lu was coming over to take a look at the carriage house, which they were proposing I market as an artist's retreat. "Creative types would love the chance for weeks of solitude. And the location is ideal." I had to admit, the idea held promise. There would be plenty of artists, especially seascape painters, salivating at the prospect. The Bluffs had the best views of the upper shoreline down to Whale Rock Harbor.

Hung over after a night of little sleep, the last thing I needed was to run around picking up the remnants of late night passion, let alone whipping up a batch of scones and making myself presentable. Still, I accomplished all but the latter. With my hair hanging damp and limp from the all-too-quick shower, and sporting ragged jeans, Converse sneakers, and a Patriots hoodie, I was quite a contrast to the always-impeccable Lu Ketchner when she arrived in her chic taupe sweater dress, colorful scarf, and treacherously high heeled pumps.

Lu reached down to pet Whistler, who'd settled contentedly between us on the porch, where we sipped our afternoon tea. "I already know of someone who would snap it up this fall if it's ready."

"October should be fine, but if the barn's going to serve as a studio for these visiting artists, I'd have to install a heating system for the winter months." I lifted my hands in helpless appeal, implying the lack of funds.

"What about writers?"

"That's a thought." Authors wouldn't need the studio, and they'd find the magnificent views from the carriage house inspiring. We were isolated enough to provide the solitude, but close enough to town and people for maintaining one's sanity.

"The library hosts a writers group, and they often invite guest speakers." The Mitchell Free Library was one of Granny Fi's legacies. I suppose in an indirect way, they should be obliged to help me. "Talk to George."

Not only did Evelyn's husband George own Hilliard House B&B, but he also served as chairperson of the Library Board of Trustees.

"You don't think he and Evelyn will consider me competition?"

"When do they ever have a vacancy?" She waved away the thought. "Besides, they're always referring people to other inns, and I'm certain they'd be delighted to help you."

"I suppose you're right." Evelyn had always offered their help if I ever needed it. I'd just been too proud to ask.

"How about we take a look at that carriage house?" Lu suggested.

After Lu gave her endorsement to the renovations, I took her to see the barn as well. When I pulled open the doors, light spilled into the large open space and onto my canvases.

Lu stopped stock still. "What are these?"

"Sorry, I didn't have time to move them." I chewed on my thumb, pondering where to store them once we started renting the space. The loft would be too cold in the winter, so until I had money to install a heating and air conditioning system, there was no other choice but the house.

Lu circled the barn slowly. Then she startled me by clapping her hands.

"I have the perfect spot for them." She was beaming. "My gallery."

I must have looked at Lu as if she were speaking in tongues, for she took hold of both my arms and said, "I'm not kidding, Cass. We are finally going to exhibit you."

She returned to the canvases, weaving through them, shaking her head in a disbelieving but joyful way.

"I knew you had talent, but rarely do I fail to notice a genius in my midst."

I turned to assess the images, trying to see what she did. It had been weeks since I'd worked on these; ever since Ashley and Vince had crated up both mine and my mother's more disturbing canvases, I'd avoided the barn, only recently venturing back in for brief stints at the easel.

"There must be a part of you that would like your work to be recognized," she coaxed.

"I guess I never thought about it much." *Never thought I was good enough.* "It's always been my escape." I pretended to rub Whistler's neck, but really I was trying to hide my shame.

"Well, I'll be blunt. You've had plenty of reasons to want to escape during these past few years. You've had more than your share of disappointments. Ethan?" She shook her head and made a sour face that spoiled her prettiness.

I let go of Whistler and stepped closer to Lu, touching her arm gently. "Not now. Please?"

She covered my hand with her own and said, "Right. We must look forward. And I am excited by what I see. The seascapes are exquisite. And your landscapes have an Andrew Wyeth quality, only fresh, more vibrant."

Lu clicked her tongue in exasperation. "If that sister of yours had ever gotten the courage to come home? Well, we would have made a star of you in the art world long ago."

I was about to ask why Zoe would need courage to return to Whale Rock, but wasn't given a chance. "Besides, timing is everything. It's just as well these have been preserved for a more advantageous time. Otherwise, Ethan would have spent all your earnings, and you'd be back to where you are now."

This time I didn't even try to hide my misery. "Does everyone think I'm a total loser?"

"Of course not. And I do apologize, sweetie." She hooked her arm in mine. "Let's have a closer look at these paintings."

During the more thorough inspection, Lu uncovered two other canvases I'd managed to hide from Ashley and Vince—portraits of them I'd planned to give them as parting gifts.

I stared intently at their likenesses, searching for a clue in their expressions. *What happened? Where are you? Are you safe?*

"You've captured something with these." Lu tapped a perfectly varnished index finger against her chin. "There's an interesting merging of qualities—mystery, sadness, innocence—but with universal appeal." Lu chewed on her lower lip before adding, "We can't forget there's some notoriety attached to them. You may or may not want to capitalize on that aspect. But I think we should include these as well."

"Let me give it some thought." I was torn. I had no interest in prospering from the situation, but perhaps exhibiting their portraits would be a way of keeping them in the forefront of peoples' minds as the search continued.

"Why have you never finished any of these?" Lu had turned her attention back to the land and seascapes.

It was a good question, for which I had no answer.

"Never mind," she said after taking a hard look at me. "I think you have some work to do. Are you up for it?"

"I am up for anything if it will help me save The Bluffs."

"Good. Then let's go back to the house and compare our calendars. I want to set a date."

Lu also promised to make a call to her client who might want to rent the carriage house, at least for October and possibly November too. That would be a big help with the looming mortgage payment.

Reading my expression of relief, she said, "We shall request payment in full up front."

"Are you going to tell Zoe about the exhibit?" I asked.

"Of course. She'll be thrilled. Unless—?" Lu peered at me as if evaluating a piece of art. "Is there some reason I shouldn't?"

"No." Though I couldn't decide if I was more worried my sister wouldn't show up or terrified that she would.

I walked Lu to her silvery-blue BMW convertible. When Whistler nudged her hand, she glanced uneasily toward the house. "I expect it's comforting to have a canine companion now that you're living out here alone."

"Whistler's great company. I'll miss him when . . ." I was too superstitious to speak the words.

"I don't want you to think I'm rude for not asking about the young couple in your portraits."

Why couldn't people call them by name? It's not as if the people in this town didn't make it their business to know everything about everyone.

"Ashley and Vince." My tone was sharper than I'd intended, causing Lu's face to flush.

"Right. I heard from Brooks that there's been no new information. I'm sorry."

"I didn't mean to snap. I just can't get over it. You would think there'd be some trace, some lead, but there's been nothing."

"While you're talking to George about the writers' group, maybe you should also have a word with Evelyn."

"About?"

"Isn't that where your—?" She checked herself. "Didn't Ashley and Vince stay at Hilliard House before moving in with you?"

"They did. But surely both George and Evelyn have already been questioned? By Brooks as well as the FBI."

"Yes, she mentioned your, ah, friend stopping by." Lu's eyebrows lifted slightly, and her face brightened with a wry smile. "But you know Evelyn."

"You mean her flair for the dramatic?"

"She is a bit of a drama queen." Lu looked to the sky, making her own theatrical display. "Lord, the fuss she made over having been the first to meet the missing tourists, hinting that she knew things from their stay."

"Then she's probably told everything she knows to the authorities."

"Maybe. But don't forget, Evelyn interprets everything quite literally. If they didn't ask the right questions in the proper way, they weren't likely to get a helpful answer. Perhaps you'd be better at drawing out some hidden clues."

"I'll give anything a try." I had to think the FBI were trained at getting information from even the most difficult sources, but also didn't want to sound dismissive to the person who was offering to help me save my home.

I watched Lu's BMW disappear round the curve before walking to the carriage house to check on the progress. I'd have to press Steve to finish by the end of the month if I was to have a tenant in October, and Lu was confident I would. I'd also have enough money to pay his bill and make two mortgage payments. It seemed solitude was going for a rather high price these days.

I was pleased to see all that remained to be installed were the finishing touches like window treatments, moldings, and hardware. As I walked toward the stairs, I glanced down into the trash receptacle, empty except for a knotted piece of rope at the bottom. I reached in to retrieve it, thinking it might have been discarded by Vince and could offer another link to my theory of a code. I noticed a corner of ruled notebook paper with familiar handwriting stuck fast to the bottom. It appeared to be a letter; I tried to make sense of Ashley's scribbled words, but could only see the beginning of three lines. *Sorry we . . . a rush . . . trust.* What was she apologizing for, and why were they in a rush? But most importantly, to whom had she written this message? Had she torn up the letter after thinking better of sending it? Not wanting to risk compromising the legibility by trying to pull it free, I ran to the big house and grabbed my digital camera. Out of breath by the time I climbed the stairs to the loft, I was thrilled by the possibility of a new clue.

After downloading the photos, I sat before my laptop, then took a deep breath and reached for the phone.

# 18

A day later

I was feeling embarrassed about the voicemail I'd left for Daniel, reporting on the scrap of paper I'd found with Ashley's handwriting, sure I sounded like a thirty-something Nancy Drew wannabe. Worse yet, he hadn't returned my call.

To shake off the nervous energy, I took Lu's suggestion and ventured to town for a lunch date with George and Evelyn. I parked toward the end of Harbor Drive so I could admire the beautiful waterfront homes on my walk to the large wharf area at the heart of Whale Rock. I strolled to the end of the pier and filled my lungs with the intoxicating salt air and waved off one of the Mitchell Whale Watcher Tour boats as it left the harbor. I hoped never to have to go begging a job from Johnny Hotchkiss again.

I turned my gaze to the quaint village. Whale Rock was a quintessential New England harbor town. Restaurants, mom-and-pop merchants, boutiques, and antique shops were interspersed between private homes, churches, and municipal buildings on the three-tiered streets of the town. A few of the clapboards could use a fresh coat of paint, and here and there shingles were missing, but to my mind it was perfect.

Hilliard House was a focal point, its tidal basin blue color standing out amid the many traditional white clapboards. The three-story Victorian offered stunning harbor views with a fabulous turret room.

I checked the time on the large seaman's clock at the center of Harbor Drive. With a few minutes to kill, I popped into the post office.

"Well, if it isn't Miss Cassandra!" I was greeted warmly by my favorite postal employee. Tommy Turner reminded me of the Scarecrow in the *Wizard of Oz*. His cheerful outlook and animated smile, complete with dimples, coupled with a quick wit made him hopelessly appealing.

I was relieved Tommy was on duty. He'd be more helpful than Postmistress Sylvia Trask, who was steadfast in her duty to uphold the privacy rights of every American citizen.

"Since you've gone part-time, I'm not always lucky to see you."

"A stepping-stone to a condo in Boca. I'm easing into retirement." He made a gliding gesture with his hands.

"Don't break my heart. What will I do without you?"

"Frigid winds, snow drifts, wicked cold." He pantomimed a scale. "Warmth, sunshine, and unlimited golf days. You'll manage." He winked at me. "Whatcha got for me today?"

I laid a photo of Vince and Ashley on the counter.

His forehead crinkled, and he kept his gaze on the photo. "Your young couple?"

"Yep."

"Since you're showing me this, I assume they're still missing." He gazed at me over the top of his cheaters.

I nodded. "But I'm still hopeful. And you might be able to help if you have a good memory."

He tapped his index finger to his balding head. "My best feature."

"I have reason to believe one of them sent a letter not too long ago, and it would be helpful to know where it was headed."

Tommy's expression dashed my hopes. "If either of them came in here, I'm sorry to say it wasn't while I was working. I only recognized them from the news. Sylvia would have waited on them. The good news, hard as it is to believe, is she's got an even better memory than I do."

"But will she help?" I was doubtful.

"I'll work on her. She'll be in tomorrow."

"You're a peach, Tommy. Call me if you learn anything?"
"You betcha."

~

*Eighty years ago*
*A month before the fire at Battersea Bluffs*

Celeste ran to the porch when she heard the horn of the Plymouth. It was Samuel Lawson, Whale Rock postal service.

"Good afternoon, Samuel." What couldn't wait for Percy to pick up on his way home? A stop at the post office first, and then a quick one at the tavern. That was his ritual.

"Afternoon, Mrs. Mitchell." He waved an envelope. "Special delivery for you."

She grasped the railing for support. *Bad news about Ambrose?*

"All the way from London, England."

Her hand went automatically to her heart. *Thank goodness.* Ambrose was safe. But who could have sent it? Her parents had died years ago, and Percy's family was in Wales now. Special delivery was too dear for her old friend Mattie O'Connell, and besides, she'd just had a letter from her last week.

Samuel handed her the letter with all the special stamps.

"Thank you for making the trip out here."

"Don't mind at all, Mrs. Mitchell. One of the prettiest spots on Cape Cod, if you ask me." His gaze turned out toward the cliffs. "It's a wild one out there today."

Celeste pulled her sweater tighter. "It is at that. Since you've gone to the trouble, can I tempt you to stay for a cuppa and some freshly baked oat cakes?"

"I could smell them as I rounded the bend. It pains me that I can't stay. Deadlines, you know. But you wouldn't have to twist my arm to take one with me for the trip back to town."

Celeste had a reputation for her delicious baking. Her cakes and buns and cookies were always first to be snatched up at church bazaars and holiday bake sales.

She sent Samuel off with a few cookies, leaving her alone to confront the mysterious letter. She sat at her desk and opened the envelope with shaking hands. Her breath caught when she read the signature: Robert Toomey.

The first paragraph was enough to distress her. Robert Toomey was coming to America.

She hadn't a chance to read further when there came a timid knock on the front door.

"Why, it's Fiona Patrick." Celeste tried to be gracious, though her mind was preoccupied with reading the unfinished missive. She gazed beyond the young girl to see if someone had driven her.

"I walked." Fiona said.

"Well goodness, come in child. And what brings you all the way out here on such a blustery day?"

The girl crumpled into a tearful mess. "I'm in awful trouble, Mrs. Mitchell."

Celeste ushered Fiona back into her library, where she quickly folded up the letter and placed it in the tin box Ambrose had given her last Christmas. It would have to wait until this child's problems were heard.

When Fiona finished the telling of her predicament, Celeste was overcome by emotions that ranged the spectrum from sheer joy to bone-chilling fear. But she maintained her composure for the sake of the frightened young woman, who sat knotting her handkerchief with worry.

She clasped her own hand over those young, twitching fingers. "Never you worry, Fiona. You have two families now."

"Ma and Pop might be so mad that they'd ship me off to live with an old maiden aunt somewhere in the hills of Kentucky."

Celeste forced back a smile, doubting the Patrick family had any relations west of the Massachusetts border.

"They'll do no such thing." Though she remembered her own parents' plans to dispose of her along with her sullied reputation to the nearest convent. "But if they threaten to do so, you may come live with us."

"Mr. Mitchell won't think me"—she lowered her eyes—"a tart?"

"Mr. Mitchell will be thrilled when I tell him. But I won't just yet."

Celeste made a pot of tea, and the two women, confident they would one day be mother and daughter-in-law, chatted about baby cribs and nappies and the like until Fiona checked the captain's wheel clock and stood hastily, nearly stumbling over her chair.

"I must be getting back. I was to help with the afternoon delivery, and look—it's getting on two o'clock."

"That clock needs to go to the shop. It's running a quarter hour fast."

"Still, I'll be late."

"Can you ride a bicycle?" When Fiona nodded, Celeste trotted her out to the barn. "This is Ambrose's old bike. It's rusty, but the tires are good."

She watched as the pretty young woman pedaled away, turning once to offer a wave of gratitude.

Celeste knew what she had to do now. She would face the words of Robert Toomey, and then she would try to make peace with the man. It might be the only way to put an end to that dreadful curse, and she had a grandchild to think of now. It was up to her to make it right for them. Percy would never be able to see the logic, for his pride and anger stood like fierce sentries against reason. She would write her reply today and get it in the post tomorrow. She would welcome Robert Toomey to America, to Whale Rock, to her home.

~

Present day

"Hello?" I called out in the cozy but unusually empty lobby of Hilliard House.

"Oh, Cassie, love." Evelyn bustled in from the back, a dusting of flour on her shirt, but that didn't deter her from taking me into an affectionate hug. She released me and pushed me gently away for inspection. "How are you holding up?"

"I'm okay, Evvie."

Evelyn pursed her lips and gave a slight unconvinced shake of her head. "You're too thin."

I couldn't argue and followed her toward the large dining alcove.

"I've got a pot of chili and a batch of corn muffins in the oven. Everything should be ready by the time we brew up a fresh pot of coffee. Or would you prefer something else?"

"Coffee's good." I needed something to take the chill off after my walk.

Sitting at one of the tables were the affable George Hilliard and Lizzie Davis, another of Zoe's high school cronies. Lizzie had been a fixture at the inn's front desk for as long as I could remember. She and George were sharing an amusing report from the *Whale Rock Weekly*, which could claim no higher level of journalism than a newsletter.

"Cassie's here," Evelyn sang out excitedly.

"Baby Cass!" George stood and opened his arms wide. As a huge fan of the Mamas and Papas, he'd christened me with the nickname when the gang used to babysit for me.

Evelyn started singing "Dream a Little Dream of Me" in her lovely soprano tone. George and Lizzie joined in, a flat tenor and pitchy alto.

"Good old times." George smiled broadly and clasped his hands. "If only Zoe were here."

Lizzie and Evelyn glanced furtively at each other. Did they know what was behind Zoe's aversion to Whale Rock? I'd never felt comfortable broaching the subject with my sister's friends, but maybe I should.

"Why've you been such a stranger?" the oblivious George gently scolded.

"It's been . . . um . . ." I looked down at the table, not trusting my emotions. There were a number of people I'd avoided since Ethan left, especially after learning I'd been a favorite topic of Whale Rock gossip. But the warm welcome these kind old friends were extending made me regret cutting off what could have been a comforting support system during the challenging times.

"Honey, you know Cassie avoids town like the plague, in season." I blessed Evelyn for coming to my rescue as she whisked her husband through the archway into the kitchen. "Help me with the muffins?"

Lizzie pulled out the antique rush-seat dining chair beside her own. "Take a load off, kid."

"I'm not such a kid anymore." I gestured toward the beginnings of crow's feet.

"To us you'll always seem that way." She smiled affectionately. "So how are you managing?" It was a broad-reaching question. She could have been referring to any or all of my current troubles: my failed marriage, my financial woes, or the disappearance of Ashley and Vince.

"As well as can be expected." I offered an equally general answer and then decided to give Lizzie a shot. "Can I ask you something about Zoe?"

She raised her eyebrows.

"How often do you talk with her?"

"It's been awhile. Ev and Lu check in on her pretty regularly. Why?"

I decided to be direct. "Do you know why she won't come home?"

Lizzie shifted uncomfortably in her seat. "What's this about, Cass?"

"She hasn't come back home in years."

"I doubt she thinks of Whale Rock as home." Not exactly an enlightening response.

"Something must have happened to make her hate it here."

"Hate's a strong word." She finger-doodled on the tablecloth.

"But accurate, wouldn't you say?"

But Lizzie did not yield, nor would she look at me.

"Please tell me."

"Tell you what?" Evelyn asked, setting a tray with steaming bowls of chili on the table.

Lizzie finally met my eyes, sending the clear message not to ask any more questions. Whether or not it was for Evelyn's benefit, I couldn't be certain.

"Anything you can remember that might offer a clue about the Jacobsons?" I switched subjects quickly.

Evelyn plopped herself down at the table and rested her head in her hands. "I've been racking my mind, trying to think of what I might have missed."

George held out a basket of corn muffins. I selected one and began removing the paper baking cup.

"Brooks mentioned a hasty checkout?" I'd put it out of my head when he first told me, but maybe there was a clue hiding in the details.

"Something had them spooked," George offered after swallowing his first spoonful of chili. "One day they were talking about extending their rental, and the next day they checked out despite a week remaining on their reservation."

"I should have charged them for not giving notice," Evelyn added, "but we guessed they were having money problems, and didn't have the heart."

"What made you think they had money troubles?" I dipped my spoon into the thick and fragrant chili.

"It was something the girl said about not having planned very well."

I was thinking the comment could have had many different meanings, but said nothing.

"I'll go get the registration book," said Lizzie. "See if there's anything in there." She returned a moment later with the old-fashioned ledger they used for checking in guests.

I laid my hands flat on either side of the book, surveying the dates and names. Brooks had mentioned earlier that they'd checked out a couple days before showing up at The Bluffs. I hadn't given it much thought then, but now I was wondering, where had they stayed in those days between?

"Where's Fiona's ring?" Evelyn asked.

I pulled my hand back. "It's become loose, so I'm not wearing it."

She accepted the lie and motioned for me to eat up. "You've lost too much weight."

"Did they give any hint as to where they were headed?"

George and Evelyn shared a look.

"I get that you didn't trust them, but as far as I'm concerned, they were my friends. They saved me."

That pretty much hushed them until George broke through the uneasy silence.

"I offered them a ride, what with the two bikes and the dog and no car. But they declined."

I tried to imagine the scene of them donning their filled backpacks and walking the bikes with Whistler on his lead.

"I got the impression they didn't know where they were going."

I narrowed my eyes, and he held up his hands. "Just an impression."

"No . . . I was just thinking. What direction did they head?"

"The last I saw them they were down at the harbor," he answered, which essentially told me nothing.

"Did Brooks question all of you?"

"He did." Lizzie answered. "So did the FBI."

"That Agent Benjamin." Evelyn began to fan herself. "He's quite the looker."

Lizzie rolled her eyes at Ev, but I suspected she was trying to lighten the mood.

"Is he? I hadn't noticed." That should set some chins into motion. "Did Agent Benjamin or Brooks make a copy of your check-in log?"

"The FBI agent did." George frowned. "I thought Chuckles was off the case."

"It's true, the FBI have taken over. Can I get a photocopy of the days leading up to their departure?" Maybe someone else who was staying here had spoken to them, and I could make a few calls to people who were guests at the same time.

"Sure." Lizzie left us briefly, then returned with the copy. "I had to black out the contact information."

*So much for that plan.* I folded up the copy and tucked it into my pocket.

"So has the FBI made any progress?"

"They don't have a lot to go on. I thought I'd check with you to see if any details might have come to mind since you spoke with anyone officially. For instance, can you remember anything Vince or Ashley might have told you about their personal lives that didn't come up when you were questioned?"

"There wasn't much opportunity," Lizzie said, to which Evelyn nodded agreement.

"Did they keep to themselves?" I continued to play with my chili.

"They were with us in May when we were busy getting ready for the summer season," George explained. "Besides, we usually don't get to spend as much time with people who stay in the cottage, because they have their own kitchen."

"But they seemed like a nice couple, friendly and curious about Whale Rock," Evelyn said.

"And everyone loved the dog," added George.

"I didn't love that dog," a croaky voice came from the kitchen, and a woman I didn't recognize shuffled through the archway in Uggs, an incongruous accessory to the shiny blue polyester two-piece outfit that might have been plucked from a museum of fast-food workers' uniforms.

"Cassie, this is Cindy." George made the introduction. "She started working for us at the beginning of the season."

She nodded a hello in my direction.

"Nice to meet you, Cindy." I smiled. "Whistler lives with me now. Did he misbehave?"

"Aw, he weren't a bad dog. He was just a *German shedder*." She offered a goofy smile at the pun. "Took me near a day to vacuum up all that durn hair for the next guests."

"Did you ever talk with Ashley and Vince?"

"Sure. Lotsa times. After they checked out, I even sometimes ran into them at Wizards." Cindy cocked her head to inspect me more closely. Was she there the night they dragged me to that dive? If she'd witnessed my foolish behavior, I could only hope she'd been as drunk as I was.

"Do you remember them saying anything about where they lived before coming here?"

The housekeeper scrunched up her face, as if thinking was a painful business, then shook her head. "Nah."

"Well, if anything comes to mind, please let one of us know." Lizzie was clearly dismissing the housekeeper.

Cindy made to leave, then stopped and waved her finger. "What about that T-shirt they left behind?"

"Something was left in their room?" Evelyn's tone was reproachful. "Why didn't you turn it in?"

Cindy fidgeted, realizing her slip. But I didn't want to lose the thread of a clue to a scolding.

"No worries. It was just a T-shirt." I sent a reassuring smile.

"That's right. And it weren't new or nothin' nice. It was behind the garbage can in their room, like they meant to toss it," Cindy added defiantly and stepped closer to the table. "I'd thought to use it as a rag."

Thought to, but my guess was it ended up in her own wardrobe instead.

"Do you still have it?" Proverbial fingers crossed.

She shook her head. "I gave it to the cops."

"That's odd," George puzzled. "Brooks never mentioned anything about it."

"It weren't Chief Kincaid. The other'n took it."

"Agent Benjamin?" I asked.

Cindy's expression clouded.

"The man who came to talk to us after the chief was here," Lizzie offered helpfully. "He wore a navy windbreaker."

The housekeeper's face lit up. "He's the one who took it."

A swift queasiness descended upon me to learn Daniel had been withholding information.

"What did the T-shirt look like?"

"It was gray. Had some writing on the front." Again the painfully scrunched face as she pointed to the upper left side of her chest. "And the back had this great big head of a red bird with an angry look."

My thoughts went straight to a phoenix.

"Do you remember the words on the front?"

"I can't be sure. Some sorta Jewish school, maybe?" An exaggerated lift to her shoulders followed by a muttered, "Sorry."

"That's okay." I reached over and touched her arm. "You've been very helpful."

And I was thrilled for a new clue to pursue.

She shuffled an Ugg. "They were always nice to me."

"If you think of anything else—"

"—or find anything," Evelyn interrupted with a stern warning.

"—please be sure to tell one of us," I finished more kindly.

Cindy gave me a quick smile, nodded contritely at her employer, and trudged out.

George leaned in and told me in a hushed tone, "We're not sure what Cindy's story is. Maybe she smoked a little too much weed in her youth, or it could be she's just naturally a little off."

"But she's a super cleaner," Lizzie added. "And we can always count on her to show up."

"I can't be happy about her keeping that shirt, though." Evelyn tossed down her napkin. "Now we'll have to keep an extra eye on her."

"To be fair, she did come clean." I tried to mitigate Evelyn's distrust. "And she did the right thing by turning the shirt over to the authorities."

But Evelyn's lemon-sucking expression proved she remained unconvinced.

"It was just a ratty old T-shirt," Lizzie said, and then as an afterthought, "Who knows? Maybe they did leave it behind on purpose."

\* \* \*

On the drive home, Lizzie's last comment was a persistent nudging. An uneasy feeling came over me to think Ashley and Vince had ditched the shirt intentionally. Unlike most twenty-somethings, I couldn't recall either of them wearing anything of a personal nature—nothing that advertised schools, favorite sports teams, bars, etcetera—nothing that offered a glimpse into their pasts. Theirs was a generic wardrobe: jeans, khaki shorts, plain T-shirts or hoodies.

I noticed a missed call and message from Daniel.

"Cassie, it's Daniel. We're still coming up blank on the rope. No message or code there. And my guy who's examining the photo is out sick today. I presume he took the file home by mistake, because we can't locate it." His voice had been all business to this point, but then, "If he's not in tomorrow, I promise to go pick up the file myself. And I would love to see you this week."

It suddenly struck me as odd for Daniel to risk a personal relationship with someone so closely connected to the victims of a case he was working on. Maybe with retirement nearing he felt he had little to lose. Otherwise, he probably shouldn't be sleeping with me. Unless . . . ? No. I could not go there. If I learned Daniel was somehow using me in this case, I'd never hold it together. A creepy image of myself sporting Raggedy Ann togs flickered into my mind. Perhaps I did need to grow a spine. I'd be more selective in what I chose to share with him in the future.

As I passed through the library, my laptop came whirring to life.

"What the devil?" I'd shut it down before leaving this morning. The screen displayed an image of Ashley and Vince taken the day we visited the Mitchell family cemetery. Their heads nearly touched over one of the gravestones. I was curious to see which one and zoomed in on the photo and saw it was Robert Toomey's: "Thief of life, with burning strife, actions caused for mourning rife."

"Percy, I do not need any of your technical pranks today." And not giving much more thought to the photo, I shut down the laptop and closed the lid.

My head was crowded with questions, so I called Brooks to try to answer one of them.

"I forgot to ask if you ever learned anything about that receipt the FBI took from the guest room."

Daniel had said the FBI hadn't turned up anything concrete, but I was hoping Brooks and his team might have had better luck.

"Oh yeah. You had the name wrong." I could hear him flipping through papers. "It was from Sinclair House, a pawnshop in Orleans."

*A pawnshop?* "Did you follow up?"

"I was about to, but then *your* Agent Benjamin took control."

"He's not *my* agent." Annoying as he was, it wouldn't be productive to pick a fight. "Can you do a little digging?"

I held my breath until he said, "The owner's helped me on some other cases. I'll see what I can find out from him."

"Bless you."

When Brooks called back an hour later, I regretted having asked him to get involved.

"They pawned a ring."

My heart sank as I rubbed the empty space on my right ring finger. Preparing myself for more bad news, I closed my eyes and asked, "What kind?"

"The guy doesn't know. He was on vacation when they brought it in and never got a look at the item."

"It's not still at the shop?"

"Nope. And the gal who was working for him has gone back to school."

"Is there any way we can get a description of the ring?"

"What's going on?"

I must have sounded panicked, which I was. "Nothing. Just thinking it might provide a clue."

"It might have, if they hadn't reclaimed it."

"Ashley and Vince?"

"According to the owner's records, the same people who pawned the item came back in for it." He let that sink in a minute before adding, "The day before the Jacobsons disappeared."

"How much did they get when they pawned it?"

"Two hundred dollars."

*It was worth much more than that.* The words almost slipped out before I caught myself.

"People are never given the real value for their items and then they have to pay more to get them back. It's basically a loan with high interest."

*If they'd pawned Fiona's emerald ring and then bought it back, where was it now?*

"You still there?"

"Just thinking."

"Well here's something else to chew on. It seems Agent Benjamin went straight to Sinclair House after he first discovered the receipt."

"He never mentioned it to you?"

"No. And that was before I'd been asked to step down from the case." He paused a moment. "I don't know what his game is, Cass."

"You're assuming he has a game." I found myself suddenly defensive.

"Trust me, he's playing at something, and he's keeping his cards close to the vest."

After we hung up I contemplated Brooks's mistrust of Daniel. Was it sour grapes for having lost control of the investigation? Or were they legitimate misgivings?

# 19

Three weeks following the disappearance

was putting the last touches on the canvases Lu had selected for the exhibit when her lilting "Yoo-hoo!" filled the air. In her red mega pumps and zebra wrap dress, she looked as out of place in the barn as a ballerina in the midst of an ice hockey game, but effortlessly breezed through an agility course of sawhorses and easels. She was all grace gliding across the uneven planks of the rustic wood floor.

"Hi, hon." She sent an air kiss, smart enough to avoid a hug and certain smudges of paint on her expensive outfit. "Are we almost finished?"

"Soon." A perfectionist I was not, but I did have my standards.

"It's getting down to crunch time, baby."

"I know." I set down my brush and wiped my hands on a rag. "When's the deadline for these last paintings?"

"I'll need a couple days to figure out the design of the exhibit once we have the final list. Add in the framing time. End of the week?"

"Then I guess you'll have them by Friday." What choice did I have? "But I'm done for today. Join me for a glass of wine?"

She checked her watch. "A quick one."

Back at the house, Whistler slipped out for a run as we entered through the front door. I headed to the kitchen, but Lu hadn't followed. Retracing my steps to the entrance hall, I found her staring at the recently hung portraits of my great-grandparents.

"Quite the resemblance to Zoe, isn't it?" I shared with her how Ashley and Vince had found and rescued the paintings and installed them back to their rightful places.

"Amazing story," she said, now tagging along to the porch as I carried a chilled bottle of Fume Blanc and two glasses.

*Not nearly as amazing as my mother's paintings of Percy and Celeste.* I'd keep that disquieting tale to myself, as well as the existence of my own paintings that so eerily mirrored my mother's.

Lu settled into a wicker rocker with comfy, fluffy pillows and touched her glass to mine.

"To your first show. Excited?"

"More like terrified." I took a large gulp before asking the question I'd put off long enough. "Has Zoe mentioned her plans to you?"

"Plans?" Lu took a ladylike sip and pretended not to follow.

"Does she intend to come east for the exhibit?" I barely succeeded in keeping the irritation from my voice.

The chair began to rock in rhythm to her nervously bouncing leg. "Look, Cassie—"

"You don't need to say another word." I held up a halting hand. "I can tell you already know she's not coming. But I'd have appreciated it if she'd at least given me the courtesy of telling me herself. When was she going to let me know? The day of?"

"I know how disappointed you must be, but give her a break."

"Of course I'm disappointed." I didn't want to hear a defense of my sister's selfishness. "She's my only remaining living relative and she can't be bothered to make one trip home?"

Whistler returned from his romp and flopped down at my feet.

"Especially in light of everything else happening in my life." I shook my head. "A little sisterly support would be nice."

"Zoe has always been supportive of you."

"I'm talking about a physical presence, not just money or a voice on the phone."

Lu released a defeated sigh. "There's so much you don't know about why Zoe left."

"I don't know *anything* about why she left *or* why she refuses to come back." I blurted this out before recalling Zoe's confession about the pervasive smell of burning flesh in The Bluffs.

Lu tilted her head and pursed her rosy, glossed lips. "Have you ever asked her?"

I stalled by swallowing the remaining wine from my glass. There were many reasons for not betraying Zoe's admission of a haunting odor, not the least of which was having to explain about the spirits who lingered in my home.

"I have asked her on countless occasions to come home since Mama and Papa died. For Fiona's memorial service, my wedding—"

"Your wedding? Zoe told us all you and Ethan eloped."

"Not exactly. We married here on The Bluffs. Judge Jordan presided over the vows, and Brit was the only other witness. We popped the cork, made a quick toast, and the festivities were concluded." I poured myself a second glass of wine. "I didn't want much. A small, informal affair. I asked Zoe to come—pleaded actually." I took a gulp of wine, knowing I should stop, and yet still forged ahead with my version of the injustice.

"I'd hoped she would help me plan the ceremony and reception, go dress shopping with me. But she said the timing was difficult, the firm was making all kinds of demands on Oliver, and she couldn't possibly get away just then. I'd offered to postpone it to a more convenient date to make it easier for her, but she wouldn't hear it. *'We'll celebrate later. Come to the West Coast for your honeymoon. We'll treat.'* And that was the end of the discussion."

"Perhaps she was punishing you for turning down that opportunity to study in France."

*An opportunity to break up Ethan and me.* Zoe and Oliver had offered to pay for a year of study at a renowned art school in the heart of Paris. It was a dream course that any artist in their right mind would have jumped at. Not to mention they were planning to rent me a pied-à-terre in the 7th arrondisement. In retrospect, perhaps it would have been best for me to go. But I just couldn't bring myself to leave The Bluffs.

"She was always trying to control my life. Instead of being a part of it."

"Well, that certainly backfired, didn't it? Did you ever take that honeymoon trip?"

I shook my head. "I grew tired of having to be the one to travel in order to see my sister. It never seemed authentic, catching up at some sterile resort or, when I did stay at Zoe and Oliver's, always being forced to attend boring cocktail parties with the phony executive wives club. Anything not to have to spend time getting to know me."

"Zoe's just always had this"—Lu shook her head—"confused interpretation of your relationship. You know? Part sister, part mother."

"Tell me about it," I groaned.

Lu set her glass down and patted my hand. "Trust me. She loves you more than anything."

I took hold of her hand and leaned forward. "Then please tell me. Why won't she come?"

"Your sister's issues are complex." She picked up her glass but didn't drink, her crossed leg bobbing again. "The ending to Brooks and Zoe's love story was . . . unfortunate."

"But she was the one to break it off."

"She told you that?"

I had to stop and think about it. "Not exactly. But she came back from that spring break trip to Mexico mooning over the *fascinating and handsome* Oliver Young. I assumed he was why she ended her relationship with Brooks."

"You know what they say about assumptions." She took a sip from her glass.

"What are you telling me? That Brooks dumped Zoe? That's crazy. He adored her."

"Still does as far as I can tell." Lu's pretty mouth turned downward. "If you want to know more, you will have to persuade your sister to tell you."

"Did you know they still talk?" I persisted in my probing.

"I'm not surprised. But I can't say anything more on the subject of your sister's past or why she left, why she can't come back."

"Can't or won't?"

"Either way it's the same result, isn't it?" Lu set her glass down and began to rub her temples. "I've got to run. I'm meeting with the caterer for your exhibit."

My breath caught at the possibility of Billy Hughes' presence in my life again.

Lu inspected me closely, then offered a shrewd little smile. "Didn't I tell you? I'm going with Feast. Have you heard of them?"

I shook my head, too relieved to speak.

"It's a wonderful little shop that just opened in Whale Rock. I like to patronize new businesses when I can. Besides, it's so much more convenient than La Table. Don't you agree?" She winked and grabbed her purse. "Ta' now."

Were there no secrets in Whale Rock? I reconsidered the question and laughed. There were secrets aplenty in this small burg. Unearthing mysteries hadn't been the problem; solving them had.

Less than ten minutes after Lu departed, a familiar gray Avalon rounded the curve of the drive. Whistler must have recognized the vehicle, for he stopped barking as soon as it came into view, wagging eagerly and waiting for the driver to emerge. A sense of distrust had been edging its way into my heart, but as Daniel sauntered toward the porch, my body's response was entirely contradictory and desirous.

"So what brings you all the way out here this time of the day, Mr. Benjamin?"

"Should I be worried?" he asked.

"I don't know, should you?"

"I'm not sure I like the formality of your greeting, *Ms. Mitchell.*" He directed his gaze to the half-empty bottle of wine and two glasses. "I see you've had company."

"That's right." I offered nothing further, letting him wonder who might have been drinking out of that second glass and hoping he couldn't see the telltale trace of Lu's lipstick. "I presume you've driven all the way out here because you have something important to tell me?"

He blew out a lungful of air and eased himself into the rocker Lu had occupied just moments earlier.

"You've found them." My eyes started burning from the tears I would not let flow.

"No, Cassie." He reached for my hand. "They're still missing."

Part of me was relieved because it meant there was still a chance they were alive. But Daniel was not projecting a good-news persona.

"Something's not right, though."

He hesitated, releasing my hand and reaching down to pat Whistler's head, obviously not looking forward to whatever it was he'd come here to tell me.

"Daniel?"

"The agency has lowered the priority for the case."

"How can they? It's only been—what?—three weeks since they disappeared?"

"We'll still be working on it. Every lead will be followed, but the problem is a lack of clues to pursue."

"What about the photo? The rope?" I just couldn't believe they were giving up.

"Neither has turned up anything of intrinsic or forensic value."

"Then I want them returned to me." I was hurt and angry and responded childishly.

"You can't have them back." His voice had a condescending edge. "They're part of the evidence we're required to keep on file. As I said, people will still be working on it."

"People? What people?"

He didn't respond.

"So *you're* abandoning them too?" I shook my head in disbelief.

"I've been reassigned to a higher level case. But I'll still consult when any new leads turn up."

"What a comfort." I was spoiling for a fight, and although Daniel appeared wounded, he didn't rise to the bait. I wanted to confront him about what Brooks had learned from the pawnshop but knew it would cause trouble.

We sat in prickly silence until I recalled my conversation with Cindy.

"What about the T-shirt?" I watched him closely to gauge his reaction.

He gave me a quizzical look.

"The one the cleaning lady at Hilliard House gave to you. I'm not sure why you didn't tell me about it before, but I'm now aware of its existence."

"Cindy?" He shook his head dismissively. "She wasn't exactly a reliable witness. We interviewed her on three separate occasions, and her answers were all over the place. No consistency equals no credibility. But we did run the T-shirt through rigorous testing. Only the housekeeper's DNA was discovered. So our conclusion was that if it had once belonged to the missing persons, it had likely been washed."

"Do you remember the image on the T-shirt?" I asked.

He forced out his lower lip. "It was a bird, I think, but I don't have a clear memory. I submitted it immediately for forensic testing, and I haven't seen it since."

At least he was telling the truth about the bird. Or was he merely giving me enough to keep me believing in him?

"What about the wording?" I asked. "Cindy said there was something written on the T-shirt."

"Did she remember what it was?"

"No." Suspecting he was holding back, I mentioned nothing about the Jewish school.

He pulled his phone from his jacket pocket and punched in a number. "Could you sign out the evidence box for the Jacobson case and pull the article of clothing? It's a T-shirt." He paused to listen. "That's right. Take a photo of any images or print and email a copy to me as soon as you can."

He ended the call and said to me, "I promise you will have the answer to your question today."

"Just so you know, *I* am not giving up on finding them."

Daniel stood and slowly stepped off the porch. "We haven't given up either, but we require solid leads. We're the FBI, not Harry Houdini."

"My intention is only to find my friends, not to bruise any egos."

"No egos here." Daniel's guard came down, with a rare glimpse of anger. "We are all working toward the same good end in this matter."

"I hope so." I lifted my chin defiantly.

He rested both hands atop the porch railing. "Cassie, let's not allow this to interfere with the terrific thing we have going between us."

His pleading eyes were pulling me under, and I had to force myself to look away.

"The trouble with *us* is, there is only one me, but there are two Daniel Benjamins, and right now it's kind of hard to keep you separate."

He gave a sad but brusque nod and turned on his heel.

At six thirty I still hadn't heard from him or received a photo of the shirt in question. Tired of waiting, I made the call.

"I'm in a meeting." Daniel's voice was hushed. "A little problem has developed on this end."

"What kind of problem?" *And how little?*

I heard muffled voices, then the sound of a door closing. "I only have a minute."

"Okay. I'm listening."

The first ten seconds of that minute was dead air. At last he told me, "The evidence box for the case has been misplaced."

This was followed by more silence. *Misplaced? How could that happen?* It was the FBI, for pity's sake.

"Cassie? Are you still there?"

"Yes." It was barely a whisper.

"It will turn up. I promise."

I'd had enough of Daniel Benjamin's empty promises and no longer felt confident in his ability or his interest in helping me find Vince and Ashley.

"Cassie, did you hear me?"

"I'm done," I said. *We're done.*

"You've got to listen."

"No, Daniel, I don't." I disconnected the call, and within seconds the phone was ringing again.

My anger was suffocating. Compounding the problem was an overwhelming sweet aroma of burning sugar, which I tried desperately to ignore. But there was no avoiding the confusing signal from Percy and Celeste save to bolt from the house. The Miata was my escape accomplice, and I found myself nearly to P-town when Wizards popped into my head. I hadn't spoken with Ashley and Vince's friend Teddy since the night they disappeared. I found the nearest opening in the median and made a U-turn. Maybe the young bartender would remember the T-shirt or some other identifying items the couple may have worn or carried with them. Perhaps Vince and Ashley had dropped some type of hint about where they were from or where they were headed for Ashley's job. It was certainly worth a try.

\* \* \*

It took a moment for my eyes to adjust to the poorly lit tavern. Soon I recognized the genial Teddy working his magic behind the bar. In no mood to fake conversation with strangers, I climbed up onto a barstool at the far corner away from the crowd.

"Cassie, right?" Teddy asked, his disarming smile the only bright spot in the dim bar.

"Good memory." I returned the smile.

"What can I get you?"

"Diet coke with a lime?" Having already downed two glasses of wine, I thought it prudent to cut myself off.

"You got it." As he filled the glass from the dispenser, he asked, "Has there been any news about Ash and Vince?"

"Sadly, no. But I was hoping to ask you a few questions."

His gaze took in the busy bar scene. Probably an inopportune time for an interrogation.

"Just a minute," he said and walked to one of the booths bordering the room. He leaned in and whispered into the ear of an older woman, who nodded and then replaced him behind the bar.

Teddy motioned for me to follow him into a windowless dark-paneled office rife with the stifling stink of tobacco. In an automatic reaction, my hand shot up to cover my nose and mouth.

"Sorry. The owner's a chain smoker, and her office is the only private place to talk." He spritzed the room with air freshener, then offered me a seat while turning another chair backwards and straddling it. "So what did you want to know?"

"I'm not really happy with how the FBI is handling the case. In fact, they seem to be losing interest in finding Ashley and Vince." That's not all they were losing, but I refrained from sharing that depressing detail.

"Bummer." He looked genuinely distressed.

"I know. But I'm hoping maybe they mentioned something to you about where they came from or where they were going."

Teddy frowned, triggering an odd feeling of familiarity.

"Nothing's coming to mind."

"How about clothing? Someone else mentioned a T-shirt with a big red bird on it. Does that sound familiar? That would stand out well enough."

"Not a shirt." Teddy cocked his head, making me hopeful. "But there was something. Damn. What was it?"

"Something with a red bird?" I asked.

"Not sure." He shook his head, and my hope dissolved. "I'll think on it. Is there anything else I can help you with?"

"Would you mind sharing with me the type of questions Agent Benjamin asked?"

"The FBI agent?" He shrugged. "He asked when I last saw Ash and Vince, what I was doing the night they disappeared—that kind of stuff. He might've asked if I knew where they were from . . . yeah, actually he did. So did Brooks." There was that familiar frown again. "It just came to me." He snapped his fingers. "I'm not sure if it means anything, but Vince had this really cool money clip. It was the letter 'T' and made of silver. At the time, I figured it was his last name initial."

"But their last name was Jacobson."

He nodded. "I'm aware now from the newspapers, but I don't know many of my customers' first names, let alone their last, and they were strictly cash-paying customers, so it's not like I ever saw a credit card."

"Jacobson may have been an alias."

"Alias?" Teddy scratched his head. "Were they in some sort of trouble?"

"I don't know."

He pulled out his cell phone to check the time. "I'd better get back out there."

"Sure. If you think of anything at all, please give me a call." I wrote down my number and handed it to him, then returned to the barstool and finished the soda in solitude, contemplating my next steps. Teddy returned to my end of the bar to offer a refill.

"Just the tab."

He smiled. "On the house."

Remembering what Ashley said about him being too generous, I set a five-dollar bill onto the bar and hopped down from the stool. "I insist."

He picked up the money. "Thanks."

"One more question. Did you ever see Vince and Ashley outside of Wizards? I mean, did you socialize with them other than here?"

His straight-faced expression belied a disquieting hesitation. But then something on the other side of the room caught his attention, changing his bearing dramatically. The amiable young bartender momentarily morphed into a scowling, hostile being. I turned to follow his gaze but was distracted when I saw Brooks walking directly toward me.

"Hey, Ted. This one giving you trouble?" His tone jovial. He'd probably recognized the Miata and decided to look in on me. No doubt he remembered the last time he saw me here.

"Nope. Cassie's cool."

"No argument there."

"Hi, Chuckles," I said for his ears only.

Unexpectedly, he winked instead of blushing angry. "Hello, Cassandra."

"You need something?" Teddy asked in a clipped tone.

"Just thought I'd check in, have a beer before heading home for the evening. But maybe tonight's not the best time, huh? Forget the beer." He looked down at me. "Join me for a little supper at the Whale Rock Diner?"

I glanced at Teddy, who was drawing a beer from the tap for another customer but aiming a chilly glare at Brooks. I'd like to find out what that was all about, but right now I had other pressing matters on the table.

"Why don't you come out to the house instead?" I suggested.

"Oh?" Brooks's left brow lifted in a randy twitch.

"Down boy. I have something important to discuss with you, and there are too many curious ears at the diner."

"Sounds intriguing." He rubbed his chin. "All right, I'm in."

I followed Brooks through the crowded bar and, before passing through the door, turned back and gave Teddy a little wave. He nodded, and I was glad to see the scowl had been replaced by his usual cheerful grin.

"How 'bout I make a quick stop at Panda Gardens for takeout?" Brooks suggested as we walked to my car.

"Perfect. You know what I like."

"Veggie Moo Shoo. Four pancakes. Plenty of hoisin sauce."

"And extra fortune cookies for Whistler," I called out to him.

On the drive home, the cruiser not far behind me, I weighed the pros and cons of revealing everything to Brooks. Not that I thought he'd sit on the information, but first I'd have to read his reaction to the misplaced evidence and the status change of the case before divulging the additional evidence I'd uncovered.

I may have given up on Daniel, but I hadn't abandoned my mission to find out what happened to Ashley and Vince. And it certainly wouldn't hurt to have someone who knew the workings of the law on my side. Still, I wasn't convinced Brooks could seriously buy into my theories. If he did and was game for the challenge, I'd at least know I was dealing with someone trustworthy, which would be a refreshing change.

\* \* \*

Never having mastered the art of chopsticks, I used my fork to stab a chunk of sesame chicken from Brooks's plate. "You weren't going to eat that, were you?"

"I guess not." He knocked back the last of his Tsingtao. "So what was it you wanted to tell me that you couldn't risk having anyone else overhear?"

"I doubt anyone would care about the subject matter. I just prefer not to toss the gossip mongers any bait."

A look of astonishment contorted his features. "This from the woman who has tossed out some juicy lures of her own recently?"

"I haven't a clue what you're talking about."

"Then you, my friend, live in a fantasy world. But go ahead and pretend that your *rendezvous* with the mysterious Agent Benjamin aren't stirring up a buzz around The Rock."

I felt my whole being grow warm with indignation. I spoke deliberately in an attempt to keep the irritation from my tone. "They. Were. Business. Dinners."

"If. You. Say. So." He parroted and reached for a fortune cookie. "Here you go, Whistler. Let's see what your fortune says. *Anger begins with folly and ends with regret.* Ooh. I think this cookie was meant for someone else."

Fortunately, Brooks had sensed the boundary he was nudging and changed the subject. "Would I be correct in assuming this little meeting has something to do with your missing tenants?"

"The FBI is not giving their due diligence to the case."

"Specifically?"

I explained about the priority status change and the missing evidence.

His eyes narrowed.

"And what would all this have to do with me?"

I fiddled with the last fortune cookie wrapper, not having the courage to meet his skeptical gaze. "I thought you might have a local interest in reopening the investigation. You know, the small-town boys showing up the big-city guys."

"I'm not sure I can help you there."

It wasn't a definite no, so I remained quiet while he continued to chew on my suggestion.

He leaned back in his chair. "It was made very clear to me who was in charge and that my involvement was no longer needed or wanted. Besides, I was never made privy to the aspects which placed the case under federal jurisdiction."

"A missing person's case wouldn't normally be handled by the FBI?" I asked.

"Not unless there was a federal correlation."

"Like what?"

"It could be as simple as a family link to someone of interest to the Bureau. Quite possibly the connection didn't pan out, which would diminish interest for pursuing the case further."

"That stinks. Why didn't you tell me this earlier?"

"You were so smitten with *Mr. FBI* I didn't think you'd hear me. And if you did, you'd just get angry with me for interfering."

I was considering a scenario in which Daniel might have engineered the situation to allow his involvement in the case to continue for my benefit. I so wanted to give him the benefit of the doubt and to believe his feelings for me had that much influence. But now I felt his abandonment of the cause had pretty much doused that possibility.

"Are you *forbidden* to work on the case?" I asked.

He tilted back further and was gazing toward the ceiling.

"Even when you're off duty?" I persisted. But still there was no response, so I reminded him, "You did look into the pawnshop receipt."

Finally, he shook his head. "What did you have in mind? You want me to pick up where the Feds left off? Just like that?" He snapped his fingers. "Well that's not the way it works. They have all the files, so I'd be starting from scratch."

"Lost the files," I reminded him. "What if I told you they don't have everything?"

"Withholding evidence is a crime, Cassandra." It was always Cassandra when I was in trouble.

I shrank back from the rebuke. "I was about to tell Daniel, uh, Agent Benjamin, but he told me that there were no additional clues to follow, so the case wouldn't be worked on until they found a new lead to pursue."

I began closing up the cartons of Chinese food.

"And you didn't think it was a good idea to tell him you *had* something new for his team to pursue?"

"I was angry. And I didn't trust they were properly handling the evidence I'd already given them. Besides, Daniel's been reassigned, and I don't know who's in charge of the case now. Not to mention it's a good thing I didn't give him everything because now it's all missing."

How could Brooks argue with that? He stood and walked to the refrigerator for a second beer, popped the top, and took a long chug.

"So, what do you have?"

"Oh, Chuckles." I placed my clasped hands against my heart. "I knew you'd help."

He pointed a finger of warning. "I am not making any promises until I know everything. And I do mean *everything*. Understood?"

"Understood."

"Okay then." He returned to his seat across from me. "Let's hear what you've got."

"First let me show you this sequence of knots on the rope." I proceeded to illustrate the various knots. "It begins with an Ashley stopper. This is a thief knot, followed by a half hitch. But I don't think Vince was using this rope to practice sailing knots, because look at these next three. I haven't a clue what they are and I know my sailing knots."

"You think it's a code?" He sounded doubtful.

"It's what I hope it is."

After showing Brooks the rope, the letter, and all my research notes, I'd convinced him to join me on my quest.

"Why do you have these?" He held up the copies from the Hilliard House check-in book for the days before Vince and Ashley checked out.

"I thought I might contact people who were staying there at the same time as Ashley and Vince. But they wouldn't give me the contact information."

"Why is this name circled?" He squinted to read the handwriting. "Henry Beamer?"

"Remember telling me something had prompted them to check out early?"

He nodded.

"And then I told you how they'd seemed concerned about someone from upstate New York?"

"Yeah?"

I pointed to the circled name. "You can make out part of this guy's address. He's from Albany and he checked in the night before Ashley and Vince checked out in such a rush."

"Okay. I'll check this guy out." Brooks began to gather up all the items spread out on the table.

I grabbed the rope before he had a chance to add it to the rest of the evidence. "Do you absolutely have to take this?"

"Afraid I'll lose it too?" He was annoyed.

I had to admit the possibility made me anxious, but there was more to it. I fingered the rope before responding.

"I always carry it with me. It helps me keep faith." I held the rope to my chest. "I truly believe there is some sort of message here."

"How do you expect me to help you figure out what the message is if I don't have the rope?"

"Let me show you." I flipped through the notes I'd copied for him. "I've listed the names of all the knots in the same order they've been made on the cord, and here are the illustrations I've downloaded." Vince had never returned Papa's book so I'd had to resort to the internet.

Brooks took a look at my descriptions. "It would help to actually have the rope."

"What if I made a duplicate for you?"

He pulled a face. "Like the one you used to deceive Agent Benjamin?"

"But I wouldn't be deceiving you."

"True." He hesitated; then, "Okay. How quickly can you make a copy for me?"

I looked down at the knotted line in my hands but said nothing.

He let out a scoffing snort. "That's another copy, isn't it?"

I nodded. "It helps me to duplicate the knots in trying to work out the code."

"If there is a code."

"Either way, *I need* to hang on to the original." I pleaded with my friend.

Brooks issued one last warning. "If I find out you're keeping more information from me—*anything at all*—you're on your own. You have exactly one chance."

"Okay. I get it."

Whistler started whining, prompting a glance at the captain's wheel clock. "I didn't realize how late it was. He needs to go out."

"And I need to head home."

Brooks waited with me on the porch while Whistler completed his final shrub-watering duty of the day.

"I'll get started tomorrow. I know a guy who might be able to identify some of those other knots, and I'll see what I can come up with on college bird mascots. Plus I have an assignment for you too."

"Whatever you need."

"Think back to the last few days before Vince and Ashley disappeared. Try to remember anything out of the ordinary, something they may have done or said that seemed strange or unusual to you. Write it all down for me."

"Will do. What else?"

"I hear you have some paintings to finish up in the next couple of days for your exhibit." He was leaning against the porch post, arms crossed casually.

"You've been talking to Lu?"

"Among others." With only the light of the moon illuminating his face, I couldn't read his expression but could guess to whom he was referring.

"Why does Zoe hate Whale Rock so much?" Figuring he was part of the inner circle, I saw no harm in asking. I waited for an answer, but it wasn't forthcoming.

"Why won't she come home?" I placed my hand on his arm.

He exhaled a mild grunt of dismay and stepped away, releasing himself from my grasp.

"It's a long and thorny story, and I've got an early morning."

"Maybe another time?" I said hopefully.

"A little advice, Cassie. Leave the buried past where it is. Digging up old secrets won't be in anyone's interest, including your own. Believe me when I say you'll regret what you unearth. You will hate how it changes you."

After Brooks drove off, I reached for the phone to call Zoe, but thought better of it. I remembered having silenced the ringer earlier and turned it back on to check the incoming history. No messages, but eleven missed calls from Daniel, the last one just before midnight.

Good! Let him wonder where I was at this late hour. I felt a sense of empowerment, though it was hard to ignore the compelling whiff of caramel stalking me through the house.

*No, I will not call him.*

"Come on Whistler. It's way past our bed time." My new canine sidekick curled himself up at the foot of my bed and within moments was sleeping peacefully.

I rolled my tired body under the down comforter, craving the oblivion of dreams, but it was another unkind night. Sleep was elusive, and the hours crept at an interminable pace. As the sun broke through the early morning clouds, Brooks's words were still reverberating in my head. *Leave the buried past where it is. You will hate how it changes you.*

I could not dismiss the stern caution against unearthing the past. I wasn't certain my fragile sense of self could bear the burden of any more regrets. But how could I leave the past alone when the mysteries of my family persisted? What, if anything, could dispel the enduring curse lurking like an ominous shadow over the Mitchell family tree? Which would win the battle, my desire to unravel family secrets or an inherent instinct for self-preservation?

The dilemma continued to gnaw away at me.

# 20

Early October ~ four weeks following the disappearance

I was awakened by sirens. The curtains were billowing, and the breeze was cool, but the sheets were soaked through, and my body burned hot. I raced to the window, and though the alarms were still sounding, I could not see the fire truck. In a panic, I made a run for the stairs, but my foot became stuck under the edge of the area rug, flinging me forward and landing me back atop the bed. The siren was so close now, like it was coming from inside. As I shook free of the remnants of a nightmare, it finally came to me what the culprit was, and I retrieved my still ringing cell phone from under one of the pillows.

"I'm here," I gasped, not bothering to check the caller ID.

"Cassie?" When I heard Zoe's voice I began to sob.

"What is it, honey?"

It took some moments to compose myself, and my sister waited patiently for me to calm down, though tremors of fear were evident in her murmurs of reassurance.

"The lighterman," I finally managed. It was all I needed to say.

"Just a dream." Zoe's tone was soothing and kind.

"A nightmare! The same nightmare," I reminded her, grabbing a towel from the bathroom and mopping the perspiration from my neck and face.

"Still?" She would be remembering the many nights I'd awakened screaming during my childhood. "I thought you'd outgrown them."

*How do you grow out of something your subconscious will not release?*

180

"They don't occur as frequently as when I was a kid," I said to allay her worries.

"I guess, as we mature, we must be able to exert some control over those buried memories, huh?"

*We? Buried memories?* "You had nightmares too?"

"Yeah." It was nearly a whisper.

"I didn't know." Brooks's severe warning flickered into my mind, but I pushed it aside. "Zoe? Can I ask you something?"

"About the dreams?"

"I'm not sure if there's a connection." I sat on the bed and wrapped myself in the comforter because now I was cold. "Why won't you come home?"

"Whale Rock is no longer my home." Her tone had chilled. "And I don't think this is a good topic for discussion, Cassandra."

"Let me just ask, and if you don't want to answer, we'll leave it at that. Okay?"

There was a moment's hesitation before she relented. "All right, ask me then."

"I know you're not coming east for the exhibit."

"That's not a question, but I presume you want to know why I can't make it?" She began her usual spiel. "Well, Oliver has—"

I cut her off. "There always seems to be a convenient excuse, either a conflict with Oliver's work or your board obligations. I understand you're busy people, but I don't believe it's possible that for nearly twenty years, *each and every time* I invite you, something else more important than coming to see me is happening in your life." I shamed her into silence. "My question goes much deeper than scheduling issues. What is it about Whale Rock that keeps you from returning?"

"You're not being fair. Didn't I come when Mama was sick? And I stayed for her memorial service and to help you sort through all her things. And I was there for Papa's funeral."

I managed to hold back the sarcastic retort tickling my tongue. Mama was ill for years, yet Zoe didn't come until the very end. She had abandoned our parents, and I hated it when she laid claim for any contribution to their care.

"You didn't even bother to come when Granny Fi died," I said out of spite. I was determined to discover the reason behind Zoe's desertion of our family and our home.

"I know you adored her, but we had a very different relationship."

"Different how?"

"She was around more for you."

Again I bit my tongue. Nobody could deny Fiona's nurturing presence while we girls were growing up. Mama was constantly pregnant or recovering from her multiple miscarriages, and she'd been of a delicate bent, susceptible to various illnesses; Papa had clearly needed the help. I can remember watching fretfully from my bedroom window as my parents walked along the cliffs, worried that Mama's wispy silhouette would be carried away by the wind if Papa didn't hold tight.

"What's more," Zoe added, "I could never forgive her."

Now this was laughable. "Why would *you* need to forgive *Fiona*?"

"She was responsible for Mama dying so young."

"That's absurd." I couldn't believe the audacity. "Fiona loved and cared for Mama as if she was her own daughter. Don't forget, I was here. I was a witness to it all."

"Sometimes people stand right beside the truth and still don't see it."

"I'll tell you what I did see." I tried to hold back but couldn't. "Granny Fi was here every day, tending to the cleaning, the laundry, the marketing, the cooking. And when Mama could no longer take care of her personal needs, who do you think bathed her and got her dressed every day? Certainly not Papa. He was a wreck. All he could manage to do was hold her hand and maybe read to her when she wasn't sleeping. Fiona would *never* harm Mama. That I know for certain."

"You don't know everything, and I refuse to discuss this further. So find another question, or forget about it."

Leaving the subject of our grandmother was fine with me.

"What I really need is for you to tell me why you won't come home *for me*."

Quietly and patiently, I waited for the response to the issue that had plagued me for so long. Zoe sniffled and blew her nose, provoking feelings of self-reproach for pushing so hard.

"There's something evil residing within the walls of The Bluffs.

I told you about that odor." Her words were measured, with a slight quaver to her voice. "But it's even more than that."

She left the thought floating across the miles between us, but I waited her out.

"I lost so much there." She sniffed again. "You could never understand, Cassie. And I don't wish to speak of this again."

\* \* \*

The ringing of the landline startled me, but a state of inertia prevented me from rising and walking the few steps to the opposite side of the bed, where the phone sounded from my reading table.

The answering machine played the greeting: *You've reached Battersea Bluffs. Please leave a message.*

"It's Daniel. I know you're angry with me right now, but I'd really like to see you. I understand you might not be ready, but if that's the case, could we at least talk? It's important. Please call me back when you get this message." He cleared his throat, and then, "I miss you."

Aggravation was the catalyst to rouse me, and I crawled across the bed to push "Delete" before sinking back onto the pillows. My nostrils began to fill with the familiar sweet aroma.

"I don't care what you think." But to whom was I speaking? Percy? Celeste? Some wicked otherworldly being according to Zoe? But I couldn't allow myself to believe there was an evil presence in my home. Bolstering that mindset was the returned burning sugar essence of Percy and Celeste. And yet I too had been tormented by what might have been the same insidious odor as Zoe remembered. There also remained the question of why that acrid pervasive odor appeared and disappeared. I didn't recall being aware of it before Ashley and Vince arrived, nor had I smelled it since they went missing. Had it dissipated because they were gone? Had it arisen to drive them away?

I moaned, flinging one arm across my head in despair, and searched out the comfort of my warm, furry companion with the other. But when all I felt was the still damp sheets, I jolted upright and alert. For the first time since I awoke from the dreadful dream, I was mindful of Whistler's absence.

# 21

Later that day

"After checking every closet and bathtub, I finally found him in the cellar." I reached down to offer Whistler a reassuring chin scratch. "He has a fear of sirens."

Brooks raised his hands in question. "Where was the fire?"

"No fire. My ringtone is a fire alarm."

He gave me an odd look. "Have you thought of changing it?"

"I will." Actually, I had changed it multiple times, but to no avail. The ringtone repeatedly changed back on its own. It seemed Percy was partial to the sound, or at least someone or something was. During the light of day, the notion of sharing The Bluffs with a strange and hostile spirit seemed an even more remote possibility.

"How did he get down there?" Brooks had stopped by for a strategy session and was sitting at the kitchen table.

"I must have left the door ajar. I'd been down there yesterday, gathering some painting rags. Anyhow, Whistler was buried under a pile of old towels. But look what I found down there mixed in with them." I held up a baseball cap for him to see.

"You think it belonged to Ashley or Vince?" he asked.

"I don't know, but it's not mine."

"Ethan?"

I fingered the cap. If it was Ethan's, it would punch a huge hole in my theory that Whistler had searched out something familiar belonging to his owners.

"Right. That's a closed book." Brooks misread my silence.

"Ethan didn't wear ball caps, but I guess we can't rule it out completely." I handed over the hat. "Do you recognize the team?"

"Sure." He thumped the hat to life with his fist. "It's an old Minnesota Twins cap."

"How do guys do that?" It never ceased to amaze me, the male brain's capacity to retain every minute detail involving professional sports. "I can recognize a total of three sports team logos. The Boston Red Sox, the Celtics, and the New England Patriots."

"It's in our genetic makeup. Women remember recipes and men remember sports."

"That might be the most sexist comment to ever come from your mouth."

"Get over yourself. I think I've proven myself more evolved than the average Whale Rock cave dweller."

"I'll give you that." I pointed to the ball cap. "Can you have DNA testing done?"

"I'd have to get the FBI involved again. They have most everything."

"Had," I reminded him again.

"DNA samples wouldn't have been with the evidence file. They'd be able to pull up computer reports and do a comparison."

I made a face.

"Look, it might work to our advantage."

"Why? Because they've done such brilliant work so far?"

"How can it hurt having two teams working this investigation? We can continue with our plan and offer them select tidbits to keep the case alive. And if they think the WRPD is being helpful, we gain access to their information without them even knowing they're assisting us."

I didn't want any contact with Daniel, but I also had no desire to get into all the messy details with Brooks. For one, I'd have to hear about it from Zoe. Because I'd bet my last dollar (which could be found in my pocketbook) that he'd be calling her after our meeting today.

"I don't know what's going on between you and Agent Benjamin—" Brooks began.

I opened my mouth, but he cut me off, his next words providing me an out.

"—and I'd like to keep it that way. It's best if the FBI doesn't know you and I are collaborating. Frankly, I'm less likely to let something slip. Especially after a few pops."

My face flashed hot at the reference to my inability to keep secrets when under the influence. But I chose to ignore his jibe in the interest of progress.

"You're in charge. Besides, Daniel and I haven't been in touch recently."

Smugness flickered across Brooks's face.

I picked up my notebook. "Shall we get to work?"

"Let's do it." He opened a file, from which he pulled a stack of artwork. "Here are all the colleges and universities with red birds for mascots."

I took the pages and began to study them.

"Brandeis is the only one that might be considered a Jewish college," he said.

"Which makes no sense."

"Why?"

"It's right here in Massachusetts. They were enjoying a summer of exploration, checking out a place they'd never been before. Who goes to Brandeis and never sees the Cape? Besides, I don't believe Vince ever lived anywhere close to the water."

"We can't get stuck on the uncertainty of assumptions."

"What do you mean?"

He held up his fingers for emphasis and began to tick off all we didn't know about the T-shirt Cindy had turned in to the FBI.

"The shirt might not have belonged to them. It might've come from a friend, a sibling." He indicated the pages I was flipping through. "And frankly, Cindy isn't exactly the most credible person."

Daniel had said the same thing, but still I found it to be an exasperating excuse.

"I think we can rest assured she'd know a red bird when she sees it."

"True, but what made her think it was a Jewish college? Maybe it wasn't even a college at all."

"Okay. Okay. I get your point." I was drowning in a sea of missing pieces.

"Don't be discouraged. It's still a clue and one worth pursuing. Why don't you take those to show to Cindy? See if any of them stimulate a memory."

"I'll do that today." As I reached the end of the photos, my heart gave a flutter at the image of a strange bird rising from flames.

"Do you recognize something?" he asked.

"It's a phoenix." My hand automatically went to my lower tummy, as if to hide what was already covered by my jeans. The image of Skunk popped into my mind and along with it a spark of a memory from that fateful night. But I couldn't hold onto it long enough for it to be helpful.

Brooks plucked the page from my grasp and looked first at the image and then intently at me. "You're remembering something, aren't you?"

I realized I could inform my friend of the connection to Vince and Ashley without revealing my own drunken folly.

"They both had tattoos of a phoenix on their shoulders. It was a joint symbolic act."

"Can you elaborate?"

"Ashley said they'd lost something important in a fire, got drunk, got tattooed. End of story."

He considered this thoughtfully for a moment before saying, "Maybe that *wasn't* the end of the story. And then again, maybe it was a complete fabrication to conceal the real truth behind their tattoos."

I nodded, unable to come up with a rational argument other than my belief in them. Still, I felt a twinge of betrayal at the possibility they'd lied to me, and not just about the tattoos.

"What about the rope and the letter?" I asked to change the subject.

"We're making progress. All the knots have been identified."

I took out my rope and notes and Brooks helped me fill in the blanks.

"This is a rapala knot, used in fishing." He pointed to one of the last knots then counted upward. "And this is a savoy knot, which has no practical use. It's decorative."

Including an ornamental knot gave more weight to my code theory. I fingered the knots, trying to interpret them as a blind person would read Braille. Still nothing came to me.

"Were you able to locate the guy from Albany?" I asked.

"We've hit a dead end on the contact information I was able to wheedle out of Evelyn. This Henry Beamer guy isn't answering the phone, and he doesn't live at the address he used at check-in."

"So he lied?" I reflected on the potential threat he posed to Ashley and Vince.

"Or maybe he's just moved in the last four months. We're still trying to track him down." He closed his file and drummed the table. "Your turn."

"I did what you asked and tried to review what happened in the days before Ashley and Vince disappeared." I opened up my notebook and began perusing my jottings. I flipped a page and uncovered the napkin I'd been doodling on when talking with Teddy at Wizards the other night. I must have shoved it into the notebook without thinking, but the sight of it stimulated a brainwave.

"He said something about a silver money clip with the letter 'T.'"

"Who did?"

"Teddy. The other night at Wizards, before you stopped in, I was talking with him, and he mentioned something about a money clip Vince carried. He said it was an unusual 'T' shape." I picked up the ball cap that Brooks had set on the table between us and waved it at him excitedly. "Wouldn't you say this is an unusual 'T' shape?"

Brooks pushed out his lower lip and nodded.

"This could be a big break. Before you send it off for DNA testing, can I show it to Teddy?"

"I'll handle it." His voice was clipped, almost angry.

The change was markedly abrupt, compelling me to ask, "What is with you and Teddy?"

"I don't know what you're talking about." He busied himself organizing his notes.

I didn't buy it. The tops of his ears and his cheeks were tinged a rosy shade. There had been undeniable tension between the two men at the bar earlier.

"Are you keeping tabs on him for some reason? Has he been in trouble?"

"I'm not at liberty to discuss official business with you."

"So I'm right." I slapped the table. "What did he do?"

"Leave it alone," he warned. "The subject is closed. I'll handle the cap. Now let's move on."

For the second time in a day, my desire for answers had been shut down. I wondered if Zoe and Brooks conspired to frustrate me.

"Fine." I raised my hands in surrender and returned my attention to my notes. "Let's see. They mentioned knowing someone in Provincetown. Nobody specifically, just that they could crash there if they weren't up for biking back to my house."

"You still have photos of them?" he asked.

I slid a snapshot of the couple across the table.

"I'll have copies circulated in P-town to see if anyone recognizes them out there. What else?"

"I'm relying on a fuzzy memory for this, but there was a place they mentioned, a bar I think, but maybe a restaurant. Anyhow this place had two first names, one male and one female. Something like Johnny Beth's or Johnny Sue's. It was in an area close to where they lived during graduate school. And it was in an area that also had a unique name. I can't remember except that it had something to do with a fish. This bar served a brand of beer which Vince evidently thought was a local brew because he was surprised when he learned it could be purchased here on the Cape."

"Do you remember the name of the beer?"

"Dog something. Dog Head, maybe?"

"What a memory. Johnny something. Fish something. Dog something." At least the dourness had faded. "When you drop by Hilliard House to show Cindy the bird pictures, why not make a stop at the package store and see if any of the beers look familiar?"

I added it to my list.

"Is that all you've got?"

I took another look at the bulleted questions I'd jotted. Vince and Ashley had reacted so passionately to the unknown boy's grave, but what would compel two strangers to go to the trouble of leaving a memorial? And what was Ashley doing at the graveyard the day they disappeared? Vince had appeared agitated when he thought he'd misplaced the rope. Was Ashley hiding it so I wouldn't see it? If only I could remember if there were already knots on the rope. They'd packed such a large quantity of food for just one day. Were they planning to meet someone? And why had they been so resistant to taking Fiona's picnic basket? A wisp of a memory, something to do with Ashley and Whistler, but it flitted away.

It all left me with a sick feeling. I looked up from my notes and forced myself to ask the unsettling question which had been nagging at me for the past two days.

"Do you think Vince and Ashley knew they weren't coming back?"

# 22

Five weeks following the disappearance

"I have bad news." I told Brooks on the phone.

"So do I," he said. "You go first."

"I was unable to show Cindy the photos." I nervously paced the kitchen. "She's gone."

"What do you mean? Did Evelyn finally fire her?"

"No, apparently she quit. At the end of her shift on Monday, Evelyn said Cindy told them it was her last day. I checked with her landlady. Gone from there too. And no forwarding address."

"What about her phone?"

"This is where it gets weird. Evelyn tried to reach her by cell to ask where she should send her last paycheck."

"And?"

"The number is no longer in service."

Brooks said nothing.

"You still with me?"

"Uh-huh. And you're right. That is weird. I'll see if I can run a search."

"So what's *your* bad news?"

"Not as bad as yours. I showed the Twins cap to Ted. It's not the same 'T' as the money clip."

"Crap. I really thought we had something."

"It was a long shot."

I knew he was right, but I'd been hopeful for any kind of lead. "Did he give you any other helpful information?"

"Not really." Brooks blew a breath into the receiver. "I don't think he knows anything."

I thought back to the night when I'd asked Teddy if he'd ever hung out with Ashley and Vince. He hadn't answered because we'd been interrupted, but I wondered if there was something more to be learned. It was definitely worth a little more digging. I'd see what I could learn on my own before sharing those details with Brooks.

"You're right. I've no doubt he'd help us if he could."

Again, Brooks went silent.

"Does he remind you of anyone?" I asked.

"What? Who?" The shuffling of papers made me think he was perhaps only half-listening.

"Teddy. Sometimes he makes this expression that reminds me of someone, and I just can't put my finger on it. Maybe it's an actor."

"Probably. He has one of those classic looks."

"He is a nice-looking kid," I agreed. "One day it will come to me."

"What will?"

"Are you busy?"

"Yes. And we have more important matters to think about right now. The FBI agreed to do a DNA test to determine if the cap is a match."

"Oh, goody," I mumbled, wondering—but not about to ask—if Brooks had spoken directly with Daniel.

"What's that?"

"Good work. Hopefully, they won't lose it."

"It's our only option. I don't have a large budget, and besides, I'm working on this case unofficially, remember?"

"Yep." Still, it really got under my skin that we had to entrust another piece of evidence to the sloppy hands of the FBI.

"Enough of this for today. Might I remind you there's an art exhibit opening tomorrow?"

I checked the captain's clock. "Speaking of which, I'm expected at the gallery. Lu wants to make sure I'm happy *with the flow*. Can you imagine? I'd never imagined having my work shown, let alone being consulted on how it should be staged. It's all so surreal."

"Nervous?"

"The more you ask me, the more nervous I become."

"How many times have I asked?"

"At least a dozen. You *are* going to be there." This was a command.

"I wouldn't miss it."

"It's good to have someone to count on. You're the closest to family that I'll have there." Not that there was any other family besides Zoe. We were, after all, a dying bloodline.

"Don't be so hard on her."

"Sure, take her side."

"I'm not taking anyone's side."

Whistler began barking an alert, and seconds later the doorbell rang.

"Hold on a sec." I rested the phone on the counter and returned with a large vase of gorgeous autumn wild flowers. I plucked the card from its holder and picked up the phone again. "Are these from you?"

"Are what from me?"

"I guess that's my answer. I've been sent flowers." I opened the card and the persistent aroma of Percy and Celeste overpowered the scent of the bouquet. The inscription on the card read: *All the best. You deserve that and more. Affectionately, Daniel.*

"Zoe sent you flowers?"

"Hmm? Yes." It was a truth of sorts. There would be an enormous arrangement from my sister and Oliver, prominently displayed by Lu at the gallery, letting it be known to all of Whale Rock that they were there in supportive spirit.

"So you see? She does care."

I tried but failed to tamp down a sardonic reply. "She cares enough *to send* the very best."

"I'm sure glad I have a brother. Sisters bring way too much drama."

"As Papa used to say, '*I need a break from the emotion commotion.*'" I flopped down into one of the kitchen chairs, suddenly zapped of energy. Whistler nudged my hand for a pet, then nestled content-edly at my feet.

"Don't laugh," I said, looking down at the black-coated beauty.

"Have I ever? No, wait. Don't answer that."

I smiled at his attempt to cheer me.

"Okay, I promise not to laugh."

"I'm not sure how or why, but I have a strong feeling Whistler is somehow a link to solving this whole mystery."

Brooks kept his word and didn't laugh, but he also said nothing, a sure sign he rejected my hunch. The silence was becoming painfully embarrassing when finally he said, "You said that about the rope too."

"I still believe there's a message there. Can't there be more than one link to the truth?"

"This whole case is like a broken cobweb, with too many drifting strands to chase after. Let's tie up one before we get sidetracked by another. I'll see if I can track down Cindy. In the meantime, take the weekend off. Concentrate on enjoying your big night. We can hit the ground running on Monday. How does that sound?"

"It's a fine plan." I needed to take a break from my new, exhaust-ing sleuthing avocation. If only my mind would cooperate.

I fingered Daniel's card thoughtfully. *Maybe he deserved another chance.*

# 23

The day of the exhibit

On the kitchen desk before me, my laptop again came to life of its own accord, or perhaps at the hands of a mischievous old spirit. There was that photo again of Ashley and Vince. The burning sugar fragrance had been persistent the past few days, and I'd written it off as Percy and Celeste enveloping me in their haven of good will as I prepared for the exhibit. But the sudden appearance of this photo only served to confound me. Whatever they were trying to tell me would have to wait until Monday. I shut down the computer and picked up my keys.

I'd had a fitful night, with strange dreams invading the few moments I'd actually slept. Was it nerves? Or was it all the unresolved fragments of Ashley and Vince's disappearance floating aimlessly in my head? One sliver I was able to grasp onto was that I'd never heard back from my favorite postal clerk.

Fifteen minutes later, I was waiting in line for my turn at the post office. When Tom Turner saw me, his usual cheerful expression turned woeful.

"The old bean surely failed me this time." He shook his head in dismay before turning to the formidable postmistress. "Remember when we were talking about that missing couple the other day?"

Silvia Trask nodded solemnly. "I'm afraid I won't be much help to you, Cassie."

I mistook this as an unwillingness to cooperate until she continued.

"I wish I could remember where the letter was heading." She frowned. "If my daughter went missing, I'd hope anyone in a position to do so would help however they could."

"It might come to you," Tom encouraged his boss. Then he turned to me with a hopeful wink.

"All I can remember is that the young woman did post a letter shortly before they disappeared. It was a busy day, and I recognized her because she'd been in a few weeks earlier to buy some of those touristy Whale Rock prestamped postcards, and we'd chatted a bit."

"Do you recall the conversation?" I was eager for any clue.

"Mainly pleasantries." Sylvia held up her finger. "She did mention wanting the postcards to send to her little brother."

It was a small detail, but I grabbed on to it, since the only other aspect I knew of Ashley's personal life was that her father was a Baptist minister.

"Maybe if you go through it step by step you'll remember something else from that last time," Tom suggested.

Sylvia closed her eyes in concentration and narrated her recollections. "She waited out in the lobby for the longest time before coming in. She was gabbing on her phone, and I remember thinking she should do her business before the lunchtime rush. But it wasn't until it got crowded in here that she made up her mind to come in. She asked to have the letter weighed to make sure it was light enough for a regular stamp."

"And was it?" I asked.

Sylvia nodded. "Well under, in fact. It was already stamped, so I tossed it right into the bin without a glance at the destination. There was a line behind her."

Was it possible Ashley had used the letter weighing to divert Sylvia from looking at the destination? I rubbed my forehead. But why not just put it in a postbox or mail it from somewhere else, like Eastham or Orleans? She could've mailed it while they were out biking. Unless Ashley hadn't wanted Vince to know she was sending something . . .

"Did anyone from the FBI question you?" I wondered if Daniel had thought to check.

"No, should they have?" Sylvia looked concerned.

Tom cleared his throat, prompting Sylvia to turn her glowering eyes on him. "Thomas?"

He scratched his head and smiled sheepishly. "I may have forgotten to tell you."

"Tell me what?" Sylvia fixed him with a stern look.

"There was a gentleman from the FBI, stopped in one day when you were off."

Sylvia was still glaring at him.

"I know." He was flustered. "I should have told you."

"No harm, no foul." I jumped to Tom's rescue. "He didn't know anything."

"I guess you're right." The postmistress softened. "But I'm hoping you'd see fit to call me if Bruce Springsteen happened to wander in one day."

Now I got it. To have missed the appearance of the FBI must have been a disappointment. To keep Sylvia on my good side, I leaned in conspiratorially and said, "Did you hear that Cindy, the housekeeper at Hilliard House, left town without a trace?"

Sylvia's eyes twinkled. "Not exactly."

\* \* \*

On my way back to the car, I passed the window of Coastal Vintage Wares, feeling a twinge of sadness to see an old Pinocchio doll in the spot occupied for years by the bronze Winnie the Pooh. When I was little, my mother would bring me here as a treat, to look for special treasures.

The tinkle of the doorbell brought the eager proprietor from the back room.

"Well, look who the wind blew in. Why, I barely recognized you." Mr. Stanfield came around the counter to greet me with a fond hug. "Little Miss Cassandra Mitchell."

Archibald Stanfield was a fastidious and effeminate man. As teenagers, we'd assumed he was gay until he shocked us by marrying our high school principal, Miss Peeper. It had seemed preposterous at the time, but that was nearly twenty years ago, and they'd remained quite happily together.

"Not so little anymore." I picked up an old-fashioned letter opener with a mother of pearl handle engraved with an ornate "M," turning it over to check for a price.

"I've been holding on to that for you. The woman who brought it in to be consigned said it once belonged to the infamous Celeste Mitchell."

"How did she come to have it?" I fingered it lovingly.

"It was apparently uncovered during an estate sale. The letter opener had the original newspaper article about the Battersea Bluffs fire folded around it. Probably one of those items that walked away, just like the crystal and the silver." He winked at me and walked his fingers across the display glass.

"If it weren't for you, Granny Fi would never have gotten back any of those treasures."

"Glad to have helped." He waved away the thought. "Anyway, I persuaded the woman to let me return it to its rightful heir. I've just been waiting for you to come by the store."

I pulled out my wallet to pay him.

"Put that away! It's yours."

"Thanks, Archie. I'm always grateful for another keepsake." I told him about the recent good fortune in finding Percy and Celeste's portraits at the library.

"Wasn't there a clock too?" he asked.

"That's right. Still hanging in the kitchen." The captain's wheel clock had been out for repair the day of the fire. Fiona had saved up all her pennies from working at her parents' shop to buy it. She'd wanted at least one memento from the Mitchell family for her son. At the time, she couldn't have guessed he'd one day be owner of The Bluffs.

~

Eighty years ago
One month before the fire at Battersea Bluffs

It was six weeks after Ambrose left when Fiona Patrick walked out to Battersea Bluffs. She was pregnant and desperate.

When she arrived, Mrs. Mitchell had been reading a letter and appeared distressed. Fiona fingered the beautiful letter opener while Ambrose's mother made them tea. She was glad she had told Mrs. Mitchell about the baby. She'd been so kind, and the news seemed to chase away the sadness that had been upon her when Fiona arrived.

"Will you tell Mr. Mitchell?" Fiona had asked.

"When the time is right. But you leave that to me. You must send word to Ambrose at once. And your parents must be told."

But she had done neither. She wrote a letter to Ambrose but never posted it. As for her parents, she had yet to find the courage. And on the single occasion Mrs. Mitchell stopped into the store, Fiona ducked into the storeroom so as to avoid a questioning glance. *Have you told them yet, Fiona?* She hadn't wanted to disappoint. She had also been afraid to tempt fate. If she admitted to Ambrose a child was on the way, would he be more vulnerable to that awful curse? Would their unborn child?

~

Present day

"Let me wrap that for you." He busied himself with the tissue paper and ribbon.

"Thank you, Archie. I will treasure it always."

He gave a small gallant bow.

"I miss seeing Pooh in the window. I'm surprised it never sold before."

He stopped his fussing and smiled impishly. "It was never for sale."

"Then how?"

He nodded. "I see you already know *who* acquired it."

"And they did something very special with it."

He leaned an elbow onto the counter next to the antique cash register. "Well then, do tell."

I hoped sharing the story would open him up to reciprocating with some details helpful to the case.

"You remember the unknown boy who was found drowned in the Cape years ago?"

"Barnacle Boy?" Like Evelyn, the shop owners on Main Street Whale Rock made it their business to know all the local folklore.

"That's right. For some reason, Ashley and Vince took a particular interest in the child. One day I was up in the cemetery, weeding, and I noticed they'd planted a perennial garden around the gravestone and placed the statue of Winnie in the center. It's really quite special."

"Indeed." Mr. Stanfield dabbed the corners of his eyes. "I'm rather pleased to know old Winnie's watching over a young soul."

"I'd love to know what made you decide to sell after all these years."

"Oh, I didn't sell him."

"You gave it to them?" I tried not to sound too surprised, but it did seem rather generous.

He made an indignant snort. "Nonsense. They were mere strangers."

"They didn't buy it and you didn't give it to them, so . . . ?" I lifted my hands in question.

"They traded for it. Your young couple had an item I couldn't resist."

I was stunned. What was so special that he'd give up his precious Winnie the Pooh? My first thought was of the emerald ring, but the timing was off. Plus, there was a risk that Archie would've recognized Fiona's ring.

"What did they trade for it?"

He pursed his lips and strummed the counter with his fingertips. "Unfortunately, I'm not at liberty to tell you."

I was stung at the thought, and the hurt must have shown, for he reached over and patted my hand.

"I am not to reveal *to anyone* what I received in trade. That was the condition, and I must abide by it."

"What's the point of owning something you treasure if you can't show it off or share it?"

"It's only temporary. I agreed to keep the item secreted away for six months."

Was there a significance to the six months? Another tactic came to mind for drawing a hint from those exceptionally tight lips.

"I don't mean to be presumptuous, but since you know the Jacobsons are missing, don't you feel compelled to mention that you're in possession of an item that might offer a clue?"

He looked at me shrewdly. "Rest assured. I did contact the authorities."

"Who did you speak with?"

"As if you didn't know." He waved his hand in the flamboyant manner he had.

"Agent Benjamin." It wasn't a question. I tamped down my annoyance for Daniel withholding yet another significant detail. "When was this?"

"A couple weeks ago. Peeps and I were out of town when the couple went missing. We didn't hear about it until we returned and were catching up on the back issues of the *Times*. I got to thinking maybe someone in authority should know about the"—he stopped, tapping steepled fingers to his lip—"our little exchange."

Daniel had likely stopped by on a day that coincided with one of our dates. It steamed me to think I was just a convenient stop after official business had been conducted.

"Did they examine it? Take fingerprints?"

He shrugged. "I imagine that's what they're doing with it."

"The FBI still has it?" This was an unexpected little detail.

"They do."

"Is the item insured?" I asked casually, not wanting to alarm him.

"I hadn't gotten around to it yet. It had been locked up in my safe until your agent friend took it. The way I see it, my little treasure is in the hands of the premier protection agency of the United States. Where could it be safer?"

*Where indeed?* I hadn't the heart to tell him about the misplaced evidence files.

"So, it's truly valuable?"

"I'm not one to brag," he answered with a self-satisfied smile.

# 24

The exhibit

"Perfect!" Lu exclaimed when I walked into the gallery. At her suggestion, I'd dressed conservatively. A simple but elegant little black dress and my mother's triple-strand pearls.

"You want the patrons to notice you, but not be too distracted. The focus needs to be on your art."

"As if?" I had to laugh, for Lu's outfit could only be described as total shimmer. "All eyes will be on glamorous you."

"My approach is always carefully thought out, Cassie. The LK Gallery is exclusive. And when prospective buyers are speaking with me, I want them to understand they are purchasing premier art creations and will be paying accordingly."

"I get it. The artist can be understated, but the gallery owner needs to make a statement."

"You're a quick study."

Who was I to question Lu? Her reputation was impeccable. And she'd earned her international standing through years of careful research, dedicated networking, and hard work. I had every confidence in her abilities. It was my own self-assurance that stood on shaky ground at the moment.

Even the gallery had been designed to inspire. The converted former bank was a granite Greek Revival with white ionic columns and high ceilings, ideal for the dramatic wrap-around second-floor loft.

"Are you ready?" Lu filled a champagne flute with some bubbly and handed it to me.

"Do I have a choice?" I sniffed the glass and grimaced.

"It's sparkling pomegranate juice."

"You don't think I can handle myself?" I assumed Brooks had been telling tales until she corrected the notion.

"It's one of my strict rules. None of my artists are permitted to drink during their showings. When people are nervous, the drinks go down much too quickly. Early in my career I witnessed the collapse of more than one fledgling artist because they said or did something stupid or inappropriate. I insist on a preventive strategy."

"I see your point. But why do I need to drink anything?"

"If you're drinking, the patrons are drinking. And when the patrons are drinking, they're more likely to . . ."

"Fall in love with my art?" If I'd been holding a glass of real champagne, I'd have swallowed it quickly to wash down the insult.

"That's not at all what I was about to say. People will recognize your extraordinary talent, and they will love your paintings, with or without the champagne. However, there's a financial motivation for this exhibit. Am I right?"

Of course she was right, and I felt embarrassed for my cynical reaction.

"So, if our guests are enjoying a bit of champagne in a relaxed and elegant atmosphere . . ." She let the thought drift.

"As they become looser, so do their purse strings?"

She smiled slyly.

"I didn't mean to be so sensitive."

"Don't worry. This is your night, and all I want is for my newest protégé to embrace and enjoy your moment. Can you do that?"

"I'll try." I set my glass down so I could properly hug her. "Thanks for taking a chance on me."

"Trust me, kiddo. By the end of the night, I'll be the one thanking *you*." She released herself from my hug and gently squeezed my arms for encouragement.

A string quartet began to tune up, prompting Lu to take her leave for one last consult with the caterer, offering me the opportunity for a moment's reflection. The thrill of having my own exhibit was somewhat tempered by all that had led up to this night. It was little more than six months since Ethan had departed my world, yet so much had changed. Would I be standing here today if my husband had not left me in such a sad financial state? I couldn't imagine where I'd be now if it hadn't been for the fortuitous day Ashley and Vince wandered onto the cliffs and into my life. Would I be living with Zoe and Oliver in California? Renting an efficiency apartment on the wharf and waiting tables at the diner or cleaning rooms at Hilliard House? How ironic that those two vibrant young people, who'd saved me from losing my home and losing myself, were now lost themselves.

A light tap on my shoulder woke me from this reverie.

"How's my girl?" I turned to find Brooks holding a dozen long-stemmed pink beauties.

"Aw, Chuckles." I leaned my head into his chest. "They're lovely."

"They pale in comparison." He lifted his glass of champagne.

I raised myself on tiptoes and kissed him on the cheek. "Thank you for being here. I'm really nervous."

"You don't look it. Besides, once this place crowds up, you'll be fine. And you can count on me to be your helicopter."

I shot him a quizzical look.

"You know? Hovering nearby at all times."

"I'm a lucky girl."

"That you are." He winked.

"So were you able to find Cindy?" I kept my voice low, although the only people milling about at the moment were those putting their final touches around the gallery.

"Not yet."

I frowned. "It could be a tremendous help if she identifies the bird."

"Hey, listen." He placed a hand on my shoulder. "No talk of Cindy or birds or missing persons. This could be a pivotal night in your life."

"You're so wise."

"Or am I just a wise guy?" Brooks had me smiling, and for a moment the jitters remained at bay.

Lu stopped for one last inspection on her way to open the gallery doors, and within minutes a crowd was streaming in. I was truly astonished by the turnout. There were the usual suspects who always showed for town functions in support of Whale Rock: local politicians and business owners like Evelyn and George Hilliard, Lizzie Davis and her beau-du-jour, Tommy Turner and his wife, Archibald Stanfield and the former Miss Peeper—even Sylvia Trask was there. But many of the faces gathered to see my work were unknown to me, patrons of the arts lured by Lu's persuasion or her reputation. And she really knew how to work the crowd, seamlessly gliding from one guest to the next, introducing them to her featured artist—me—and guiding them toward the pieces she felt would be most suited to their tastes.

At one point, I gazed around the room and was surprised to see Teddy there, grinning at me. He was wearing a wild retro sports coat, loose tie, and tight jeans, but the oddly thrown together ensemble worked for him. I walked over to where he stood with a disparate group of young people.

"You clean up well, Teddy. Thanks for coming. And for bringing your friends."

"Oh, yeah. These are my bros, Marco, Benz, and Cav." They were an awkward group, but each of the young men uttered a polite hello. "And this is Jess." Teddy placed a possessive hand on a young woman's waist.

"Nice to meet you." Teddy's date took in the room. "Your work is impressive."

"Thank you." And I was in turn impressed by Teddy's good taste in girlfriends. Jess was engaging, attractive, and poised.

"Yeah, really cool stuff," Marco added, looking around uncomfortably. The other two friends, Cav and Benz, nodded in wholehearted agreement, though I suspected this was probably the trio's premier introduction to the art scene.

But Jess presented an air of sophistication, a noticeable contrast to the uneasiness of the young men in the party. I wondered if Jess and Teddy were one of those age-old Cape Cod stories: daughter of a wealthy tourist becomes infatuated by the irresistible charms of a local boy. Those summer romances didn't usually end well, but maybe they'd beat the odds, as my parents had done.

"Your paintings of Ash and Vince are awesome." Teddy nodded toward the alcove where the small grouping had been placed.

"They had a special bond, didn't they?" Jess asked. "You captured that."

I was taken aback. "Did you know them?"

Teddy didn't give Jess the opportunity to answer for herself. "Sure, Jess knew them from Wizards."

"That's right." Jess seemed to have taken the cue. "They came into the bar a couple of times when I was there. You can just tell from your paintings they were a close couple."

Now was not the time to delve further, but I was quite certain my earlier hunch was correct about Teddy being more familiar with Vince and Ashley than he was admitting.

Instead, I asked, "How did you know about the exhibit?"

"Your friend Brooks told me." He nodded to where Chuckles was sharing a laugh with George Hilliard.

"I hate to interrupt." Lu sidled up to me. "Some buyers are dying to talk to you."

I turned to Teddy and his entourage. "If you'll excuse me?"

"Sure thing."

"It was lovely meeting you," I said to the three amigos, and each mumbled a somewhat clumsy reply.

"And you too, Jess." Then I leaned in and whispered. "Teddy's a lucky guy."

She was positively luminous from the compliment. "Good luck tonight."

"Teddy, it means a lot to me that you came."

"Enjoying it. Who knows? I might even buy something."

Lu was quick to intervene, offering her own sparkling smile and adding, "If you find a treasure you just can't live without, we can discuss a payment plan. And of course, Cassie offers a discount to family and close friends."

I gave her arm a subtle pinch to lay off the sales pitch. Taking my cue she added, "Absolutely no pressure. Please enjoy the show. There's plenty more champagne."

"Old habits," she apologized and whisked me across the room, whispering in my ear, "I also wanted to let you know your handsome FBI guy is here."

"What?" I nearly stumbled and turned quickly to look. Fortunately Lu had a good grip.

"Tell me you haven't had any of the real sparkling wine." She gauged me closely.

"I just wasn't expecting Daniel to be here tonight."

"Something up with you two?"

"I'm pleased he's here." And it was true. But could I trust his motivations? For all I knew, he was returning the mystery item to Mr. Stanfield and just happened to see the flyer in the antique shop.

"Is there a *but* at the end of that thought?"

"It's complicated, Lu. I cut it off with Daniel a few days ago."

"It doesn't appear he got the message. He's hardly taken his eyes off you since he arrived, at least until a moment ago."

"Where is he now?"

"At the wine bar having a little tête-à-tête with our good friend Chuckles."

An involuntary groan escaped my lips.

"Is there something going on between you and Brooks?"

"What? No!" Whatever made her think that? I needed to get this discussion off the subject of my personal life. "So who wants to talk with me?"

She negotiated the crowd and directed me toward two nattily dressed middle-aged gentlemen who were beaming as we approached.

"Edgar. Jimmy. Here she is: our new star of the local art scene."

I knew Lu had a job to do, but it made me uncomfortable to be described in such immodest terms.

"A pleasure to see you again." Edgar Faust extended his hand and covered mine with the other in a warm and familiar manner. "Funny, we hadn't run into you for years, yet here were are meeting for the second time in the space of just a few weeks."

"That's right. Café Muse."

"You were with that tall, super-delicious drink of water standing right over there." Jimmy Collins was looking around the room. "Now wherever did he go?"

"I promise we'll track him down later," Lu swooped in for the save, relieving me from any discussion involving Daniel.

"I'm so glad you came tonight."

"We wouldn't have missed it for the world."

"Edgar was just saying how he'd love to write a sequel to his story about Battersea Bluffs for the *Cape Cod Times*," Lu enthused.

"Especially in light of the newest mystery surrounding the Mitchell family." Edgar was glowing at the prospect of another story.

Before I had a chance to respond, Jimmy interrupted. "I must apologize for my partner, Miss Cassandra. But I will make amends by offering our concerns for your young friends who have so sadly disappeared."

"I appreciate that."

"You have mine as well." Edgar looked chagrinned. "Jimmy's right, and I do apologize for my overeagerness. Nevertheless, perhaps one day you will permit me the opportunity for a little chat."

"You'll come down to Alcyone. I'll make lunch," offered Jimmy, taking my hand and leaning in close. "I predict we are going to become very good friends."

I was drawn in by their charm and would be pleased if Jimmy's prediction came true. "What's Alcyone?"

"Our humble abode in Chatham."

"If you grant us the favor of your company, I'll tell you the tale of how we decided upon the name," added Edgar.

"It's settled," Jimmy said. "We can make a day of it. And I promise not to let Edgar monopolize your time."

Lu took the prompt from Jimmy for her pitch. "Perhaps you could make it a dual opportunity and find the ideal spot for those canvases you're planning to purchase?"

"Oh, we already know where they're going."

"We have the perfect space that has been waiting for just the right collection." Edgar nodded delightedly in agreement with his partner.

"And since *The Enduring Mysteries of Cape Cod* did win a New England Book award—and Edgar attributes much of the credit to the story about Percy's Bluffs—we just have to have the grouping of paintings from the three different vantage points."

"They so capture the essence of the cliffs, the rocks below, where Percy Mitchell met his fate. And that majestic house with the incredible views of Cape Cod."

"Edgar fell in love with that view the day he came out to interview you. I've heard about it time and again, and now that I've seen these paintings, I finally understand what is so compelling about the setting."

"Then you must come out and see it in person one day," I offered.

"I would love that." Jimmy pulled out his checkbook and said, "Now, down to business. Name your price. I'm ready to buy an anniversary present for Edgar."

Edgar was obviously moved by the gesture, and the adoration these two men shared was enviable.

"I'm honored you chose my work." I left the business details to Lu and excused myself. Pretending to mingle but hoping to find Daniel, I strolled from room to room, exchanging pleasantries with the guests.

Lips caressed my ear and whispered, "If you're looking for your boyfriend, he's gone."

I turned to face Brooks and flashed angry. "It's not nice to sneak up on someone. And besides, I don't know what you're talking about."

He cocked his head. "Is that right?"

"If you're talking about Agent Benjamin, I knew he was here. But truly, I couldn't care less."

"If you say so."

"I do say so." I kept my voice low but intentionally frosty.

"Aw, come on. I was just teasing. Don't let it ruin your night." He put his arm around my shoulder and gave a fond squeeze. "Still friends?"

"I suppose so." How could I resist that disarming smile? "Especially since, to quote Granny Fi, you keep showing up like a bad penny."

"She was an awfully nice lady, your grandmother." He picked up a flute from a passing waiter's tray. "Lu's trying to catch your attention." He thrust his chin toward the opposite side of the room.

Indeed, Lu was waving me over to where she was standing next to a short, plump, elderly woman glittering in diamonds.

"Her latest prey. I'd better go." But before I did, I touched his arm and asked, "You going to stick around for a while?"

"You betcha. Why don't we celebrate afterward?"

"I hope there's reason to do so." I hated to brag, but I did want to tell Brooks the good news. "Actually, I did sell three paintings. Isn't that amazing?"

"I'll bet you sold more than that. At least one more I'm certain of." His ears were turning red.

My heart melted, but Lu had now crossed the room, hooked her arm in mine, and was pulling me back toward the dazzling dowager.

The rest of the evening was a bit of a blur. After the last lingering guests bid farewell and the catering crew was completing its cleanup, I kicked off my heels and plopped onto one of the elegantly upholstered settees decorating the gallery.

Chuckles was with Lu in her office, settling the sale for the painting he'd selected of Whale Rock Harbor, the place he'd called home his entire life. His father was founding partner of a prominent law office on Main Street and had restored one of the original Victorians on the harbor. Mr. Kincaid loved more than anything to be out on the open water, and with his home and office both but a mere stroll from the harbor, he could hop on his sailboat at the slightest whim. When the elder Kincaids retired to Florida, they took the boat with them but signed over their cherished Victorian on Whale Rock Harbor to Brooks.

"I'll have them delivered tomorrow," Lu said as they exited her office. She settled herself beside me on the settee. "Well, tonight went exceptionally well. I'll know more tomorrow when I hear definitively from several other interested buyers. It's a game we play in the art world. Oh, but Margaret Devon did purchase the schooner. Did you know it was her son's? *The Lady Slipper*?"

"I had no idea. It just happened to be anchored out by Simon's Reef when I started that seascape."

"He died a few years ago." Brooks shook his head. "Cancer."

"I'd forgotten. Tragic."

"Yes, but Margaret was thrilled when she saw *The Lady Slipper* in your painting. She bought it for her grandson, Jonathon's oldest."

"So, if nothing else, I made someone very happy tonight. As far as I'm concerned, it was a success."

"Trust me. Your success surpassed bringing some joy to Margaret Devon. But right now, I'm exhausted, so I'm kicking the two of you out of here." Lu stood up and made a graceful waving motion toward the door.

Brooks picked up an unopened bottle of champagne. "One of the perks of being a buyer tonight?"

"It's yours. Just go." Then she kissed me on both cheeks. "We'll talk tomorrow."

*   *   *

Brooks and I strolled leisurely through town, reminiscing about which family had lived in what house and the shops that had been open since we'd been kids. I told him about my visit to Mr. Stanfield's antique store and Celeste's letter opener. The harbor was fully illuminated by the moon and with a bit of chop to the water, the masts of the moored boats were swaying in a dancing rhythm.

"So, I saw you talking to Agent Benjamin tonight. Has he cross-referenced the DNA?"

"He submitted the cap, but DNA testing isn't quick. It could take up to two weeks."

"You must have scared him off."

"He got paged. Besides, I thought you '*couldn't care less*,'" Brooks said, quoting my earlier denial.

"I couldn't." I repeated the lie.

We walked along the marina without speaking, my mind on Daniel and his quick departure. He'd sent flowers and made an appearance, but he hadn't even said hello.

The afterglow of my exhibit was becoming tainted, and Brooks must have detected the change in mood, for he held up the bottle of bubbly and suggested, "Why don't we go to my place and enjoy this under the stars?"

"Why not?" I took his arm, glad for a respite from thoughts of Agent Daniel Benjamin.

We walked straight to Brooks's backyard. "Have a seat." He motioned to the faux wicker sectional, centerpiece to his dramatic terraced patio facing the water. "Be back in a sec."

Moments later he returned with two flutes and a bucket of ice.

"It's exhausting being famous." I fell back against the pillows and rested the back of my hand across my forehead in a dramatic gesture.

"Soon you'll forget all the little people," Brooks joined in as he popped the cork. "Might I have your autograph now before your star rises too high?"

"I signed your painting—isn't that enough? Or would you have me strain the tool of my art?"

Brooks uttered a low chuckle, quite like the one having earned him his nickname. "Cassandra Mitchell and fame would be such a dangerous combination."

I swatted his arm. "I wouldn't change."

He handed me one of the filled glasses and rested his large frame on the pillow back beside me. "May you retain the virtue of humility. Always."

We tapped our flutes together. "No worries. My aspirations are simple. If I can save Battersea Bluffs, I'll die a happy woman."

"You'll succeed." He finished his first glass and then poured himself another.

"By the way, thanks for buying the painting. You didn't have to, you know?"

"It wasn't a charity buy. Truthfully, it's one of the best depictions of Whale Rock Harbor I've seen."

"Quite the compliment." I set my half-empty glass down and turned to look at him. "Lu said something about having *them* delivered, as in plural. I thought you only bought one."

Brooks turned his eyes up toward the sky. "You must have misunderstood."

I didn't think that was the case, but Lu would tell me tomorrow.

As Brooks continued his stargazing, I couldn't help but admire his handsome profile. He was a very appealing man. What had happened between him and Zoe all those years ago? I was about to make another attempt at uncovering the answer to the mystery when Brooks downed his second glass of champagne, set it on the table, and made his move.

I was in such a state of shock I was unable to react, other than giving in to his kiss. Or at least that was the excuse I made to myself later to assuage the guilt.

My senses returned and I gently extracted myself from the passionate embrace.

"Aw, Chuckles." I placed my hands affectionately on his cheeks. "I'm not Zoe. Not in any way."

"I know damn well who you are." His voice was hoarse, and he turned his head away, leaving my hands to drop heavily into my lap.

After sitting in lamentable silence for what seemed like hours, I summoned the nerve to speak. "I have always had the deepest affection for you, Brooks."

"Please don't patronize me." He was no longer turned away, but his eyes were closed.

"I'm not. But please let me tell you how I'm feeling about this . . . complication, for lack of a better word."

"'Complication'? Not a better word."

"Will you just listen to me for one minute?" I took in a deep breath to calm my frustration. "I can't imagine not having you in my life, okay? You are that important to me. You're one of my closest friends. So as much as I wanted the same thing you wanted a short while ago—and believe me, I did—it was an *in-the-moment* emotion. And you can trust that I know how dangerous those types of impetuous actions can be. If you'll recall, it's how I ruined my marriage."

"You and Ethan were on the path of destruction long before Billy Hughes made his encore performance."

"That's beside the point."

"So what exactly is your point?" His words echoed off the water.

I tried to take his hand, but he wouldn't let me. "You are far too special to me. I could never consider getting involved if there was a risk of losing you. I think you'll agree I have a talent for screwing up relationships."

"Yeah, I've noticed."

"At least we're in agreement on something." My stab at humor was wasted. "I'm going to tell you something I've never shared with anyone. Not even Brit."

"You should have maintained that strategy." A definite dig for Brit's blabbing about Billy, but the tone more conciliatory.

"I had the biggest crush on you when I was a kid. But you were so in love with Zoe, you hardly knew I existed. I spent half my days fantasizing of ways to get rid of her so I could win you over for myself." I laughed softly. "But that's the point."

"What is?"

"Zoe. She was, is, and always will be the most obvious of obstacles. Don't you see? We would never be able to escape the shadow of her memory."

He rubbed his hands over his face and up through his hair. "Damn the ghost of Zoe Mitchell. Will she never stop haunting me?"

*　*　*

It was half past one when I finally left Brooks to his brooding. I'd said all I could to placate his bruised ego, and only hoped our friendship would remain unscathed after one unfortunately timed attempt at romance. It would have been far worse if we'd abandoned good sense and awakened in the morning with regrets.

I was still fretting about it when I pulled the Miata up to the house, but worries over Brooks quickly vanished when the orange glow of a burning cigarette tip caught my notice. My pulse raced—who was on my porch at almost two in the morning? The mystery stalker? I quickly reversed the car to aim the headlights at the smoker and was both relieved and confused to see sitting there on my porch a scruffily clad woman and her signature Uggs.

"I heard you was asking about me." Cindy crushed her cigarette butt into the gravel driveway as I let Whistler out to do his thing. When the dog was finished, he ran back for a proper greeting. "Hey there, old fella."

"He remembers you fondly," I observed.

"I used to give him the table scraps. You know, eggs and bacon left over from breakfasts. I reckon it don't matter if Evelyn finds out. She can't very well fire me now." Cindy cackled at her own joke.

I noticed she was shivering. The wind had kicked up, and there was the smell of frost in the air.

"Let's go inside. I'll light a fire and put on a kettle for tea. Are you hungry?" I had many questions for this woman, and it was prudent to keep her comfortable.

"I could go for one of those cookies," she said when we walked into the kitchen.

"Cookies?"

Cindy inhaled deeply. "Smells like somethin' just came from the oven."

I could do nothing but stare at her for a moment, disbelieving this woman had the perceptive power to pick up on Percy and Celeste. I subtly sniffed the air myself, and yes, they were clearly making their presence known.

I retrieved a tinned coffee cake from the pantry. It would have to do.

"How did you get here?" I asked, setting plates on the table.

"Hitched." I must have looked startled, for she added, "With a friend of mine. I never get into a car with strangers no more. Ever since those two kids went missin', my policy is to only go with people I know."

Cindy must indeed have been hungry, because by the time the tea was ready, she'd already eaten two large pieces of coffee cake. "Homemade is always the best."

*If only she knew.*

"If you don't mind my asking," I sat in the chair across the table from her, "why did you leave Hilliard House?"

She gave a wave of her hand. "Aw, you know how Evelyn is."

I did, but that surely couldn't have been the only reason to leave a decent paying job in this economy.

"But you didn't even give them notice or a forwarding address for your last paycheck. They thought you'd left town altogether."

"Yeah. Well." She shrugged and offered nothing more.

"Did you find another job?"

"Nah. I'm thinkin' of retirin'."

"Not that it's any of my business, but can you afford not to work?"

Cindy took on the look of a trapped animal.

"I only want to make sure you're alright."

"Tha's okay." Again the wave. "I came into some money, so I'm doin' just fine."

Sudden wealth didn't exactly fit with her tattered appearance or the lack of an automobile or even a jacket. Still, I wouldn't pursue it further for fear of alienating her.

"So what was it you wanted to see me 'bout?" She blew the steam away from the top of her teacup.

I went to my desk and pulled from the drawer the file of bird mascots. "Do you remember telling me about the shirt with the angry red bird on it? The one you found in Vince and Ashley's room?"

Her face clouded. "You bringin' that up again?"

"Only as a means of helping to find them."

"I don't see how it'll help." She cut a third slice of cake.

"Look. My reason for asking about the shirt is to see if I can track down where they came from. Maybe someone in their hometown or where they went to school might have information about them. But until we know where they're from . . . ?" I lifted my hands. "It's a big country."

Cindy snickered. "Sometimes not big enough."

I would love to know her story, no doubt a colorful one, but I had to keep my focus. "So, will you help me?"

She pushed her plate aside and wiped her lips with the back of her hand. "A'right. Lemme see what you've got."

I opened the file and began to flip through the pictures of college mascots Brooks had assembled. "When something looks familiar to you, just let me know."

She made a job of inspecting each drawing or photograph, squinting and holding the pages close.

"That's not it. Nuh-uh. Neither is this one." She placed the rejects facedown while puzzling over others. I was losing hope as she neared the end, but finally she punched an image with her index finger. "This is the one. This one right here."

My pulse quickened as we moved one step closer to figuring out where Vince and Ashley came from. But I also had to smile now that I understood why Cindy thought it had been a Jewish school. It was *Temple* University's mascot.

"You're certain?"

"Hundred percent." She handed me the sheet of paper. "What are ya gonna do with this?"

"'*Now there's the rub.*'" The quote from *Hamlet* appeared lost on Cindy, who responded with a vacant stare.

I looked at Temple's red owl mascot while considering my two alternative paths for this new information, neither of which was particularly appealing at the moment. Should I give Brooks a day or two to cool down? On the other hand, could I trust Daniel to act on it? And almost as important, did I trust myself to keep an emotional distance from him?

"What to do, what to do?" I said under my breath.

"'*That is the question!*'" Cindy beamed her crooked-toothed smile, making me speculate whether dumb was just an act for her.

# 25

The next morning

"Come on, Brooks. Pick up." It was the third time I'd tried to reach him, but he wasn't answering. Another call came in, so I didn't leave a message this time.

"Good morning, Lu." I was curled up on the bay window seat, sipping my coffee as I looked out at the rough waters of the Cape.

"It's not too early, is it?" she asked.

Under normal circumstances it would have been, but I hadn't even made it to bed yet. It had been very late—or early—when I'd returned from dropping Cindy at the Orleans Stop&Shop. She wouldn't let me take her to wherever she was living these days.

"I was too keyed up to sleep." I stifled a yawn.

"Are you sitting down? Because this is really big, Cassie."

"I'm listening."

"After you left, I was waiting for the caterers to finish, and a gentleman walked into the gallery. I'd seen him earlier at the exhibit, but he disappeared before I had a chance to introduce myself."

"What did he look like?"

"He was wearing a navy blazer and khakis, no tie."

I had to laugh.

"I know," she chuckled along with me. "The standard uniform of male Cape Codders over thirty."

"Which covers most of the men who were there last night," I added.

"Except perhaps for that adorable group of young people."

"Teddy and his pals."

"The blondish, tall, good-looking kid? Funky jacket?"

"Yes, that's Teddy."

"Getting back to this other guy—he was a lean, distinguished, pleasant-looking man with salt and pepper hair, mostly pepper."

"Dimpled chin?"

"That's him. He came back asking for another look. I'd already affixed sold stickers on the paintings purchased last night and also put out a few 'Sale Pending' signs, wanting to set aside the works being eyed by the usual buyers. It's not good to whip up an interest and then not have the final product available for them to purchase."

"But?"

"*But* I had a feeling this man was a serious buyer, and my instincts proved correct." She stopped for a breath, but her eagerness was contagious.

"So? What happened?"

"After I walked him through the exhibit, he said—and I quote—'I'd like to purchase the balance of the collection.' Can you believe it? The balance of the collection."

I couldn't. *Everything* had sold?

"A solid offer, higher than the asking prices totaled, I might add. All sold!"

"How much?"

"Hold on to your hat." She named a figure, and I made some quick calculations in my head. "But Lu, that's way over the value you placed on the *entire* collection."

"True," Lu agreed. "But you have to remember, it's a significant collection that you've been assembling for a number of years. Perhaps I underestimated the worth your talent would draw."

My heart had been doing cartwheels of joy until the center of all my emotions took control and my stomach began churning with apprehension. Something was rotten in the state of Denmark, to borrow yet another quote from my old pal Hamlet. There was no logic in someone offering such a significantly higher price than asking.

"No," I said, rather emphatically.

"Yes, it's true." She had misunderstood.

"I mean I won't sell to him, Lu."

An involuntary squeak of anguish came through the earpiece. "Are you crazy?"

"Quite possibly." But I had to know the truth behind this unbelievable sale. "Are my paintings still at the gallery?"

"Yes, of course. A purchase this large requires special arrangements. A buyer doesn't simply walk out with the paintings. Each has to be specially packed for shipment."

"Shipped to where?"

"Mr. Bernard, Michael—that's the buyer—hasn't given me all the details yet. I'm meeting him this morning to finalize the sale. He's having a cashier's check drawn."

"Tell him I will sell my collection to him on one condition. I want to meet him first."

Lu was quiet for a moment, probably to form a composed response. "I just want you to understand, such a proviso could very well jeopardize the sale."

"Don't you find it odd for this stranger to materialize in our midst and fall in love with a debut artist's work, so much so that he buys everything and offers more than they're worth?"

"Extremely odd. But the art world is chock full of eccentrics. Who are we to question their whims? Especially if they can afford to indulge them."

"Is there anything in our contract forbidding me from making this condition?"

"No. Just common sense, which apparently is in short supply today."

"I have a sense, all right. The sense of a mystery lurking within this collector's motives."

"And again I say, so what? You need the money. Why question the buyer's intentions?"

"Humor me."

Lu blew out a defeated sigh. "I'll do my best. What should I do if he refuses?"

"Why would someone who is so keen to buy up all my completed works not be thrilled for the opportunity to meet me in person?"

"I hate to admit it, but there you have a point."

"What time is the meeting? Shall I be at the gallery early or would it be better to keep the buyer waiting?"

"I've got a better idea. I'll suggest he might also want to see some of your works in progress. That way I can bring him to you."

"I like the way you think."

"What? Like the captain who doesn't want to go down with her sinking ship?"

I pushed aside the guilt of putting the screws to all Lu's hard work.

"And one more thing, do you think you might spring my little stipulation on this Mr. Bernard after you've determined the shipping destination?"

"When did you develop such a devious mind?" she asked, and when not answered, "Oh, all right. The agent always seems to get the dirty work."

*Along with a healthy commission.* "You're a peach, Lu."

"Remember that sentiment when the bank forecloses on your house." She let the thought sink in before ending with, "You're the boss."

\* \* \*

At nine o'clock, the phone rang again. I thought it might be Lu, but it was Zoe's voice singing into the phone.

"Good morning, little sister. How does it feel to wake up knowing you've taken the art world by storm? A sellout! And this your first exhibit."

I didn't respond immediately.

"Don't be mad. Lu was so excited last night. She had to tell

221

someone, and it was too late to call you. What with the time difference and all, telling me was the next best thing. You would have called me anyhow to tell me, right? I could hardly sleep last night. This is such wonderful news. When will you get your check? Will it be enough to pay off the mortgage?" She was chattering away, not even pausing to let me answer.

"You're making me dizzy, Zoe. How many cups of coffee have you had already today?" It was only six o'clock out there.

"Can't I be excited for you? Fortunately, Oliver had an early tee time, so he's up too."

"Congratulations, Cassie," Oliver called out from a distance.

"He wants to know when we'll get a Cassandra Mitchell original."

"You already have one," I reminded her. "The portrait of Fiona?"

"Yes, of course. I'll be sure to show Oliver one day."

"Where is it? Tucked away in the attic somewhere growing mold?" It was still a sore subject.

"Let's play nice today, okay?"

"Sorry. Oliver still in the room?"

"No, he's headed for the shower."

"Just wanted to check if everything's okay between you two. The last time we spoke, you seemed a little upset."

"We're fine. But let's not talk about it now. I want to hear all about last night. Who was there? What were they wearing?"

"This wasn't the Oscars, Zo-Zo."

"Sue me for wanting to share your special night."

My first reaction, which I managed to stifle, was to shoot back with "If you truly wanted to share my special night, you'd have been here. We'd be having this conversation in person, over coffee at Mama's old oak table." But the shame from my kiss with Brooks was keeping me in check.

"Then let me start at the beginning. Lu was absolutely dazzling." I delivered a fairly detailed account of the evening, listing everyone in attendance that she would remember, describing what they wore. We talked of all her friends, who had changed, who looked the same.

"I presume Brooks was there?" She slipped the question in.

"Of course." I tried to make my voice equally as casual, which was difficult. Thank goodness we hadn't started Skyping yet. She'd see right through me.

"How does he look?" She was killing me.

"As handsome as ever." I needed to get off the subject of Brooks but was grasping at straws for a new topic. "Let's see, who else was there? Mr. Stanfield and Miss Peeper. Edgar Faust. He wrote about The Bluffs years ago for his book about Cape Cod lore. Do you remember that?"

"Barely." Her tone had gone oddly chilly.

My call waiting beeped, and not a minute too soon. "Lu's calling."

"Keep me posted."

I didn't have the heart to tell her I hadn't yet agreed to the sale.

I transferred to the incoming call. "Guess who just called me from California?"

"Oh." She paused. "Sorry about that."

"You know I would have told her anyway. Only it would have been smarter to wait until the offer had actually been accepted."

"Cassie, trust me when I say that I couldn't have conceived of it not being accepted."

"That's fair. Let's hope it works out because I don't want to have to deal with Zoe flipping out if this falls through."

"She's not the only one you'll have to answer to."

"I know how hard you've worked putting this exhibit together for me. But as you said last night, before this offer even came in, the show already had the makings of a success."

She sighed. "You're right. But I haven't given up yet. It's arranged. They'll be out to your house in ten minutes."

"They?"

"Well, here's the thing. Michael Bernard, the man who made the offer? He's not the actual buyer."

"Who is then?"

"A man named J. Aaron Welkman. Michael's his personal assistant."

"Did you meet this Mr. Welkman?"

"No. But you will."

"Why aren't you coming too?"

"They had their own condition, which was a private meeting with you. Maybe they want to sweeten the offer and cut me out of the deal."

"You know I would never do that."

"I'm not worried, at least not about that. But how do you feel about two strangers coming out to the house with you there alone?"

"I have Whistler to protect me." Although it *was* a bit unsettling.

"Maybe we should call Brooks and let him know just for the sake of caution."

"I don't think that's such a good idea. He had a little too much to drink last night, and we should let him sleep it off."

Lu hesitated but ultimately gave in. "Okay, but check in with me after you meet with them. If I haven't heard from you in an hour, I'm going to drive out there myself."

I waited for my guests on the porch; when Whistler began his normal warning routine of barking viciously, my stomach lurched as a black Lincoln Navigator with darkly tinted windows drove toward the house. *Maybe I should have let Lu call Brooks after all.*

A man I vaguely recognized from last night got out of the driver's side while Whistler continued growling and pacing in front of the vehicle. I didn't call him back. It was better for my visitors to think him threatening.

To avoid Whistler, the man—presumably Michael Bernard—walked behind the SUV to assist an older gentleman in sunglasses, whom I assumed was Mr. Welkman. I wondered why he required assistance; he was not a frail man—quite the opposite, he was in decent physical shape. Then Whistler did something totally unexpected. He stopped snarling and with ears laid back flat to his head and his tail doing a low wag, he slowly approached Mr. Welkman, then dropped to a down position.

"Hey, fella." The older man pulled something from his pocket and Whistler licked greedily at the extended fingers. "Good boy. *Up.*"

But instead of sitting up, the dog rolled onto his back and whimpered delightedly as the man stooped down to offer a tummy rub.

*So much for my protector.* I walked toward my guests, stunned.

"I've never seen him take to a stranger so quickly. What's in those treats?"

"Secret recipe." He patted his pockets. "I've always had a way with animals, especially of the canine variety. I even managed to charm a pack of dingoes once long ago."

I dipped my head. "Pardon?"

"You heard right. He said 'dingoes.'" The younger of the two shook his head as if he himself didn't believe it. "Aaron's a regular Dr. Doolittle. You should see him with a congress of baboons."

"Baboons? My, you keep strange company."

"May I introduce myself? I'm J. Aaron Welkman, but you can call me Aaron." He reached his hand out as the other man guided him toward me.

"Cassandra Mitchell."

"Pleasure. This is my assistant and good friend, Michael."

We both nodded cordially to each other. Aaron removed his sunglasses, and it was immediately obvious what his condition was. "I'm not blind yet. Low vision is what the doctors say. Macular degeneration is a most unpleasant disorder, particularly for those who enjoy drinking in the beauty of this world."

"Aaron was a photographer of some renown before his sight began to fade." Michael said this in obvious admiration. "If you've ever flipped through a *National Geographic* magazine, you've probably seen his photographs."

"Impressive. Now I understand the reference to baboons." Lest he think I was making light, I rushed to add, "I'm sorry for your sight loss. As an artist, I can't imagine how devastating it would be to have to give up my passion."

"Fortunately, I am able to live vicariously through others. I've passed the baton to my protégé here." Aaron patted Michael's shoulder. "As for your own passion, it is a special talent, Ms. Mitchell."

"Or so you've been told?" I looked directly at Michael as I said this.

"Might we go sit somewhere?" Aaron suggested, ignoring my comment.

"Of course." I motioned for them to follow.

Traitor that he was, Whistler stayed close to Aaron's side until he was seated in the living room, where he rested at the older gentleman's feet to receive the treats so generously being doled out.

I chose the settee opposite from the two men, who were sitting either side of the fireplace.

"I made you a generous offer, Ms. Mitchell." Aaron got right down to business. "Are you prepared to accept it?"

I hesitated, prompting Michael to utter an offensive insinuation. "Unless you're holding out for more?"

"The offer was more than fair, even beyond generous. Initially, I was prepared to accept it because it is extremely tempting. But I cannot ignore the mystery surrounding your interest."

"Are you suggesting Aaron is trying to deceive you?" Michael's insolence sharply contrasted to his well-mannered first impression.

Aaron held up his hand. "Please, Michael."

"The word I used was 'mystery,' which doesn't imply you're being unscrupulous. I simply don't understand why someone would offer more than the value of the collection for a complete unknown. Especially—and please don't take offense—since you can't even see them."

"I understand your misgivings. But I assure you, I only wish to purchase your paintings as a gift for someone who holds dear to their heart this area of Cape Cod. I trust Michael's eye on these matters. I know he sees in them what I would have seen."

"But why would you need to purchase the entire collection? Some of the paintings are near duplicates."

"This isn't the first time Aaron has given a newcomer a break," Michael explained. "He scooped up every photograph in my first exhibit."

"Well, in that case, I appreciate the confidence and the compliment.

However, what I don't understand is why you'd pay over the asking price. Do you see why I might be troubled by the motivation behind such a significantly higher offer?"

"What *I* see is a breakout artist with a chip on her shoulder."

"I'm begging you, Michael," Aaron admonished his assistant.

At the same time, the fireplace flames suddenly flared as if doused by a shot of kerosene. Aaron hadn't noticed, but Michael sent me a nervous, questioning look as he moved his chair away. I comforted Whistler, who had abandoned his post at the hearth for the safety of the settee.

I took the eruption as an alert from Percy and Celeste, but I was already a step ahead.

"Gentlemen, I'm not so easily fooled." If they'd played this game six months ago, no doubt I would have accepted the offer without question.

"I beg your pardon?" Aaron's brow had bunched, but Michael's complexion was becoming red and blotchy.

"I feel like I'm in the middle of a not very-well-acted good-cop/bad-cop routine." Michael's expression morphed from indignation to embarrassment.

"I'm afraid the jig is up for us." There was a subtle slump to Aaron's shoulders as he said this. "We underestimated you, Ms. Mitchell, and for that I'm sorry."

It was a backhanded apology; his regrets were only for the failure of their ploy. It burned me that they'd just assume I'd fall for their little act.

"Might we start again?" Aaron held out his hands in appeal. "I am still serious about this transaction."

"And I'm still serious about wanting to understand the nature of your interest."

"You must believe me, the less you know, the better for everyone involved." He did not state this as a threat, but more as a resigned truth.

"That sounds rather ominous."

Aaron rubbed his forehead. "There is no danger to you no matter what you decide about selling the paintings to me. But for others?" There was a subtle lift to his shoulders. "I can say no more on the subject."

"May I at least have a day or two to think it over?" I needed to buy some time.

"We're leaving today," Michael protested mildly, and then he offered for clarification, "We have to be in Boston for some business concerns. We're scheduled to fly out on Thursday morning."

"I'm confident we can conclude those dealings by Wednesday," Aaron interjected. "Does that give you enough time for thoughtful consideration, Ms. Mitchell?"

Four days was more than I could have hoped for. "I promise to have an answer for you by then. Shall I call you?"

"That won't be necessary. Michael and I will plan to return here on Wednesday afternoon."

I was positive Aaron was not the type of man to give up easily. He'd have another plan of attack at the ready if my answer was not to his pleasing.

The two men stood, and Whistler followed suit, wagging happily. When we arrived at the Navigator, Aaron reached into his pocket and retrieved another morsel.

"Good boy." The dog devoured the treat before darting off for a romp in the meadow. Aaron winked in my direction. "Bribery is the key."

"I'll remember that next time I find myself surrounded by a congress of baboons."

He was amused but then became serious in his final petition. "I do hope you will decide in my favor."

As he held out his hand, the signet ring he was wearing caught the sun. In that brief glimpse there was a familiarity to it, but I was unable to manage a closer look because Aaron grasped my own hand firmly.

"I promise to consider it carefully."

Michael helped Aaron into the vehicle and closed the door. He turned to me and said, "Please don't let our little attempt at trickery have a bearing on your decision."

"It's forgotten," I lied, sensing something else at play. I was dying to know what lay at its root.

I watched them drive off, but as I walked up the front porch steps to make the promised call to Lu, Whistler started barking another alert. A gray Avalon came into view at the curve of the drive.

"Who was in the fancy ride I just passed?" Daniel asked, receiving an affectionate greeting from the dog. I folded my arms across my chest as he approached.

"A buyer from last night's exhibit."

"So I presume it went well?" He seemed genuinely pleased.

"Better than I could have predicted."

"That's because you don't have confidence in your talent." He stepped up onto the porch, my heart quickening as he drew near.

"Maybe my work would suffer if I was conceited." I took a casual step back, and he leaned against the railing to give me berth, folding his arms in a mimicking gesture.

"There is a difference, you know, between confidence and conceit. But you may be right. Your work has an aura of vulnerability."

"Listen to you, Mr. Art Critic."

"What can I say? The Sunday Arts section of the *Globe* is a wealth of information. Besides, I know what I like, and I liked what I saw last night."

"Thanks." I didn't ask why he'd left without saying hello. I didn't want him to think I cared. But I did care and had been hurt. "I assume you're here to see me on that other matter."

"Yep." He yawned, making me wonder if he'd driven out from Boston or was crashing at his friend's cottage in East Falmouth.

"I'm sorry for texting at an ungodly hour." I was grateful he'd answered last night after Cindy had identified the mascot.

"No problem. I haven't been sleeping well lately anyhow." He offered a sad smile. "But we were able to access enrollment information for Temple University."

"I'm impressed."

"The FBI is a twenty-four/seven operation. Unfortunately, there are no records of an Ashley or Vince Jacobson having gone to school there."

I sat down on the porch rocker, feeling as if all the air had been knocked out of me.

"Don't lose heart yet." He sat in the other rocker. "I emailed their photo to the Philadelphia office. The campus is located in the heart of the city, so it will be easy for them to send someone out to see if anyone recognizes or remembers them. Is there anything else you can recall? Names of friends or professors?"

"Their apartment was very close to a fire station. Whistler was terrified when the alarm sounded. He bolts whenever he hears a siren."

"Ah. So that's why he disappeared that night?" He gave me a meaningful look, which made me flush hotly with the memory of the first time he'd stayed the night and the fire alarm ringtone of my cell phone that had sent Whistler cowering in the guest room.

He was jotting notes in a small notebook. "Anything else?"

"They frequented a tavern called Johnny-something which served a microbrewery beer called Dog Fish Head, one of Vince's favorites." I suddenly felt disloyal to Brooks. I'd forgotten to pass along this information after I'd found the beer again at the package store.

"I'll have one of the research people conduct a search, see if they can come up with some type of geographical match."

"Thank you for doing this," I told him. "I mean it."

He flipped the notebook closed and reached over to caress my cheek. "I miss you."

I missed him too. But I didn't trust myself to say the words and only took his hand in mine and nodded.

Whistler, who'd presumably been involved in his favorite pastime of chasing chipmunks at the side of the barn, came running in the direction of the driveway as a Whale Rock Police Cruiser rounded the curve.

I became slightly nauseated as Brooks walked toward the house.

"Hello, Cassandra." He nodded at me then reached his hand to Daniel. "Agent Benjamin."

"Chief Brooks."

The two men maintained a challenging stare before releasing their grips.

"Cassie, may I use the restroom?" Daniel asked, walking toward the door. He then added, no doubt for Brooks's benefit, "I know the way."

"What, may I ask, is he doing here?" Brooks hissed his rebuke after the door closed.

"I might ask you the same thing." I tried the defiant approach.

"Lu called me because you weren't answering your phone, and she was worried because you were out here *alone* with *two strange men*."

"Well, I was on my way in to call her when Daniel showed up."

"Out of the blue?" He looked at me suspiciously. "He just happened to drive all the way from Boston, a second time in under twenty-four hours, no less?"

Now was not the time to share details about Daniel's possible stopover at his buddy's cottage on the Cape.

"I didn't know he was coming." That part was true.

"So this is a personal visit?" he asked.

I looked away. "Not exactly."

"And thus, I repeat my question. Why is he here, Cassie?"

"Oh, all right." I gave him my most withering look. "When I got home last night Cindy was here."

His eyes narrowed. "I thought she left town."

I'd also forgotten to pass on the information I'd learned from Sylvia Trask.

"Evidently she's been hiding out, and somehow she heard that I'd been asking about her."

"And who would have relayed such a message to her?" he asked.

"I don't know." It was a lie to protect Cindy and Sylvia, but I also didn't want to give Brooks any more reasons to be angry with me. "But that's not relevant."

"For your information, we've been trying to locate Cindy on an unrelated matter. But it's good to know you're the one determining what's germane to Whale Rock police investigations these days."

I brushed aside the affront. "She was able to identify the red bird. It's the mascot for Temple University."

"I see. And instead of calling me with that crucial information—?" He looked pointedly toward the house.

"I did call you. I phoned your home number and your cell phone and left two messages."

He pulled his phone from a front jacket pocket to verify. "That was at six this morning. Didn't you think I might be sleeping? You couldn't have waited another hour or two before bringing in the big guns." He practically spit out those last two words.

"When you didn't answer or return my calls, I thought you were—" I paused, assuming he'd grasp the inference.

He tilted his head. *Was he really going to make me say it?*

I lowered my voice to a whisper. "I thought you were mad at me about last night and probably avoiding me."

He shook his head disdainfully. "You sure do rebound quickly, though, don't you?"

I decided to ignore the unkindness and give his bruised ego the benefit of the doubt.

"Look, I needed to get somebody working on this lead. You were not available. Besides, it was your suggestion that we consult with the FBI again."

"I suggested *I* consult with them. You are not supposed to be involved in any type of investigation. And, lest you forgot, you agreed never to withhold any information from me. It was a clearly stated provision of my reopening the case." He lowered his voice. "However, our little deal seems to have conveniently slipped your mind."

"I wasn't going to keep this from you, and I didn't see the harm in contacting Daniel. You said it yourself: the FBI has the resources. Isn't that why you have them conducting DNA testing on the ball cap?"

Brooks didn't have the chance to respond because Daniel's footfalls could be heard crossing the creaky kitchen floorboards.

"I should be going," Daniel said when he came back out to the porch. "I hope to have some answers to you soon."

"Actually, call Chief Kincaid the minute you know anything. He's the one you should be dealing with on this case, not me." I concentrated on petting Whistler, to avoid looking at Daniel. "I only called you because Cindy appeared at my door, and you told me I could call any time, day or night, with information. I probably should have waited to pass on the details to the chief so he could have contacted you in an official capacity."

There: that should set things right again with Brooks.

When I finally brought my gaze up, it was to Daniel's wounded eyes. "Whatever you say, *Ms. Mitchell*."

*Touché.*

Daniel turned to Brooks. "I guess you'll be hearing from me in a couple days."

"I'd appreciate it." Brooks sent me a self-satisfied smirk while patting Daniel on the back and guided him away from the porch. "I'll walk you to your car."

The two men spoke for several moments and then got into their respective vehicles and drove away without either one giving even so much as a farewell glance in my direction. The message was clear. I was officially out of all loops, personal as well as investigative.

I trudged wearily back into the house only to face the overpowering force of my great-grandparents' sweet aromatic communiqué.

"Which one would you have me choose?" I shouted. Then I withdrew from the cupboard a giant bayberry-scented candle, usually reserved for the Christmas holiday centerpiece. I lit it in hopes of masking the scented message from my ancestors. "I'm begging you for a little peace today."

I reached for the phone to call Lu. I'd relinquish my role in the missing Ashley-Vince puzzle for a day or two while the dust settled. In the meantime, I had the distraction of the new mystery that had presented itself in the way of one J. Aaron Welkman.

\* \* \*

"Montana?" That was where Michael Bernard had instructed Lu to ship the paintings.

"Bozeman, to be specific," she added.

"I've never heard of it. What's in Bozeman?" I flipped open my laptop to begin a Google search and staring back at me was that same photo of Ashley and Vince in the cemetery, which I promptly closed while cursing Percy under my breath.

"Evidently, J. Aaron Welkman."

"That is a very long way to travel to see a small-town art show." When she didn't respond, I thought to add, "Nothing against your ability to draw people in."

"No offense taken."

"Can you give me the exact address?"

"Five-five-five Industrial Parkway, Building eleven."

My heart sank as I wrote down the information. "Is there a name of a company?"

"No. I'm to send the shipment in care of J. A. Welkman."

"A storage facility."

"I certainly hope it's climate controlled," Lu added, always keeping the integrity of the paintings at the forefront.

If the paintings in fact made it to Bozeman, I sensed they would never again see the light of day.

"Bozeman. Fourth largest city in Montana. Beautiful surrounding mountains and scenery." I perused the Wikipedia listing of notable residents. "Well, what do you know? J. Aaron Welkman, renowned photojournalist."

"At least you have some backup that he is who he says he is. What was he like?"

"Um, to begin with, he's blind."

"I'm sorry?"

"You heard right. The man can't see. Or rather, he is in the process of losing his sight."

"That explains why he didn't attend the exhibit. Did he tell you why he's interested in your work?"

"He said the paintings were a gift for someone with fond memories of the Cape."

"Do you believe him?"

"I'm not sure what to believe at this point."

"'*Curiouser and curiouser*,'" Lu mumbled.

"Yes, but do I want to go down this particular rabbit hole?"

"Your initial instincts might be right, Cassie. I'm also starting to get the feeling there's more to this than a case of an eccentric art collector. His assistant, Michael, was quizzing me about the paintings we'd already sold."

"In what way?"

"He wanted to know who the buyers were."

"Did he offer any kind of reaction when you told him?"

"I *did not* give him those details." Lu took umbrage at the suggestion. "I have my clients and a reputation to protect. The sale of art is a private matter. If the buyers wish to share, that's up to them."

I was reminded of Brooks's insistence he'd purchased only the harbor scene painting. "Did Brooks buy just the one painting last night?"

"He bought one for himself and one as a gift. But you didn't hear that from me." *So much for protecting the buyers.*

A gift? For who? For his father, who had a great love of Whale Rock Harbor? I hoped it wasn't for Zoe; that would be a slippery slope.

"Your handsome Agent Benjamin was all set to buy a painting of the *Queen Jacqueline* until a call came in on his cell and he departed quickly. But not to worry, I set it aside in case he comes back."

Highly unlikely, after the shabby treatment I'd dished out earlier.

"So, what are you going to do about your prospective buyer?" Lu asked.

"I'll have to come up with a new plan."

"Maybe Brooks could offer some help?" Lu's suggestion sounded innocent, but who knew what she and Chuckles discussed. Their friendship was over three decades strong.

"He's a busy man. I don't want to involve him just yet." Maybe never, if he stayed mad at me.

"Edgar Faust called me this morning, begging for a peek at anything else you might be working on. He and Jimmy are genuinely interested in your talent."

"That was a very touching gesture, not to mention generous. Those were the three most expensive pieces Jimmy purchased for Edgar."

"Don't be fooled by who wrote the check."

"I'm not following."

"Without Edgar, Jimmy would be as poor as a church mouse. In fact, he was bussing tables down in West Palm Beach when Edgar stepped in and rescued him from poverty twenty years ago. But Edgar didn't want anyone judging Jimmy as a gold digger, so he created, and has continued to perpetuate, the illusion that Jimmy abandoned a posh Palm Beach lifestyle for the sake of love."

"What would it matter?"

"To you or to me? Not a whit. But there are plenty of snobs in this world, especially the world into which Edgar was born."

"Why are you telling me this if it's not for public knowledge?"

"It's not really a secret anymore. These days, anyone with an interest and internet access could find out. Besides, most everyone in Edgar's circle already knows about Jimmy's meager beginnings, but he's so charming and fun and good to Edgar, people just play along and accept the story. I would even go so far as to suggest that anyone who ever knew the truth, including Edgar and Jimmy themselves, have probably forgotten all about it by this point."

"It makes me like them even more."

"Oh, I almost forgot. Edgar mentioned something to me about wishing to return some Mitchell family correspondence he'd recently come across in his files."

"I didn't give him anything." The only correspondence I had was the letter Ambrose gave to Granny Fi when he shipped off to the Navy. "Where could they have come from?"

"I'd imagine your sister."

"Zoe?" I was incredulous. What correspondence could've been in her possession that I didn't know about? Add one more sisterly secret to the heap guarded closely by Zoe.

"Come now, Cassie, you're not the only descendent of the infamous Percy and Celeste Mitchell. Edgar talked to Zoe too."

"When did she tell you this?"

"She didn't. Edgar mentioned it to me back when his book was published."

I was still trying to figure out how Zoe came to have any Mitchell family letters without my knowledge, when Lu added, "Look, you need to cut Zoe a break."

This only served to inflame my resentment.

"My sister tells me nothing and has an impenetrable fortress of friends protecting her secrets. No matter how much digging I do, instead of coming closer to the truth, I end up more confused."

"'*Stop digging and climb higher. You don't have to climb too far up the mountain to get a clearer view.*'"

"I didn't expect you to get all philosophical on me." Although I had to smile. Lu was quoting another of Granny Fi's gems. As a kid, Lu spent more time at our house than her own and had often heard Fiona spouting her sage counsel.

"Maybe Zoe confided something to Edgar when he was interviewing her for the article. You should ask him."

"That was years ago, and how many articles since written? He'd have to have an excellent memory."

"He does. And I know he keeps impeccable records and never tosses out a shred of his notes or research. According to Jimmy, he keeps all his notebooks in a vault. What do you have to lose?"

Nothing, except for time. *And right now, time was not a luxury I had.* It's what Vince had said to Ashley not long before they disappeared. However, I would make the time to set up a meeting with Edgar to at least retrieve the letters I hadn't known existed. Perhaps they would somehow open up a new door to understanding the Mitchell family legacy.

"All right. I'll do a little climbing." I was still scanning the Wikipedia entry about Bozeman when something grabbed my attention. "Speaking of climbing . . ."

"What's that?"

"Nothing. I think I'd better see what more I can find out about our prospective buyer and his sidekick."

"Keep me apprised." Lu said and rang off.

~

Eighty years ago
Christmas Eve ~ eleven days after the fire at Battersea Bluffs

Less than three months after Ambrose shipped off for the Navy, triple tragedy struck the Mitchell family in the form of his and his parents' deaths. Fiona Patrick coasted about in a haze of private grief while rumors and allegations spun amok in Whale Rock. Working in her parents' market, Fi was privy to every aspect of small-town chin wagging, especially the whisperings about the stranger who'd traveled from England to exact his revenge on Percy and Celeste. Now she understood why Ambrose's mother had taken the oath seriously, fearing—quite rightly—she might be bidding a final farewell to her last remaining son the day he left.

Fiona walked the three miles from town to Battersea Bluffs. The tire had fallen off the rusty old bike Mrs. Mitchell had lent her the last time. She could have asked for a ride, but then she would have had to offer an explanation. How could she explain the need to mourn the death of the husband she would never have? The father whom this baby she was carrying would never know? The in-laws who would never have the chance to spoil their grandchild? The holidays they would never share? She could make herself crazy listing all she had lost when that house was set aflame. She hadn't even known at the time that Ambrose had been killed. The official documents made it to Whale Rock a few days later, and she'd lived with the awful truth for a week now. But the messenger who delivered the cable on the day of the fire said Percy had read the news in his presence and reacted with deep anguish. So he'd died knowing his last remaining son had been killed— but not that Ambrose had left behind a child. Would it have made any difference?

When she reached the top of Lavender Hill, Fiona was out of breath. A coyote was digging at something in the rubble. She tossed a rock in the vicinity of the wild animal to shoo it away. The animal stopped its rooting, stared benignly as she approached and then reluctantly trotted off. She rested on the rock wall that meandered through the estate. When the stones were originally laid, there was probably some sense to their placement, but now it seemed incongruous to the property. Fiona admired the charred but still proud framework of the house. She truly was a grand dame, her magnificent bones still standing in defiance to the fire. Of course, nearly everything inside had been ruined by smoke. She walked around this house of ashes and sniffed the air, her nostrils filling with a strange scent.

A brief flicker of sun through gray clouds glinted off a shiny object near the foundation. She pushed aside debris to uncover a tin box. After brushing away the ashes, Fiona pried it open and quickly flipped through the contents. They were Mrs. Mitchell's letters, and Fiona knew she'd keep the tin, knew she would read the letters.

A white speck landed on her cheek, and soon the flakes became larger and fell faster. The first snow of the winter. It didn't seem cold enough, but maybe she was just numb. She tucked the tin box under her arm and, with one last solemn glance about the ruin, took her leave. On the long walk back to town, Fiona contemplated the striking contrast to just weeks ago, when she'd confided her news to Mrs. Mitchell. She had been filled with such optimism that day.

Though she'd managed to keep her pregnancy a secret thus far, it couldn't go on much longer. She reckoned she had another three months at best to plan and prepare. Her hope was that her parents would happily accept the baby as Mrs. Mitchell had. But what if they didn't? More than her parents' wrath, she feared the consequence of being sent away from Whale Rock.

Fiona withdrew her hand from her pocket to admire the lovely emerald ring. Besides the child she was carrying, it was all that remained of the man she loved. She vowed to keep them both close to her always.

# 26

Two days after the exhibit

C hatham was a charming harbor village with beautiful ocean views, delightful shops, and unequalled dining to attract the summer crowds. However, after the tourists and seasonal residents departed in the fall, Chatham resembled a ghost town. But Edgar and Jimmy loved the serenity of the off season, and after indulging in the party atmosphere between the obligatory days christened Memorial and Labor, they tucked in like clams. Of course, their home was no ordinary clamshell.

Jimmy met me at the front door of Alcyone.

"Welcome to our little acre of paradise." He leaned in for a peck on both cheeks.

From the front entrance, I could see through the expansive open living space, with its cathedral ceilings, to the wall of windows along the back of the house and the unobstructed views.

"This is breathtaking."

"Come and see." Jimmy guided me to view the immaculately manicured lawn gradually sloping down from the large terrace, like green velvet flowing into a private little cove and spilling into the ocean beyond. There was a barrier island in the distance that served to shelter the cove during angrier weather.

"Edgar doesn't need paintings of the sea. He *has* the sea." I was referring to Jimmy's comment about Edgar's description of Percy's Bluffs.

"Ah, yes, this personifies tranquility." I turned toward Edgar's voice. "As the pendulum swings in the opposite direction, Percy's Bluffs has a certain passion that infatuates the spirit. It is the compelling nature that you've captured in your paintings. Percy saw it. That's why he chose the spot to build his home."

"Still, there's nothing wrong with peace and calm."

Edgar raised his brows to Jimmy. "Did you already tell her?"

"I most certainly did not," he answered in feigned offense. "This is one intuitive lady."

"Tell me what?" I asked.

"How we came upon Alcyone for the name of our home. But let's go to the sunroom, where it's bright and cozy. We can talk in there while Jimmy creates his magic in the kitchen."

"Just a few finishing touches," said Jimmy as he sashayed through one archway, and we ambled under another into what I would consider the perfect room. It was spacious and open, yet cozy and bright from the natural light, fresh white woodwork, clean colors, and cheery decor. There was, of course, the same stunning ocean view from southern-facing windows and French doors out to the terrace. But the scene continued through tall westward windows as well. On winter afternoons, this would be where I'd want to curl up with a book, basking in the warmth from those west-facing windows, a crackling fire alight in the large corner hearth, beautifully finished with exotic sea creature tiles.

I turned to see another dramatic feature; on either side of the archway were floor-to-ceiling bookshelves filled with leather-bound volumes. And there was one of those cool library ladders on gliders I'd always thought to put in my own library at home, but had never gotten around to it, mostly due to lack of funds. The single remaining wall was decorated with an exquisite piece of art portraying a magnificent winged woman painted against a starlit night sky, the wind whirling about her being as she hovered above an inky sea.

"I would never leave this room." I inhaled deeply. The scent was fresh, like the sea.

"When Jimmy's not sleeping or in the kitchen, he can be found in here. Please." Edgar indicated one of the plump inviting sofas for me and he took the nearest side chair. "I need a straight back. Disc problems, I'm afraid."

"Too much time bent over a keyboard?"

He offered a rueful smile.

"You were going to tell me about Alcyone." I prompted.

"I imagine you've heard of halcyon days?"

"Restful, untroubled times?" How I longed for those.

"That's right. Well, the ancient Greeks believed the halcyon birds were responsible for bringing us those days of peace and calm. But do you know how those birds came to be?"

I shook my head.

"According to Greek mythology, Alcyone, daughter of the god of the winds, was the devoted wife of Ceyx, son of the morning star. They had a blissful life together until tragedy struck when Ceyx set off on a sailing venture to consult Apollo, god of prophecy. Having spent her childhood watching storm clouds and lightning dance around her father's palace, Alcyone was fully aware of the power of the wind and feared something terrible would happen to Ceyx. Her dread was not without merit, for a violent storm destroyed her beloved's ship, drowning all aboard. When her husband did not return, Alcyone asked the gods for a dream to tell her what had happened. They granted her plea by sending the dead Ceyx to tell her the truth. She awoke grief-stricken and wandered to the shore, where she looked out upon the gentle waves and saw Ceyx's dead body floating homeward. Alcyone threw herself into the sea to go to her husband, and upon seeing her deep anguish, the gods breathed life into both her and Ceyx again and gave them wings. The couple was turned into halcyon birds flying happily across the sky, a symbol of the unbreakable bonds of love."

My breath caught at the familiarity of the story. From what I'd learned from Lu, I could see how Jimmy and Edgar would be inspired by the symbolism of Alcyone and Ceyx. However, to my mind the Greek allegory was a much more striking parallel to what happened to my great-grandparents: Percy's pain and sorrow had been so strong and compelling that he'd hurled himself and his soul mate over the cliffs and into the sea, only to rise again and live on as the protective spirits of my home. I wondered if Edgar had made a similar connection.

"So that's Alcyone." I gazed up at the painting of the winged woman.

"Edgar is my Alcyone." Jimmy had returned and affectionately placed his hands on the other man's shoulders. "He leapt into the ocean to save me when I was drowning."

"Love triumphs over tragedy." He reached up to pat Jimmy's hand, giving me my answer. He preferred Jimmy's interpretation.

It was a concept I wanted to believe, but sadly—at least within the last few generations of the Mitchell family—tragedy had been the victor. First Percy and Celeste, followed by Fiona and Ambrose, then Mama and Papa, recently Ethan and me. There was a reason the Mitchell lifeline was teetering on extinction. The cycle of misfortune needed to be shattered.

Edgar broke through my lugubrious reflections. "Jimmy has a deep fascination with Greek mythology."

"It's those Greek gods who so beguile me." Jimmy winked suggestively. "Anyone hungry?"

*  *  *

After a lunch that could only be described as scrumptious, Edgar and I retired to his study, located on the opposite side of the house. The views still amazed; however, this room was darker, more masculine with its leather chairs and dark hickory wainscoting. I could envision immediately where my paintings should make their home, specifically the unadorned area above the fireplace, which could handle the drama of Percy's Bluffs. Edgar's desk backed against the opposing wall, giving him the advantage of the views, the fireplace, and presumably my paintings.

"So, what do you think?"

"It suits you."

"My hiding place from the world." He made a theatrical swirl with his raised arms. "Jimmy thinks it a dreary room."

"Inspiring, not dreary. The perfect atmosphere for writing. When I first stepped into this room, I knew my paintings belonged here. I'm honored you would want my work for your"—"man cave" was both an inaccurate and an indelicate description for the retreat of such a cultured and dignified man—"exquisite sanctuary."

"These walls have remained spartan far too long. But we never

243

found anything that worked, until now. Come back again after they've been hung. We'll drink a toast to Percy."

"Speaking of which, would you mind if I took a look at those letters?"

"Of course. Please sit by the fire, where it's toasty. I'll just get my files." He shuffled off to a built-in cabinet as my anxiety mounted over what would be learned from those ancient missives.

"Here we are." The leather creaked as he sank into the armchair next to mine. He settled his glasses onto the edge of his nose and began to flip through papers. "These are the letters your sister sent to me."

*So Lu was right.* I took the small pile of envelopes he held out to me and touched them reverently before setting them on the side table.

"I hadn't been aware she helped with the article." I hoped my tone didn't betray my bitterness.

"Oh yes. I interviewed Zoe by phone on several occasions. I even have a notebook dedicated to our conversations."

I may have been cross with Zoe for keeping these from me, but I was saying a silent thank-you to Lu for making the suggestion to visit Edgar.

"Could I see it? Maybe take it with me?"

Edgar squinted at me over his glasses in a way that made me squirm. Evidently, I had presumed too much.

"I never allow my annotations to leave this sanctum." His voice was stern.

"I didn't mean to be so bold."

His expression softened to kindness again. "But stay if you like. You are welcome to peruse any of the notes and research pertaining to your home."

"Could I come back in a week or so?" I suggested, knowing the lengthy to-do list I had before Aaron returned from Boston.

""Of course. Shall we go find Jimmy to say goodbye?"

"Before I go, I'd like to ask you something." I took a deep breath before leaping into the mire. "From all the research you've gathered and the people with whom you've spoken . . ."

"Yes. Go on." Edgar leaned forward and offered an encouraging smile.

"Do you believe my home is haunted?"

He fixed a serious gaze first at me and then into the fireplace flames. "Wouldn't you be the best person to answer that question?"

"I do know the answer."

He appeared startled.

"I'm curious why, in the many hours we spoke, you never asked the question of me."

He sat pensively before responding. "I felt it would be intrusive. I worried the question might disturb you, so I danced around the subject, making subtle innuendos and waiting patiently for you to offer your own insight."

I probably wouldn't have admitted it for fear of being quoted in the book and looked upon by everyone in Whale Rock as *that crazy Mitchell girl*. "I would still like to hear your thoughts."

He removed his glasses and rubbed the bridge of his nose. "I found your great-grandparents' story to be fascinating, suggestive of a Greek tragedy. In fact, more like Alcyone and Ceyx than any other true life story I've heard about."

*So he had grasped the significance after all.*

"I first heard the tale of Percy and Celeste at a Halloween party many years ago. We were talking of Cape Cod ghosts, and someone mentioned Battersea Bluffs. That's when I began to gather research for my book. I tried to interview your grandmother shortly before she passed, but she'd have nothing to do with it."

I did not find this to be a surprising revelation. Granny Fi was very protective of the Mitchell family secrets.

"It seems you did well without her input." I pointed to the framed award. "And thanks to you, the Mitchell family will never lose their place in the annals of Whale Rock lore."

Edgar dipped his head, taking it as a compliment. He paused reflectively before asking, "Have you read it lately? The chapter about Battersea Bluffs?"

I shook my head. "Actually, not for many years."

I'd read it when it was first published, then had filed it away. I knew the story well enough. Didn't I live it every day?

"You might want to do so."

"I will. But you haven't answered my question."

"I think you will discover the answer in what I wrote. We'll talk more when you come back."

It was the best I was going to get today, so I tucked the packet of letters inside my backpack.

"By the way, I found the journal entries to be as enlightening as the correspondence," Edgar said. "I apologize for not returning those to you years ago, but I'd quite forgotten I had them until just last week."

*Journal entries? What gold mine had I stumbled into?*

\* \* \*

I was so eager to read the documents Edgar had given me that, after saying my goodbyes, I found a small diner, empty save for a waitress playing solitaire and the cook who stood at the counter, reading the newspaper. I sat in a corner booth, and in the quiet privacy offered by the afternoon lull, I poured over the old-fashioned, cursive handwritten words on crinkled, yellowed pages.

~

October 22

Dearest Celeste,

I write to tell you of my sailing to America. The journey will not be easy, as I have been unwell. If the Lord is willing, the sea air might restore me. If not, my time in this world will not be long. But I must attempt to see you one last time before I die.

It's been bad blood between myself and Percy, and he may forbid you seeing me, I know. Still, I must try. If I am able, I will send word in advance of my arrival. It will be sometime in December. Until then.

Yours,
Robert

~

November 1

My dearest friend,

Forgive me for not writing often enough. Willie has been down with the fever, and Lottie's little Mick is a handful. Just like his grandfather that one is.

But no time today for idle news from home. I write to send you fair warning. There is talk that Robert Toomey is crossing the Atlantic to America. I know not of his intentions, but surely you would want to know and not be caught unawares if he were to show up at your door. My Michael says that Percy would shoot him on sight. So I pray you hide the bullets. I don't know what the prisons are like in America, but if they are at all like ours, I would not want to see our dear Percy locked up in one.

Your sister in friendship,
Mattie

On a sticky note attached to two other letters:

*These are dated the day my*
*great-grandparents were killed.—Z*

December 13

Dear Ambrose,

Your father and I are fit as fiddles. You remember how fond I always was of the Christmas holidays. This year will seem strange without you and your special Christmas grog, but we will try to make do. I'll be starting my baking soon now that my larder is full of butter, flour, and all the fine sugars. It's not nice of me to be making your mouth water, now is it?

I am hopeful your days are full of the adventure you were seeking. It gives a mother the greatest of pleasure knowing her son has found happiness. I had a visit a few weeks ago from your young Miss Patrick. I've not mentioned it sooner, as I knew she wanted to be the first to tell you the wonderful news. I was quite taken with Fiona and wanted to assure you that I approve of your choice. I also wished you to know that your father and I will watch over your bride-to-be and the baby, when it arrives in the spring. I selfishly hope the happy news will hasten your return to Whale Rock and your loving mother's arms. Of course, now I will have to share you, but I don't mind.

I am planning to tell your father this weekend. It's his birthday, and I can't think of a more special gift. I know you never took the curse of Robert Toomey seriously, but it was hard for your father to do otherwise after the deaths of Jerome and Edwin. The news of a grandchild on the way will uplift his spirits greatly, especially with you being so far away.

I will be inviting Fiona and her family for Christmas Eve, to begin a new tradition between our families. We will raise a glass to you and to your safe return.

With love always,<br>Mother

~

December 13

Dear Mattie,

I hope you and your dear ones are in good health, especially your Willie, who had the fever last time you wrote. Even though he's wedded, it's still a mother's healing hands a son finds most comforting. I suspect Lottie inherited your sweet nature and must be a fine mum. And I can envision our old Michael, the proudest grandpapa, following little Mick around like a guardian angel.

I have news of my own to share, although I fear the simple act of writing the words will make us vulnerable to the curse. But tell you I must, and it is not with an ounce of shame, our Ambrose has gone off and joined the Navy and left behind a local girl with child. The girl is called Fiona, and she wears an emerald promise ring my son gave her before he shipped off.

She swears he didn't know, and I believe her, for certainly my Ambrose would have stayed and made things right. She is clever and pretty and has a sweet disposition. She will make a good and true wife.

Indeed, Robert Toomey is coming to America. I've received a letter from him but have not yet told Percy, as I fear what he will do. I pray for an end to the hatred.

Mattie, a stranger approaches on foot. He limps. I must see what he wants and tell you of it later.

Another sticky note attached at the end:

*One could speculate the stranger was*
*Robert Toomey.—Z*

~

Included in the stack was an older letter from Celeste's mother, telling her of Robert Toomey's destruction of their fleet of boats. There was also an original newsprint article, written the day after the fire, in what was then known as the *Cape Cod Standard Times.*

The headline read: **Fire Brings More Devastation to Prominent Whale Rock Family ~ Percival Mitchell's Last Words: "I am not finished!"**

Having read it before, I almost dismissed the article but then noticed a second page I didn't recall having seen previously and which I now read with interest.

From page 1 . . . Rescue workers noted an oddly pleasant smell at the house, not the normal bitter odor of ash and debris. Some men said it smelled of vanilla, others claimed it was the smell of burning sugar or molasses. It was deduced that the odor originated from a pantry that had been stocked with sugars and other baking ingredients. Celeste Mitchell was a baker of renown, and with the holidays approaching she had received a large shipment days before the fire.

The Constable has posted a guard at Battersea Bluffs after unnamed persons were witnessed removing items from the property. One woman admitted to having taken just a small memento from the fire, as it was likely to be famous one day.

As of this printing, it has been learned that a gentleman visiting from England has claimed a relationship with Percy and Celeste Mitchell and will be questioned by police once he's dried out from a bender at Whale Rock Tavern. Lloyd Grant, proprietor, has told officials that the man all but confessed to setting the fire. Grant told us, "He kept mumbling over and over again, 'Lake of fire, lake of fire.'" In the Englishman's bible, a page marker opened to the book of Revelations, with these verses boldly underlined: 'And the devil who deceived them was thrown into the lake of fire and brimstone, where the beast and the false prophet are also; and they will be tormented day and night forever and ever. This is the second death, the lake of fire.'

Attached to this article was a yellowed piece of paper scribbled with some date notations, the first written boldly in ink: *E.M. & J.M. 30/06/1932.* This was followed with a barely legible pencil scratching: *A.M. 12/12/1937.*

My breath caught at the significance. *Was this the page marker from Robert Toomey's Bible mentioned in the article?* As far as I could tell, the handwriting matched that of the letter he sent to Celeste. The dates noted by Robert Toomey represented the deaths of Percy and Celeste's three sons, as if he'd been keeping track. I wondered, had anyone else ever pieced this together? Surely Granny Fi had. But had Zoe?

I opened a small manila envelope and found the journal entries of which Edgar had spoken. My stomach twisted upon seeing they were in Mama's handwriting. I was too shaken by my latest discovery to read these now, and feared facing what assuredly were the heartbreaking meditations of my mother. Quickly flipping through the pages, I discovered another sticky note with Zoe's handwriting.

Dear Edgar,

I've enjoyed our phone conversations and am glad I've been able to assist with your research. Here are the letters and journal pages I told you about. When my grandmother passed, I was sent a box of her personal effects, which included some correspondence that belonged to my great-grandmother. I've enclosed those items I thought might be helpful. Good luck in completing the book.

Sincerely,<br>Zoe Mitchell Young

At least now I knew how Zoe came to have these letters. But who had sent them to her in the first place? Was it Evelyn, who'd been so helpful when Granny Fi died? Had Mama's journal been among Granny Fi's personal effects? And where was the journal now?

But those questions would have to wait. I had more pressing matters to deal with, and I started by calling Wizards. Teddy wasn't working, but I persuaded the woman who answered to give me his cell number, and fortunately he accepted my invitation to drop by. It was a short drive to his marsh-facing cottage near First Encounter Beach in Eastham.

"Thanks for letting me intrude on your day off," I said when he answered my knock.

"It's cool." He opened the door to a neatly kept and surprisingly well-appointed abode.

"Nice place. I'm impressed."

"Between my mom and Jess?" He lifted his hands. "I have no say in the matter."

He motioned for me to sit. An early edition of *Moby Dick* was lying open and facedown on the coffee table.

"You said you needed to ask me something?" He casually placed a bookmark and set the novel aside.

"It's about Ashley and Vince, and I'll be frank. Something you said makes me think you knew them better than you let on."

He fidgeted uncomfortably but said nothing.

"Did you ever socialize with them outside of Wizards?"

"We may have hung out a few times." He shrugged nonchalantly. "We went sailing once. Not much else."

"You have a sailboat?" I don't know why I found it surprising.

251

He leaned back on the sofa and clasped his hands behind his neck. "We borrowed one."

"Did they ever say anything about their plans? Where they were headed when they left Whale Rock?"

"Only that they'd be leaving soon."

"That's it?"

He squirmed under my disbelieving gaze. "Jess asked Ashley where they were going."

"And?"

He shrugged again. "Ashley started to cry and said she couldn't talk about it. We just thought it was because she was upset about leaving. They really liked it here. They really liked you."

I felt a warmth deep within. "It was mutual. Then what?"

"Two days later, they disappeared."

"Remember telling me about Vince's money clip?"

He nodded.

"Do you think you could draw it from memory?"

"I can try."

I took a notepad from my backpack and ripped out a sheet of paper onto which he sketched an image. "It looked something like this."

I must have looked pleased. "So that's helpful?"

"You've provided a missing link of sorts." Or at least I hoped so. Teddy had just drawn a near duplicate of the "T" in the Temple University logo, which matched the T-shirt with the Temple owl Cindy found in Ashley and Vince's room. If Aaron Welkman's signet ring also bore a Temple "T," there was more than coincidence at work here.

Backing out of the driveway, I noticed Teddy's gray Jeep, which sparked a memory. The friend who'd delivered Percy and Celeste's portraits had been driving a gray Jeep, and it wouldn't be a leap to assume it had been Teddy. No doubt he *had* been closer to Vince and Ashley than he was admitting. But why? What more was he hiding?

# 27

Forty days following the disappearance

Two days had passed since Daniel and Brooks gave me the collective brush-off. I'd heard nothing since then from either of the men who hovered uncertainly in my life. It was clear that I would have to assume the role of the grown-up. What other choice did I have if there were to be some resolutions before Wednesday's return of Misters Welkman and Bernard?

I absently spun my phone on the kitchen table, pondering who to call first. For the sake of peace here in The Rock, Brooks won the silent debate. However, according to the clerk who answered the station phone, the chief was tending to an official police incident, and would I like his voicemail? I left a vague message with a couple of dangling carrots to pique his interest.

Then I made the uncomfortable call to Daniel. I was sent straight to voicemail, but this time I left no message, thinking he might be more intrigued by the missed call. The strategy worked because within two minutes he phoned back.

"Someone recognized them," he said without even a hello. But I was too excited to care.

"Who did? Where was this?"

"Wait a minute. Shouldn't I be taking this through the proper channels?" Now he was being just plain mean. "I wouldn't want to challenge the authority of your mighty Chief Kincaid."

"I get it. You're angry, and not without good reason."

"I only wish to keep this investigation within *official* boundaries."

I was trying mightily to control my irritation. "Look, I was in an awkward spot. By all rights, I should have taken the information to Brooks first, but I was blindsided by my eagerness to figure out what happened to Ashley and Vince."

"I believe you've been blindsided all right, but by something else. Strike that—*someone* else. How about explaining what's going on between you and good ol' Chuckles?"

I was stunned by the insinuation. What had Brooks led him to believe? Or had Daniel's finely honed instincts picked up on some unconscious pull between Brooks and me? And where on earth had Daniel found out about Brooks's nickname? Had I let it slip?

I shook my head free of all the question marks dancing the cha-cha-cha in my brain. Now was not the time to venture into the complexities of my friendship with Brooks, so I lobbed back an indignant reply.

"Have we not evolved to the point where a friendship between a man and a woman can be accepted without inference of something more intimate going on?"

This was met with silence, which I hoped was from shame.

"Anyway, I called to let you know that while I understand if you can't share with *me* any of the information *you've* discovered, *I've* come across some details that might be of interest to this investigation."

"I'm listening."

"Do you remember the black Navigator you passed coming up my drive the other day?"

"The art collector interested in your work?"

"That's right." I paused to consider how much I should tell him. "I think he's in some way associated with our missing friends."

"What drew you to this theory?" I was trying to gauge the subtle change in his voice. Was he mocking me or was there a genuine interest?

"I've learned of a connection difficult to explain away as a fluke."

"You're going to have to give me more." Not mocking me, but definitely skeptical.

I lowered my voice. "I don't feel comfortable talking about this on the phone."

I could hear the tapping of a pen on his desk. He was at least thinking it over. Finally he asked, "So, where do you feel comfortable talking about it?"

I had him hooked. He was taking an evening flight out of Boston, so we chose to meet at the Sagamore Inn, a place halfway between the airport and Whale Rock. I didn't mind the drive. For one thing, it got me out of the house and away from the confusing signals Percy and Celeste had been bombarding me with of late. Their scent signals had been hard to decipher lately, and they'd practically hijacked my laptop. I also preferred to eliminate the possibility of Brooks seeing us together. Speaking of whom, a call came in from none other on the drive to my rendezvous with Daniel. I hit the "Speaker" button.

"So what's this about a ring?" Apparently today was not a day for good manners.

"And hello to you too."

"Look, I'm busy. Do you have something for me or not?"

"J. Aaron Welkman was wearing a signet ring."

"Who is J. Aaron Welkman?" That's right. I hadn't told Daniel or Brooks the name of my prospective buyer. And evidently Lu hadn't mentioned it to Brooks either.

"He's the man who wants to purchase my collection. Anyhow, he was wearing a signet ring, and although I only got a quick look, there was something familiar about it."

"I'm not following."

"After Cindy identified the red bird as the mascot for Temple University, I did some online digging, and that's when it came to me that this buyer's signet ring may have had the same 'T' in the Temple emblem used on their rings."

"And where had you seen it before?"

"Remember Teddy mentioning that Vince carried a money clip

with an unusual 'T'? Well, I stopped by his place yesterday, and he drew it from memory. The image is pretty darn close to the Temple emblem."

He was quiet a moment, I hoped not because I'd overstepped by contacting Teddy directly. Then he asked, "So you think there's a connection?"

"There has to be."

"How do you reconcile the fact that Agent Benjamin has not turned up the names of Ashley and Vince Jacobson in any association with Temple?" So Brooks had been conferring with Daniel on the case, even if he wasn't up to date on the latest findings. I found myself in the middle of a precarious bridge linking the two investigations and the men in charge, and it was not a comfortable spot.

"Is it possible the names we knew them by were aliases?" I decided to lay another card on the table. "I think Welkman is related, especially given the Temple connection. And the 'J' in J. Aaron Welkman's name is for 'Jacob.' Jacobson." I let that sink in for a moment.

"That's the link? It's a stretch, Cassie." He blew out a breath. "But still worth pursuing. Frequently, when criminals devise false identities, they like to hold onto a personal connection."

"Criminals?" I found the suggestion offensive. "How could you even think of them as criminals?"

"Calm down. There are a multitude of reasons people seek out new identities. If your friends went down that road, we can't eliminate the possibility they were in some kind of trouble. I'll get on it after I finish up here."

"Thank you for hanging in there with me, Brooks." I could hear a siren blaring on his end, followed by squealing tires. "Where are you?"

"Orleans."

I swallowed hard. "Cindy?"

"Yep. Gotta go."

What had Cindy done to bring upon herself the hot pursuit of the WRPD? Her trapped-animal reaction to my question about her financial stability came to mind, and I hated thinking her recent windfall was from ill-gotten means.

I had an uneasy feeling as I pulled into the parking lot of the Sagamore Inn a few minutes later. Daniel was sitting at a window table, perusing the menu. He stood and pulled out the chair next to him.

"Have you been waiting long?"

"Five minutes. I've got an hour. Might as well order dinner, airplane food being what it is these days. You hungry?"

I shook my head. My stomach was too knotted up to eat.

He signaled for the waitress.

"What can I get for you folks?" Dottie, her name tag revealed, was a skinny woman with leathery skin and the gravelly voice of a heavy smoker. She wore the bored look of someone who'd been waiting tables at the Sagamore Inn since its doors opened.

"Should I go with the lasagna or Shirley's Famous Pot Roast?" asked Daniel.

"You can't go wrong with either one. Our lasagna recipe was Nonna Bianco's. She opened the place back in the 1930s." I revised my estimation of Dottie's tenure. She couldn't be quite that old.

"In that case, I'll try the lasagna. And a glass of Chianti."

Dottie jotted the order on an old-fashioned cashier tablet then looked expectantly at me.

"Just a ginger ale, please."

Her crinkled smile faded with the realization of a diminished tip. "I'll be right back with your drinks."

"So who was it that recognized Ashley and Vince?" I asked after Dottie deposited our beverages, Daniel's salad, and a basket of warm bread.

Daniel's mood had mellowed since our phone conversation, and he was more forthcoming. "The owner and some of the staff at a place called Johnny Brenda's in the Fish Town area of Philly, not far from Temple."

"Fish Town! That's it." I slapped the table. "That's where their apartment was. Maybe it will help narrow the search for student apartments located near a fire station."

"Still a big area. But." He forked up a bite of salad and chewed it slowly, sipped from his wine glass, then dabbed the napkin to his lips.

This attempt to heighten the suspense was mildly annoying.

"You were saying?" I smiled innocently.

"Oh yes. The faces were recognized with no problem, but the names they were remembered by were not Ashley and Vince Jacobson." He buttered a piece of an Italian roll and tucked it into his mouth.

"What were the names?" I asked before he had a chance to cram in another bite.

"There's a difference of opinion among the wait staff. Laura, Lori, or Lauren for her and for him the possibilities were Jay or JJ."

*Jay. Short for Jacob, maybe?*

"Any last name?"

"Working on it. There's not a lot to go on. But we're still circulating the photos around the university." He pushed his salad plate away.

"Did you learn anything else?"

"The last time they were at Johnny Brenda's, they both got really drunk, which was apparently out of character. Their waiter overheard part of the conversation and said "Jay" seemed especially distraught."

"Did he remember what they said?"

Daniel retrieved a notebook from his pocket and flipped through the pages until he found the notation. "Jay repeated more than once to Laura, 'All that work. Up in smoke. Nobody will ever believe us now.' And Laura said . . ."

"Here's your lasagna, nice and hot." The dish was placed unceremoniously before Daniel, and Dottie asked, "Can I get you folks anything else?"

"I've changed my mind." With mouth-watering aromas drifting from the kitchen, my own appetite had returned. "Could I have an order of eggplant parm?"

"Of course, hon." Dottie's wrinkly face beamed at the prospect of a growing gratuity. After she left, I nudged Daniel, "You were about to tell me what Ashley—"

"Laura," Daniel corrected.

"You were about to tell me what she was overheard saying."

"That's right." He flipped the notebook closed and stared purposefully at me before repeating the quote. "She said, '*Out of the ashes, the phoenix will rise.*'"

I flushed hot at the memory of Daniel's fingers tracing the outline of my tattoo. And his wickedly sensual smile was transparent enough for me to know he was also remembering the first time we made love.

"I keep thinking to myself, now where have I heard that before?" He sucked his bottom lip suggestively.

A strong yearning arose within me, and I found myself wishing Daniel was not bound for Logan Airport. I stopped myself short of suggesting he take a later flight, which was just as well since my desire quickly fizzled when he next spoke.

"So what have you dug up about Aaron Welkman that makes you believe there's a connection between him and our missing persons?" he asked casually, returning his attention to the lasagna as Dottie set the steaming eggplant dish before me. But I was suddenly nauseous. I was positive I'd never shared the identity of the art buyer with Daniel. So how did he come to know the name Aaron Welkman?

"Something wrong, hon?" the waitress asked. "You don't look so hot."

"I'm fine." And not wanting Daniel to become aware of his gaffe, I began to eat. "Mmm. Delicious." I decided to plow forward with my information. "I think Aaron Welkman wears a Temple University signet ring. And I remembered something Ashley mentioned one day."

Daniel was chewing again and lifted his eyebrows in question.

"Thinking back on it now, it was probably something they hadn't intended to share, since Vince redirected the conversation."

"What did she say?"

"She was bragging about Vince being a triple legacy at the college they'd both attended." There was no reaction, so I plodded on. "So I wondered if this Aaron Welkman and Vince might be related."

He gave me an odd look before parroting Brooks's initial response earlier. "Because *maybe* they both went to Temple? That would be a real stretch, Cassie."

"But Aaron's first name is Jacob."

"So?" He wasn't usually slow on the uptake.

"Jacob. Jacobson. If they were using aliases, they might have chosen names with a—"

"Another code?" Daniel jumped in before I could finish. "That's pushing it, don't you think?" His smile was mocking and his attitude just short of insulting. His insinuation about nothing materializing from the knotted rope hit a nerve and had me thinking how glad I was the jerk had a plane to catch.

"Had you let me complete my sentence, I was about to suggest the possibility they chose aliases that had an association with something of a personal nature, like their families."

There was a subtle eye roll before he emptied his wine glass, pulled out his wallet, and withdrew some bills. "My treat. I've got to run. But you stay and finish."

"You don't think it's at least worth checking into? If there are other Welkmans on the Temple Alumni list, maybe they fit Ashley and Vince's descriptions?"

He frowned as he stood, but said, "Sure, why not? I'll have someone take a look. Still, I wouldn't get your hopes up. The Temple connection, *if* it proves to be a valid scenario, could be purely coincidental."

Was this not the man who less than a month ago told me that he did not believe in coincidences? That every variable, even the most improbable, must still be examined?

"You'll let me know what you find out?" I asked as he began to walk away.

"Who should I call first? You? Or Chuckles?" He said over his shoulder, but didn't wait for an answer.

Daniel was playing a role, I had no doubt. I watched him cross the parking lot, phone to his ear. He looked worried.

\* \* \*

"You've been quiet lately," my sister said. I should have ignored the call.

"It's been a bit busy on this end." Not wanting to get into the details of the investigation or what was going on with Aaron Welkman, I picked a much safer topic. "Steve Morrison finished work on the carriage house, and the first tenant arrives in two weeks."

"You don't sound very excited."

"There's still a lot to do to get it ready. I'm sure he'd like to have sheets and towels and dishes."

"So it's a man?" The mother-hen voice. "What's he like?"

"I haven't met him yet."

"Have you at least had Brooks conduct a background check?"

"I don't think it's necessary."

"You are far too trusting. Haven't you learned anything from your most recent fiasco?"

Amazingly, I resisted the snappy comeback dancing on the tip of my tongue and offered a brief bio of my new tenant. Though I was truly surprised Lu hadn't already told Zoe everything about him, since she's the one who found him.

"He's an illustrator for children's books, with a January deadline. He's booked through the end of the year and will be going back and forth between here and Rhode Island, where he lives with his wife and three teenage daughters. In addition to needing a quiet refuge for his work, I'm guessing he'll be delighting in a respite from his estrogen-infused household. I think I'll be safe."

"Hmph." Zoe's murmur could have meant anything. "Nonetheless, you might not need the additional income, what with your new artistic success."

"I don't see why I can't do both." I was actually looking forward to an influx of creative types taking up temporary residence in the carriage house. "I'd like to maintain a viable Plan B."

"So have you deposited that large check yet?"

I hadn't been able to gauge where Lu's loyalties rested now that I was a client, but suspecting the bonds of lifelong friendship would win out, I chose the more prudent route.

"Lu's waiting for all the sales to be finalized."

"Why the delay?"

"Don't worry. I'll repay your loan." First I had to pay Steve Morrison, but there would be enough to cover all my debts, even without Aaron Welkman. I would be starting clean and solvent again.

"I only wanted to share in your joy."

When it came to my sister, I had a constant internal tug-of-war between anger and shame. Anger at Zoe's ability to so easily assume the role of martyr when it suited her, and then embarrassment for hurting her feelings through defensive reflexes.

"Sorry. I'm just tired." It was the truth. I was exhausted from trying to weave into place all the unraveling threads to the mysteries consuming my world.

"It hasn't been a kind year, has it?"

"No." I exhaled the stale breath of fatigue. "It hasn't."

"But things are looking up, right? Especially with this new buyer?"

"He had some pressing business in Boston, but he's coming back out to Whale Rock on Wednesday."

"Do you have any reason to think it could fall through?"

"Only if he's discovered another unknown but up-and-coming artist in Boston." I made my voice playful to ease her concerns.

"That's unlikely."

"Don't you think it strange, though, that someone would want to buy up my entire collection?"

"Maybe. But a buyer is a buyer." *Denial.* It was always the easier route. However, that was my usual modus operandi, not hers.

Time to cast the lure. "Remember my telling you Edgar Faust was at the exhibit?"

"Vaguely."

"Did Lu mention that he bought three of my paintings?"

"No, I don't think she did." Displeasure was seeping into her tone. "Actually, I'm quite sure she didn't."

"Anyhow, Edgar and his partner invited me out to their home in Chatham."

"Why would they do that?" Her voice was sharp.

"They wanted to show me where they planned to hang the paintings. They selected three of The Bluffs, which is fitting. Did you know he won a literary award for the book he wrote?"

"No, I wasn't aware. Honey, I'm going to have to get going. I have a meeting." *Avoidance.* There was no meeting. It was code for not wishing to continue this line of discussion. We really were doing a role switcheroo today.

"Okay. But before you do, let me ask you something."

"Make it quick."

"Can you send me Mama's journal? I'd very much like to read it."

I'd poked the bear with a short stick just as I entered a dead zone, and for once the call was dropped at a most convenient time.

Moments later the phone chimed again, but it wasn't Zoe—it was Brooks, asking me to meet him.

"I'll be in Eastham in about twenty minutes. Do you want to meet at Wizards?" I suggested.

"Where are you now?"

"On my way back from Hyannis. I had an appointment with an acupuncturist." It was the only thing I could come up with to avoid explaining why I wasn't in or near Whale Rock.

"Not Wizards. The Jail House is closer."

\* \* \*

During Prohibition, the Jail House Tavern was home to the town constable, who also used it as a lockup for rum runners on the Cape. Turning it into a tavern seemed ironically appropriate. Tonight it was empty, save for Brooks enjoying a piece of apple pie a là mode near the fireplace.

"Hey, there." I sat heavily as the bartender brought over a pot of coffee to refill Brooks's mug and a menu for me. I waved it away and said, "Just decaf for me."

After a steaming mug had been placed before me, and we were alone, Brooks asked, "Why are you having acupuncture?"

I rubbed my wrists.

"Occupational hazard." It wasn't an outright lie.

"Does it work?" he asked after finishing his last bite of pie.

"We'll see. So what happened with Cindy?" I briskly directed the talk away from my fib.

"She's too slippery."

I secretly cheered for her.

"Can you tell me why you're pursuing her? Or would that be breaking the rules?"

"Allegedly," he emphasized the word, "she tried to sell a rare Greek gold coin at the Metal Exchange."

Bizarre, but hardly illegal. "Since when is that a crime?" I thought about the recent windfall she'd mentioned, but decided it best not to say anything to Brooks—at least not yet.

"It's not. But the dealer claimed Cindy was acting strange."

"She *is* strange," I argued in her defense.

"True. He also began to question how Cindy came into possession of such a unique coin."

"Maybe it's a family heirloom?"

His expression was dubious. "It was the second time such a coin had been brought into the Exchange in recent weeks, which is suspicious. I need to take a look at that coin, if Cindy hasn't already unloaded it."

I was stirring sugar into my coffee and thinking about what a mess Cindy might have landed in.

"More to the point," Brooks continued, "there's a potential connection with another case. The coin in question apparently bears an interesting symbol."

"How so?"

"It's imprinted with"—he inhaled deeply—"a phoenix."

I sat motionless, blinking at him, letting the words sink in.

"The phoenix," I whispered, laying my hand atop my tummy. Another flicker of a memory surfaced. I looked down at my bare ring finger. Suddenly I had a very good idea where I might have left Fiona's emerald ring.

"Weird coincidence?"

"*Too* weird to be a coincidence. The phoenix tie-in? Cindy

working at Hilliard House with access to the Jacobsons' room?" He took a gulp of coffee. "Not to mention the dealer's description of the man who brought in the first coin. Tall, dark hair, mid to late twenties. Sound familiar?"

I swallowed hard and nodded.

"*And*, it's apparently quite valuable. However, the young man—let's call him *Vince*—had been eager to cash in, so it was a lower take than had he waited for the dealer to sell it at auction."

"I gather Cindy was eager to cash in too?"

"You got it. Have you heard from her?" Brooks's voice held a sternness that made me wriggle like a naughty child.

"Not since the night she showed up at my house."

"Do you know how to get in touch with her?"

"I'll ask around." No need to involve Sylvia or Tommy in this mess.

"You do that." He stared fiercely.

I nodded, taking a sip of my coffee so as not to have to speak. I was an easy read.

"I did some checking. Besides Aaron, there was only one other Welkman enrolled at Temple University, some thirty years ago."

"Aaron's son?"

"Nope. *Her* name was Viola."

"Okay, so Aaron's *daughter*?" I told him about Ashley's triple-legacy comment. "I'd assumed that meant son, father, and grandfather. But of course it could be Vince's mother, right? And that likely means Vince has a different last name."

"Let's not get ahead of ourselves."

"Well, there is something else. Promise not to be angry?" I asked meekly.

"What have you done?" He pushed back his chair from the table.

"Not until you promise."

He groaned. "What are we, in junior high school?"

I held my ground.

His hands rose in submission. "I promise."

I took a deep breath and forged ahead. "Ashley and Vince's photo was recognized at a bar called Johnny Brenda's near Temple University in Philadelphia. But the staff remembered them as Laura and Jay."

To his credit, Brooks didn't scream or storm from the room, though he had to know the source of that information.

"I have a theory."

"Of course you do."

"I think they may have changed their identities as a way to hide. Ashley told me they lost something important in a fire. That's the night they got their tattoos. Apparently, they were both in a state of near hysterics one of the last times they were seen at Johnny Brenda's. The staff overheard them talking about losing something and being upset because now nobody would believe them. I'm thinking that whatever was lost could be the key to understanding this mystery."

Brooks stared at me, drumming his fingers on the table. He was giving me nothing.

Even though we were alone in the bar room, I leaned in and whispered, "Do you think they could they have been in the witness protection program?"

"Impossible." He scoffed, sticking a pin in my hope-filled balloon. "When someone from the witness protection program settles into an area, local law enforcement must be informed. Scratch that part of your theory."

"Oh pooh." *Pooh?* Another thought popped into my head. Could it have been a phoenix coin Ashley and Vince traded for the bronze Winnie the Pooh? That would certainly cement the connection between the Greek coin Cindy was trying to sell with Ashley and Vince, and it was valuable. A visit to Archie Stanfield's shop was added to the list.

In the meantime, Brooks was killing me with his silent contemplation.

"What do you think?"

"What I think . . ." He rubbed his face with his hands, then sighed heavily, "I think we have some work to do before your art benefactor returns."

"Oh, Chuckles, thank you." I'd regained an ally.

* * *

When I got home, the lights in the den were flickering, and my laptop was on, showing that same photo of Ashley and Vince in the cemetery.

"Okay," I cried out, and the lamps calmed. I sat down at the desk and stared intently at the picture on the screen. What was I supposed to see here?

I was startled by the phone's shrill ring and snatched it up quickly.

"Hi, Cassie? This is Jessica Tanner."

"I'm sorry, who?" I clicked to zoom in on the photo.

"Teddy's girlfriend. I met you the other night at the gallery?"

"Oh, of course. I'm sorry I didn't recognize your voice."

"I need to tell you something"—she lowered her voice to a whisper—"about Ashley and Vince."

"Where are you?" I gave her my full attention.

"At Teddy's. He's in the shower, so I only have a few minutes. He wouldn't want me to call you. When I told him I wanted to report what I knew, he thought I'd be causing more trouble for Ash and Vince. But I've been struggling."

I didn't want to seem pushy, so all I said was, "It's been hard on everyone involved."

"I've been so worried about them."

"What can I do to help?"

"I'm not sure how important or useful this is, but I'd rather some-one in a position of authority make that judgment. I would have told Chief Kincaid, but you can probably guess why that wouldn't be such a good idea."

"Sure." I couldn't really, but I was too focused on what she had to say about my missing friends. "You did the right thing by calling me. Can you tell me now? Or I can meet you somewhere?"

"Let me go outside for a minute." I heard the soft creak of a door hinge. "Please don't tell anyone where you came by this information. I don't want Teddy angry with me."

"We never had this conversation."

She let out her breath. "I think they may have been on the run from someone or some threat."

"What makes you say that?" I didn't let on that I'd been imagining the same thing.

"One night the four of us were at Teddy's, and I found Ashley crying in the bathroom. She was a little drunk and said she was missing her family, especially her little brother. It was his birthday, and she was upset because she couldn't call him."

"Did she say why not?"

"This is where it becomes troubling. I thought maybe she didn't have her phone, so I offered mine and suggested she call him right then. But she shook her head and said, 'Too late. We're dead.'"

I felt icy fingers on my spine.

"Is there anything else?"

"Yes. She started crying again and said something like, 'That damn file changed our lives forever.'"

"She said 'file,' not 'fire'?"

"Yes. File. I'm sure of it because she freaked out so much as soon as she said it, begging me not to repeat what she'd told me, and not let on to Vince that she had. She said he'd made her promise not to say anything to anyone. It was sorta hard to follow, but it sounded like maybe they'd told the wrong person about it before, and it had caused all kinds of problems."

My head was filling with questions. Had a file been lost in a fire? If so, what information had the file contained? "Did she seem frightened?"

"Yes."

"When was this, Jess?"

"Just a few days before they disappeared. I wanted to keep my promise to her, but I couldn't live with myself if I withheld information that might help find them."

We were both silent for a moment before she added, "I know. I should have told someone sooner."

"It wasn't an easy decision."

"Do you think any of what I've told you will help?"

"It might. Did Ashley mention anything about where she was from? Her brother's name? Any family details?"

"Not really. I know she's from down South, but I'm vague on where."

I was too.

"I have to go, I think Teddy's out of the shower," Jess whispered.

"Please call me if anything else comes to mind."

"I will."

"One more thing," I added quickly. "Is Teddy a good sailor?"

"Oh yeah, he's excellent."

I hung up with a gnawing in my stomach. If Ashley and Vince were frightened of being pursued, had it been by the stalker in the woods? Or Henry Beamer from Albany? Or *was* Henry Beamer the stalker in the woods? Most importantly: had whoever it was already caught them?

I clicked the mouse to bring the laptop screen back to life. But instead of the cemetery photo I expected, it was the photo of my grandfather looking back at me. Years ago Ethan had restored what few old family photographs there were and saved them on my laptop. The photo had been taken in front of the *Femme Celeste*, and it must have been right before Ambrose shipped off, because he was flexing his muscles to show off his new tattoos. Vulcan and Neptune. *Vulcan*. The night I was getting my tattoo, Ashley had mentioned a statue of Vulcan in her hometown.

*Thank you, Percy and Celeste.*

How many Southern towns could there be that boasted a statue of Vulcan? Only one, according to Google—on Red Mountain in Birmingham, Alabama. As I was considering how this information might be useful, the phone rang again.

"That was quick," I said to Brooks.

"Viola Welkman-Prince, J. Aaron Welkman's daughter, was killed in a crash with her husband, Alex Prince, back in 2003, when the plane Prince was piloting crashed into Whistler Mountain."

"Whistler Mountain? Where's that?"

"It's in Canada. British Columbia."

I looked down to where the German shepherd was sleeping at my feet. I thought back to the story Vince told me about how he had named Whistler. It had not seemed authentic at the time, and now I was certain it was a fabrication.

"Could you find an obituary? Did it mention children?"

"No obit I saw, but I was able to find a tribute article to Alex Prince in a skiing magazine. Prince, Americanized from Alexis Princolas, was a former Olympic skier, originally from Greece. They were survived by one child. A son named Jason." *JJ. Jay. Jason.*

The mounting parallels between Vince Jacobson and Jason Prince were adding credence to my theory. "I feel we're getting close to breaking through this mystery."

But then Brooks threw a bucket of ice water on my enthusiasm.

"Agent Benjamin called. The FBI has closed the case."

* * *

Less than five minutes after ending my call with Brooks, the phone rang again. I wasn't surprised to see who was calling. Daniel confirmed the bad news.

"Why would you close a case that's still unsolved? Is there nothing you can do? Even unofficially?"

"My hands are tied."

"Well, mine aren't."

"Be sensible, Cassie. You need to step back."

"Give me a good reason."

In a quieter voice he pleaded, "You have to trust me on this."

"Like I trusted you with the evidence you lost?" My anger had me pacing the floor.

"*I* didn't lose it. And only a portion of the evidence was misplaced by a tech. It will show up." This was a different version from his earlier story.

"Why did you lie to me about the ring they pawned?"

"I didn't lie to you. I wasn't at liberty to discuss details of the case. Besides, we hadn't determined its relevance."

"How about Archie Stanfield?" It was the thought that popped into my head when Brooks was telling me what he'd learned about the phoenix coin. Given the possibility of Vince actually being Jason Prince, his Greek heritage made it feel even more plausible.

"What about him?"

"He trusted you with a valuable Greek coin. Did that get misplaced as well?"

"How did you know about the coin?"

"I didn't. You just told me." *Gotcha!*

"You were guessing?" He snorted in exasperation.

"An educated guess."

"Cassie. Let it go."

But I couldn't, so I pressed on with another guess. "What about Cindy? She trusted you, and now she's in trouble."

"What are you talking about?" This bluff hadn't paid off. Daniel seemed genuinely bewildered by this claim. "What kind of trouble?"

"She's gone into hiding. She tried to sell one of the same coins Mr. Stanfield had. I presume there's a connection between those coins and Ashley and Vince's disappearance."

"You should not presume anything. You shouldn't even be involved. This is not a television crime show, for crying out loud. It's real life."

"I agree. And the real lives of two people I care about are at stake."

"I can't say anything more about it. Trust me when I tell you to walk away from this. Please." His was the voice of reason.

I inhaled the sweet scent of burnt sugar. "I wish I could." *I truly wanted to.*

I hung up feeling disheartened. All the conversation with Daniel had done was save me a trip to Coastal Vintage Wares to question Archie Stanfield. I checked the captain's clock and realized that Daniel should have been on a plane right now. Had he been lying to me about that as well?

# 28

The next day

Barely twenty-four hours before Aaron Welkman would return, and I still had several issues to resolve. And more bad news from Brooks, who told me he'd been ordered to cease any investigative work on the Jacobson case also.

"I thought you were working unofficially."

"Someone found out."

*Had Daniel ratted him out?*

"Why were you told to stop?"

"That was my question to the Massachusetts attorney general."

Pretty high up the ladder of command. "And?"

"I was told my place was not to ask questions, but to follow orders. This comes from the powers on high."

"We're getting close to something big," I said.

"Maybe," Brooks replied, "but it's something I've decided we should back away from. You in particular."

I sat down heavily. "I can't, Chuckles."

"You have to," he barked into the phone. He took a breath and softened his tone. "You have to because I can't be there to protect you."

"Do you really believe I'm in danger?" From the onset of this whole mess, I'd only been frightened for Ashley and Vince.

"I can't say for sure, but it's possible. And the risk is too great."

Changing the subject slightly, I asked, "What about the paintings? Do you think I should sell them?"

"Yes. Give the man what he wants. Take his check, thank him, and then wave bye-bye."

I said nothing, hoping he'd take my silence as acceptance.

"Promise you'll let it go."

"I'll do what you say." And I would, to a point. I'd already decided to let Aaron buy the paintings. But there were still some questions he'd need to answer as additional payment for them.

"Good girl."

*　*　*

"I've been deserted on all fronts." I was talking to Whistler as we walked up to the Mitchell family cemetery. "You're all that's left on the team, boy."

And he didn't let me down, heading straight for Barnacle Boy's headstone. I remembered seeing Ashley running toward the graveyard right before the call came in from my attorney about the divorce, the day she and Vince had disappeared.

"Good job, buddy." If I hadn't been looking for something, I wouldn't have noticed the slight disturbance of earth around the Winnie the Pooh statue.

I heaved the bronze figure aside to find an obvious burial site. However, after several minutes of digging, I determined whatever had been buried must have since been retrieved. Now it was clear why Ashley and Vince had done all the landscaping work in the cemetery. *It's the right place.* But why here? And what had they hidden? The coins, perhaps?

Whistler was nosing around one of the other graves so I went for a closer look. It was Fiona's, but nothing looked amiss save for one of the yews that had been chewed by deer.

"Don't pee on that grave. That's my granny, dontcha know."

The dog scampered off toward the house, and I followed quickly behind him. It was time for the second task on my to-do list for the day.

*　*　*

I waited in the merchandise corner of the post office lobby, pretending to select some postcards of beautiful Whale Rock Harbor until the crowd cleared out.

Sylvia Trask eyed me suspiciously. "What's up, Cassie?"

"I need to get a message to a certain somebody who presumably left town."

The postmistress's face brightened, and she responded in her own code. "I might know of a person who delivers in that area."

"I need to talk with her."

I turned at the sound of the door opening behind me. It was Mrs. Kruk, owner of the small grocery market next door, famed for its high prices and for being another hub of Whale Rock gossip.

Sylvia peered at Mrs. Kruk over her half-glasses and said, "I can take you first, Stella."

"Oh no. I wouldn't think of it." I held a grudge against Stella Kruk; she'd been one of the less kind merchants in town when I started having my financial struggles. She'd had the nerve to call Zoe and demand payment of my bill, which not only humiliated me but had also been the first tip-off to my sister that I was in trouble.

"It needs to arrive tomorrow."

"That soon, huh?" Sylvia frowned and looked down at her computer screen.

I lowered my voice. "It's fairly urgent."

"Okay, then. I'll send it Express." She winked, clearly enjoying her dabble in the covert discussion.

"What do I owe you?" I asked, subtly tilting my head toward the meddlesome shopkeeper.

Sylvia was quick on the uptake. "Overnight delivery would be eighteen dollars."

I handed her a twenty and she stealthily returned two tens along with a phony receipt. I thanked the postmistress and turned to leave, but Mrs. Kruk was a large woman and easily blocked my egress.

"Where've you been keeping yourself, Cassandra Mitchell?"

*Could the woman be so obtuse?*

"And don't give me the starving artist excuse." Her voice had turned syrupy sweet as she waved a playful finger at me. No doubt she'd heard the positive reviews of my exhibit and was eager to have me back as a paying customer.

A million sarcastic replies were bursting to be released, but the sensible angel won out over the vengeful devil.

"I promise to stop in soon." I sent a wave to Sylvia before rushing out.

As I walked purposefully to my car thinking of the next item I had to tackle, a familiar swagger rounded the corner a couple blocks ahead. *Billy Hughes.* I froze for a second before realizing I was standing in front of Hilliard House and escaping into its safe haven.

It was mid-morning, quiet time for the usually bustling inn. I found Evelyn alone, tidying up the dining room.

"Hey there, Baby Cass." She took me in a warm hug that allowed me to inhale her cozy smell of cinnamon and lavender. "George and I so enjoyed your showing. Is it true it might be a sellout?"

I waved my crossed fingers.

"What brings you here this morning?"

I decided to be completely honest. "I was ducking Billy Hughes."

She mouthed, *Oh*, and gave a dramatic and knowing nod of her head.

"Evelyn, does Zoe know about Billy and me?"

"Not from these lips." She made the motion of zipping them shut.

"But you knew." Who'd spilled the beans?

"Honey, we all knew." She took the chair beside mine. "But we wouldn't have told her. She'd've been crushed to know the truth."

"I'm her sister, not her daughter." I flared at the implied judgment. "She should have had her own brood instead of inflicting all that mothering on me." *Albeit long distance.*

And I didn't stop there with my venting. All the frustrations of recent weeks had accumulated to an eruption.

"She should have married Brooks and stayed here in Whale Rock and had a dozen kids. I could have been a favorite auntie who spoiled all my nieces and nephews. I might never have married Ethan if she'd stayed."

Evelyn was staring at her hands. She stood and walked toward the antique sideboard. "Cuppa?"

"Sure."

She set two filled mugs on the table, along with a sugar bowl and pitcher of cream, before sitting wearily.

"Sorry, Evvie."

"What you just described? That's exactly what Zoe always dreamed of for her future. But circumstances sent her down a different path." Evelyn sent me a sad smile. "She could hardly stand to be in that house. She had this crazy idea that Robert Toomey's spirit was haunting her."

*Not so crazy.* Except it wasn't Robert Toomey who was haunting her; it was his curse.

"I often wondered if your sister would have stayed here in Whale Rock if it hadn't been for those awful hallucinations."

"What kind of hallucinations?"

"These terrible smells only she could smell. She said it was horrible, like—"

"—like burning flesh," I whispered. "She told me that part," I added quickly.

Evelyn peered at me, askance, and lowered her voice to ask, "The stories about Battersea Bluffs—they are just stories, right?"

I couldn't go there right now, so I simply rolled my eyes. Despite being the person who'd done the most to perpetuate and embellish the tales of spirits haunting my home, Ev actually looked relieved.

"Well, anyway," she continued her story, "Zoe wanted to quit school and move away from home. She was making plans to go to New York, but your parents talked her into taking the semester off and staying in Whale Rock to think things through before making any rash decisions. But she was becoming more and more depressed and withdrawn. Then there was a terrible falling out between her and Fiona."

"What about?" I asked. There'd always been a lot of drama in our house as it concerned Zoe, but I'd been too young to be included in the family discussions.

"I don't know, but it was serious."

I thought about the journal pages waiting to be read, hoping they'd hold a clue.

"Anyhow, your folks were beside themselves with worry. As spring break approached, your mother arranged a trip to Mexico with a group of Zoe's sorority sisters. That's where she met the dashing Oliver Young. None of us thought she'd actually marry him. We all still held out hope she'd get back with Brooks, but you know how that chapter ended."

I nodded, even though I was positive there was much more to the story than I'd been told. But for now, I had no choice but to let it go.

We sipped our now-tepid tea in silent reflection before I asked, "Do you think she's happy with Oliver?"

Evelyn lifted her shoulders in a dramatic shrug and made a face. "Through the years, your sister has remained consistently ambiguous on the subject of her marriage."

"And Brooks?"

She raised one eyebrow and said, "I believe you might hold the more accurate barometer on where Chuckles stands."

I scowled at her.

She lifted her hands. "Gossip. It's the one drawback of living in a small town."

The bell at the front desk tinkled, and Evelyn dashed to the front hall. I carried my cup to the kitchen, where she met me with a cha-grinned look.

"An early check-in."

"I should be going anyhow. Appreciate the save."

"You mean Billy? Anytime." She walked with me to the lobby. "One more thing about your sister. Her intentions are always the best. Especially when it comes to you."

"I'll try to remember that, and I promise to be more patient." I made a scout's salute.

She leaned in and kissed my cheek. "Ah, Baby Cass isn't a baby anymore."

I left Hilliard House having learned nothing more about Zoe and her secrets. Just as well since I needed no further distractions before Aaron Welkman arrived on my doorstep tomorrow.

As I descended the porch steps, I noticed the bad boy of Whale Rock waiting for me on a bench in front of the hardware store.

I pretended not to see him and crossed the cobbled street to where my car was parked.

He called out, "Hey, Babe!"

"Piss off, Billy," I yelled back, which instigated some hearty guffaws from a few of the locals in earshot. After all these years, was it possible I'd finally grown that spine and become immune to the charms of Billy Hughes? It was a long time coming, but I had to admit, it felt good.

* * *

The high from giving Billy the brush-off was short-lived. By the time I arrived in Provincetown, my mind had clouded again with thoughts of all that could go wrong in the next few hours.

When I walked through the door of Grand Funk Ink, I was relieved to see the unmistakable Skunk sitting behind the counter, finishing up his lunch.

"What can I do for you today?" He wiped his mouth on a paper towel and stood to greet me.

"Do you remember me?" I asked. "I came in a couple months ago with my friends."

He sized me up through slit eyes before a sly smile crept across his face as he pointed and said, "Oh yeah. The phoenix."

"That's right."

"I've been waiting for you to show up." He unlocked his cash drawer and removed a small brown envelope. "I believe this is yours."

I hadn't even had to ask. I shook out the contents of the envelope and slipped Fiona's emerald ring onto my finger.

"You're one happy lady." His smile mirrored my own.

"For more reasons than I can tell you." Bits and pieces of my memory of that night had been coming back to me. I'd finally remembered taking off the ring before getting my tattoo so Skunk could take a closer look when I'd requested the eyes of the phoenix match the emerald color. "Didn't I fill out a release form with my contact information?"

"You'd had a few pops before coming in that night."

*Which was probably the reason I hadn't remembered taking the ring off.*

He pulled out the form and placed it on the counter before me. I felt my face warm as I read what I'd written for my name and address: *Dorothy the Small and Meek, Yellow Brick Road, Emerald City, Somewhere over the Rainbow.*

"We've seen worse. But I did try to call you. You must have written it down wrong."

I checked the telephone number and found I'd completely mixed up my cell and landline numbers.

"So, are you pleased with my work?"

"Very. But I wouldn't have had the courage to do it sober."

"Often the case." He nodded knowingly. "I'm glad you weren't pissed off at your buddies."

"Not at all, Sadly, they disappeared not long after that."

He puzzled for a moment before asking, "The couple that went missing from Whale Rock?"

"That was them. Do you remember anything unusual that night, anything they may have done or said?"

"I was concentrating on my art." He rubbed his chin. "But now that you mention it, they had this rope they were playing around with."

I must have smiled, for Skunk asked, "That mean something to you?"

"More like satisfies a hunch." Despite no support from Brooks or Daniel, I was still convinced that the knotted rope was key to figuring out what had happened to my missing friends.

*   *   *

It was nearly midnight when I powered off my laptop just as Whistler lifted his head and uttered a low growl. Rubbing my tired eyes, I flipped on the porch light and saw those telltale Uggs, like the Wicked Witch of the East's ruby slippers sticking out from Dorothy's fallen house. Only a house hadn't landed on Cindy: she'd somehow landed on mine.

"Come on in." I swung the door wide open, resisting the urge to ask how she got here and why she hadn't knocked.

She slunk in like a naughty child preparing for a reprimand.

"What's wrong?"

"That's zactly what I'm here to find out. I s'pose you're gonna tell me what awful trouble I'm in, with you bein' such good pals with the cops and all."

"I'm actually on your side, Cindy. I'd like to try and help you out of whatever mess you've unwittingly gotten yourself into."

She glared at me under a furrowed brow. "What mess?"

"I believe you're in possession of a coin that once belonged to Ashley and Vince."

"They gave it to me." She crossed her arms defiantly. "You can't prove otherwise."

"I believe you." I took a seat at the table and motioned for her to sit as well.

"You do?" She looked at me sideways.

"Yes, but I'm probably the only person who does. So that's why you're in a bit of a pickle right now."

"Damn that gold trader. I don't know why he just wouldn't buy it without askin' all those stupid questions."

"It's his business to be cautious. But that's water under the bridge at this point. Ashley and Vince are good kids, but I'd bet they didn't give that coin to you out of the kindness of their hearts. I'm prepared to help you, but you have to tell me what you did in exchange for it."

"I knowed there'd be a hitch." Her arms remained stubbornly crossed. "I gave my word I wouldn't say nuthin'."

"But circumstances have changed. You don't have a job anymore. No income. No prospects. You're living God knows where. And you can't sell the coin. I'd say you've run out of options."

Cindy's protruding lower lip caused the loose skin around her chin to pucker.

"Look, I'm impressed you want to do the honorable thing here, but considering your predicament, you might want to rethink your loyalties."

Cindy leaned her elbows onto the table, cupping her face in her palms, staring at me for quite some time before asking, "What's in it for me?"

We were making progress. "I'll vouch for you with the police."

"Hah! A lot of good that'll do me." Her stomach rumbled loudly, and then she stifled a belch. "Scuse me."

"I feel like a midnight snack." I went to the refrigerator and took out a block of cheese and some fruit, then grabbed a baguette from the bread box. "How about you? Care for anything?"

"Well. If you're going to go to the trouble, I wouldn't mind a lil sumpthin-sumpthin."

There was a tug at my conscience as I watched her scarf down the food, half-starved. She wasn't a bad sort, just an unfortunate soul. I hated to be forced into manipulating her, but I needed answers.

"Cindy, it's time for you to level with me," I said after she stuffed the last slice of the loaf into her mouth.

She swallowed and then whined, "But I promised."

"Okay. So I guess that's that." I leaned back in my chair. "What are your plans now?"

She looked at me suspiciously. "You givin' up? Just like that?"

I lifted my hands in defeat, hoping reverse psychology would be effective. "I can't force you to help me."

"Help you?" She sniffed. "I thought you was offerin' to help me."

"Same thing. I'm in a position to help you. But I need your help too. Have you heard the expression: If you scratch my back, I'll scratch yours?"

She puzzled on this a moment, then shook her head. "Yeah, but my back don't need scratchin'."

Maybe not, but I was thinking her palm was itching pretty badly right now.

"All you have to do is tell me what they paid you to do."

"And who will you tell?"

"Maybe nobody. It depends on what the answer is. But I promise, no matter what, I will keep you out of it. Nobody will ever know you were involved in any way."

She was picking up crumbs with her fingertip and licking them off. When there wasn't a speck of food left on the plate, she asked, "You don't happen to have any cookies?"

"I might." All I had were Oreos, but I doubted she would care.

She smacked her lips.

"I'll check, but if I do, will you give me some information in return?" I stared at her, not moving.

"Oh, ah-right." She chewed her fingernail as a stall tactic, but when I didn't move to get the cookies, she said, "I just mailed a letter."

"That's all?" I held up my end of the bargain and retrieved a package of Double-Stuffs from the pantry.

Cindy ripped into the package as if she'd not just polished off a wedge of brie, a pear, two apples, and a loaf of bread.

"Well, it wasn't as if I just moseyed into the Whale Rock Post Office and handed it over to ol' Tommy. Ya see, I had special instructives."

"What kind of . . . ? What did they have you do?"

"I had to borrow my friend Buddy's taxi cab," she said, then pulled an Oreo apart and began scraping the filling with her teeth. "To take it to an out-of-state post office."

"Okay, so where out of state?" The questioning was becoming as tedious as the answers were unenlightening.

"New York."

"You drove all the way to New York to mail a letter for them?" This was throwing me. I could see Rhode Island or New Hampshire if they didn't want to reveal a Massachusetts postmark. But why New York?

She must have predicted the next question because she added, "Albany."

*Albany?* The guest who checked in at Hilliard House was from Albany. I took a moment to digest this before asking the next question. "Do you remember who it was addressed to?"

"Nah." She looked down at the table.

"Where it was going?"

She pressed her lips tightly together and still wouldn't look at me. "Cin-dy."

Unexpectedly, she started to cry. "I can't even sell the damn coin. And I've gotta give Buddy his share or he's gonna turn me in to the cops."

I doubted Buddy would do any such thing. The creep was probably bullying her with empty threats. "If I buy the coin from you, will you tell me the rest?"

She wiped the wetness from her face, leaving gray smudges on her cheeks. She had the resigned look of someone ready to give in. However, at that precise moment Whistler rose from his position at my feet and nudged Cindy's hand. She smoothed back the dog's fur, then shook her head. "I made a promise to those kids."

We were at a stalemate, and in my frustration I considered snatching back the package of cookies. Then I remembered a ploy Zoe often used on me to pry my sealed lips open.

"What if I guess? That's not the same as telling."

The tightness in Cindy's mouth softened, and her eyebrows lifted slightly. I was betting her silence would be easier to break than mine had been as a child.

"Just give me one guess. If I don't get it right, we don't have to talk about it anymore."

"Ah-right. Take a stab." She sat upright with a sense of bravado.

I inhaled deeply, wishing I'd thought to ask for two guesses. "Was it going to Montana? A town called Bozeman?"

Her mouth dropped open, which was all I needed for an answer.

"A Mister Welkman?"

Cindy slapped the table smartly. "If you already knowed, why'd you have to hassle me?"

"I didn't know for sure. It was a gut feeling, and the only way I could be certain was if you helped me." I reached across the table and clutched her hand. "Thank you."

I left her and went to the den, only to find the laptop I'd turned off less than thirty minutes ago had powered up with that same photo of Ashley and Vince looking back at me.

"Okay, Percy," I said. "But first let me tend to this."

"Who you talkin' to?" Cindy had followed me and was looking about the room suspiciously.

"Myself."

I took my checkbook from the top drawer of the antique rolltop desk. Lucky for me I had deposited a payment from Lu yesterday. I handed Cindy the check and asked, "Do you have the coin now?"

When she saw the amount, her eyes widened even more. Then she blinked twice.

"It's not a mistake. I'll call the bank tomorrow. You won't have any trouble cashing it."

She took off one of her Uggs and worked at loosening something from the toe. "Here ya are. I guess you bought yourself a weird-lookin' quarter."

"Thank you." The gold was smooth, worn with age, but the image of the phoenix was well preserved.

"I feel like a turncoat." However, she was still gazing at the check with relief.

"What you did for them may very well have saved their lives. And by telling me—"

She waved a finger at me. "I din't tell you nuthin'."

"Fine, but it will help me find out if the man you sent the letter to is one of the good guys or a villain."

"What if he's the . . . not good one?"

It was a perfectly legitimate question.

"That's not for you to worry about."

Cindy yawned hugely. I was about to offer her a ride until I looked at the clock.

"It's late. Why don't you stay here tonight? I'll drive you back to Orleans in the morning."

She became timid all of a sudden. "Nah. I don't have no PJs or nuthin' with me."

"No worries. I've got a spare." I motioned her to follow, pretending not to notice as she pocketed a stack of Oreos. I'd tend to the crumbs in the bed tomorrow.

"By the way, why did you leave the Hilliard House?" I asked while turning down the bed in the room Ashley and Vince had used during their stay.

"When the kids went missin', I figgered the letter I delivered had sumpthin' to do with it." She shook her head in annoyance. "That Evelyn has a nose, and it wouldn't have been long before she sniffed me out." Cindy's street smarts were well honed for survival.

"You're right, but she also has a good heart."

Cindy shrugged. "I s'pose."

"You have your own bathroom if you'd like to shower." I handed her a towel and a toothbrush, hoping she'd take the hint.

"I reckon I'll sleep ah-right tonight. No money worries for a good long while." She waved the check at me, then tucked it up into the toe of her Ugg. She turned shy again and ducked her head. "I owe you, Cassie."

"Let's call it even. See you in the morning."

When I awoke early the next morning, my houseguest was gone. The bed was neatly made, with little trace she'd been there save for the scrawled note left on the table: *Don't forget to call the bank.*

I wondered where Cindy would land after Whale Rock, somewhat sad at the thought I'd likely never see her again.

# 29

Six weeks following the disappearance

I tried to remain calm as I waited for the black Lincoln to round the corner. But with each minute, my anxiety ratcheted up proportionally. What if I was wrong? What if my plan backfired? What if Aaron and Michael were dangerous? What if they didn't show? All the *what ifs* were starting to outnumber the established facts. I paced uncertainly, stewing over the biggest question: *What if I'd made the situation worse for Ashley and Vince?*

I did a visual sweep of the kitchen. The knotted rope was on the kitchen island, strategically positioned to peek out from under some newspapers near the sugar and creamer. It would be easily noticed by Michael when I asked him to bring the coffee service into the living room. My gut was telling me that Aaron and Michael's business in Boston had involved a visit with the FBI. And if I was right, they'd be looking for this rope.

My plan was to bring Whistler in after Aaron was settled in his chair by the fireplace. The dog had reacted unusually calmly during their first meeting, and though I suspected why, I wanted to be certain. And it might offer a bit of leverage if needed.

I was rehearsing my lines when the vehicle finally came into view. I walked out through the front door to welcome them, pulling my sweater tighter against the stiff cool breeze left over from last night's storm.

"I have a fire burning. Let's get out of this chilly air."

Once Aaron was seated, I asked Michael, "Would you mind help-ing with the coffee?"

He bowed slightly and followed me.

"I trust you've finished your business in Boston?" I pulled pastries from a box.

"Everything came to a reasonably satisfactory conclusion."

I nodded to a tray. "Can you put the sugar and creamer there beside the cups and bring it all to the living room?" I intentionally went ahead, leaving him in the kitchen.

"I hope you like cheese Danish," I said to Aaron, setting the plat-ter on the coffee table in front of him.

He inhaled. "They smell delightful. But you needn't have gone to any trouble."

"We have an excellent bakery in town."

A moment later, Michael appeared with the tray.

I tapped my chin. "Oh goodness, I forgot the coffee." I returned to the kitchen and collected the carafe, feeling a surge in confidence when I observed the rope was missing.

"Do you mind pouring?" I asked, handing the carafe to Michael. "I have one more item to retrieve."

I opened the door to the back stairway where I knew Whistler would be eagerly waiting. He stayed at my heels until we reached the living room and saw Aaron. The dog's ears went flat, and he let out a whimper before trotting over to the man's feet where he folded him-self into a down position.

"Ah, my friend." He patted Whistler's head. "My memory isn't what it used to be. What's this guy's name?"

I didn't answer. Instead I called out a command to the dog. "Up."

Whistler rolled onto his back in a submissive position.

"Go," I commanded, and the dog jumped up and ran from the room.

Aaron had subtly issued those directives to Whistler during his first visit. At the time, I'd been too nervous to recognize them as such, but it continued to bother me how the dog's reaction to Aaron had been so obviously different from that to anyone else he'd come across.

"I believe you and Whistler met long before your last visit to Whale Rock."

I caught Michael's uncomfortable glance at Aaron, who was now sitting with his hands folded together, head slightly bowed. A prisoner awaiting his sentence.

"Guilty as charged."

*What else might he be guilty of?*

"Was he your guide dog at one time?"

"You're quite the clever girl, Cassie."

The hairs on the back of my neck stood at attention. I'd been more formal when we first met and used my professional name to introduce myself. Cassandra Mitchell was how I signed my paintings. He'd been talking with someone who knew me more familiarly, someone who called me Cassie, and I was growing sickly assured of who the person was.

"So it was you who named him Whistler? Because—and I hope I don't misquote you—'Whistler Mountain is one of the most beautiful places on the planet.'"

Aaron nodded gravely.

"What I'm not clear on though, is how Vince Jacobson came to have your dog."

Michael fidgeted uncomfortably. I addressed my next question to him. "Why did you take the rope?"

He closed his eyes and laid his head on the back of the wingchair.

Aaron leaned forward and spoke in a calm but solemn tone. "I'd really hoped not to overly involve you in a sensitive matter, a matter that is personal and serious. I'd like to give you the opportunity now to let us walk away with the rope, no questions asked."

"And the paintings?"

"The offer remains. And I urge you to take it."

"Why buy them all when the portraits of Ashley and Vince Jacobson—even though those aren't their real names—are what you're really interested in, right?"

Neither of them responded.

"I'm guessing you're trying to acquire all evidence they were here, which was fairly easy because they'd left few telltale signs. However, my exhibit featuring their portraits was an inconvenient complication."

Aaron nodded.

"How do you know the rope is significant?" I wanted my suspicions confirmed.

"I guarantee you will find no satisfaction in knowing," Aaron said with an air of finality.

"And I can guarantee there will be no satisfaction derived from the rope Michael took from the kitchen."

"Why is that?"

"Because it's not the rope you're looking for."

Michael pointed a warning finger at me. "You are playing a dangerous game, Ms. Mitchell."

The mention of danger made me squirm, but I stood my ground. "This is not a game to me. Two of my friends disappeared under a cloud of mystery, and you know something about it."

"Let's be reasonable," Aaron began his own gentler plea. "I've agreed to pay a substantial fee for your paintings. I'll sweeten the deal by offering the same amount for just the portraits, and you're free to sell the others. You stand to do quite well from my proposition."

"It's not about the money."

"What more could you possibly want from us?" Michael implored.

"Answers. Reassurances."

"It appears you've already uncovered a great deal on your own." Aaron's tone was almost approving.

"I've only figured out parts of this maddening puzzle. And in doing so, I've also come across some information you might find useful. But this needs to be a two-way street. I need to know what happened to Ashley and Vince. I need to know if they're safe. And I think you're in a position to tell me."

"Ah, if that were only the case." Aaron nodded at Michael, and from his pocket he withdrew a folded-up piece of paper and handed it to me.

"This letter was sent to Aaron from the woman you knew as Ashley."

My gaze moved suspiciously from man to man as I unfolded it. Yet, as soon as I read the first two words my heart began to race. This was the remainder of the letter I'd found just a corner of in the bottom of a trash can. It had to be the same one Cindy mailed to Aaron from Albany. One more piece falling into place.

> Sorry we left before getting in touch. We were in a rush. O'Henry could no longer be trusted to pay our rent. We had to leave our bicycles behind. You will find them and bring them to us. Look for the woman we stayed with. Fondly, Percy Bluff

I retrieved the corner of the letter I'd found and held it beside the note Michael had handed me for comparison. "Same handwriting, same first words. She must have written a draft letter and destroyed it. But it's rather cryptic."

With only those written words to go on, I wouldn't have been able to figure out a message, let alone that they should look for a rope. No doubt Aaron and Michael had had some guidance, and I didn't have to work too hard to reason out from whom. But I still didn't understand why.

"The man you call Vince was studying criminology," Aaron said.

"Criminology? Hmm." I felt a stab of betrayal.

"Not the story you were given?"

"Vince told me he was going to teach." I chewed the inside of my lip. "But how could they have been so certain I'd take the rope?" I said this more to myself, but Aaron responded.

"Perhaps they never intended for you to remove the rope. But it's a reasonable assumption that the bikes would be returned to you eventually since this was their last known place of residence."

My head was spinning. This revelation was way offline from the conclusions I'd arrived at, though my formula included as much guesswork as facts.

"How did you know to come to Whale Rock? To look for me?"

"I will admit, we had a bit of luck in that regard. There's a small GPS tracking device attached to Whistler's collar." He clapped his hands and shouted. "Come!"

The dog swiftly obeyed.

"Good boy." I gave him a praising head rub before examining his collar to find a barely detectable tab on the inside. "Huh?"

"After we arrived in Whale Rock, it wasn't hard to determine your connection. Percy's Bluffs is quite famous around here."

I opened my mouth to speak, but he held up his hand to stop me. "To anticipate your next question, it was only by chance Michael saw the notice of your exhibit in a storefront window."

"Well, that certainly does solve one mystery." It also opened up the door to many more questions. Still I needed to stay focused on more important matters. "But actually, my next question was going to be how did you know to look for a rope?"

"If this is to be a two-way street, it would be my turn to ask the next question."

I nodded begrudgingly.

"They had in their possession something of great importance, something they would have been protecting. Do you know anything about it?"

"The coins?" I asked.

Aaron frowned.

I pulled the phoenix coin from my pocket and showed it to Michael.

"She has one of the Greeks." He placed it in Aaron's hand. This time I could clearly make out the Temple "T" on his ring.

A ghost of a smile passed over Aaron's lips as he caressed it. "That's not what I'm looking for. However, they are indeed quite valuable." He frowned again and asked, "How did you come to have this?"

"They used it to pay someone to run an errand for them. Actually, it was to mail this letter to you. They also traded one for a statue of Winnie the Pooh."

"How large of a statue?" Aaron cocked his head with interest.

"Maybe a foot high by eight or ten inches wide. Bronze. Heavy."

He shook his head. "It's probably solid. Besides, not big enough."

"For what?" When there was no answer, I said, "It's my turn to ask a question."

"Could you ask a different one?"

"Okay. Why would they bury the coins?"

"I can't see any reason they would." Aaron's forehead wrinkled. "Did they bury something?"

"Yes."

He leaned forward. "How do you know? Where was this?"

"As I mentioned, they bartered for this bronze statue and bought some plants to decorate a gravestone in my family cemetery here on the property. I discovered they'd buried something and used the statue to cover it up."

"But you don't have what they buried." It wasn't a question.

"Whatever it was, they removed it before I went looking."

"Are you certain it was they who removed it?"

"Who else?"

"God be good, let's hope it was them," Aaron mumbled.

"Was somebody else looking for whatever it is they buried?" I asked, but again my question was ignored.

"Can you take us to this gravesite before we leave?"

I nodded, then asked, "The young man who showed up here with your dog and called himself Vince Jacobson—is he your grandson, Jason?"

Aaron sighed heavily before he spoke. "Jason Jacob Prince. The best part of my life. We were very close. After my daughter died, Jason came to live with me."

I felt sorry for the man, who had aged a decade in the past few minutes.

"What about Ashley?"

"Jason's wife? Her real name is Laura Ashton Prince."

"Why the names Vince and Ashley Jacobson?"

Michael shrugged, "We didn't know they were using these names until we got here. But I can guess—Viola and Prince, to come up with Vince. Ashley taken from Laura's middle name of Ashton. Jacobson from the obvious."

"Clever, but amateurish nonetheless." Aaron shook his head in annoyance. Still, it confirmed my theory.

"And her family is from Birmingham?" I asked.

"How on earth did you determine that?" Michael asked.

I told them about her mentioning the statue of Vulcan.

"Were they in the Witness Protection Program?" Despite Brooks having denied it earlier, I put it out there.

Michael made a face, and I prepared for my suggestion to be rejected again.

"Maybe they wouldn't be in this mess if they had been." Aaron let out a deep sigh. "I don't suppose there's any harm in her knowing."

"Knowing what?"

"They were actually being prepped to enter the program when the situation turned on them, so to speak," Michael answered.

*I wasn't so far off the mark, after all.* This acknowledgement filled me with a small sense of validation. Both Brooks and Daniel had eschewed my theory—presumably, Brooks hadn't known, but I wondered if Daniel had been trying to divert my path because I was getting too close to a truth that would have exposed his duplicity.

"But they'd gone rogue." Aaron shook his head.

"And went to Albany?"

He nodded. "They were put in touch with a private protection agency. A man named Henry Beamer was their security officer. Thus, the reference to O'Henry."

Henry Beamer was the man from Albany who'd checked into Hilliard House. "They were frightened of this man?"

"Frightened?" Aaron considered the question. "I hope not. But it appears from their message they no longer trusted him."

"They were worried enough to send an SOS to Aaron," Michael added.

I chewed on this bit of information. "So, feeling vulnerable in Albany, they came up with the fake identities on their own?"

"Evidently. They must have felt it safer to take their chances elsewhere, alone."

"I still don't understand why they'd insist the letter be postmarked from Albany. Wouldn't a Whale Rock zip code be more helpful to you in finding them?"

"Possibly, but it was preestablished that any correspondence from Albany would be treated with utmost urgency. Because I travel extensively, my secretary was instructed to immediately contact me about any letter with an Albany postmark. Otherwise, my personal correspondence was to remain untouched until I returned."

"And since they couldn't risk being seen in Albany, they paid someone to deliver the letter for them."

"A logical deduction."

"But you didn't show up for weeks after their disappearance."

"It seems the person they entrusted to mail the letter forgot to affix a stamp. It's lucky I even received it. I hope you didn't pay dearly to get that coin back."

He was a shrewd man. My thoughts turned briefly to Cindy. To drive all the way to Albany and then not even check to see if the letter was stamped?

"So, the reason they went on the run has something to do with whatever they hid?" I asked. "Have you discussed any of this with the FBI?"

Both men were silent far too long, which was answer enough. It was Aaron who eventually spoke.

"The authorities in Boston are of the position there is no message on the rope; that it's a series of knots, nothing more."

I was burning at the thought of Daniel taking part in those discussions. Yet another deception.

"What do you think?" I asked.

"I believe the rope holds the key to finding out where my grandson is. And perhaps the good fellows of the FBI just aren't good enough to decode it."

This made me smile.

"Now, I've answered a number of your questions and I need—or rather, Michael needs—to look at the rope they left."

Clearly my friends had wanted Aaron to find the rope and the message it contained, so I could no longer deny them access. I escorted them to the kitchen and brought out the rope.

We sat together at the table while Michael examined the rope, comparing it to a sheet of paper he'd extracted from his messenger bag. After nearly half an hour of deep concentration, he set the rope down, rubbed the bridge of his nose, and admitted defeat.

"Nothing's coming of this, even with these notes from the FBI about the knots."

"Maybe you've done a better job coming up with some kind of message?" Aaron suggested.

"May I?" Michael handed me a photocopied page of knots similar to the ones I'd downloaded. When I was first teaching Vince to sail, I'd loaned him my father's original copy of *The Art of the Sailor*, a basic handbook with illustrations of sailing knots. Unfortunately, I hadn't found it among the belongings Ashley and Vince had left behind.

I opened my folder and quickly appraised the notations before sliding the top sheet of paper across the table for Michael to translate to Aaron while I explained.

"There are three sets of knots, each separated by a length free of knots. Let's take the first set. See where I've listed the knots in order?" I pointed to each knot on the rope as I recited the names. "Ashley stopper. Grief knot. Half hitch. Eye splice. This one I believe is a noose knot but it looks different since it's not at the end of the rope. This one isn't used in sailing, but a consultant working with the Whale Rock police determined it to be a savoy knot. And lastly the thief knot."

I pulled out another page where I'd written A–G–H–E–N–S–T and showed it to Michael. "This is an anagram using the first letter of each knot. To me they're nothing more than a jumble of letters, but to someone who knew them more intimately, it might hold a special significance."

Michael read the letters aloud and sounded them out before asking, "Does that mean anything to you, Aaron?"

The older man moved his lips as he mentally repeated the letters. Then he shook his head.

"What about this second set of knots?" Again I recited the names followed by an anagram. "True love. Eye splice. Whistle knot. Eye splice. Bowline. T-E-W-E-B."

"At one point I thought the actual names of the knots might have told a story. Especially since one of the knots was an Ashley stopper. But since you didn't know the new names they'd assumed, following that track doesn't work." I flipped through the downloaded pages.

"The problem with deciphering knots is that some of them have more than one name. For example, the bowline is also known as blindman's knot."

Aaron made a face. "You might be on to something. Could it be about Whistler and me?"

"Possibly. If these knots do have a secret code, it's safe to say that Vince was more adept at coming up with them than we are at decoding them."

While the men conferred about what I'd written, I fiddled with the rope that had been left tied to the bicycles. I then pulled out the piece of rope I'd retrieved from the trash the day I found the corner of Ashley's letter, hoping it might hold a clue. As I compared them, I noticed that on the practice rope, a grief knot had been used in place of a thief knot.

"Can you please pass my notes back to me?" I made a correction to what I'd first written. "I wonder if Vince mixed up two of the knots, which would be easy to do since the grief knot and thief knot are very similar. If he confused them, it changes the anagram."

I pushed the paper back for them to see. "Look what it says when I correct it."

"A-T-H-E-N-S—G. Athens." Michael said to Aaron, who was smiling broadly for the first time since I met him.

"Athens, Georgia? Is that where they've gone?" This fit with none of the facts I'd gathered.

"What are these other notes?" Michael ignored my question and pointed to my scribblings about the last three knots on the tale of the rope.

"The first is an eye splice, the second is a rapala knot, which is used in fishing. It took me awhile to figure that one out. And the last is another grief knot. Or it's a thief knot, depending on if he was making it correctly."

"ERT or ERG." Michael said to Aaron, who frowned and shook his head again.

As I studied those last three knots intently, something finally clicked into place. Percy and Celeste had been adamant in their message, repeatedly opening up my laptop to the photo of Ashley and Vince in the cemetery. But I hadn't understood until just this minute as that sweet familiar aroma filled the room. Eye splice = Look. Rapala knot = R. Thief knot = T. Look at R.T. *Look at Robert Toomey*.

"Any thoughts?" Michael asked me.

"None whatsoever," I lied, glad Aaron was unable to see my face. He wasn't telling me everything, so why shouldn't I keep this possible clue to myself? I might need to use it as a bargaining chip later.

\* \* \*

An hour later, the transaction had been completed. Funds had been transferred into my Seaman's Bank account, and Lu had been instructed to package up and send the portraits of the Jacobsons to the Montana address. The three of us were now standing at the grave marker for Barnacle Boy.

"He was an unknown boy who washed up on our shores. Folks around here always referred to him as the Barnacle Boy. Nobody ever figured out who he was or where he came from. Ashley and Vince had been moved by the story. When I first discovered what they'd done with the plants and the statue, I'd assumed it was a tribute to a poor little boy whom nobody knew. I felt it was a private gesture and never mentioned it to them."

Now I was wishing I had. Perhaps then they would have confided in me.

"A gesture of some significance." Aaron's sightless eyes could still show emotion.

"It's solid. No secret hiding compartment." Michael had turned the statue of Winnie the Pooh onto its side. Then with a small shovel he'd brought from the car, he proceeded to dig up the area under where the statue had been standing guard. I understood their need to check for themselves, but I also knew it would be a fruitless endeavor.

"What's the harm in telling me what you think might've been there?" I persisted.

"Some secrets are best left buried."

*Hadn't I heard that enough lately?*

"And that is all I intend to say on the subject." It was spoken with solemn finality.

Aaron had what he needed from me, and I had nothing left to barter with, at least nothing I was certain of at the moment. I stole a quick glance over at Robert Toomey's grave, wondering what my young friends might've left there.

"Ashley was obviously disturbed when she came across this marker, and you called their selection of the spot a gesture of significance. How so?" I asked.

"Remind me again how the marker reads?"

I did the honors. *"Bless this unknown boy who washed upon our shores."*

"It's not a happy story," he cautioned.

"My family has managed to survive by clinging to the fibers of its own heartbreaking tales."

"Very well. If you insist on knowing." Aaron sighed deeply. "My daughter-in-law lost a younger brother to a drowning incident when he was six years old. She was eleven at the time and was swimming with him when they both got caught in an undertow. Her father nearly drowned trying to rescue his children, succeeding in saving only her. It wasn't until weeks later that the little boy's ravaged body washed up on shore, discovered by strangers. She always felt responsible for the drowning."

"No wonder she reacted so strongly when she first saw Barnacle Boy's stone," I whispered, my eyes held tightly shut as I tried to imagine the burden Ashley carried with her.

"Her parents had another son, a late-in-life baby, of whom she's become extremely protective. I suppose it's quite hard for her not to be in touch with her little brother now."

"How old?"

"Twelve."

"He must be confused. And her parents?"

"I've kept them intentionally in the dark for their own protection, especially in light of recent events and the uncertainty of who can be trusted."

To whom specifically was Aaron referring?

"Do you think Henry Beamer knew about any of this?"

"How can we know until we talk with my grandson?"

"I'm fairly certain Beamer came to Whale Rock."

"Henry Beamer did?" Aaron's pallor intensified.

"Yes." It was unnerving to think this man, whom Ashley and Vince didn't trust, could've been following them.

"We don't know the depth or validity of their concerns. Perhaps Henry Beamer showed up here because he took his job of protecting them seriously, and nothing more," Michael suggested.

"Let us hope."

"But this"—Michael pointed to the grave—"is a dead end." He then took Aaron's arm and said, "Time to move on."

The older man patted the hand of the younger and, with fatigue christening every word, said, "We must do as they have done."

We walked back toward the house at the tempo of a dirge. The blissfully ignorant Whistler ran playfully ahead of us, offering an opening to break the spell.

"How did Vince end up with Whistler? I'm sorry—I mean Jason."

"I'd actually prefer if you'd continue to think of them as Vince and Ashley, for obvious reasons."

"Of course," I agreed, though I still lacked specific details.

"Whistler is terrified of flying. And since I travel so much," he turned his palms upward, "he needed a new home. Luckily, my grandson already adored Whistler."

"I believe it was a mutual love." I was glad for my sunglasses to mask the threatening tears. I'd fallen hard for this black beauty who had once frightened me. "So, Whistler will go with you today?"

"I hate to impose on you any further."

"He was never an imposition. I'll hate to see him go."

"And Whistler would hate to leave." Michael stretched out his arms. "All this open space."

"Michael and I do have an overseas trip to arrange."

*Overseas?* It suddenly clicked for me that the code referred to Athens, *Greece*—not Athens, Georgia—which made sense, since

Vince's father was Greek and there'd likely be family there, offering a safe haven. It likely also explained how they came to have the valuable Greek coins.

"I'll go out on a limb and make a guess—Greece?"

There was a twinkle in those sightless eyes, but all Aaron said was, "What I'm trying to ask, rather ineloquently it would appear, is could Whistler stay here with you?"

I could hardly believe what he was offering.

"It would be a gift." I was thrilled at the prospect of keeping him.

"No greater than the gift you've given me." He raised the knotted rope he'd been clutching like a lifeline to his grandson.

We had arrived at the SUV, and Aaron bent down to caress Whistler's head, choking out the words, "So long, my old friend."

"He will always be your dog. Yours and Vince's. Think of me as his caretaker until you return."

"You are a gracious woman. I understand how my grandson and his wife would have been drawn to you." He gave the dog one more head rub. "Maybe you could take some of your newly earned money and buy him a collar. The tracking device will be easy enough to change."

I examined the frayed band around Whistler's neck. "Aaron's right. Looks like you need a new outfit, bud."

"By the way, the command is *hup*, not *up*." Aaron offered a rare smile. "Humor an old man and accept some unsolicited advice?"

"I'm listening."

"Don't be too hard on Agent Benjamin. He'd been tossed into a rather thorny bush." He squeezed my fingers once, then let go and climbed up into the car.

I said nothing, no longer having the energy to wheedle further information from the man.

Michael closed the door and turned to me. "Mr. Benjamin threw himself on his own sword."

"What do you mean?"

"That's all I can say." He offered a dismissive wave. "Thank you for allowing us to stir up your life a bit. And my apologies for those times when we were, for lack of a better word, pushy."

"Oh, I'd say 'pushy' is a most fitting word."

Michael blushed sheepishly and walked to the other side of the car and climbed in.

I knocked on the passenger window for Aaron to open again. "Something else, Ms. Mitchell?"

"Will you deliver a message for me?"

He nodded.

"Tell them when their phoenix rises again, they'll always have a home here at Battersea Bluffs."

He looked bemused.

"They'll understand." I watched the SUV round the bend of the drive while patting Whistler's head.

"Looks like you're stuck with me, buddy." The dog obediently followed me as I headed toward the barn. "Shall we go see what surprise Vince and Ashley left for us?"

# 30

The next day . . .

'd forced myself to wait a cautious thirty minutes after Aaron and Michael departed before returning to my family's burial grounds, this time with my own spade in hand. After a close check to ensure nobody was watching, I'd heaved aside Robert Toomey's stone and dug until I uncovered a well-taped plastic bag. I took extra care in replacing the upended earth and marker, so as not to leave any signs the grave had been disturbed.

I'd come so close to missing the significance of those last three knots on the rope. Eye splice/rapala knot/thief knot. *Look at Robert Toomey.*

I would have continued to assume whatever they'd hidden under the Pooh bear statue had been dug up and taken away, just as Aaron and Michael believed, had it not been for the persistent appearance of the cemetery photo on my laptop screen. When I'd snapped Ashley and Vince, I hadn't realized they'd been standing beside Robert Toomey's grave. I would make the photograph my screensaver as a constant reminder to pay closer attention to what my guardian spirits were telling me.

Back at the house, I performed a mating dance of sorts with the package, testing its heft and caressing it in an attempt to determine the contents. I sniffed at it, but the clinging scent of the earth masked any other telltale odors. I let it sit for an hour on the credenza of the library while I readied myself to discover what mystery my friends had left in my charge. Extra logs were tossed onto the fire, and I poured a glass of pinot noir to calm my nerves. At last, there was nothing to be done but to open it. Inside was a thick sealed envelope, and taped to the outside was a letter-sized envelope with these instructions: *Read first.*

The letter offered a lot to digest, and I'd needed a day alone with the package before making the call. Barking announced my visitor's arrival, and I peeked out the kitchen window as Brooks emerged from his WRPD cruiser. Whistler presented his favorite chew toy for a game of fetch. For several moments, I watched the repetitive tossing and retrieving, assuming it was a stall tactic. Although I had put the awkward night of my exhibit behind me, I wasn't sure where Brooks stood on the matter. I hoped enough time had passed to wash away the sting of rejection.

After a dozen throws, I swung the door open and called out, "Give the poor dog a break."

Whistler ran into the house, panting wildly, and flopped down under the old oak table. Brooks followed, taking a good long time wiping his shoes on the porch mat before stepping into the warm and cozy kitchen.

"Smells good."

"Gingerbread. Fresh from the oven." This time I actually *was* baking. Percy and Celeste had been oddly quiet of late. Perhaps they were as tired as I was.

"Sharing?"

"Of course." I'd had enough caffeine for the day and by the jittery bearing of my friend, so had he. I filled the teakettle and lit the burner, then cut a slab of gingerbread.

"Here you go." I set it before him and took a seat across the table.

"Mmm." He savored the first taste. "Fiona's recipe?"

"Yep." It was Celeste's originally, but my Granny Fi had somehow tracked down a copy.

"How's the new darling of the Whale Rock art scene?" he asked between bites. "I hear the exhibit saved The Bluffs."

"I was just lucky." *Lucky that Aaron Welkman showed up on the scene.*

"Not true." He pointed his fork at me and spoke through the gingerbread. "You have talent."

"At least I've given everyone something else to talk about besides my failed marriage and my"—*what to call it?* Fiona would say, *"Call a spade a spade."*—"my affair with Billy Hughes."

"Most people knew you and Billy were an item back in high school. Nobody blamed you for falling back with him, especially after seeing how Ethan took advantage of you."

"Has Billy taken any heat?"

"Not really. He's a bit of a rogue, but he's also a charmer. Anyone who did know about it forgave you both."

I was glad Billy'd been given a pass by the people of Whale Rock.

"Folks were probably just glad to have Ethan out of here. He wasn't good for you, and he wasn't good for The Rock either."

The kettle sounded, and I tended to the tea, thinking how blind I'd been.

"Who else?"

His eyes tightened. "Who else, what?"

"Who else did Ethan borrow from?"

"Not going there." He jabbed the fork in the air again. "And neither should you."

"I'd like to make things right with anyone who helped Ethan because of me."

"No need. They wouldn't expect *you* to pay back *his* debts. Besides, they'd have meant it to be a gift." The way he said it made me think he'd been one of Ethan's suckers. My heart warmed, but my pulse raced to think Ethan would have used a good family friend to further his own pursuits.

I'd drop it, for now. But if I was clever enough, I could probably wheedle it out of someone, maybe Evelyn. Heck, she and George were probably contributors to the Ethan Fund themselves.

I brought two steeping mugs to the table. "Did you ever tell Zoe about Billy?"

"Me? Why would I?"

I shrugged.

"I wouldn't doubt she knows. Your sister has her informants."

"Oh, I'm aware." I leaned my elbows onto the table. "It's just that she never said anything about it, and it's not like her to keep her nose out of my business, especially when it gets messy."

"I can't speak for her, but I would imagine she'd have picked Billy over Ethan any day." He stirred sugar into his tea, then took a test sip before adding more. "And don't be too hard on your ol' pal Brit. Who could have predicted she'd become a loose-lipped Lucy after a few pops?"

"Certainly not the honorable Brooks Kincaid."

He gave me a stern look. "She was a consenting adult."

"I meant it as a compliment. You always do the right thing."

He looked at me skeptically.

"Not always." He cleared his throat before continuing. "Agent Benjamin paid a visit to the station yesterday."

A peculiar feeling came over me to hear Daniel had been in town.

Brooks gave me a sidelong glance. "You know he's retiring?"

"So soon?" He wasn't due to retire for another year. I brooded over whether this was a consequence of his involvement with me during the investigation. Had this been what Michael Bernard was referring to when he said Daniel fell on his own sword?

"Did you hear me?" Brooks interrupted my musings.

"Sorry, what?"

"I was telling you he came to give me a wrap-up on the case."

"So you know why it was closed."

"Officially, yes."

"And what do you know unofficially?"

"I wouldn't be able to share that now, would I?"

"You're evil."

He let loose that famous chuckle, making me feel safe again in our friendship.

"However." He pulled three evidence bags from his coat pocket and picked up one with the remnants of a food wrapper. "I took this from the campsite in the woods the day you and I hiked out there. We've since determined it's from Liam's Clam Shack."

"At least the mystery camper had good taste."

"Also taken from the site." The second bag he waved before me contained some thick black threads. "This got lost in the shuffle when the case was hijacked by the FBI. When I got involved again, I sent it out to a lab for analysis. They're nylon strands, consistent with material used to make dog collars."

He definitely had my attention now. At Aaron's urging, I'd purchased a new collar for Whistler but hadn't yet tossed the old one. I retrieved it from the broom closet and laid it on the table.

"Think it's a match?" I asked.

"Undoubtedly. The single hair attached to the strands was ID'd as canine. And now for the pièce de résistance." He produced one last bag that held a black rubber tip. "I went back to the site after you told me about that guy from Albany."

It still bothered me nobody had been able to track down the mysterious Henry Beamer. Brooks suspected he was using an alias, as people in that line of work often do.

"It was before we had confirmation about the dog collar strands, and I wanted to be certain there wasn't anyone still hanging around out there."

I inclined my head. "Aw shucks, you were worried about me?"

"Always." He offered a sweet, sad smile. "Do you know what it is?"

I fingered it, fairly certain, but didn't wanted to spoil it for him. I shook my head.

"It's the cap off the air tube of a bike tire. Ashley's bike was missing a cap, and this"—he flicked the evidence bag—"is a match."

"So it was the Jacobsons who were camping in the woods between checking out of Hilliard House and before moving in with me?" I braced myself for the I told you so, and was grateful it didn't come.

"That's what it looks like."

"They had good reason, Chuckles."

He raised his eyebrows. "If you say so, but they still shouldn't have lied to you."

I wouldn't argue the point, but in fairness, they hadn't actually lied; they'd merely withheld the truth.

Brooks went on to say, "Agent Benjamin also solved the mystery of the pawnshop ring."

I had never mentioned my suspicions about Fiona's ring to anyone and was relieved that I'd never had to explain where it had been.

"How?"

"He finally tracked down the summer employee from Sinclair House. She described it as a gold signet ring with an unusual T on it and a black onyx stone."

"Temple?"

"Most likely."

I contemplated their reason for pawning it and why the ring and not another of the Greek coins.

"The woman told Agent Benjamin someone else came back to reclaim it." Brooks's ears were burning red and it took some coaxing to get him to share.

"Come on, Chuckles. Who would I tell?"

"It was Teddy Howell." My friend was clearly exasperated. "And don't ask me how he managed to get it back without the receipt."

"Why would *he* reclaim it?"

"He says he found out Vince and Ashley had pawned the ring to pay him for a favor, so he decided to get it back for them." He continued to fidget.

"What favor, Brooks?"

He sucked in a deep breath, then blew it out slowly. "For helping them get off the Cape."

I shouldn't have been surprised by this revelation. For some time, there'd been a nagging whisper in the back of my mind. And it explained why Teddy had been reluctant to divulge the truth about his friendship with Vince and Ashley.

"Agent Benjamin told you this?"

"No! And he's not going to find out about it either." He narrowed his eyes. "Right?"

"Not from me." I held up my arms in surrender. I leaned forward. "Please tell me they didn't steal Johnny Hotchkiss's Mercury?"

"No, but if he had, my hands would have been tied, and Teddy would've been in big trouble with the FBI." He finished off his ginger-bread. "They sailed out on Teddy's grandfather's sailboat."

It seemed fitting my friends had escaped by sea, though I was left wondering how Brooks became privy to all the details of their escape. I was itching to know more but for now wouldn't push it.

"How much trouble is Teddy in?"

"Let's put it this way: he's used up his three strikes. Sometimes that kid crosses into dubious territory." Brooks shook his head.

"I'd want someone like Teddy on my side."

"Said the other person I know who's likely to bend the law." Brooks frowned. "Getting through to him can be like cracking a code." He gave me a hard, appraising look. "I guess you'd know a thing or two about that."

"Perhaps I would. Not bad for a lowly high school graduate." I tried not to look smug.

"I have a hypothetical question." I was finally getting to the reason for asking Brooks to come out to The Bluffs.

"Shoot." He was already digging into his third piece of gingerbread.

"Let's say a young couple is on the run, and they disappear without any explanation."

"I've heard this story before." He grinned.

"Not this part. In my story, the young couple left behind some information that could possibly disclose some details."

"I'm interested." He licked his lower lip and leaned forward.

"I thought you might be." It was fun to dangle the carrot. "The question is, would you turn this hypothetical information over to the FBI?"

"Considering recent dealings?" He made a disgusted face. "Not going to happen until I know what I'm dealing with."

Practically the same response Aaron had given when I asked what he'd do with whatever Ashley and Vince had buried. *I do not have a good answer for you at the moment. Especially in light of recent events and the uncertainty of who can be trusted.*

I left the room to retrieve the package and set it on the table between us.

"So we've left the realm of hypothetical."

I handed him Vince's letter, which explained about the file contained within the larger envelope:

I'm not sure who will be reading this first.

If it's you Granddad, please tell Cassie we're sorry for deceiving her. Cassie, if you're reading this, we didn't mean to lie to you about how we ended up on the Cape, but we owe you so much for taking us in. If it's anyone else, please handle this information delicately.

My real name is Jason Prince. While I was working toward my master's in criminology at Temple University and interning with the N. Philadelphia police force, I stumbled onto a serious case of police corruption. I worried about my wife's and my safety, so I sought help from the FBI. They were already building a case against a group of officers and pressured me to testify, but someone tipped off the corrupt officers, and I no longer felt confident that the FBI would be able to protect us. A friend and classmate connected us with a private protective agency in Albany, who set us up in a safe house, where we hoped to stay until charges were filed and the officers were in custody.

We shared some details with the agent, Henry Beamer, about the file, which we suspect he let slip, either by accident or intentionally. We felt it was too much a gamble to stay, so we left Albany quickly. We bought burner phones but were still concerned the calls could be traced back to us if your phone was being monitored, Granddad.

When Beamer showed up at the place where we were staying in Massachusetts, we had to leave again. We were starting to run low on funds and were so lucky to find you, Cassie, and a place to crash for a while. Granddad, we sent you a letter to let you know we left Albany, but when you didn't show up, we had to assume you either didn't receive it or that there was a problem with Whistler's GPS device. There was no choice but to move forward with our own plan to leave the country. We are depending on Dad's family to help us until we can connect with you.

The attached package contains a file of incriminating evidence I discovered during my internship, but I never had a chance to hand it over to the FBI guys in Philly before we left. The file was believed to have been destroyed in a fire, but obviously it wasn't. What we don't know for certain is whether or not the dirty cops knew the file still existed or if Beamer told them about it.

Granddad or Cassie, I'm entrusting you with the file. Whoever finds this, please get it to the right people.

Brooks shook his head and passed the paper back across the table. "Holy cow, Cass. What had they gotten themselves into?"

*Holy cow, indeed.* "You can't blame them for trying to escape into new identities. If I'd been in their shoes, I'd have gone on the run too."

"You'd never leave The Rock." He was right on that count.

"But if someone feared for their life?" I took my empty teacup to the sink.

"Hmph. No wonder they were spooked every time I showed up out here," he mused.

"It probably explains why the FBI wrangled the case away from you so quickly."

"Maybe. Agent Benjamin didn't get into those specifics with me, and it's not clear from the letter whether the Philly FBI knew Vince still had the file."

I wondered how much Aaron had known and what he'd shared with the local FBI office. He'd kept those cards close to the vest.

Brooks nodded. "Have you opened it yet?"

I shook my head. Every time I reached for it, Aaron's words came rushing back to me. *'You must believe me, the less you know, the better for everyone involved.'* I wasn't afraid for myself as much as I was for Ashley and Vince.

"Is this about the fire Vince mentioned?" He waved a copy of a newspaper article dated around the time Vince and Ashley went to Albany. There'd been a fire in a Fish Town apartment building. Not a lot of damage, according to the newspaper accounting. Mostly files and paperwork. I was pretty sure I knew who was behind it.

"That, my friend, is a smokescreen. No pun intended." All their drunk talk in Johnny Brenda's about losing something valuable in a fire may have been intended to convince their pursuers that any evidence had been destroyed.

"You think they started the fire?" He looked doubtful. "How do you know it wasn't an attempt to frighten them?"

It was a possibility I hadn't considered, and one I wasn't happy to think about now.

"The biggest unknown is who, besides Henry Beamer, is aware the file wasn't destroyed by the fire?"

No doubt the same question was behind Aaron's desperation to find it.

"So what should we do with it?" Vince's instructions were to get it into the hands of the right people. "Who are 'the right people'?"

Brooks remained quietly pensive for several minutes.

"Let me have some private time with this." He took the file into the library, where he began paging through the evidence. I was too tense to wait in the kitchen and left for a walk with Whistler. I returned an hour later and found my friend staring into the remaining embers in the fireplace.

"So what's the verdict?" I tried to be light.

"As much as I hate to admit it," he rubbed his hands over his face, "this really does belong in the hands of the FBI."

"Okay then." I shrugged. "I trust your judgment. But I'll let you do the honors."

"The dilemma is, how should I say I came upon it?" He stared at me intently. "I'd like not to involve you in any way."

"Tell them it rose from the ashes like a phoenix." I added a log to bring the fire back to life.

He made a face.

"Why must you say where it came from?" I plopped down onto the opposite end of the couch.

"The credibility of the source?" He made a face that all but said, *Duh*. "How would you feel if I gave it to Agent Benjamin before he retires. I think he'd know how to handle it."

When I didn't say anything, Brooks added, "You know, Cass, he's really not such a bad guy."

"So I've been told." Another endorsement, and from a most unlikely source.

# 31

Early November ~ two months after the disappearance

Two weeks later, I received a postcard of a beautiful Greek harbor with another cryptic message: *The phoenix has risen again. Oikos modest. Doesn't compare to BB. Have been listening to "The Winds of Change" and missing him. XOXO*

I looked it up and learned that *oikos* was a Greek word for "house," so I had to assume "BB" referred to Battersea Bluffs. It took awhile to figure out the last reference was to a song that began with sad whistling. *They were missing Whistler.* If only there was a way to assure them he was doing well.

The postscript had this message: *Left* Art of Sailor *behind* Vivlio techne!

*My father's sailing handbook!* They'd left it behind, but where? I had initially thought the phrase "*vivlio techne*" to be a farewell signoff, but according to the translation website *vivlio* meant "book"— obviously they were referring to *The Art of the Sailor*—and one of the meanings for the word "*techne*" was "art." *They left the book somewhere with my paintings!*

But I'd searched every nook and crawl space of the barn and carriage house and come up empty. I'd also checked the guest room, looking for a secret hiding place I may not have known about, but again—nothing.

I hadn't slept well last night as I tried to think of possibilities for where they might have hidden that book. This morning I took my coffee into the library and lit a fire. When my laptop whirred to life on the built-in desk, the scent of burning sugar could not be ignored. But no photo appeared on the screen to give me a hint of what the message was.

"What are you telling me?" I whispered, tilting my head back to rub my neck. That's when I noticed my mother's art books carelessly stacked on the shelf above the desk where I'd quickly shoved them the day we were emptying the carriage house of all my art supplies. I began arranging them in an orderly fashion and felt a smaller book had fallen in back of the pile. I reached behind the larger books and retrieved my father's well-used sailing handbook. Vivlio techne. *"Art books." Now I get it!*

Tears came to my eyes. It may have been a tattered old sailor's guide, but for me it represented a treasured bond with my father. I flipped through the pages to read some of Papa's notations, and a slip of paper fell out. The handwriting was familiar, and it read: *Cassie— we left something important with Robert Toomey. Do a little digging.*

Getting all the incriminating evidence in the hands of the authorities was critical in bringing those corrupt cops to justice. It would also be the beginning of Ashley and Vince's journey home. They hadn't wanted to leave it to chance that someone would be able to decode the message they left on the knotted rope—let alone figure out it even held a message.

*If only this postcard had arrived earlier.* It certainly would have hastened solving the mystery of their disappearance . . . and finding that file.

# 32

Late November ~ three months after the disappearance

Finally the dust had settled in my life, and I'd found the time to read those journal entries of Mama's given to me by Edgar Faust. Memories of my childhood became more vivid. One especially stood out, of being with Mama in her studio, drawing at my child-size easel. I'd looked up from my miniature masterpiece and found her crying. I don't remember what she told me when I crawled up onto her lap, for Papa had whisked me away to Fiona's room. Granny Fi had moved in with us when Mama become so weak and needed her help.

~

Thirty years ago ~ Battersea Bluffs

"Granny Fi?"

"Yes, my darling." Fiona was sitting in her rocking chair with Cassie on her lap.

"What's a lighterman, and why does he curse?" the child asked.

"Where did you hear about such things?"

"Mama said something to Papa about it."

Zoe had come to the doorway.

"It's your fault Mama's sick all the time," she yelled at her grandmother and fled.

"Why's Zoe so mean?" Cassie asked.

"She's not mean. She's a teenager. Now let me teach you a song, and then you'll know all about lightermen. Your Papa's grandfather was a lighterman in London."

"That's in England."

"My, you are a smart one. Now hum along while I teach you the words." She began to sing in her lovely voice, "'Light is the lighterman's toil, as his delicate vessel he rows, and where Battersea's blue billows boil . . .'"

"Battersea? Like where we live?"

"Exactly. But the Battersea in the song is in England. Your great-grandparents named this home to remind them of their lives before they moved here. "'For love he has kindled his torch, And lighted the lighterman's heart . . .'"

"Granny, what does a lighterman do?"

"They captain boats. 'And the Thames Tunnel echoes the lighterman's sigh, and he glides mid the islands of soft Eelpie'."

"Eel pie? Yuck!"

"This Eelpie is a place, not a food." Fiona softly squeezed the little one's nose, which provoked a giggle.

And then Cassie grew serious. "Did my baby brother go to heaven?"

Fiona felt like the old woman she was. "Yes, m' love. He's with the angels now."

"With Grandpa too?"

Fiona twisted her emerald ring. She'd never filled the empty hole in her heart left after Ambrose was killed. "Grandpa too. And your great-grandparents, who built this house a long, long time ago."

The little girl sniffed at the air. "Granny Fi, who's baking cookies? Can I have one?"

~

Entries from Jacqueline Mitchell's journal:
*Damn that lighterman's curse, and damn Fiona for telling me about it in the first place. Too much pressure. Still, I aim to beat it and make James proud. But I shouldn't have let Cassie see me so upset. Why did I tell her she lost a little baby brother? She's too young to understand about miscarriages and curses. A child should never see*

*her mother in despair. Thank goodness James came in and took her away.*

***

*That foul odor will drive me mad. Even now, after losing the baby, it follows me everywhere. In the studio. On the Bluffs. James doesn't smell it, but his nose is useless. Fiona says it's only pregnancy sickness. I think it's causing the miscarriages. Why is it always the boy babies?*

***

*Lost another boy last night. I cradled him until I slept, his tiny finger curled around my own. When I awoke he was gone, almost as if he'd been a dream. But James was there, stroking my face, calling me his Queenie, telling me it didn't matter. The awful burning smell is back. It's that damnable curse that tortures me.*

The ravings in Mama's journal were proof she'd been deeply disturbed by the nearly choking invisible presence. I thought back to times when I'd gaze out my window to see Papa holding tight to Mama as they walked along the cliffs. I now wondered if he had been rescuing his distraught wife from replicating our ancestors' dramatic leap into the ocean.

It was finally all fitting together. I rested my miserable head in my hands. It had taken years to decipher the scents and signals being issued by the spirits of my great-grandparents, to recognize the difference between the encouragements and the warnings. I had allowed my own fears to mislead me when I became nearly overwhelmed by that repulsive smell. The burning flesh odor as Zoe had described it.

However, it wasn't the evil stench of Robert Toomey that had pervaded Battersea Bluffs. After reading Mama's journal, I was convinced it could only be Percy and Celeste's deep expression of grief. All those lost Mitchell baby boys through Mama's miscarriages and then my recent fruitless ectopic pregnancy. All would have been chances to keep the Mitchell bloodline going and, more importantly, to defy the lighterman's curse. In their deep distress, they must have emitted an odor so egregious as to match their own misery.

And had I not had a last fling with Billy and the resulting failed pregnancy, I never would have grasped the significance. A bit of good had at long last come from that enduringly complicated relationship.

It was unnerving to consider I might have followed a similar path as my mother, had it not been for Ashley and Vince to help pull me from the dark cavity into which I'd crawled when the strange and disturbing stench of grief arose. They'd guided me away from the destructive influence of my mother's paintings and helped me find the courage to overcome the grip they had taken on me.

And one last aspect would continue to mystify: How had the images of Percy and Celeste come to both Mama's and my imagination and crossed over into our art? Was it our creative natures that caused Mama and me to be more susceptible to the force of such despair? To the excessive point where it could infiltrate our minds and possess us through our paintings? This was beyond my capacity to comprehend, and would likely remain so.

I'd returned again and again to the letters Edgar had passed along to me, and in so doing made some interesting discoveries. Evidently, my sister hadn't taken care to read everything she'd sent, as stuck between the pages of one of Celeste's letters was a telling note Mama had written to Granny Fi.

Fiona ~
It is urgent that we talk. Zoe keeps a diary, and I have done the unthinkable. But she has committed an act that I fear will strengthen the curse. Can we take a walk this afternoon when James is due in town? Tell him the fresh air will do me good. It won't be a lie. That smell is so thick I can hardly breathe.
—Jacqueline

I puzzled over what Zoe could have done to have Mama so worried. That it had something to do with the curse only heightened my curiosity. I was positive there'd be more to learn from Mama's journal, but what could be so terrible?

I was desperate to see if my mother had written anything to explain those morbid paintings so similar to mine. I remained hopeful Zoe would eventually grow to trust me enough to relinquish the journal, but was prepared for a long wait.

During my last phone conversation with Zoe, as I tried again to coax the journal from her tight clutches, we touched on a number of formerly taboo subjects, including Granny Fi and Robert Toomey. Zoe confirmed my suspicion. "Mama was disturbed by the same evil presence as I was. The Bluffs is haunted by Robert Toomey."

"You're wrong about that." I searched my mind for something to convince her. "What about Edgar's book? Didn't that help you understand?"

"I could never bring myself to read it. In fact, I don't even have it anymore."

"Oh, but you must read it, Zoe." I'd send her another copy of the book, but for now I tried to explain. "I believe with all my heart Percy and Celeste are a presence here—and not a bad one. I know it sounds crazy, but if you can believe in a bad ghost, then try to have an open mind about these good spirits."

"I'll try."

"There's an entire spectrum of smells in this house. It's their way of sending messages. When it's sweet, they're guiding you or affirming something, and when it's pungent and sharp, they're trying to get your attention, send a warning, or change your mind. If you think back, what was happening in your life?"

My sister remained silent.

"Edgar says they have unfinished business."

"Let me guess what that might be," she said sarcastically. "Break the curse?"

Her bitterness saddened me, and I made one last appeal. "You read Celeste's letters. She was willing to make peace with Robert Toomey, and I think we should do the same. If you'd just let me read Mama's journal, maybe I could give you another perspective."

"I don't need your perspective. If Fiona hadn't told Mama about the curse, she wouldn't have continued trying to have a son. There wouldn't have been so many miscarriages to weaken her body and her spirit."

There had to be more than this fueling Zoe's resentment toward our grandmother, but for now all I could do was try to help her understand that Fiona always had the best intentions when it came to her family.

"Before Granny Fi died, she confessed to me her only regret was having told Mama about the curse," I told Zoe. "She said she'd only wanted Mama to understand why she was so protective of Papa, not push her to break it. Fi said she begged Mama time and again to stop, but Mama was possessed with the notion that only she could break the curse. And Papa wouldn't do anything against Mama's wishes. You know how they were."

"Siamese twins of the soul."

~

Eighty years ago
Friday, December 13th ~ the day of the fire at Battersea Bluffs

Celeste quickly folded the letter and placed it in the tin box, her eyes narrowed to better focus on the approaching stooped figure. She'd never imagined such a day. Robert Toomey, here at Battersea Bluffs. Her whole being quaked with apprehension as she opened the grand double doors. The man who stood there held a well-worn Bible in one hand, and a tattered duffel bag rested on the ground at his feet.

He tipped his hat in respect, then took in the woman before him. "Ah, Celeste. You are as beautiful as the day we first met on the wharf."

He had once been handsome, but it would be untrue for her to say he hadn't changed either over these past thirty years. So instead she asked, "How are you then, Robert?"

"I've had better days. Age takes its toll, does it not?" He pulled his threadbare coat tighter across his chest to ward off the howling winds.

"Come in from the cold." She gave him a wide berth.

He struggled with his bag, but Celeste stopped herself from reaching down to help.

"Shall I put on the kettle, or would you care for a wee drop of whiskey?"

"I've not had a drink in over a year now." She'd noticed the tremor in his hands.

"It'll be tea then." Her own were trembling as she filled the teapot. Robert came closer and reached as if to caress her face, but she abruptly stepped away.

"Did ye never feel nothin' for me, Celeste?" he cried. "I was hopin' . . ."

"Hoping what, Robert?"

"That I'd see something other than hate when you looked at me." He then began a terrible coughing fit.

She pulled out a chair for him. "I am sorry you find yourself in poor health."

"Mine was not a virtuous life," he said, stuffing his handkerchief back into his pocket. "Sins take their toll. But I've found the Lord. Or 'twas the Lord who found me." He set the Bible on the table.

"'Tis a shame He came to you too late to save my parents." She turned her back to the man who had brought such pain and lit the stove.

He bowed his head. "I never meant for your father to be ruined. It was an accident. I'd been overcome by drink that night, as so often I was back then."

"Please." Celeste whipped back around. "I can't bear to hear it."

"I've traveled cross the great pond to see you, woman." He stood, nearly toppling the heavy table and brought his fist firmly down on the hard oak. "Will ye not grant one last wish to a dying man?"

Celeste, though alarmed, tried to sound calm. "It's best you stay seated, Robert, and tell me why you've come."

"Don't ye know?" he looked at her with rheumy, beseeching eyes.

"I pray it's to take back the curse. Let this nightmare end so we may live the rest of our lives in peace." The words rushed out.

"I'm even muddling this up." He laid both hands on the Bible, as if trying to derive strength from it. "I've made this vast journey to repent. So I can meet my Maker knowing I done right. Please find it in your heart for forgiveness."

"I will forgive you if you take back the curse," she begged.

"Curse?"

"The oath you swore against Percy that took my sons from me."

"I heard about your sons. A frightful, terrible loss."

"Take it back," she commanded.

"As if I had such power. Only the Lord . . ."

"Say it!" Celeste was nearly hysterical. "I need to hear the words." Then merely a whimper, "Please, say it."

"I take it back. I swear on this." He lifted his Bible. "There is no curse against you or Percy or any Mitchell or anyone you love."

The kitchen remained quiet while Celeste composed herself. And then, "Thank you, Robert."

"I am sorry for the heartaches I have brought you."

She supposed he was. It had cost him dearly enough to be here, and she would do no more to bring the man any further down.

"I forgive you, Robert," she finally told him.

~

Present day

"I tried to exorcise him once." Zoe said, so quietly I thought I misheard.

"You *exorcised* him? When?"

"In college. The smell was driving me crazy. Evelyn decided the house was possessed, so she checked out a library book with instructions for conducting an exorcism."

"How did you do it?"

"We had to burn something that once belonged to him."

"Where on earth did you find anything?"

"Evelyn went to see Mr. Stanfield, and believe it or not, old Archie had that man's Bible."

"You burned a Bible?" I was recalling the original newspaper report about the verses Robert Toomey had underlined in the book of Revelation. Then it dawned on me that it was Zoe, not Fiona, who had likely found the page marker with the dates of death for Percy and Celeste's three sons.

"It was all we had. We did it at his gravesite. Did you ever notice the stone was changed?"

"That was you?"

"*Thief of life, with burning strife, actions caused for mourning rife.* Those were the words of the exorcism. I'll never forget them."

"Oh my god, I'm so sorry, Zo-Zo. I wish you had told me."

"You were too young then."

"But not all these years since, when I could have helped you understand."

I pondered the wisdom of sharing my own attempt to exorcise the lighterman's curse. Though my tattoo of the phoenix had come to represent something else altogether—a symbol of liberation from my own personal demons.

"You can't go back." My sister might've been holding an angry grudge toward Fiona, but it hadn't stopped her from quoting our grandmother.

"Maybe you should," I argued.

"Meaning?"

"Come home to Whale Rock and face those fears."

"Face a ghost?" she scoffed. "Right."

"I'll be here with you. We will forgive Robert Toomey, just as Celeste was willing to do."

"But did she? Forgive him?"

"We'll never know," I relented. "But isn't it worth a try? Together we'll stand strong, a united force to end the curse of Robert Toomey once and for all."

She was quiet a moment.

"Zoe?"

"I've got other pressing matters at the moment."

"Can I help?"

"Not unless you can turn me back into a vivacious thirty-year-old," she sobbed.

Oliver had strayed again.

"You can't go back," I echoed her earlier words. "But you can come home, Zoe."

~

Eighty years ago—the day of the tragic fire

"Praise God, you have lifted my heavy burden." The wretched Robert Toomey shut his eyes tightly, a tear escaping, which he quickly wiped away.

Celeste herself felt lighter. They sat quietly for a moment before she asked, "What will you do now?"

He shrugged. "Look for work."

Her panicked eyes searched his. "You cannot stay here."

"Aye, true. I made some mates on the trip. They'll find me work at the Boston docks."

She doubted he was in any shape for dock work.

"Have you any money?" she asked.

"Enough to get settled." He pulled out his pocket watch. "Ah, 'tis time I go."

At the door, she took some bills from her pocket and pressed them into his grasp.

"I couldn't."

His look was so pained, it brought tears to her own eyes. The swell of compassion was a surprise and a relief. Gone was the hatred.

"Consider it a loan. Once you get yourself a job, you'll send it back."

He balled the money in his fist and held it to his heart, but said no more.

Celeste watched Robert Toomey hobble down the lane and out of her life, hardly believing he had actually been in her home, sitting at her table. She returned to her desk with intentions of finishing the letter to Mattie, but it remained in the tin box. Instead, she gazed contentedly out at the bluffs, warmed by a sense of optimism for the first time since Edwin and Jerome's accident. She envisioned Ambrose's return, having a grandson to help raise and a daughter-in-law to befriend. Celeste had always wanted a daughter. Her dreams filled her with such happiness as she dozed.

*Hmm. What was that lovely scent?* She was enveloped by the mingling sweetness of sugar and vanilla. But where was she? It was a chore to open her heavy lids. At her desk, of course. Through the haze, she made out a delicate china cup on her desk. *The teakettle!* Had she forgotten to turn off the burner? She'd been so eager . . . for what? Oh, but she must get up. She tried, but the smoke was too thick. She would just stay in her chair for a moment. Percy would be home soon, and he'd know what to do. She'd wait for him there.

And then Celeste Mitchell drifted off into a sweet, unconscious state until the flames took her.

# 33

Present day ~ Whale Rock, Massachusetts ~ Cape Cod
Friday, December 13th

I t was the anniversary of the tragedy that forever altered the Mitchell family tree. Eighty years ago, my great-grandparents died, and their home nearly succumbed to the fire that killed them. But Battersea Bluffs still stood atop Lavender Hill, a defiant and tough old lady.

I carted a wagon of wreaths up to the cemetery, with Whistler in tow, and noticed a small group of locals already gathered at Percy's Bluffs for the annual tribute, mostly descendents of the men who'd helped save my home. I gazed out to the cliffs where my great-grandparents had met their end, wondering if I'd remain forever shackled to the wicked spell cast upon our family by Robert Toomey. When I finished decorating the graves, I left the wagon and joined the gathering in their solemn remembrance. Afterward, I invited them all to the house for hot cocoa and Christmas cookies.

Myron Kaufman, my current tenant in the carriage house, was also there. I was glad for the company. He was a fine and interesting man, safe in that he was very happy in his marriage and home life. Myron had rented the place through the end of February, and I already had another renter scheduled for the spring.

I spent the rest of the morning dragging down boxes from the third floor, sorting through Christmas ornaments and thinking about Ashley and Vince.

I smiled to picture my young friends sailing around the Greek Isles or wandering through the colorful Athens street markets I'd read about in my internet searches. At least I knew where they were and that they were safe.

I was spending a fair amount of time on my laptop these days as I began to follow the case of corruption charges brought against several members of the North Philadelphia Police Department. I was hoping for a swift conviction so Ashley and Vince could return home.

It was a quiet day, and the phone hadn't rung once. Not that there was ever a steady stream of calls, but usually somebody checked in. Often it was Zoe or Brooks, but sometimes Evelyn or Lu as well. Busy with their own holiday preparations, perhaps they'd forgotten the significance of the date.

It was mid-afternoon now, and I'd lit a fire to combat the chill that seeps in through antique windows on raw days such as this. Nat King Cole was crooning of a nipping Jack Frost and roasting chestnuts as I finished stringing the tree lights. There were two stockings on the mantle, one stuffed with rawhide treats and chew toys, the other hanging limp and sad.

Whistler lifted his head and looked toward the door, with the soft groan he gave to announce Myron's comings or goings. I pushed the curtain aside to take a peek, but instead of Myron's Blue Chevy Blazer, it was a familiar gray Avalon rounding the bend of the drive. Before Daniel even stepped from his car, the room filled with that wonderful scent of burning sugar. I realized now, it had been the absence of Percy and Celeste that had me feeling lonely all day. But they were indeed making their presence known now, the message unmistakable.

As Daniel walked toward the house, a fluttering warmth surged through me, and the sweet aroma intensified.

"Okay. I get it. You approve."

And then I proclaimed my own oath.

"'Be damned the lighterman's curse. My own phoenix will rise from the ashes of Percy's Bluffs, freeing us once and for all.'"

# Acknowledgments

I've always been fascinated by old cemeteries, as ancient tombstones have some interesting tales to tell. How fitting, then, that I became neighbor to a three-centuries-old cemetery when we moved to a home in Connecticut. I was not, however, prepared for one of its residents—a certain Oswin Dickinson—to stir up some mischief in our house.

Inscribed on Oswin's tombstone was the pledge: "He shall rise again." Apparently, he did just that. I was not a believer in unearthly visitors until we experienced a series of inexplicable events, bizarre appearances, and occurrences also witnessed by equally baffled family and guests. Even our dogs responded to the presence of our ghostly lodger. As a result, I've now become much more observant to mysterious forces that surround us.

I must admit, Oswin was a pleasant ghost to have around—even if he was behind some strange goings-on from time to time. And just like Cassie took comfort in the spirits of her great-grandparents, I find that I've missed Oswin's presence since moving from our Connecticut home. Without him, who knows how this story might have been different or whether it would have been written at all?

Though writing is a solitary endeavor, the hands and hearts of many people touch a manuscript on the long path to becoming a published novel. There are so many people to whom I am deeply indebted for their contribution and assistance in bringing *House of Ashes* to the world.

My amazing agent, Jill Grosjean, years ago recognized potential in an inexperienced writer filled with self-doubt. I lack the words to express my gratitude for her tireless and persistent efforts on my behalf and her unwavering belief in my writing.

I had the immediate sense Shannon Jamieson Vazquez was the perfect editor for my novel, not only by the way she connected with the characters and the story but also because of her genuine desire to make it the best book possible. She put me through my paces, and for that I am truly grateful. Because of Shannon's magical touches, *House of Ashes* became a much better book.

# ACKNOWLEDGMENTS

Many thanks to all the behind-the-scene folks at Crooked Lane Books who worked hard to bring the book to publication: Jenny Chen, who is as efficient as she is organized and always pleasant and eager to help; marketing and publicity specialists, Sarah Poppe and Ashley Di Dio; the copy-editing team who patiently combed through the manuscript; and Erin Seaward-Hiatt, who designed a cover that perfectly evokes the atmosphere of The Bluffs.

A writer can become too close to the story and needs other readers to point out her blind spots. My early readers were extremely helpful in working out the kinks, often reading several revisions as the book evolved. Cia Marion, Beverly Larson, Evelyn Monea, Debbie Busch, Deb Chused, Barbara Singhaus, Meredith Huse, and Geoff Marion—your constructive assistance was invaluable.

My critique partner, Rosemary DiBattista, has been fabulously helpful and is always available whenever I need her. How lucky am I that our paths crossed a decade ago at the Algonkian New York Pitch Conference, and from there such a special friendship evolved.

I could not ask for a more supportive group of friends, many of whom have been part of my world since childhood; others I've had the good fortune to meet along life's journey. All have offered endless encouragement. I can only hope to give back to them what I receive on a daily (sometimes hourly) basis.

I am grateful to the Russo family for introducing me to Cape Cod and for offering their tranquil beach cottage as a favorite writing retreat. The Cape, I've learned, is as much an attitude as it is a place, and hopefully I was able to capture its unique spirit. Though existing Cape Cod towns are mentioned in the book, Whale Rock is a completely fictional village, inspired by many visits to the area, but with a look and feel of its own. I love it when a fictional town becomes a place where readers would like to live, and hopefully that was achieved with the creation of Whale Rock. I've taken some artistic license with the topography of the area to suit the story, and I hope all the native Cape Codders will forgive any changes I've made to their idyllic home turf. Also, a fond farewell to Liam's Clam Shack's long tradition at Nauset Beach.

There are those, sadly no longer with us, who have left special imprints upon our beings. A line in the book was written with my mother in mind: *I'd felt Granny Fi's firm steering hand at my back countless times as I lost my way after her death.* My mother's essence endures, through ethereal whispers of encouragement and guiding, gentle nudges, letting me know she is still with me. *I miss you, Mom.*

And mostly, I wish to thank my husband, Geoffrey, to whom this book has been dedicated and whose support has surpassed all hopes and expectations. Being an author was never part of the original plan. Writing is what brings me peace, and I am aware of the privilege it is to spend great portions of my days doing what I love.